ALSO BY STEVE HOCKENSMITH

Holmes on the Range

On the Wrong Track

The Black Dove

The CRACK in the LENS

STEVE
HOCKENSMITH

MINOTAUR BOOKS ✹ NEW YORK

This is a work of fiction. All of the characters, organizations, and events portrayed in this novel are either products of the author's imagination or are used fictitiously.

THE CRACK IN THE LENS. Copyright © 2009 by Steve Hockensmith. All rights reserved. Printed in the United States of America. For information, address St. Martin's Press, 175 Fifth Avenue, New York, N.Y. 10010.

www.minotaurbooks.com

The Library of Congress has cataloged the hardcover edition as follows:

Hockensmith, Steve.
    The crack in the lens / Steve Hockensmith.—1st ed.
        p. cm.—(Holmes on the range mystery series ; 4)
    ISBN 978-0-312-37942-1
    1. Brothers—Fiction. 2. Cowboys—Fiction. 3. Doyle, Arthur Conan, Sir. 1859–1930—Influence—Fiction. 4. Texas—Fiction. I. Title.
  PS3608.029C73 2009
  813'.6—dc22

                                    2009007910

ISBN 978-0-312-67217-1 (trade paperback)

First Minotaur Books Paperback Edition: January 2011

10 9 8 7 6 5 4 3 2 1

FOR MAR,
FOR KEEPS

AUTHOR'S NOTE

It has come to my attention that certain people believe the late, great Sherlock Holmes to be a mere fiction—an invention of some yarn-spinning scribbler like myself. This is scandalous, slanderous, preposterous, and just plain dumb. Mr. Holmes, though no more, was a real man, as solid of flesh and bone as am I myself. I'm happy indeed to live in a world that could accommodate such an extraordinary individual as he, and it's difficult to imagine why anyone would show any reluctance to join me there.

—OTTO "BIG RED" AMLINGMEYER

The CRACK in the LENS

PRELUDE

Or, The Ties That Bind

Stop right there or I'll blow you outta your damn saddles," the fellow with the shotgun croaked, and he and two pals rode slowly out of the nighttime shadows shrouding the woods by the side of the road.

My brother and I reined up our horses. It was obvious from the dull gray glint of moonlight off the barrels that was no broomstick the man was pointing at us, and his compadres sure weren't brandishing bananas—.45s was more like it.

Funny thing, though: All that artillery didn't scare me half as much as what the men were wearing.

Their heads were, at first, mere white splotches in the darkness, but as their mounts ambled closer, I could see that those shapeless blobs were, in fact, gunnysack masks.

This wasn't a random "Who goes there?" where a country road winds too close to some jumpy rancher's spread. My brother and I had spent the last two days thereabouts digging up dirt—and now someone meant to do us some.

"Gun belts. Off. Slow," the shotgun man rumbled. He had a low,

I

unnaturally rough voice, like a fellow trying to talk while gargling pebbles.

Old Red unclasped his holster and let it drop to the ground.

I reluctantly did likewise.

The six-gun men put away their irons and unsaddled themselves, dropping to the ground with soft, muffled thuds. One took hold of our mounts by the bridles. The other pulled out a couple short lengths of thin rope.

"Hands behind your backs," said the gravel-mouthed man. He was still on horseback, holding the reins in his right hand and the shotgun in his left.

"Careful with that cannon, mister," I told him. "You squeeze off a shot accidental-like, your friends'll get as much buckshot as us."

"Shuddup," the man growled.

I aimed a peep over at my brother, looking for some signal that we should make a break for it—throw ourselves from our saddles and hope the shotgun man wouldn't fire for fear of blowing his chums to kingdom come.

Old Red shook his head. Then he put his hands behind his back.

I again followed suit—even more reluctantly, this time—and the fellow with the rope got to cinching us up.

"Well, Brother, here's another taste of that famous Hill Country hospitality you told me so much about," I said. "It positively warms the heart to see folks welcome you back the way they have."

"Sorry," Old Red said.

It worried me, that "Sorry." It's not a word I'd heard often from my elder brother, no matter how many times his detecting dragged me within spitting distance of death's door.

"Alright," Froggy said, and he pointed his shotgun at a large, low-hanging branch jutting from an elm tree nearby. "Over there."

The fellow holding our horses led them—and, by extension, *us*—beneath the branch.

This did not bode well. In fact, it boded the worst.

Behind us, I could hear the creak of saddle leather, hoofbeats coming slowly closer, a shushing sort of sound as something rough and heavy was slid out of a saddlebag.

Someone reached out and whipped my hat off my head.

No wonder Old Red was sorry. He had good reason.

We both did.

In a calm moment, you could've told me it'd all end like this, and I'd have just laughed and said, "How right! How proper! All these years tied to my brother's apron strings and then I'm hung from the same rope! Oh, that's me, alright—adangle from the last branch of my family tree!"

Only this wasn't a calm moment, and I sure as hell wasn't laughing.

Especially not when the noose went around my neck.

1

GERTIE AND ADELINE

Or, Old Red Reopens an Old Wound . . . and It's a Bloody One

I suspect you're asking yourself a number of questions right about now. For instance: "Who are these unlucky SOBs with the ropes around their necks?" And: "Where in God's name are they?" And: "Why would anyone want to string them up?" And: "Can they *un*string themselves, somehow?"

And perhaps most important of all, "Do I give a crap?"

Allow me to answer all of the above the best way I know how. Let me tell you a story.

Once upon a time, there were two young cowboys. One was named Otto Amlingmeyer—"Big Red" to his friends—and he was strapping, handsome, and as charming as the day is long and all through the night, too.

He was also me.

The other was a tad older, a good sight smaller, and infinitely crabbier. This was Gustav "Old Red" Amlingmeyer—my brother.

One day somewhere in the vicinity of July 1892, Old Red got religion. Not your usual churchgoing, hymn-singing kind, though. No, he became a Sherlockitarian. Or maybe you'd call it a Holmesodist. Either way, it was Sherlock Holmes he worshipped.

He first saw the light when I read out a magazine yarn by Holmes's disciple John (Watson). It was me reading the scripture because my brother couldn't do it for himself: He can pick out enough letters to read your average brand, but *words*—let alone sentences and paragraphs and stories and such—remain beyond him.

Yet despite this minor impediment, Old Red got it in his head that he'd make almost as good a detective as the Great One, if given half a chance. And, miracle of miracles, more than one such chance came his way—and he proved himself a top-rail deducifier. So much so that your (admittedly not particularly) humble narrator was moved to put pencil to paper and chronicle his Sherlockery. The result: Old Red found his true calling as a sleuth (albeit an unemployed one), I found my true calling as a tale-teller (albeit an unpublished one), and the both of us were finally striving for a higher purpose than not starving between roundups.

End Part One.

If you're going to forge on with Part Two, I suggest you make yourself comfortable. It takes up the rest of this book.

It begins when—instead of the "No thank you" or "Not for us" or silence I'd become accustomed to from publishers—I recently received a contract plus two hundred dollars to show it was good for something besides wallpaper. One of my yarns would soon see print.

My ever glum brother had been especially sulky of late, so I left it up to him what to do with the windfall.

"We're goin' to Texas," he announced after a day of mute, moody pondering.

"Oh?" I said hopefully.

We were pushing brooms in a Petaluma, California, hatchery at the time (both detecting and drovering jobs being scarce thereabouts). So the hustle of Houston, the bustle of Dallas, the more easygoing allure of Austin or San Antone . . . any of it sounded good to me.

Old Red nodded firmly, eyes aglint with a grim purpose that withered my foolish hope before he even spoke.

"San Marcos."

"Oh," I said, and it was a very different sound this time—knowing and sad and tinged with trepidation.

At last, our future looked bright . . . or something other than hazy gray, anyway. Leave it to my brother to turn back to the dark past.

Now, among the many things Gustav's not (funny, sunny, as good-looking as his kid brother, etc.) is chitchatty. So there was no idle gab as to whys or wherefores. I knew, more or less—mostly *less*—and that'd have to do until my brother couldn't justify silence another second.

The moment finally arrived soon after we stepped off the train in San Marcos, a big town/small city (take your pick) dangling off the eastern edge of the rolling Hill Country north of San Antonio. Old Red led us straight to a dingy downtown hotel called the Star (a place I won't label a fleabag lest I give offense to fleas) and promptly checked us in.

"Alright, we've put off plannin' long enough," I said, dropping my carpetbag onto the bed and myself on after it. "How we gonna start this thing, Brother?"

Gustav let his own bag drop to the floor with a thud.

"We done started." He closed the door behind him and began moving slowly through the little room, gaze sliding up and down over the sparse, stained fixtures and furniture like he was touring the Smithsonian. "This is where my Gertie was murdered."

I hopped up off the bed so quick you'd have thought I'd stretched myself out on a hot griddle.

"Right here? In this room?"

My brother shrugged without looking at me.

"Could be. She was sent to the Star, and somebody done her in. That's all I was ever told."

"Gustav," I said, and the soft, solemn sound of my voice turned him around to face me.

Up to that moment, all I'd known was that Old Red—normally so bashful about women he'd blush at the sight of a bustle in a dry goods store—had loved a girl once. A chippie who'd met a bitter end. In San Marcos.

It had taken him years to get around to telling me even that much. Like I said, not a chitchatty man. So I'd never prodded him for more. He'd tell me in his own good time, I reckoned.

But now here we were. Good or not, the time had come.

"Don't you think you oughta lay out the whole story?" I said. "I mean, sweet Jesus, Brother—till a second ago I didn't even know the gal's name."

Gustav drifted over to the room's one window. Its smudged, cracked glass afforded a scenic view of the brick of the neighboring building and a trash-strewn alley below.

He stood there, his back to me, as he told the tale.

"Gertrude Eichelberger—that was her name. A Hill Country gal. Grew up on a farm not thirty miles from here. Run off 'cuz of . . . family troubles. Well, a gal on her own, no money, knowin' nothin' but farm chores and a little sewin'. You know what's gonna happen to her. So . . . that's what happened.

"I met her in the local bawdyhouse—the Golden Eagle. I come into town with some other boys from the spread I'd signed on at, and me bein' a little feller and skirt-shy to boot, naturally I ended up with the new filly who's just as scrawny-thin and scared as me. 'Adeline,' that's what they called her at the Eagle. I guess 'Gertie' don't have the right sound to it for a . . . woman in that line. Anyway, when she and me went off to her crib to do our business . . . well . . . she up and *cried* on me.

"You know me. I ain't sentimental nor particularly soft-hearted, but just about nothin' I ever saw broke my heart as bad as that little thing a-bawlin' the way she was. So though I ain't much of one for words around women, this one I *had* to talk to, just to soothe her down some. And the more we talked, the more it turned out we had things in common—her comin' off a farm, her pa bein' a *Deutschsprecher* just like *Mutter* and *Vater*. Why, it coulda been Greta or Ilse sittin' there."

The mention of our mother and father and sisters—all long dead—added to the lump in Old Red's throat that had already started to choke off his words. He had to hack out a couple coughs to keep going.

"After that, me and Gertie . . . Adeline . . . we got to be friends, and then more than friends, the more I come back to check on her. The first three, four times I saw her, we didn't do more than talk. Eventually, though . . . you know. At the time, I was sendin' most of my money back to the family in Kansas, but before long I was holdin' back a little extry for me and Adeline, so I could be with her every chance I got. Cuz true love or not, of course, them damned pimps of hers expected me to *pay*.

"Adeline, she started layin' some cash aside, too. Which wasn't easy to do, livin' as she was—most of them 'workin' gals' ain't much more than slaves, you know. She had her a hidin' place where she'd tuck the tips and gifts the fellers give her, though. And when the time was right, she was gonna put her kit with my caboodle, and we'd run off to Kansas."

Gustav paused again. He didn't just have a lump in his throat now—his voice was so strangled it sounded like he had a watermelon wedged in there. After a few more coughs and a sigh, he managed to forge on.

"I couldn't get into town more than once a week, so I wasn't around when it happened. I was out to the ranch I was workin'. The Lucky Seven. Hadn't been in San Marcos in days. Then a friend of mine—a hand who'd been sent to town after supplies—he comes flyin' in to tell me something's happened to Adeline. She's dead, he says. *Been* dead. Murdered, two days back.

"I jump on the nearest horse and point it north and dig in my spurs and ride. When I get to the cathouse, they just send me straight on to the cemetery—and there she is under a cheap pinewood marker I didn't even have the letters to find without flaggin' someone down for help, that's how useless *I* am.

"After that, I tried askin' around, lookin' to make somebody pay, but I didn't learn much. Her macks, they sent gals to the Star for special customers didn't wanna be seen in no brothel. Drummers and the bigger cattlemen and such. Respectable men. So Adeline was over here on a call . . . and some *respectable* piece of shit up and slit her throat.

"Of course, I didn't have Mr. Holmes's method to call on at the time. I didn't know what to do. So eventually, I just let my friends drag me back to the Seven in a daze."

My brother turned his head to the side, looking away from the window yet still not meeting my gaze.

"This was in October of 1888, exactly five years ago. *Five years . . .* you understand?"

"I understand," I said.

That part of the story he didn't have to tell me. I knew it well.

It had been five years since a flood swept over our family farm, the only flotsam left breathing being me. Gustav came back to Kansas to collect me, and ever since we'd been on the drift together.

So in a matter of weeks, he'd lost the love of his life and most of his family and gained a big-mouth ball-and-chain kid. Yet Old Red never let me see anything you might call pain. Irritation, yes— morning, noon, and night—but not weakness. Not hurt. Till now.

"So here we are, after all these years . . ." I took a deep breath and tried to say with conviction what so often felt like mere bluff: "Detectives."

Gustav snuffed out a snort.

"Or so we keep tellin' ourselves—but things ain't always worked out so good with my deducifyin', have they? I mean, we get our answers, sure, but folks always get hurt along the way, and things don't ever seem to tie up neat. It's got me thinkin' . . . maybe I've had it all wrong. Maybe I ain't really meant to be a dee-tective. Maybe I'm just meant to track down one killer . . . and then leave well enough alone."

Well, what was I going to say to that?

You can't stop detectifyin' now . . . I just got me a publishin' contract!

No.

I walked across the room to Old Red—a journey that took my long legs all of three steps, teeny as our wee cigar box was.

"I reckon there's only one way to know for sure," I said, and I reached out and placed a hand on my brother's shoulder. "Let's you and me catch the bastard."

2

NOT-SO-EMPTY NEST

Or, We Go Looking for an Eagle and Find Two Bad Eggs

We'd seen where Adeline had died (or its vicinity, anyway). Next we'd see where she'd lived.

Our second stop in town would be the Golden Eagle. The whorehouse.

The plan: ease in, find a few familiar faces, finagle what clues we could, then ease out again, all on the q.t. My brother didn't come right out and say it, but it would be best to avoid the management.

The management of such places is *always* best to avoid.

Old Red led the way with his usual quick, purposeful stride, and as we walked through San Marcos we passed a sampling of the local citizenry: shopkeepers sweeping their front steps, workmen stringing up telephone lines, ladies pushing prams or toting home groceries, men in sharply tailored suits on their way to or from the county courthouse in the town square. This may have been a young Texas cow town, yet it felt as comfy-cozy as any burg you'd find back east.

Oddly enough, it was I, who'd never been within a hundred miles of the place, who got whatever smiles and nods were to be had as we went striding along the tidy sidewalks. Gustav might as well have been a dog I was walking for all the notice he received.

"Say, Brother . . . you notice how everybody's only bein' neighborly to—?"

"It's your duds," Old Red said.

"My duds?" I looked down at my San Francisco–bought suit. "Ahhh. *Yours*, too, I reckon."

With his scuffed boots, sweat-ringed Stetson, and weathered work clothes, Gustav looked like what he'd oh-so-recently been: a down-on-his-crappy-luck cowhand. I, on the other hand, had taken to dressing city style, in sack coat and brogans and black bowler.

From the look of the two of us together, I could have been a business-minded swell fixing to swindle some penny-ante rancher out of his hard-earned cash. Which would make *me* the respectable one among folks who fancy themselves "forward-looking."

"Well, that's what you get for dressin' like a saddle bum even when we finally got dollars in our pockets," I said. "Has it occurred to you that we mighta landed us real detectivin' jobs by now if you'd just wear a suit and tie from time to time?"

Old Red shrugged. "I ain't a suit-and-tie man."

"You ain't a chaps-and-spurs man anymore, neither," I said. "That cowboy you keep dressin' like—that *was* you. Not who you are now. Not who you could be."

"We'll see about that."

Whereupon my brother employed one of his favorite conversation killers: He sped up and left me behind.

I let him go. Folks aren't always in the mood for wit, charm, and truth, and I find it so darned difficult to dam up the stream.

Gustav disappeared around a corner a half block ahead. When I followed I found him stopped cold, glowering hatefully at, of all things, a wallpaper store.

"Something wrong?"

"There sure as hell is." Old Red jerked his chin toward the store. "The Golden Eagle."

"Oh," I said. Then, since "Oh" didn't seem to quite cover it, "Shit."

What little trail we had to follow had already come to an end.

The whorehouse was gone.

"You sure that's where it was?" I asked. "Five years is a long—"

"Of course I'm sure! I ain't gonna forget a thing like that!"

I studied the building across the street.

You'll find many a "front" for brothels—boardinghouses, gentlemen's clubs, dance halls, melodeons, saloons—but a *wallpaper shop* . . . with samples in the window and everything?

Next door was a shoe store. On the other side was a dentist's office. Up the street I could see a drugstore, a bakery, and even, way off at the end of the block, what was either a massive, gleaming new church or the White House recently relocated from Washington, D.C.

"Looks like this part of town's come up in the world since you left," I said. "Still . . . we oughta do us a little wallpaper shoppin' all the same. Just to see what we can wheedle out about the Eagle without rufflin' any feathers."

Gustav nodded glumly. "I suppose you're right."

"It has been known to happen. And here's something else I can tell you: You should let me do the talkin'."

"And why is that?"

"Well, Tex," I said, and I gave my brother's cowpuncher clothes a haughty-faced up-down, "when was the last time you saw a bunkhouse papered with anything but the Monkey Ward catalog?"

With this he could not argue: I made a much more convincing wallpaper purchaser than he. So when we went inside, I took to looking over the sample books, all the while blathering at "Tex" about the paste he should use to put up the paper and how long it would take him and whether he should next move on to grease the wheels of my surrey or clean out my gutters.

For his part, Tex responded with a series of curt "Yessirs" that sounded quite convincingly surly.

The audience for our act was a small one: a single frock-coated, bald-pated little clerk. He watched us from behind a long, sample-strewn counter (undoubtedly the bar back when this had been a showroom for a different kind of merchandise), his smile growing brighter the more my tone with Tex grew stern. He even gave me an approving nod when I warned Tex not to try watering down the paste and spending the savings on drink.

"Gotta watch him every minute," I said, waggling a thumb at my glowering handyman.

The salesman nodded again knowingly. "I understand, sir."

"This one, he's like a stage magician. First chance he gets—*poof.* He disappears in a puff of smoke . . . only to rematerialize inside the nearest saloon."

The salesman frowned at Tex. "Shameful."

"That it is." I gave my brother the long-faced look of perpetual-disappointment-unto-hopelessness he's perfected over the years on me. "That . . . it . . . is."

Tex shot back a look of such naked aggravation I could've sacked him on the spot.

"Speakin' of shameful," I said, turning back to my new chum the clerk, "you should've seen this street not all that long ago. I've been gone a few years—followed some business up to Houston for a spell—and it is a wonderment to me how this part of town has turned around. Why, sir, do you know what sort of low-down place once occupied this very spot?"

The salesman's hands gripped the edge of the counter. "You won't find such things in San Marcos anymore."

"Well, I'm glad to hear it. I just wish more towns knew how to sweep out the riffraff like that! How'd it come about here, exactly?"

"Oh, goodness, really . . . you don't want to hear about all that," the clerk spluttered. The truth obviously being that *he* didn't want to *talk* about it. "Have you found a pattern you like? We have a wide variety of—"

"Come now, friend," I cut in. "Don't let propriety stand in the way. It's just us three gents here." I eyed my underling with disdain. "Or two gents and a Tex, anyways, and you could no more scandalize him than you could a wild boar."

Tex looked like he was about to tender his resignation—with a swift swat to the side of his employer's head.

"If you please," the salesman said softly, "I'd rather not discuss it." There was a sample book on the counter nearby, and he flipped it open to a random pattern. "Art papers like these are all the rage, and we have several rolls on hand for less than fifty—"

"I guess I am just one of those insufferable people," I said. "The more someone tries to steer me off a subject, the more I gotta stick to it. So I ain't steppin' off this one till you break down and tell me: What happened to that brothel?"

"*Please,*" the clerk said, and his beseeching eyes flicked, for just an instant, to the right—toward a big staircase at the back of the store. "Could we just talk about wallpaper?"

"Sons of bitches," Gustav hissed, face flushing red. He turned and started stomping toward the stairs. "It's *them*, ain't it? They're here."

"Stop," the salesman called after him halfheartedly. "You're not allowed up there."

My brother stopped at the foot of the stairs, but not because he'd been asked to. He wanted to make someone come to *him*.

"Ragsdale! Bock! You up there?"

"Please, sir!" the clerk begged me. "Tell your man not to do that."

"Sorry," I said with a shrug. "What Tex does during his time off is no business of mine."

"Come out and face me, dammit!" Old Red roared. "*Ragsdale!*"

Sounds from upstairs finally silenced him.

Footsteps. The creak of a door. Then more footsteps, clunking down the stairs.

Gustav backed toward me, right hand drawing in close to his side, fingers brushing the leather strapped against his thigh.

He was dressed like a cowboy, alright—all the way down to the Colt slung from his gun belt.

Me, I wasn't packing at all. I hadn't seen the need—and what's more, a holster would've wrinkled my trousers. If there was going to be any gunplay, I'd be useless to my brother as anything but breast-works.

When I caught sight of the men coming down the stairs, I was relieved to see they weren't heeled themselves—not in plain sight, anyway. Nor did they appear to be toughs of the sort who might pull knives or knucks on us. They were, in fact, dressed as businessmen, albeit rather clownishly so, like kids done up for a masquerade dance.

One was tall and fair and lean, the other short and swarthy and stout, but their attire was identical: dark frock coats, checked trousers, oversized ties, and, though we were indoors, silky-shiny top hats. The tall one's pant legs didn't come within half a foot of his ankles. The short one's coat was so long it almost swept the floor.

Their appearance would've been outright comical if not for the expressions on their faces, which could've killed any smile within a five-mile radius. The one with all the height kept his head tilted back at an angle so that he literally looked down his beakish nose (and past his puckered, sneering lips) on everything. Contempt flowed from him like water over the Niagara.

The one with all the girth was actually more disturbing to look upon, however, for his face betrayed not only no emotion but no sign that it—or its owner—was capable of registering human feeling at all. It was a dead face, immobile, lacking even the phony spark of life you might see shining in a stuffed crow's black marble eyes.

"Alright, here we are," the tall one said. He and his pudgy partner stopped at the bottom of the stairs side by side. "Who the fudge are you?"

(A quick word here about fudge. In truth, *I* am fudging what was actually said in the interest of shielding delicate sensibilities. More worldly readers can, most likely, imagine what word it is I have chosen to omit . . . and omit and omit and omit.)

"Answer the man, motherfudger," the squat fellow said to Old Red, his words coming out slow and sleepy. "Whadaya fudgin' want?"

"I want answers," Gustav growled. "About what happened to Gertrude Eichelberger."

"Who the fudge is Gertrude Eichelberger?" the blond one scoffed.

"No, I don't guess you'd remember her real name, would you? How could you keep track of all the gals you've ruined?"

My brother turned his head and spat on the floor.

"Listen, fudgehead," the fat man said, his tone still so flat and listless he seemed on the verge of slipping straight into snores, "this is a legitimate fudgin' place of fudgin' business, and we don't fudgin' tolerate any fudgin'—"

"Y'all called her Adeline," Old Red said.

Skinny and Stout both scowled. Though they said nothing for a moment, I could hear what was echoing in their heads like a roll of distant thunder.

Fuuuuuuuuudge.

"Brother," I said under my breath, "you can't mean them two was—?"

"Oh, they surely was." Gustav nodded first at the beanpole, then at the pumpkin-gut beside him. "Allow me to introduce Pete Ragsdale and Gil Bock . . . Adeline's pimps."

Bock shifted his dead-eyed gaze over to the clerk, who stood frozen behind his counter looking like he wanted to blend into the very wallpaper he made his living selling.

"Mr. Coggins, would you kindly fudgin' fetch Mr. fudgin' Bales?"

Coggins bolted for the door so fast he was already on the sidewalk by the time he finished his "Yes, sir."

The lean, mean-faced fellow—the one Gustav had called Ragsdale—jutted his chin whiskers at us. "Do we know these stupid fudgers?"

Bock's eyes met mine, and I could've sworn the temperature dropped forty degrees.

"Never saw the big fudge before," Bock said, "but the little loud-mouth's Gloomy fudgin' Gus. Adeline's fudgin' boyfriend."

"Oh. Fudge, yeah. I see it now," Ragsdale said, nodding. "Didn't fudgin' recognize him underneath that mustache. Looks like he's got half a fudgin' fox stuck up his fudgin' nose."

The two men looked at each other, carrying on their conversation without words.

I tried to hold the same kind of talk with my brother, clearing my throat and throwing my eyebrows up high. *What in the world do you think you're doing?* I was trying to say. Getting into pissing matches with pimps was nowhere on the docket.

"Gloomy Gus" ignored me.

"There ain't a pocket picked or a throat slit in this town you two don't have a hand in one way or another," he said. "So you can't stand there and tell me you don't know who done Adeline in."

"We sure as fudge can and we sure as fudge *did*," Ragsdale sneered. "Five fudgin' years ago. Or were you too fudgin' drunk to fudgin' hear us?"

My brother's face went even redder—which was truly something, as there *isn't* anything redder than crimson.

"Anyway," Bock said tonelessly, "we don't fudgin' talk about such fudgin' things here. So unless you wanna buy some fudgin' wallpaper, you'd better get your fudgin' ass out the fudgin' door."

"You wanna talk wallpaper?" Old Red took a step toward Rags-dale and Bock—neither of whom backed up an inch. "Well, then, how-zabout I paper these here walls with your greasy guts unless you—"

"What's going on here?"

The voice told me *lawman* before I even turned around. It had that blunt, heavy, hammer-hitting-anvil sound to it. You could hear the impatience, the sourness, the assumption that someone needed his ass kicked, and hard.

I turned and there he was, a badge on his chest and a frown on his face. Aside from the Colt Lightning on his hip, though, the rest of him hardly seemed lawman material. He wore spectacles, for one thing, and the eyes behind them lacked the flinty-hard coldness sheriffs, marshals, and constables work so hard to cultivate. And there was a softness to the rest of him, too. Not just that he was plump—though he did spill out over his gun belt a bit—but while he was older than my brother and myself, somewhere on the north side of thirty, there was a boyishness to him, a green streak even his don't-give-me-shit squint couldn't quite hide.

"My God—if it ain't Milford Bales!" Old Red said, and the malice poured out of him like beer from an upturned bottle. He almost even *smiled*, which would have been the eighth wonder of the world, sure to attract awestruck gawkers from far and wide had it lasted longer than a split second.

This Bales was a friend, it appeared. An ally. A decent man in a position to help us—or so I assumed until the man's scowl deepened, and all the softness I'd seen in him hardened to steel.

"Gustav Amlingmeyer," he said slowly, every syllable dripping with disgust. "What the fudge are you doing here?"

3

THE SPEECH

Or, The Long Arm of the Law Reaches Out to Give Us a Slap

The little salesclerk, Coggins, peeked out from behind the fellow with the badge—the man my brother had called Milford Bales.

"That's him, Marshal," Coggins said, lifting a trembling finger to point at Old Red. "He's the one."

Gustav was still agape, obviously shocked by the spite with which the scowling lawman had greeted him. Which left it to me to mount his defense.

"He's the one *what*?" I said. "The one been makin' conversation? Askin' a few questions? Well, alright, then—he *is* the one. What's wrong with that? There some law against talkin' in this town?"

"No," Bales said. He'd stopped outside the store, just beyond the door, as if the threshold was some line he couldn't cross. "But there is a law against causing a disturbance in a legitimate place of business."

That snapped Old Red out of his stupor.

"Legitimate place of business? Feh!"

"See, Marshal?" Bock waved a languorous hand at my brother. "There you go."

"We are fudgin' respectable, law-abidin' fudgin' taxpayers tryin' to fudgin' conduct fudgin' business," Ragsdale added, squint-sneering at Bales down the double barrels of his long nose. "And we don't have to fudgin' put up with that kind of fudgin' talk in our own fudgin' store. So do your fudgin' duty and fudgin' throw the fudgewit out, would ya?"

Bales glared at Ragsdale and Bock for a moment, seemingly torn between doing his "fudgin' duty" and putting bullets betwixt their eyes.

When he'd made up his mind, he turned to me and Gustav and said one word: "Out."

"Now, just one minute, Milford," my brother began.

The marshal hit him with the same look he'd just given Ragsdale and Bock. "*Out.*"

I wrapped a hand around Old Red's arm and tugged him toward the door.

"Time we got goin' anyhow, Brother. They might not peddle tail in here anymore, but the place still has a scummy kinda feel to it, don't you think? Like a man could catch the clap just from breathin' in the air."

"Fudge you!" Ragsdale called out as we walked away.

I waved my free hand over my head without looking back. "*Vaya con* fudge you, too, *amigo!*"

As Old Red and I stepped outside, Bales and Coggins swung from our path like batwing doors. The second we were on the sidewalk, the clerk sidled around us and scampered inside with a cringe so craven it sparked in me the sudden, near-overpowering desire to plant a brogan toe between his butt cheeks. Yet something told me this would be a bad idea—my common sense, perhaps. I can't be sure, for it and I usually aren't on speaking terms.

"My, what big cockroaches y'all have around here," I said instead.

"Leave him alone," Bales snapped.

He still didn't strike me as imposing physically—with his tidy clothes and soft features, he would've been right at home behind a sales counter with Coggins—but the rage in his eyes was a warning not to push him any further.

A warning I didn't heed. There was something about the naked loathing on his full moon of a face, the impression that he was about to pop, that spurred me on.

What can I say? Give a little boy a box of matches and a stick of dynamite and just see what happens.

"You're right," I said. "Why take it out on poor little Coggins? It ain't always a feller's fault who he has to take orders from. I mean, just look at you and them two law-abidin' taxpayers back there."

Bales eyed me warily, torn between disbelief and disgust. "Are you *trying* to piss me off?"

I shrugged. "If you have to ask, I must not be doin' it very well. Tell you what: I'll try harder next time. We don't wanna detain you any longer here, though. You got important work to do. Why, at this very moment, there might be fearsome desperadoes like ourselves ter-rorizin' defenseless pimps all over town. So you just toddle along and do your duty, and we'll promise not to inconvenience any more of your constituents today."

That was it—Bales finally exploded. Only not in the way I'd expected.

It was an explosion of *laughter* that erupted out of him, one big burst of bitter amusement, too short-lived and barky to be what you'd call a guffaw. Maybe just a guff.

He looked me up and down again, sour gaze lingering on the flaming red hair that's such a perfect match for my brother's. "You must be Otto."

I went pop-eyed with amazement. "Yessir, that's right."

Bales shook his head. "You're an even bigger pain in the ass than I'd imagined."

"Well, I'm pleased to see that my legend precedes me," I said, and I shot a cocked eyebrow at Old Red—my standard (and oft-employed) "What the . . . ?" look.

"Milford here's a fr—" Gustav cut himself off with an awkward cough, then started over. "Mr. Bales and I were acquainted when I lived down here."

"Oh, you don't say," I said with a solemn nod.

And my brother likes to accuse *me* of stating the obvious.

Old Red turned to Bales. "I never pegged you for a lawman."

"Yeah, well . . . people will surprise you, won't they?" the marshal snarled, his hostility flaring up hot again in an instant. "I just decided there were things that needed changing around here. Things that needed to be stopped. Enough people agreed to get me elected."

Bales sucked in a quick breath that puffed him up like a hissing cat—and his left hand slid toward the black grip of his Lightning.

"I don't intend to let those people down, Amlingmeyer. So let me be clear about this: Cowboy bullshit is no longer tolerated in this town. Nowadays, men who play rough get played even rougher. So the first chance I get, you're going to see just what kind of lawman I am—and believe me, you're not going to like it. You understand me?"

Gustav nodded. "I understand."

Bales gave us an extra moment's glare, then turned and stomped out of sight.

"Well, you gotta give him this much," I said. "That was the best don't-mess-around-in-my-town speech we've heard in a right long while. Maybe a tad too much of the stage about it, though. And didja notice?"

"What do you think?" Old Red snipped.

Translation: Of course he'd noticed.

Bales's left hand—the one hovering over his gun—had been trembling so bad you could hear the fingertips rattle-tapping against the holster leather.

"Don't let that fool you," my brother said, staring off the way Bales had just gone. "My experience, a man with the shakes is more likely to draw than one without."

"Yeah. Maybe."

I stepped in front of Old Red so he'd have to look at me instead of gawping off at nothing. "So . . . what'd you do to piss the man off, anyway?"

Gustav rubbed his chin, still brooding. "I honestly don't know. I mean . . . I think I threw a punch at him the last time I saw him, but I didn't think he'd hold that against me."

"You *think* you threw a punch at him?"

Old Red nodded.

"But that shouldn't have bothered him?"

My brother nodded again.

"That settles it," I said. "Come on."

I started off up the sidewalk with my brother in tow. He wasn't accustomed to following my lead, so the only way to be sure he'd come along was grab an arm and drag him again.

"Come on where?" he grumbled.

"Seems to me you've got another story needs tellin'," I said, "and the place to tell it also happens to be the best place to dig us up some gossip on Ragsdale and Bock and your ol' pal the marshal. All you gotta do is point the way."

Old Red jerked his arm free—and said, "Turn here."

For all our tramping around town that day, I'd seen little that truly seemed seamy. In fact, the most sordid den of iniquity I'd spied was a billiard hall.

But left and then left again and there it was: a sleazy little saloon, dark and dank and fit only for the dregs of society. Which, to judge by our experience with the local law, now included us.

So in we went.

4

A FOUNTAIN
FILLED WITH BLOOD

Or, Old Red and I Fish for Gossip and Catch Hell

The name of the saloon was, apparently, Saloon, as that was the only word on the dingy sign out front. Along the same line, the solitary bartender inside could have been named Mr. Bartender, so standard a dive barman was he: dirty-shirted, stubble-faced, slump-shouldered, sallow.

As for the clientele, you'd have to label them "nonexistent." Gustav and I were the only two patrons—and only one of us was welcome.

In Saloon, it seemed, the social order of San Marcos was turned on its head. Now it was my brother receiving the (snaggle-toothed) smile, while I was judged unworthy of more than a curled lip.

It was irritating, but hardly surprising. The place was tucked away on a dusty side street across from the railroad stockyard—which made it a cowboy joint. In such establishments as that, a respectably dressed fellow like myself would get no respect at all.

Once Old Red and I had our beers (mine already half-emptied thanks to the slamming-sloshing way Mr. B slapped the glass down before me), we claimed a table in the corner.

"So . . ." I tried to take a sip but got nothing but suds. "Tell me about Bales."

My brother took a long, *long* pull on his beer before speaking. He usually doesn't do more in a saloon than wet his whistle, but now he was really giving the thing a good soaking.

"Man's a barber. *Was* a barber, anyhow. The local postmaster, too. That's how I got to know him. Used to help me fill out the money orders I sent up to y'all on the farm. So he knew I was . . . unschooled. After a time, it got so's he'd help me with other things, too. Like the notes you used to send me."

I chuckled, thinking back on my dispatches about flying-ship trips to the moon and President Cleveland's latest visit to beg our dear old *Mutter* to marry him. When you're a crazy-bored farmboy, the excitement you put into a bullshit tall tale's about the only kind you're likely to get.

"So that's how Bales knew of me," I said.

Gustav nodded. "He ended up knowin' a *lot* about me. I think you could even say he was a friend."

"So naturally you tried to knock his block off."

"Yeah . . . I reckon I did." Old Red foamed up his mustache with another glugging swig. "After I found out about Adeline, I went on a real tear, and Milford ended up in my path one night."

"A tear? You?"

Not only had I never seen my brother drunk, I'd never even seen him truly tipsy.

"Yeah, me," he said miserably. "If I'd had the slightest clue what to do, if I'd had me any *method*, it wouldn't have happened. But Mr. Holmes was a long ways off for me still . . . so I just went and got stinkin' drunk. Made a big scene at the Golden Eagle, stumbled around town ragin'. Somewhere in there, me and Milford tangled—though I can't recall over what. That was the last I seen of him till today."

"Well, looks like your ol' pal can hold a grudge."

"So it would seem." Old Red polished off his drink, finishing in the manner prescribed by cowboy etiquette—by dragging his shirt-sleeve across his face. "Just don't fit him, though."

"Neither does a badge."

My brother stared down into his empty mug and made a neutral, thoughtful sort of sound—"mmmm." Then he pushed the glass across the table with his fingertips, putting it as far from his reach as possible.

"What do *you* make of the man?" he said, and he turned toward the bar.

Mr. B looked up with wide, innocent eyes. "Huh? You talkin' to me?"

He'd been busying himself as all barmen will when killing time. Swiping at the counter with a rag. Spit-polishing shot glasses.

Eavesdropping.

"Yeah, yeah," Old Red said, impatiently waving off the man's phony confusion. "Bales—what kinda marshal is he?"

"The do-gooder kind," the barkeep growled, scowling. He was obviously one of those fellows who consider the doing of good un-manly and more than mildly repugnant. "All the holier-than-thous got together to throw out the old marshal and put Bales in his place."

"So he's some kinda reformer, is he?" I asked.

"Worse than that! The bastard's *honest*! First day in office, he actu-ally starts enforcin' the damned laws!"

I shook my head and clucked my tongue. "Scandalous!"

"Marched right into the Golden Eagle with a bunch of deputized busybodies and closed the place down," Mr. B went on, ignoring me (which, I grant you, is often for the best). "Did the same to the Bull's Head and the Bon Ton, and now there ain't nowhere in town a man can get himself a piece of ass with his head held high. Can you imag-ine? I mean, this is *Texas*, dammit! That's supposed to stand for some-thing! Am I right or am I right?"

"Both," I said, and I saluted him with my mug.

"If Bales is such a crusader, why's he put up with Ragsdale and Bock?" Gustav asked. "Not half an hour ago, we saw the three of 'em together, and it looked like Bales was at their beck and call."

The bartender shook his head and snickered as some will when admiring the audacity of particularly naughty boys. "Bales *is* at their beck and call . . . though no more than for anyone else in town. You see, Ragsdale and Bock had to close the Eagle, sure, but they still owned the building fair and square. So what did they open there a couple weeks later but a wallpaper store! Nothing illegal about that. Meanwhile, at the very same time, them two rascals was puttin' up a whole new cathouse—only this one's half an inch over the city line, out where the law's not beholden to no bluenoses. So if Marshal Bales so much as sets foot in the place, Ragsdale and Bock could have the sheriff arrest the meddlin' SOB for trespassin'! Ever since then, they've been rubbin' the town's face in it, struttin' around in top hats like a couple Vanderbilts on their way to the opera!"

Mr. B laughed. I joined in out of common courtesy.

My brother, being uncommonly uncourteous, frowned.

"Sounds like Ike Rucker's still county sheriff," he said.

The barkeeper nodded. "Will be till the day he dies, so long as the cattlemen and cowboys have the votes. Ol' Ike's never come between a man and his fun. Hell, he's too busy havin' fun himself!"

Old Red's already sour expression curdled even further. "This new bawdyhouse . . . how would we get there?"

Mr. B cocked his head to one side and said nothing. Then he sighed, reached under the counter, and produced an ancient carbine that looked like it was already rusted out when it saw service at Gettysburg.

I put up my hands. "You'd rather we bought a map?"

The barkeep snorted, then laid the rifle on top of the bar. "This ain't for you. It's for them." He jerked his head toward the door. "Sometimes I have to remind 'em to stay outside."

"Remind who?"

Gustav shushed me, and I finally heard it, too.

The sound of distant singing.

"Them?" Old Red said.

The barman nodded. "If you're wonderin' how your old buddy Bales got elected—and why my tavern's empty—just look outside and you'll find your answers."

As the singing grew louder, a feeling of familiar dread draped over me. Even before I could make out any words, I knew it was a hymn I was hearing—the drony, groany moans of the choir told me that.

Why is it, I wonder, that so many songs meant to lift up praise to heaven sound so much like the wailings of the damned in hell? You'd think folks on their way to paradise would sound a mite more cheerful.

Certainly there was little cheer to be found in the hymn we were being subjected to: that peppy little ditty known as "There Is a Fountain Filled with Blood."

> *There is a fountain filled with blood*
> *Drawn from Emmanuel's veins.*
> *And sinners plunged beneath that flood*
> *Lose all their guilty stains.*
> *Lose all their guilty stains.*
> *Lose all their guilty stains.*

After that, the lyrics get *really* depressing. "Camptown Ladies" it is not.

"The new brothel—where is it?" Old Red asked again. The choir was right outside now, and he practically had to shout to be heard above the dreary din.

"Just follow San Antonio Street west till it turns into a trail. You'll hit the place soon enough. The Phoenix, it's called."

Old Red nodded and stood up. "Alright. Let's go."

And off he went.

Mr. B didn't seem particularly sad to see us go—though I think he would've preferred it had more of our money stayed behind.

Night was falling, and we found maybe twenty people, men and women alike, crooning away in the dusky gloom outside the saloon. All of them were draped in flowing robes that glowed faintly gold in the dim light.

As we walked past, a tallish fellow separated himself from the rest of the choir, one arm stretched out before him. His robes and hair—even, it seemed, his eyes—were coal black, and as he moved closer I could see a frown chiseled so deep into his square face it might as well have been chipped from a block of granite. Had he not spoken a word, it still would've been obvious to me: Here was a preacher of the sort who dined on brimstone and breathed fire.

"The stench of death is upon you," he boomed as his heavenly host went on wailing behind him. "The putrescence of sin and damnation! Only the blood of the Lamb can wash it away! Only the blood of the Lamb can save you!"

He was pointing a finger at us that seemed as long and straight and sharp as the spear that pierced Christ's side. But when Old Red and I drew even with him, he suddenly flipped his palm up, and the Finger of Doom became an outstretched hand.

"Come join us in prayer before it's too late. Come join us and be cleansed!"

"Can we take a rain check on that?" I said. "Saturday's my usual bath night, and anyway we gotta run on out to the Phoenix tonight."

The preacher gave us the Finger again as Gustav and I walked away.

"Hellfire awaits you!" he roared. "You will burn! You will both *burn*!"

And it's kind of strange to reflect on, me not being a religious fellow or prone to fright at bad omens or spooks—but that preacher's prophecy?

It came true.

5

THE PHOENIX
Or, I Discover That Clothes Do Indeed Make the Man . . . a Target

I wasn't just guying that sky pilot about heading out to the cathouse. It was obvious that was where my brother intended to take us next. First, though, there was an errand to run: We returned to the Star long enough for me to strap on my gun belt. The wrinkles in my fine trousers would be an annoyance, yes—but not nearly so much as a bullet through my liver.

"You're gonna keep your iron holstered 'less we really need it, ain't you?" I asked Old Red as we trudged off toward the edge of town.

"What the hell kinda question is that?"

"A mighty simple one."

"Well, the answer's yes. You know I ain't one to throw slugs around willy-nilly."

"Usually, yeah, but you got a little hot when you laid eyes on Ragsdale and Bock. A lot hot, actually. In fact, I'd say you didn't handle the whole thing very . . . uhhh . . . Holmesily."

My brother picked up his pace.

"I ain't feelin' very goddamn Holmesy," I heard him mutter before he hustled out of range.

I let him have his distance again. There was enough crowding him already without me treading on his toes.

Full-on darkness had fallen by now, yet for the first half mile or so we had plenty of light to see by: On each corner was that shining beacon of civilization, the electric streetlight. Some of the businesses and even homes were strung up for electricity, too.

The twentieth century might be all of seven years off, but San Marcos—at least some of it—seemed to be getting there early.

The Phoenix, on the other hand, was the 1880s encased in amber. Yes, barbed wire and railroads have put an end to the big cattle drives. Yet the heyday of the drover had never passed, to judge by the hullabaloo out at that brothel.

From a distance, the Phoenix looked like nothing more than a big, newly raised barn just off the road—albeit one where the animals were obliged to stay outside rather than in. There must have been forty ponies ringing the place, and from their lean yet sturdy builds, the way they were tied, and the saddles they wore, it was obvious who the Phoenix catered to. And if all that didn't make it plain enough, all you had to do was stop and take a listen.

When a cowboy gets a crack at the fun he prefers—the kind mixing liquor, women, and gambling in equal measure—it's said he's "cutting his wolf loose." To hear it, you'd think that's just what was happening, for punchers get to yipping and howling like a pack of wild dogs. I guarantee you a dozen drunk dentists or lawyers or even sailors don't put up half the racket of one whiskey-soaked cowhand, and it sounded like there were a hundred in the Phoenix that night.

"Got a plan for inside?" I asked when Old Red let me catch up.

He'd stopped at the spot where a little path to the bawdyhouse veered off from the main trail.

"Don't make a fuss. See who we see."

"That's it?"

My brother nodded. "That's it."

"You know how that seein's probably gonna go, don't you?"

33

"I know," Gustav said, and he gave me a "What's a man to do?" shrug.

Five years is a long time for either a cowboy or a floozy to stick to one place—excepting, of course, if that place is a grave. Most of the folks Old Red would've known thereabouts had most likely drifted on or been plowed under.

Still, there we were, and as my brother's shrug had so eloquently put it . . . well, what's a man to do?

We headed up the path to the Phoenix.

There was only one door in sight. Torches burned on either side of it, and as we approached I could make out a figure standing alone in the flickering light. A dark curve of polished wood glinted dully at his side.

The grip of a holstered gun.

This, it seemed, was the maître d'. Even a place as shady as the Phoenix has standards, you know. Low ones, but standards.

I hailed the gunny with a cheerful wave. "Sounds like the boys have got the place good and warmed up for us!"

"Take off your guns," the man snapped.

Old Red and I stopped.

"We got some kinda problem here?" I asked.

"Not if you give up your hardware," the gunny said.

He was a hard-eyed customer who looked about as friendly as a bear trap to begin with. But, for me, he seemed to feel a special disgust.

"Well?" he said. "I'm waitin', greenhorn."

For neither the first nor the last time, I got the feeling I'd switched to dressing city-style a mite early for my own good.

"Alright. No need to get snippy," my brother said, and he started unbuckling his holster.

"Ain't nothin' personal," he whispered to me, and he jerked his head to the gunny's left.

Two crates sat in the shadows behind the man. Both were piled high with holsters and hoglegs.

We weren't being singled out. Going in unheeled was house policy.

"Don't tell me there's a county ordinance against packin' in a cathouse," I said as I took off my gun belt. "I wouldn't think y'all would give a shit."

"We wouldn't, and the sheriff wouldn't neither," the gunman said, and he stepped aside so Gustav and I could add our Colts to his collection. "Last week some asshole shot up the chandelier, that's all."

"Oh? Anybody get hurt?"

The gunny gave me one of those scowls that told me I had, for the millionth time in my life, asked a stupid question.

"Yeah," he said. "The asshole who shot up the chandelier."

He waved us past, his squint already sweeping out toward the trail again. We weren't worth speaking to any further—which was fine by us.

We walked into the Phoenix.

Pandemonium in a ten-gallon hat—that's the only way to describe what awaited us. Or the quickest, at least.

To take a little more time with it, I'd have to mention the cacophony of shouted conversation; the cackles of chemise-clad goodtime gals coaxing customers toward the stairs at the back of the broad, high-ceilinged hall; the hunched, perspiring piano player hammering at the keys to make "Sweet Betsy from Pike" heard above the din; the madly grinning cowboy making the piano man's job all the harder by clog dancing atop his upright; the impromptu game of Keep Away being played with another drunken puncher's pants; the overpowering stench of sweat, smoke, liquor, and upchuck.

Hanging above it all was a glimmering double-tiered chandelier that would have been fit for a grand opera house . . . if a quarter of the glass hadn't been busted and one of the arms lashed together with bailing wire and twine.

"Looks like the move to the country ain't hurt business," I said.

"Feh," Gustav snorted. "This here's a Sunday prayer meetin' compared to the old days."

He started to work his way toward the bar. Not a dozen steps into the crowd, though, and he was spinning on his heel to turn his face the other way.

"Spot someone?" I asked, pivoting around beside him.

"Get a gander at that big feller with the bartenders."

I threw a casual glance over my shoulder.

The dark mahogany bar ran the length of the room just like the counter in Ragsdale and Bock's wallpaper store. But the "big feller" standing behind it was a different story altogether from trembly little Coggins the clerk. You'd have to add three Cogginses together just to make one of him, then throw in a bushy black beard so thick yet another Coggins could hide inside it.

Though he was on the working side of the counter, he wasn't fetching bottles or pouring drinks. That he left to the lesser men who darted around him like squirrels scampering about at the foot of a giant redwood. He just stood there as still as said tree, keeping silent vigil on the commotion before him.

"Stonewall," Gustav said. "Ragsdale and Bock's top-screw asskicker."

"Well, I sure didn't peg him for the maid. The question is, have his bosses warned him to be on the lookout for you—and, if so, would he know you by sight if he *did* spot you?"

"That's two questions," my brother grumbled. "And the answers are 'How should I know?' and—"

"Well, lookee at Mr. Fancy Pants!"

A passing puncher came to a tottering stop before me, an empty beer glass clutched in one grimy hand.

"What are you supposed to be, then?" he said, his words coming out as wobbly as the rest of him. "A lawyer, a storekeeper, or a schoolmarm?"

There were laughs all around, and just like that we had an audience.

Guffawing cowboys put down their drinks and playing cards to leer at us from the nearest tables, their eyes blazing-bright with anticipation. A dustup is, without peer, every drover's favorite floor show, especially if it leaves some uppity so-and-so mussed and bloody. Tonight I'd been pegged as the so-and-so.

"Huh, li'l missy?" the swaying cowpoke said, taking a lurching step closer that brought me within range of both his knuckles and his nostril-scorching breath. "You get lost on your way to the sewing bee or what?"

There were more hoots. Enough, I saw over the drunkard's shoulder, to turn Stonewall our way.

Fortunately, I make quite the formidable wall myself. I turned to fully face the braying drover—and position myself between Stonewall and my brother. Old Red's needled me on occasion about the (supposedly) extra pounds I carry around, but I'm sure he was grateful for every ounce just then.

"You got me all wrong, pal," I said.

"I ain't your pal, ya damn greener!"

The waddie looked as gristle-tough as any hand, but he wasn't a large fellow, and it would take but one swat from my big paw to remove his empty head from atop his shoulders. Who knew how many cowboys would pop up to take his place, though? I didn't dare spark a fracas with Stonewall eyeing me.

I pasted on my best shit-eating grin and held out my hands.

"Just look at them calluses, would you? You think I got those buttonin' up a business suit? Naw, I earned the things the same way you got yours—throwin' rope and muggin' calves. This slicker getup's just a put-on."

"It's you he's puttin' on, Wishbone!" someone called out.

"Yeah!" another rough voice added. "You gonna take that from some snotty city pansy?"

My shit-eating grin was choking down a seven-course banquet, but I managed to keep it in place.

"Now, now, boys," I said. "You wanna know why I stand before you as frilly-assed as a·lace doily? Well, that's how you need to do when you're tryin' to make time with a preacher's daughter. And why am I now here dirtyin' my scrubbed and starched self in a low-down clap factory like this?" I turned back to Wishbone and shot him a wink. "Because I succeeded, of course . . . and now I'm gonna celebrate!"

There were jeers and catcalls of the "Oh, go on!" and "Bullshit!" variety, but the scoffing had a jovial feel to it now, like the roughhousing and friendly ball-breaking of hands in the bunkhouse. I'd won the audience over.

Even Wishbone wasn't grimacing at me so menacingly anymore, and the fire had faded from his eyes. Either he bought my story or he was about to pass out. Whichever, I knew just how to seal the deal.

"Tell you what, Wishbone," I said, "let me buy you a drink and I'll tell you the whole story."

Wishbone flashed me a crooked grin.

The cowboys either cheered or groaned.

Stonewall pointed his stony stare elsewhere.

And Old Red?

He, I discovered when I turned to toss him a triumphant smirk, was long gone.

6

BIG BESS

Or, My Brother's Disappearance Leads to a Real Pain in the Butt

My first thought was that Stonewall had somehow arranged to have Old Red snatched away and handed a harp.

My second thought was that my brother had slipped off to rustle us up an arsenal—a couple empty bottles, say, or a derringer pilfered from the gunny's pile outside—in case I couldn't talk my way out of a tussle.

My third thought was that Gustav was a sneaky little son of a bitch.

This last thought stuck with me a while, for after a frantic survey of the room, I spotted proof of the truth of it.

There was Old Red laughing it up with some punchers over by the piano, his back to Stonewall at the bar . . . and his arms wrapped around a giggling floozy. He acknowledged me with a small nod, the jolly expression on his face going as stiff as the mask it truly was. Then he turned his attention back to his new pals.

While I'd made a spectacle of myself, he'd slipped off to do some detecting.

It was the smart thing to do, I suppose, and one could infer from it an unshakable faith in my bullshitting abilities. Yet it still rankled that my brother hadn't stood behind me, literally or figuratively. The hunt for clues had come first.

"Hey," Wishbone said, his smile starting to droop, "we gettin' a drink or ain't we?"

"My friend, you're askin' the wrong question," I said. "What you oughta be wonderin' is what kind and how many."

"Well, I say rye . . . and lots!"

"Done!"

I clapped a hand on the boozy cowhand's back and steered him toward the bar. Seeing as all I was good for, apparently, was providing distractions, I parked us right across from Stonewall.

"Rye for me and my compadre here!" I crowed, slapping down two bits.

"S-sorry, S-Stonewall," Wishbone stammered, sliding my quarter down the counter to one of the men actually tending bar. "I think he's n-new around here."

"Not for long," I said with cheerful (and feigned, for once) obliviousness. "I expect I'll be a regular soon enough. You got a real nice place here, Mr. Stonewall. Well, maybe 'nice' ain't the right word—but that's what I like about it, ho ho!"

The look Stonewall gave me wasn't so much staring daggers as dropping an anvil. You felt it squash you flat.

"Well, uhhhh . . . where was I?" I said, turning back to Wishbone. "Oh, yeah, the preacher's daughter! Mary Jane's her name. Ahhhh, what an angel—and what a saucy little devil!"

With that, I launched into a long, sordid story about a trip into a church baptistery to wallow in rather than wash away sin. Suffice it to say, it was exactly the sort of thing men like Wishbone (and, I hoped, Stonewall) could not resist. Even surrounded by jiggling, half-naked woman-flesh as we were, real live prostitutes are no match for imaginary preacher's daughters.

As I jabbered away, Stonewall went on playing watchdog, though I fancied I spied a faraway look in his eye the dirtier my story got. Wishbone, meanwhile, was soon hunched over the bar with such a slump to his back he looked like a giant question mark. When he was no more than a puddle on the floor—which would be soon, at the rate I was pouring whiskey into him—I'd slip away and rejoin my brother. Assuming I could find him.

"Wha' culuh wuh deh?" Wishbone asked as my yarn neared its climax.

"Her bloomers? White, of course."

The cowboy shook his head wistfully. "White bloomuhz," he sighed. "White bloomuhz . . ."

"Erf!" I said. Which is not something I say often, but then again, it's not often someone smacks me on the ass.

I peeked over my shoulder to find a woman behind me so broad of beam I had to turn all the way around just to take in her entirety. She was a vista, a whole horizon unto herself. Stonewallina, they could've called her. Leviathette. Goliathene. Her sweat-stained chemise might have served as a whaler's sail, while her round face sported so many chins I hadn't the time to count them all.

And it wasn't just her body that was big. Her personality was oversized, too.

"If you ain't Big Red," she blared at me like a foghorn, "then I just slapped the wrong fanny!"

"No, you got the right fanny," I said, rubbing my still-tingling cheek. "Not that I didn't enjoy it, but would you mind tellin' me why I've been so honored?"

"Cuz I've been sent to fetch you, that's why! Your little friend's waitin' for us upstairs in the Bridal Suite. He's sprung for a twofer with Big Bess, you lucky dog!"

The woman grabbed me by the arm and tugged with all her considerable might.

"Go on!" she boomed as I was swung, stumbling, away from the bar. "Get a move on, boy—I got work to do! What do I look like? A damned drover? I gotta herd you? Alright, then—*git*!"

She got her point across with another couple swats to my keister.

"Yes'm! Yes'm!" I said, and as I scurried up the stairs the room erupted with rafter-shaking howls. I didn't have a chance to say so long to Wishbone, and it actually makes me feel kind of bad as I think back on the man: It only occurred to me this instant that he never got to hear what happened to Mary Jane.

Once I was at the top of the steps, I waited for Big Bess to catch up, as it took her considerably longer than me to lumber up to the second floor.

"That way, sugar," she wheezed, waving a flabby hand at the end of the hallway. "Last room on the left. You go on ahead."

As I set off, I could hear Big Bess's colleagues hard at work behind the doors lining the hall. Of course, there were no such sounds coming from the room Big Bess directed me to. Though that was only to be expected, something about the silence there froze me in place before I could reach for the doorknob.

"So," I said, "by my 'little friend,' I assume you mean who I think you mean."

Big Bess came waddling down the hall toward me, her bulk filling the narrow corridor so fully I couldn't have squeezed past her had I tried.

"Christ, you're a cagey one," she said. Her voice was quiet now, weary, with none of the forced merriment of a minute before. "What . . . you think this is some kind of trick?"

I shrugged.

I didn't think it, exactly, but I *was* thinking it had been quite a while since I'd laid eyes on Old Red.

"Me . . . coaxin' a man into a trap." Big Bess shook her head as she stepped up close, walling off any escape as efficiently as brick and mortar. "Now, I ask you—what kinda bait would a fat-ass like me make?"

"Very temptin', ma'am."

"Ha," she said. Not laughed. *Said.* The sound was just as flat and fleeting and joyless as it looks on paper: ha. "They only keep me around for comedy and novelty, and I know it. Another year or so and they'll finally decide I'm too—"

"Ma'am . . . you haven't answered my question."

Then she didn't have to. The door swung open, and there was my "little friend" looking like he wanted to cuff me upside the head.

"For chrissakes, get in here," my brother hiss-whispered at me. "You think we got all night for this?"

I stepped past him into the room. The Bridal Suite, Big Bess had called it downstairs. But it wasn't pure and virginal in any sense but one: Lord knows it had never been touched by either scrub brush or broom. It was probably a good sight larger than the Phoenix's other "cribs," though, sporting as it did an actual four-poster bed instead of a mere cot or mat. There were other cozy touches, too—a threadbare rug on the floor, a portrait of Abraham Lincoln (with inked-in eyeglasses and devil horns) on the wall, a nightstand upon which sat a stained chamber pot and a cracked vase holding a single black, shrivel-petaled rose.

"Very romantic," I said.

"Yeah, well, it's the best we got around here." Big Bess shuffled straight to the bed and spread herself out upon it. Trollop and bedsprings alike let out a loud sigh. "This is where we take the big spenders. Any other room, and Stonewall'd get suspicious if I wasn't back in ten minutes."

"I don't aim to be here longer than that anyhow," Gustav said. "We wasted enough time already haulin' my brother up here."

"Keep your shirt on, Gus," Big Bess said through a yawn. For a woman who did most of her work on her back, she sure seemed tired. "Like I said before—down there he'd just get himself in another brawl." She pointed her next yawn at me. "What were you thinkin', comin' in a place like this dressed like that?"

"He'll tell you," I sighed, nodding at my brother.

"We *weren't* thinkin'," Old Red said.

At least he'd made it a "we." That was more than I'd expected.

"So you two know each other?" I said to Big Bess.

"Gloomy Gus and me? Oh, we go way back."

"Bess worked at the Eagle with Adeline," Gustav explained. "She was the only gal downstairs I recognized."

Big Bess nodded, her multitudinous chins doubling with each downward dip.

"Yeah, me and Squirrel Tooth Annie are the only ones left outta the whole bunch."

"Squirrel Tooth's still around? I didn't spot her workin' the floor."

Big Bess shrugged. "Must be with a customer."

"What happened to the others? Sunshine and Belle and the rest?"

"Oh, you know. Married local hands or took sick or got too old."

The chippie's sleepy-eyed gaze drifted over to the painting facing her from the wall, though she seemed to see something there other than Honest Abe—something she didn't care for. Her future, perhaps, approaching fast.

"The usual," she muttered, "but it's not all them others you're here to talk about, is it?"

"That's right," Old Red said. "What can you tell me about the night Adeline died?"

Big Bess stroked her wattles. "Ohhhh, nothing you ain't heard before, I expect. She got sent over to the Star and she never come back. I hate to say it, but I was busy at the time, y'know? Workin'."

"Who told her to go?"

"Mr. Bock, most likely. He's always been in charge of the 'room service' at the Star."

"That's still goin' on? Even with Bales crackin' down in town?"

Big Bess scoffed. "Bales? What can he do? There's no law against a woman rentin' a room . . . or wanderin' into the wrong one 'by mistake.'"

"How about that night five years ago?" Old Red said. "Did Bock or Ragsdale ever mention who Adeline was sent over to the Star for?"

"Oh, yeah. Pete . . . Mr. Ragsdale. He came right out and told us who done it."

My brother took a lurching step toward the bed, eyes wide. If only it could be this easy . . .

"*Who?*"

"Some stranger passin' through. Signed into the Star under a fake name and skipped out that same night."

Gustav sagged—head bowed, shoulders slumped.

Then Big Bess went on, and he wilted even worse.

"Mr. Ragsdale says he never came back. Ain't nobody seen hide nor hair of the man in five years."

7

FRAME JOB

Or, Gustav and I Find Ourselves Painted into a Corner

My brother looked as wobbly at the knee as my chum Wishbone downstairs, and for a second I almost thought he was going to crumple onto the bed next to Big Bess.

"A stranger . . . just passin' through," he said, voice hoarse.

Then he snapped his spine straight, and his gaze turned into something hard and sharp—a blade aimed at Big Bess. The woman even flinched.

"If that's all there is to it," he snarled, "why didn't you say so before we came up here?"

"Hey, you said you had questions about Adeline, so here I am. If you don't like the answers, that ain't my fault."

"She's right, Brother," I said, "and she's stickin' her neck out just talkin' to us, y'know. Instead of grousin' about what the lady's got to say, we oughta just hear it through quick and get the hell outta here."

"Alright, alright," Old Red grumbled. "I'm sorry, Bess. I'm just . . . edgy, is all."

"Sure, I understand. Some things never change." The "lady" threw me a wink that reminded me of the Big Bess I'd first seen downstairs—

the one who was all wisecracks and frolics and hustling the customers. "So who else you talked to since you hit town?"

"Well, all we've really managed to do is—"

"Hear it through quick, you said," Gustav snapped at me. "So let's not get off the trail, huh?" He turned back to Big Bess, and his tone softened. A bit. "When was it Ragsdale told you about this supposed stranger?"

Big Bess furrowed her considerable brow. "When? I don't know. A long time back."

"*Think.* Could it have been the first time he sent one of you gals over to the Star after Adeline died?"

"You think Ragsdale was lyin'?" I asked Old Red. "So his chippies wouldn't be afraid to make house calls?"

"I don't know. I do know him sayin' something sure as hell don't make it true."

Big Bess gave her head a quick, firm shake. "No, no . . . I remember now. It was the night Adeline died. That's when Mr. Ragsdale mentioned the stranger at the Star, I'm sure of it."

"That very night?" Gustav said. "Around what time?"

"What *time*? Christ! It was five years ago!"

"Well, if you can't gimme the when, what about the how? I'm guessin' Ragsdale didn't just bring it up in the midst of friendly conversation. Cuz from what Adeline used to tell me, once that bastard has a gal in harness for him, he'd as soon spit on her as speak to her. It's all 'Yes, Mr. Ragsdale—no, Mr. Ragsdale' and a slap to the face for anything more."

Big Bess's face flushed as if *she'd* just been slapped.

"I asked him what happened to Adeline, and he told me," she said. "That's all I remember."

"You gotta admit, Bess," I said, "it wouldn't be beyond a feller like Ragsdale to lie."

"Feh," Gustav spat. "It wouldn't be beyond that son of a bitch to kill Adeline himself and whip up some bullshit story to cover it."

"Why would Mr. Ragsdale do that?" Big Bess asked.

"Well, there's the money Adeline was savin' up, for one thing," Old Red said. "What happened to it?"

Big Bess shrugged. "I never heard about any money."

"Really? Adeline told me all you gals sock cash away around the cathouse, cuz them two slave drivers of yours would take—"

"I don't know what you're talkin' about!" Big Bess boomed. For just an instant, her gaze flicked away to the wall, seeming to settle on the portrait of Lincoln behind us. There was sullen spite in her eyes, and I couldn't help thinking it wasn't fair, Honest Abe getting the evil eye like that. But, hey . . . this was Texas. The woman was probably a Democrat.

"Look," Gustav said, "the week before she was killed, Adeline told me her kitty was up to three hundred dollars. Now, that much money don't just—"

Big Bess leaned back and barked a harsh laugh up at the ceiling. "Three hundred dollars? Well, ooo-la-laaaaaa!"

"What's that supposed to mean?"

When Big Bess looked back down at my brother, her face wasn't so much changed as unveiled. The anger and contempt etched deep into her blubber had been there all along, just underneath the grins and winks.

"It means Mr. Ragsdale and Mr. Bock wouldn't wipe their asses on three hundred dollars, let alone kill a good earner like Adeline for it. She could hump up more money than that in a month."

Old Red stiffened, his jaw clenched tight.

"Oh . . . you didn't know that about her, did you?" Big Bess went on. "That she was popular with the boys? Well, she was. *Real* popular. I tell you, that bird-with-a-wounded-wing act of hers sure worked. She must've had twenty dumb drovers on her string, all of 'em thinkin' they was her one and only. You want the truth about your sweet Adeline, well, there it is: You didn't mean any more to her than any other horny ranch hand plunkin' down his dollar."

Gustav just stood there, utterly still, utterly silent. Lot's wife in a Stetson and blue jeans.

"Oh, hon . . . I'm sorry," Big Bess said, her tone suddenly turning tender, remorseful, sickly sweet. "I should've told you nicer. But the important thing is now you know, and you can save yourself a lot of trouble. Adeline always said you was thick, but I never believed it. You're smart, I can tell. And a smart man wouldn't tangle with Mr. Ragsdale and Mr. Bock. Not for *her*. You don't owe that lyin' bitch a thing. Just go. Now. Before it's too late."

Old Red made no move to go, though. He made no move—no sound—of any kind.

"Brother," I began. I'm not even sure I had more to say than that. I was just reminding him I was there. That he wasn't as alone as Big Bess's words might make him feel.

Then words finally came to him again, slow and low.

"Tell me again . . . who sent Adeline to the Star that night?"

"Mr. Bock."

"Hmm." Gustav turned away, head bowed, and began pacing around the room with heavy, deliberate steps. "And who was it told you about the stranger?"

Big Bess hesitated, like this was some kind of trick question.

"Mr. Ragsdale."

"Uh-huh."

As Old Red was passing the picture of Lincoln, he stopped, then pivoted again and leaned back against the wall next to it. His face and gloomy old Abe's were perfectly even, and it was like there were two men staring at Big Bess now.

"Just one more question, Bess," Gustav said. "Why are you still callin' both them bastards 'mister' when ain't neither of 'em around to even hear it?"

"Oh. Huh. I don't know." Big Bess's wide mouth twitched into an overcooked smile of the sort she'd been serving up for the customers.

"Habit, I suppose. It's like you said a minute ago—them macks of mine get awful persnickety if us gals get too familiar."

My brother shook his head sadly. "Oh, Bess . . ."

And he swung up his right hand, the index and middle fingers stuck out in a *V*, and poked Abe Lincoln right in the eyes.

Even more shocking than that, the Great Emancipator *spoke*— though the Gettysburg Address it was not.

"Fudge!" he screeched. "Ow ow ow! Oh, that fudgin' mother-fudger!"

Lincoln's eyes took on a dull glow—light shining through from a room on the other side of the portrait.

The eyes were empty slits, I now saw, the canvas cut away to make two wee peepholes. And the man who'd been doing the peeping was staggering around on the other side shouting, "Get in there and fudgin' kill that little fudger!"

"Sweet Jesus," I said. "Is that Ragsdale?"

My brother's only answer was "Run run run!"

This seemed like sensible advice indeed, and as I was closer to the door I reached it first and jerked it open—and found myself facing Stonewall, a Peacemaker looking puny in his huge sausage-fingered fist.

"Remember, now," I said to him. "Your boss told you to kill the *little* fudger."

Stonewall wasn't the sort to let such niggling details stand in his way, however.

He thumbed back the hammer and pointed the gun at a spot midway between my eyes.

8

FUDGIN' FUDGERS

Or, Ragsdale and Bock Take Suite Revenge for Our Meddling

"Don't," someone said.

To my great amazement, it wasn't me. Had it been, I assume Stonewall wouldn't have listened.

He didn't just have a clear shot at my forehead. He looked eager to take it.

"Inside," the voice said, and Stonewall stepped into the Bridal Suite, herding me back with his .45.

Round-bellied, blank-faced Gil Bock walked in after him. He was still wearing the top hat and oversized frock coat we'd seen him in earlier that day, and as before his dead eyes registered no emotion—not even satisfaction at seeing me and my brother cornered.

"Against the wall," he said.

We obliged him, backing up till we were lined up three abreast: me, Old Red, Abraham Lincoln.

Remembering how things had turned out for Abe did *not* cheer me up.

"Ohhhhh, fudge fudge fudge *fudge* . . ."

Pete Ragsdale stumbled in rubbing his eyes. He closed the door behind him, then blinked at us blearily.

"Why the fudge are these fudgin' fudgers still fudgin' alive?"

"Questions first," Bock said.

Ragsdale sighed like a farmboy who's been told he has to slop the hogs before he can go fishing. He had a chore to do . . . *then* he could have his fun.

"Get back to work," he said to Big Bess.

She fought to haul her flab up off the bed.

"Come on, come on," Ragsdale said, clapping his hands. "Get a fudgin' move on. You're done here."

Big Bess finally got her feet planted on the floor and headed for the door. Old Red stared at her hard as she waddled past.

"Oh, don't look at me like that," she sneered. "After all these years you decide to stir up old shit, and you actually expect me to help?"

"Maybe not," Gustav said, "but I wouldn't expect you to sell me down the river to these—"

"Shut your fudgin' mouth," Ragsdale said to my brother.

"Hurry the fudge up," Bock said to Big Bess.

Charming conversationalists, those two—and it would only get better.

"So long," I said as Bess shuffled out. "Thanks for the royal screwin'."

She slammed the door behind her.

"Well. Well well fudgin' well . . ." Ragsdale sauntered over to the nightstand near the bed and leaned over the old, withered rose in the vase atop it. He lifted it to his beaklike nose, gave it a sniff, then began idly picking off the brittle black petals. "Where to begin?"

"How about with you goin' to hell?" my brother snarled.

Ragsdale snickered.

"Bales," Bock said.

"Right. Fudgin' Bales." Ragsdale plucked the flower down to nothing, then stuck the thorny stem through his lapel hole. "What did you two fudgeheads talk to the marshal about after you left our store this afternoon?"

Gustav said nothing.

I said nothing.

Stonewall said nothing—he just pushed the muzzle of his gun so close I had to go cross-eyed to look at it. Which said plenty, actually.

"Oh, we chatted about this and that," I said. "The weather. Recipes. Neighborhood gossip."

The gun whipped out of sight . . . but only because my head was jerking to the side, lights flashing in my eyes, cheek stinging, ears ringing.

"What did you talk about?" Ragsdale barked.

He'd swooped in and slapped me, pimp style.

"We didn't talk about nothin', alright?" I said. "It was Bales talkin' and us just listenin'."

Ragsdale brought up his hand again, palm flat.

Stonewall still had his gun on me.

I steeled myself for the blow.

It never came.

"Bales was warnin' us off!" Old Red blurted out. "Said he didn't want us stirrin' up any trouble in town. You two didn't even come up, if that's what you're worried about."

Ragsdale glanced back at Bock, looking pleased.

"The timing," Bock said.

Ragsdale nodded. "Why'd you fudgers show up now?" he asked us. "After all these fudgin' years?"

"We just never got around to it before," I said. I wasn't even trying to be a wiseass this time. It was the only answer I could give that wouldn't take an hour to get out.

Ragsdale raised his hand again—and this time he was making a fist.

"There ain't no special reason, ya bastard," Gustav said. "I just finally *had* to come back, and that's all there is to it."

Ragsdale dropped his hand. "I told you these motherfudgers had squat," he said to Bock. "Can we be done here?"

"The picture," Bock said.

"What about it?"

Bock nodded at Honest Abe watching over the proceedings with his sad, empty eyes.

"Oh. Fudge. Yeah," Ragsdale said. "*That* picture."

"You know, don't you?" my brother muttered. "You dirty sons of bitches know who killed Adeline and you're tryin' to—"

Ragsdale drove a fist into his stomach.

Old Red oofed and doubled over and grabbed his gut with both hands.

I reached out to help steady him.

Something cold and hard pressed against the side of my head.

"Back."

I did as I was told, but the cold spot—the muzzle of Stonewall's Colt—stayed against my skull.

Ragsdale had one more question—and when he was done, it seemed, so were we.

"When it was just you two and Bess," Ragsdale said, "how'd you know someone was fudgin' watchin'? And don't say it was just cuz that fudgin' lard-ass kept callin' me and Gil 'mister.'"

"Adeline," Gustav wheezed. "She told me there was a room y'all used when you wanted to peep on folks at the Eagle. For blackmail and . . . 'special requests,' she called it. Wasn't much of a stretch to guess you'd have one in your new pl—"

"Oh, don't worry, honey!" a new voice cut in, and I heard the door swing open behind me. "I'm always welcome to use the Bridal . . . shit."

Then that cold spot on my temple came in real handy, actually, for the moment Stonewall turned to look over his shoulder, I felt it waver.

I shot up my left hand, snagged Stonewall's wrist, and pushed the gun toward the ceiling. My right hand, meanwhile, was busy bloody-ing Stonewall's nose.

The Peacemaker spat a slug upward, and a puff of gunsmoke sur-rounded us. The recoil made it all the easier to pry the gun from Stonewall's grip, and when I had it firm in hand, I gave it back to him. Over the top of his head.

Stonewall went down like the walls of Jericho.

"Come on!" Old Red hollered, and through the gray haze around me I could see him charging toward the doorway—and the extremely slender, extremely shocked customer standing there with an equally stunned floozy by his side.

My brother darted between them, but I (being about twice as broad across) had no such option. So I went *over* them.

Ever the gentleman, I made way for the woman as much as I could . . . which meant I gave the man the worst of it. I got a good look into his goggling eyes before he bounced off my chest and disap-peared beneath my feet. He had the leather-tough look of someone who doesn't usually let folks walk all over him, and I couldn't help but notice (as I stepped on it) that he had a holstered gun at his side.

"Stop 'em!" Ragsdale roared. "Don't let those motherfudgers get away!"

I looked back just long enough to spray the hallway with lead. All of it toward the ceiling, of course—no killer of innocent (or not so innocent) bystanders am I. Still, the barrage was enough to clear the hallway and keep it clear. When the Colt was emptied, I tossed it aside and went bounding down the stairs after my brother.

"Some drover just went crazy and shot Stonewall!" I wailed at the top of my sizable lungs. *"And the SOB's reloadin'!"*

If the Phoenix had been merry chaos before, now it was *panicked* chaos multiplied by bedlam plus anarchy squared.

Women screamed. *Men* screamed. A few brave souls rushed past us up the stairs. Another, much larger bunch stampeded for the exit.

Still others made the most of Stonewall's supposed demise by rushing the bar and helping themselves to whichever bottles came to hand.

The gunman from out front passed us before we reached the door, wriggling against the fleeing throng like a salmon trying to make its way upstream. I looked back and saw Bock and Ragsdale and that slim/tough customer trapped halfway down the stairs amidst a swirl of milling cowboys. All three were bellowing and gesticulating wildly in our direction, but their words were swallowed up in the general hubbub, and Gustav and I were outside before the gunny could figure out what they were so fired-up eager to tell him.

"Ain't got no choice, Brother," Old Red said, dashing toward a string of horses hobbled beside a barberry bush.

"I never figured it'd come to this," I panted as I sprinted after him. "You and me . . . horse thieves."

"You wanna walk back to town with them bastards on your heels, you go ahead."

I pointed at a pretty palomino.

"Dibs," I said.

We rode into San Marcos at a gallop, but rather than retreat directly to the Star, Gustav insisted we leave our borrowed mounts in front of the courthouse in the town square.

"Ike Rucker, the county sheriff—he keeps office here," Old Red explained as we tied the horses to metal hitching posts in front of the building. "And whoever these belong to, they'll have to go to Rucker to report 'em stolen. So this way, they'll get their ponies back quick—"

"And nobody'll want to hang us for stealin' horses."

"That's the idea."

"What if Rucker spots us out here, though? He'll have us red-handed."

Gustav shook his head, finished his hitch, and hustled away.

"Rucker ain't in town tonight," he said when I joined him in the shadows of the nearest side street.

"How do you know?"

My brother glanced over at me, and even scurrying through the dark, I knew the Look when I saw it. I was being dense.

"Didn't you notice?" Old Red said. "That feller you flattened back at the Phoenix was packin'."

"So?"

Then, before my brother could even answer, "Oh."

The Phoenix had a no guns rule.

Then, "Oh" again.

Rules don't apply to everybody.

And finally, "Oh, hell."

The customer I'd rolled out like a pie crust?

That was Sheriff Ike Rucker.

9

GIBES AND SNEERS

Or, I Throw Questions at Gustav, and He Throws the Book at Me

Y ou want first watch or second?" Old Red asked when we got back to our ratty little room at the Star.

"Oh, I ain't sleepy after all that fuss tonight. I'll go first. Only . . ."

I patted my thigh where a .45 should have been hanging. We'd been in such a hurry to leave the Phoenix in our dust, we'd left our Colts, too.

"Somebody comes for us, what am I supposed to hold 'em off with? My toothbrush?"

"You could always clobber 'em with this."

Gustav swiped something black and blocky off the bed and tossed it across the room to me.

It was his copy of *The Adventures of Sherlock Holmes*.

"Fair enough," I said. "You've hit *me* over the head with Holmes often enough."

My brother grunted out a non-laugh, tossed his hat onto a nearby chair, then sat on the bed and got to tugging off his boots. A moment later, he was stretched out still dressed, hands behind his head, eyes pointed straight up.

This was his usual nighttime repose, part of the ritual we'd initiated a little more than a year before: He lies down on his back staring up at nothing, and I read out a Holmes yarn before turning out the light (or turning away from the campfire, should we be on the trail). Then I awake in the morning to find Gustav still gazing into infinity and wonder to myself whether the man sleeps at all anymore.

This night would be different.

"No stories," my brother said. "Ain't got no use for fairy tales just now. I got enough to chew on already."

"You wanna do that chewin' out loud?"

Old Red didn't even take his eyes off the stained, crack-webbed plaster above.

"Not really."

"Well, too bad. Cuz I do," I said. "What the hell happened tonight, Brother?"

Gustav rustled the sheets with a halfhearted shrug. "We got snookered."

"That much I figured out myself. It's the details I'm wonderin' about. Like was that a trap from the get-go or did our luck just go bad?"

"Trap from the get-go," Old Red sighed. "There wasn't time to fetch Ragsdale and Bock in from town after we showed up. They must've been upstairs already. And the way Big Bess steered us into the Bridal Suite—that smacks of a plan. So the whole time we was tryin' to milk Bess for data, she was tryin' to milk *us*."

I grimaced. "I do wish you'd take more care with your metaphors."

"Seemed fishy, Big Bess insistin' on you and me both bein' up there," Gustav went on. "I had no choice but to play along, though. Far as I knew, that was gonna be my only chance to talk to—"

I put up my hands like I was flagging down a wagon about to roll right over top of me. "Whoa whoa whoa! Are you sayin' you guessed it was a snare before Bess even brung me up?"

Old Red finally looked over at me. "It was just a feeling. I figured I had to take the risk."

"Well, it wasn't just you takin' it, was it?"

"Look, I don't think they meant to kill us . . . not at first, anyway. They're hidin' something, and best for them if we was to mosey on of our own accord rather than draw attention by turnin' up dead. That's why Big Bess was feedin' us lies. Like that tripe about the 'stranger' at the Star. Or Adeline and all her other beaux."

"Assumin' that *was* tripe."

My brother's face flushed. "It was."

I was about to ask a dangerous question indeed—"How do you know?"—when another, even thornier thought occurred to me.

"If they was just servin' up swill hopin' we'd swallow it and go," I said, "why not pretend it worked? You say, 'Thank you, Bess—guess we came here for naught,' and you stroll out and I follow and that's that. Instead you go and poke Ragsdale in the eyes, and the whole thing blows sky high."

"That's hindsight talkin'," Gustav growled.

"Not for you, it ain't. You walked into that room half-cocked for a trap, and when Ragsdale and Bock didn't spring it, why, you went and sprung it yourself. On the both of us."

"Alright, I made a mistake. I was pissed and flustered and finally it was me doin' something dumb instead of you. So I ain't Sherlock Holmes! I ain't perfect! If that puts a streak of yellow up your spine, you can just pack your bag and hightail it off to—"

"Oh, don't give me that horseshit," I snapped. "You know I'm stickin' with you to the end. I just don't want the end comin' any sooner than it has to. And that means I don't like stupid risks we don't gotta take."

To this, my brother did not reply. He did not retort. He did not offer riposte or rejoinder or rebuttal.

No, he bounced off the bed and he *roared*.

"You think *I* like it, ya jackass? Well, I don't! But stupid risks is all we got! We're here five years after the fact, and there ain't no clues to be found. 'Can't make bricks without clay,' that's what Holmes used to say. Well, we ain't got the clay to fill a thimble, let alone build bricks. So we gotta dig for it—gotta root around in the mud for it! And if that means I take stupid risks, then I take stupid risks. And if I make mistakes, I make mistakes. And it ain't horseshit to say if you can't stomach it, you need to get the hell gone!"

I blinked at my brother, stumped for once for something to say.

Our nearest neighbor, on the other hand, wasn't tongue-tied in the slightest.

"Hey!" a muffled voice called out, followed by three thumps that sent flakes of plaster snowing down from the wall behind our bed. "Shut up over there!"

Old Red spun around and gave the wall his pounding fist seven times in quick succession.

"I . . . am . . . sorry!" he hollered, one word to a wallop. "Good . . . night . . . to . . . you . . . sir!"

Then he dropped back down on the bed, rubbing his fingers.

"Ow," he muttered—and nothing more. He just grabbed his Stetson, stretched out on his back again, and, as he often will when readying himself for heavy-duty sleep or cogitation, plopped his hat over his face. Then all was still.

Silences, of course, are by no means my specialty. Yet I managed to ride this one out for a good four or five minutes before I spoke.

"Brother."

No response . . . but no snores, either.

"Brother?"

Still nothing.

"Alright. Suit yourself."

I braced the door with the room's one chair, then settled myself on the floor and did something I'd never done before. I opened up *The Adventures of Sherlock Holmes* not for Gustav, but for me.

There was a passage I was thinking of, one that Old Red—despite his fondness for quoting Holmes—almost never mentioned. It was just a little aside in the yarn called "A Scandal in Bohemia," a few tidbits Johnny Watson tosses off before getting down to the facts of the matter.

Holmes, Watson wrote, distrusted "the softer passions," never speaking of them but with "a gibe and a sneer." Love he dismissed as "a distracting factor which might throw a doubt upon all his mental results," "a crack in one of his own high-power lenses."

I read through all this again, then had to sit there and wonder: If love could crack a lens, what could a *lost* love do? What could the thirst for vengeance do?

Because it seemed to me I was seeing cracks aplenty in my brother. And the longer we stayed in San Marcos, the more likely his whole "lens" would up and shatter to pieces—and maybe the man with it.

10

CITY LIMITS
Or, We Visit the Town's Greasiest Spoon—and Dine on Ashes

When I was through reading *The Adventures of Sherlock Holmes*, I used it for writing: Balanced against my knees underneath a sheet of paper, the book made a decent desk.

Doc Watson's chronicles were my foundation in more ways than one, for it was a mystery tale I was working on—a short story for my new publisher, Mr. Urias Smythe of Smythe & Associates Publishing, Ltd. Though I had yet to see any of the yarns Mr. Smythe had bought from me in print, I felt at last like a real, professional writer and not just a drifter with an overactive imagination.

Every so often, I was jerked from my work by footsteps in the hall, but each time the sound passed by our door without Stonewall busting through it. Eventually my eyelids and my pencil both got to drooping, and I found that the last "sentence" I'd written was nothing but a long, scraggly scrawl. It was time to call it a night.

As usual, Gustav roused so easy I had to wonder if he'd been asleep at all, snatching the hat off his face and saying, "I'm up," the second I started toward him. My own slumber came on so quick and deep I can't even remember making it to the bed, and the next thing I knew the light of day was flooding the room.

The *empty* room, I noticed through a groggy half-sleep haze.

The empty room someone was fiddling with the door to get into.

I snatched up the nearest weapon—my pillow—and let it fly as the door swung open.

It sailed right over my brother's head.

"You want that back, you can go get it yourself," Old Red said, "and I wouldn't dawdle, I was you. Place like this, someone's liable to grab it and hold it for ransom."

He was cradling a pile of whatnot in his arms, and by the time I was back with the pillow, it was all spread out on the bed.

Levi's, flannel shirt, vest, spurs, boots, bandanna, and, to top it all off, a Boss of the Plains, round-crowned Texas-style. Beside all that was the *real* topper: a new gun belt, a gleaming Colt nestled in the scabbard.

It was the cowboy's uniform, dutifully worn by myself for so many years it got to be like a second skin—a skin I'd been happy to shed. The thought of slipping back into it made me itchy.

"You know," I said, "if you're gonna give me a coronary sneakin' in like that come morning, the least you could do is bring me what I really want."

"Which is what?"

"Whadaya think?" I popped the hat on my head. Its tall-peaked top made me feel like I'd just put on a dunce cap. "Doughnuts."

"Don't worry. We'll fill that tub gut of yours before we go."

I patted my stomach. It did jiggle a bit, I admit, but I still felt myself wronged.

"This ain't no tub. It ain't even a chamber pot. Why, I could work it down to . . . hold on." I looked up at my brother. *"Go?"*

"Yeah, go. I thunk up a new plan. If we can't get anything outta the gals at the Phoenix, I figure we should try the next best thing. Their clee-on-tell."

"Meanin' punchers? So we're headed out to a ranch?"

64

"*The* ranch. The one I used to work for—the Lucky Seven. What with Ragsdale and Bock and all the law around here set against us, it's about time we rounded up some folks for our side."

I nodded.

"Makes sense."

"Oh, I'm so pleased to hear you think so." Old Red snatched up the Levi's and pushed them against my chamber pot. "Now stop jawin' and get dressed. I thought you was hungry."

He thought right. So when we got to the little hole-in-the-wall lunch counter Gustav had picked out for our morning repast, I ordered everything on the menu. Which wasn't hard to do, actually: The menu, written on a chalkboard the approximate size of a handkerchief, was only three lines long.

> BAKIN & EGGS—5¢
> FRY'D TATERS—5¢
> COFFY—5¢

The little hash house was of a kind with a thousand others you'll find attached like ticks to a cowtown outskirts. It was spitting distance from the stockyards and railroad depot—which was appropriate, as spitting was exactly what a man was wont to do after taking a sip of the gritty black sludge slopped into his COFFY cup. Yet the dozen or so other customers weren't complaining, them being cowboys or railroad men long accustomed to Arbuckle the color and consistency of axle grease.

I was pleased to see my new clothes were already paying off in one regard: I received nary a sneer from our fellow diners . . . for a couple minutes, at least.

"Mornin', Ike!" the greasy old coosie who ran the place called out, and within seconds nearly every other man there had taken up the call. The exceptions being my brother, who opted for a hissed "Shit," and myself, who nearly spit out a mouthful of half-chewed BAKIN.

I peeked over my shoulder to find a tall, lean man with a star on his chest sauntering into the cookshack.

There was a red splotch high up on his left cheek the exact size and shape of a shoe heel.

In San Francisco's Chinatown just a few weeks before, I'd run across the notion of yin and yang: two things that are equal though entirely opposite. Taking my first good look at Ike Rucker, I got the feeling I was seeing Milford Bales's yin. Or maybe his yang, though that sounds vaguely vulgar.

Where the town marshal was baby-faced and soft-bellied, the county sheriff was as sinewy as a rawhide whip. While Bales had to work hard to put up a tough front, a layer of sweat glistening over the nerves all a-jitter just under the skin, Rucker looked like he'd been born wearing a badge. He seemed at ease, amused, but with an air of command that wasn't so much haughtiness as complete and utter confidence.

Rucker and Bales may have both been the Law thereabouts, but the men—and the Law as they embodied it—couldn't have been more different.

"Boys," Rucker said to the customers lined up along the sagging plankboard counter, and he smiled and touched the brim of his hat.

"What'll it be this mornin', Ike?" the cookie asked.

"Oh, just a cup of coffee and—"

That's when Rucker pretended to spot us.

"Oh, my. Could that be Gloomy Gus over there?" He walked to our table and pulled out one of the empty chairs. "Mind if I join you fellers?"

He was already sitting as he said it.

"Not at all, please, go right ahead," I said. If Rucker wanted to fake conviviality, then I'd show him how it was done. "Truth is, we'll feel safer havin' you with us. I hate to tell you this, Sheriff, but you've got some mighty unsavory characters in your county."

It looked like Rucker was giving me a friendly grin until I noticed something strange: The man didn't blink. His eyes just kept boring into me, and I had to fight the urge to blink on his behalf or look away altogether.

"I don't believe we've met," he said.

"Not formally, I suppose, no. I'm Gloomy Gus's brother, Unstoppable Otto. Three guesses how I got my nickname."

Rucker casually plucked a piece of bacon from my plate and tore off a bite.

"Boy, they sure wasn't lyin' about you," he said as he chewed. "You are a stitch."

He stuffed the rest of the bacon in his mouth.

He wasn't laughing.

"What else you heard about us?" my brother asked him.

"Well, for one thing, that you borrowed horses off a couple Circle B boys last night."

"Oh, that couldn't be," I said, wide-eyed innocence personified. "We don't *know* anyone from the Circle B."

The cook came over with Rucker's coffee, and after thanking him, the lawman picked up my brother's fork and helped himself to some home fries.

"I'm also told you been harassin' some of our local business leaders," he said around a mouthful of tater.

"Golly, Sheriff . . . you make it sound like we blew up the Elks Lodge," I said. "As I recall it, *I* was the one with the gun to his head last night."

Rucker gave me a glower, then turned to my food, poking at a yolk until it bled gold all over my plate. He sopped up the mess with my egg's mangled remains and stuffed his mouth full, leaving a yellow slime trail up his chin.

"We wasn't harassin' nobody," Old Red said. "Just askin' questions."

"It ain't for the likes of you to ask questions. That's my job." As if Rucker's badge couldn't be more tarnished in my eyes, he tapped it twice with his fork, leaving a smear of yolk and grease. "And let me tell you something else . . ."

And just like that, Rucker's voice rose and his back straightened and his head went up high. It was almost like he was giving a speech— and from the way the rumble of conversation and the clink and scrape of cutlery came to a sudden stop all around us, I knew he was.

"Pete Ragsdale and Gil Bock provide a service this county needs. That's what this stick-up-its-ass town doesn't understand anymore. Oh, yeah, we've got a fancy school up on the hill and telephones and electric lights—but the money for all that? It still smells like cowshit, no matter how much perfume these townsfolk sprinkle over it. It's cattle that made something outta San Marcos and cattle that'll keep it something. And you can't push men as hard as ranch work does with- out lettin' 'em blow off a little steam at the end of the week. So the boys whore. So they drink. So they get rowdy. *So what?* At least they ain't rapin' and robbin' and shootin' up the county courthouse. And that's just what they'd do, run wild through town, if they didn't have some- place like the Phoenix to turn to."

I caught a flurry of motion out of the corner of my eye, a little ripple that spread from table to table.

Nods. Cowboy or railroader, it didn't matter—they agreed with Rucker.

He may have been a rotten lawman, but as a politician he was first-rate.

"Sheriff, with all due respect," Gustav said, and from his grating tone and gritting teeth, it was clear not much *was* due. "I don't give a damn about any of that. I just wanna know who killed my Adeline."

Rucker nodded, an expression of benevolent tolerance on his sun- leathered face . . . even as he reached out and speared another helping off my brother's plate. When he spoke, his voice was quiet again, muffled by a moist mouthful of fried egg.

He'd stepped down off the stump.

"Look, Gus . . . I sympathize. I knew that little gal myself, and it's a shame what happened to her, but you know what she was. It's a rough business, and people get hurt. That's just the way of it, and you'd best accept that."

Old Red's lips squeezed tight but his jaw was working, almost squirming beneath the skin. He looked like a man trying to figure out what kind of bug just flew into his mouth. He finally washed the sour expression away with a long slurp of coffee.

Rucker's coffee.

"So," he said, slamming the mug down hard in front of the sheriff, "you 'knew' Adeline, did you? You usin' that word biblical-like? Cuz obviously it ain't just ranch hands who turn to Ragsdale and Bock for their fun."

Rucker had been polishing off the last of my potatoes when Old Red got going, and now he froze midchew.

"And tell me, Sheriff," my brother rolled on. "Them 'people' who 'get hurt sometimes.' Who would you be talkin' about, exactly? Cuz if the son of a bitch who sliced Adeline up has done the same to anyone else since then, that's blood on your hands. And another thing—"

Gustav was cut off by a nerve-shaking clatter—Rucker tossing the fork he'd appropriated onto my plate.

"Listen here, you little shit." Rucker snatched my napkin off my lap, wiped his mouth with it, then threw it back into my chest. "Do you have any idea why I sat down to talk things through with you all polite like this?"

"Because you were hungry?" I ventured.

Rucker kept his unblinking gaze on Gustav.

"Cuz we're inside city limits," my brother said.

"That's right. Milford Bales's badge trumps mine here in town. But out there?" The sheriff pointed a long finger to the east, then did the same to the north, west, and south. "And there and there and there? That's all me, and the law is what I say it is. *Right* is what I say it is. Wrong, too. So sittin' here in San Marcos, I can only try to persuade you to see reason. But the second you cross the line . . . ?"

Rucker leaned toward Old Red and dropped his voice to a whisper.

"I can gun you down easy as swattin' a goddamn fly."

Then, quick as that, he was on his feet.

"Quit buzzin' in my ears, boys."

Before he turned to go, he smacked an imaginary fly on his shoulder, brushing its little invisible carcass away with a couple casual slaps of the hand.

He was all smiles again as he made his good-byes and left.

Me and Gustav—we were all frowns.

11

SUICIDE

Or, A Visit to the Lucky Seven Is Abruptly Deep-Sixed

Well, now it's official," I said to Old Red. "We've been threatened by every livin' soul in San Marcos."

My brother just glared hatefully at Rucker's back as the sheriff ambled out the greasy spoon's door.

"Eatin' a man's eggs," I said. "That is just plain wrong. Say, Cookie . . ."

I turned toward the belly cheater at the griddle, thinking I'd order us another round of eats. I found the old man already glowering our way, a spatula gripped tight in his hand like a flyswatter he was fixing to squash us with.

"You two clear out," he said. "I don't need no troublemakers in here."

"Oh, come on, Pop," I started to protest.

"You heard the man," snarled a grungy puncher at the counter. "Get."

"Yeah," his equally scruffy buddy threw in. He left it at that, apparently assuming it said enough.

He was right, too, and a quick glance around the cookshack confirmed it. We were surrounded by scowls. Our choices were get or get got.

"Guess I was wrong before," I sighed. "*Now* we've been threatened by everyone in town."

We had our revenge, though. Gustav and I made for the door without leaving the old coosie a gratuity. That'd show him.

After that, alas, it was a breakfast of general store crackers and jerky, and then we were riding off for the Lucky Seven on mounts rented from a local livery. It felt good to be putting San Marcos behind us for a while, though our departure clearly wasn't permanent enough to suit some: As we trotted by the railroad depot, we passed Milford Bales himself chatting with the station agent, and the marshal stared at us with such open revulsion I had to look down to be sure we'd remembered to put on our pants.

I tipped my hat.

He curled his lip.

Given all the ill will coming our way lately, some serious slinking seemed in order. So though there was a well-trod trail to the outlying ranches, my brother insisted we ride along the San Marcos River, which bubbles up out of springs just north of town.

While it's fed by the occasional stream as it winds its way south, the "river" rarely lived up to the name its first few miles. It seemed no deeper than your average bathtub, and in some spots was so narrow I could have stood with a foot on each bank. About four miles south of town, though, the San Marcos joins up with the Blanco River, and the water not only widens considerably, it picks up some foamy white. Here my brother steered us to the southwest, and we left behind the lush green undergrowth and looming trees lining the river in favor of craggy, hilly grassland.

After that, we gave the horses our heels, and not just because we no longer had to watch for coiling vines and low-hanging branches.

We were out in the open, exposed, and a man with a Winchester or carbine could pick us off with ease.

It wasn't long, though, before this open country started to close in as it has everywhere else out West: with a lot of barbed wire. We'd reached the fence line of a big and obviously busy spread, for cow-smell was in the air all around us. Which meant cow*boys* would be all around us, too. It was October, time for the fall roundups, and those beeves wouldn't be leaving the summer pastures of their own free will.

"This it?" I asked.

"Yup. The Lucky Seven."

My brother had a dreamy, faraway look in his eyes as he took in the rolling meadows on the other side of the wire. He seemed to be as much in the past as the present just then, though whether the memories he was reliving were happy or sad, I couldn't say.

A flurry of movement ahead jerked him back to the here and now—and jerked our hands to our holsters. It was no bushwhacker, though, and the both of us relaxed . . . a little.

A family of turkey vultures was tucking into the mangled carcass of a calf just over the fence, cleaning up after a wolf pack's midnight snack. As we passed by, they screeched and flapped up into the sky, barely getting above the treetops before circling back to their banquet again.

"Well, that's a good sign," I said.

"How so?"

"They didn't start followin' *us*. Speakin' of which, I been wonderin'— what kinda reception we gonna get at the Seven, anyway? Ain't no one in town baked us a cake yet. You really think it'll be any better out here?"

"Depends. I got along good with the boys in the bunkhouse. The superintendent, too. The straw boss, though . . ." Gustav sighed. "Let's just hope he finally took a hoof to the head."

"He have something against you?"

"Yeah. Mostly that I thought he was a stupid son of a bitch . . . and told him so before I lit out the last time."

"Christ, Brother," I said with a laugh. "You burned more bridges than Sherman."

"Maybe, but all we need's . . ." Old Red twisted around in his saddle, looking back. "You hear that?"

"Hear what?" I said—which surely answered the question.

"Get in the brush," my brother snapped.

I turned to look back, too.

We'd been rounding a low, flower-dappled rise, and up above it I could see, just for a second, the flutter of big, black, flapping wings.

Something had startled the buzzards again.

"You think we're bein'—?"

"*Yes.* Now get outta sight, goddammit."

"What about you?"

"I'll draw 'em out, you cut 'em down. Now go!"

There was no use arguing—and no time for it, either. Whoever was behind us would round the curve of the hill any second.

Off to the east, about thirty feet from the wire, was a tangle of trees and brush. I hopped off my horse, tugged her into the shady chaparral, and wrapped the reins around a low-hanging branch. Then I filled my hand with iron.

Old Red, meanwhile, just sat there, slump-shouldered, both hands on the saddle horn, looking as relaxed as any hand lollygagging between chores. If it was Death he was facing, he'd meet it like an old friend.

A moment later, our shadow came galloping around the hill: one man on horseback, on the Lucky Seven side of the wire.

I squinted down the barrel of my Peacemaker.

"Suicide!" Gustav shouted. It looked like he was committing just that, too, for he sat up straight, making a nice big target of himself with his Colt still holstered.

The man slowed his horse and came toward Old Red at a trot.

With his big brush-popper chaps, coiled rope, and general air of dirt-caked grit, he could be nothing but a puncher. An old hand, by the look of him—he might have been as ancient as twenty-nine or thirty.

If he reached for a gun, I'd see to it he never got any older.

"Hey, Gus," the cowboy said. He reined up near the fence. "You mind tellin' your brother he can leave my head on my shoulders?"

"Sure, sure. Come on out, Otto! Suicide's a friend."

That last word—"friend"—seemed to poke the drover like a pin-prick, and a little wince puckered his tanned face.

"That ain't an easy thing to be these days, Gus," Suicide said. He greeted me with a nod as I stepped from the thicket. "You two ain't very popular around here. In fact, I shouldn't even be talkin' to you. We got orders to run you off if you come around."

"Joe Koska's still straw boss, is he?" Old Red said.

"Yeah, and he ain't forgot how you said good-bye to him." Suicide coughed out a grunt that might've been a chuckle under happier cir-cumstances. "That ain't the all of it, though. The Circle B, the Lazy Diamond, the Slash—they're all closed up to you. You won't find a hand in the county who won't spit in your eye."

"Well, there's *one*," I pointed out. I was up to the fence by then, and I stretched an arm over the wire. "Otto Amlingmeyer. Big Red to friends."

Suicide leaned down for a reluctant handshake. "I know who you are—and I'd be spittin' at you, too, if any of the boys was around." He gave my brother a miserable shrug. "Sorry, Gus, but I gotta get by around here."

"It wasn't just luck it was you who spotted us, was it?" Old Red said.

Suicide nodded. "I've been 'roundin' up strays' over here all morn-ing. Figured you'd come this way sooner or later."

"Well, there you go." My brother waved the puncher's shame away with a single swipe of the hand. "So . . . what's got everyone so riled?"

"That ruckus y'all kicked up at the Phoenix, for one thing. There were hands from all the big spreads there last night, so word's got 'round fast about it."

"Why would anyone hold that against us?" I said. "Fellers must be raisin' hell at the Phoenix all the time."

"Not fellers like you."

"What's different about us?" Gustav asked.

Suicide took in a deep breath. He looked like a man who's been asked to tell a long, sad story he'd just as soon forget.

"Look, Gus—things have changed since you been gone. Before, there was a little chafin' between San Marcos and us out here in the country. Now everything's rubbed raw. A bunch of them townsfolk went and got religion—the hellfire and damnation, no whorin', no drinkin' kind—and closin' down the Golden Eagle won't be enough for that bunch. It won't be long 'fore they're tryin' to vote the whole county dry . . . and you know that don't sit well out here. It's got so there's only two ways to line up: with Marshal Bales and them reformer types or with Sheriff Rucker and everybody else."

"And 'everybody else' thinks we're in with Bales?" Old Red asked.

Suicide looked confused. "Ain't you? That's what Ike Rucker's been goin' around sayin'. And everyone knows you and Bales used to be pals."

"Used to be is right. Now?" Gustav shook his head. "Milford don't even enter into it, though. I ain't here to help him. You know what really brought me back."

Suicide nodded slowly. "Sure. It ain't like Gloomy Gus Amlingmeyer to leave a job undone. I can't help you on that score, though. I don't know anything more about it than I did five years—"

"Put your gun on us," Old Red cut in.

"What?"

Suicide's Peacemaker was still in its scabbard, but Gustav put up his hands all the same.

"Some feller just come over the hill behind you," he said.

76

I peeked past Suicide's shoulder and spotted the man myself: another puncher, not a hundred yards off and headed our way fast.

I put up my hands, too. "Looks like you got the drop on us, you wily devil."

Suicide finally got the idea and whipped out his artillery.

"One more thing you oughta know, Gus," he said, talking fast. "Bob Harris bought part of the Seven—that rocky patch that dips into Guadalupe County. Got himself a homestead and his own little herd, of sorts. You want answers, maybe you oughta look there."

As Suicide spoke, the hand behind him came galloping down the slope so fast it looked like he aimed to jump the fence. At the last moment, though, he reined up hard, and his horse kicked up dust and clods of dirt as it skidded to a stop mere inches from the wire.

It sure made a statement, an entrance like that.

I am a reckless halfwit.

He was young, even by drovering standards—a true cow*boy* of perhaps fifteen, with wispy fair hair and apple cheeks and freckles he probably wished he could shave off like the whiskers he hadn't yet sprouted. He was trying to scowl at us like a hard man, a real tough hombre, but the effect he achieved instead was more a gassy baby.

"That them?" he said to Suicide.

"Yup. Caught 'em skulkin' around the wire here."

"Meddlin' sons of bitches." The kid caressed the grip of his gun—a Smith & Wesson .45 that bulged on his hip like a two-ton anchor tied to the side of a rowboat. "What should we do with 'em?"

"I already gave 'em the lay of the land." Suicide threw us a depressingly convincing sneer. "They know they ain't welcome here—nor anywhere else outside town."

"We was just leavin'," my brother said.

"Yeah, you do that." Freckles straightened up in his saddle, puffing himself up to what he fancied was man size. "Run on back to your streetlights and Bibles, and do it quick. Cuz the next time you get caught out here in the hills, you'll be *buried* here. You get me?"

It was a little much to take from a squirt who didn't look any tougher than a slice of angel food cake. So I didn't take it.

"Alright, alright—don't get your diapers in a bunch, junior." I turned my back to him and started walking off toward the trees. "We'll go and let you get back to playin' cowboys and idjits."

When I led my mount from the thicket a moment later, I found Freckles waiting with his .45 drawn.

"Why don't you try that again, asshole?" he snarled menacingly— or would've if his voice hadn't cracked. Still, his S&W was menace enough for me.

"May I have your permission to flee in terror now?" I said. "Sir."

"That's better," the young puncher said. "Sure. Go. And don't come back."

As I saddled myself, he kept the gun aimed so as best to remove what little brains I have.

There was no way to thank Suicide or say a proper farewell, so Old Red and I just rode off, leaving the only friend we'd met so far to glare at us from behind a mask of contempt.

The kid, meanwhile, stared bull's-eyes at our backs. The thing I tried not to think about (and thought about all the more as a result) was that there were dozens more like him between us and San Marcos.

And us and the truth.

12

BOB'S PLACE

Or, I Smell a Trap, and a Foul Wind Blows Our Way

We rode north hard all of five minutes before my brother veered off eastward. Another five minutes of that, and he was veering once more, to the southwest this time. Fifteen minutes later, we hit barbed wire again, and from then on we followed the Lucky Seven's fence line due south.

We were doubling back, albeit in a roundabout way. Doubling back to where and why, though, I had but a vague notion—and no way to test it out. Our mounts were moving too fast to allow for any talk. There was nothing for me to do but hang on and try to enjoy the ride. And there would have been plenty to enjoy, if I'd been in the right frame of mind, for a Hill Country autumn's a beautiful thing to see.

Rolling knolls stretching out to the horizon like waves on a choppy sea. Tall junipers and yellowed oaks battling to lord it over dark pockets of shinnery. Thick carpets of bluebonnets and verbena so blinding-bright with color they made the cloudless sky above look as gray as dishwater.

All of it so lush, so lovely, so scenic.

So perfect for an ambush.

The glint of sunlight off rifled steel—that's what I was straining my eyeballs to see. We might as well have been riding through a coal mine for all the pleasure I took from the scenery. All I saw around me was a pretty, pretty grave.

Fortunately the Lucky Seven's fence gave out before my nerves did. Round about noon, the big ranch's taut, straight wire gave way to the raggedy lines and rotting posts of a smaller outfit, obviously undermanned. We didn't have to search for any gate—the fence was down in so many spots we had our pick of places to enter.

So enter we did. Old Red finally slowed his horse to a trot and steered us onto the new spread.

"A bit bold, ain't it?" I said. "Invitin' ourselves onto a stranger's land?"

"This ain't a stranger's land."

"Ahhhh. Bob."

It was as I'd suspected. We were paying a call on the fellow Suicide had mentioned: Bob Harris.

"Who is he, anyway?" I asked.

"Another old hand from the Seven. A friend."

"Yeah, well, I gotta say, Brother . . . friendship don't seem to count for much around here. Just look at Bales and Big Bess—and it was nice of Suicide to point us the right way and all, but I wish he'd had the guts to stick up for us."

"He did enough. Got his name for takin' crazy risks. Can't blame him if he finally got over the habit."

"Has it occurred to you there might be more to it than that? Like maybe he's pullin' a Big Bess on us? Settin' us up to get dry-gulched? Cuz it *has* occurred to me."

"Why should he do that? He had a gun on us already. He could've done whatever he pleased."

"Yeah, I suppose. But what about this Bob feller, then? Friend or not, he ain't seen you in five years. He might take us for rustlers and go for his rifle."

"Ain't gonna happen . . . and if you had eyes in your head 'stead of rocks, you'd know why."

I looked around, trying to use my eyes and my brains and my rocks and whatever else I had in my head to read trail sign with. A stony rise, a zigzagging trail up the slope, sparse greenery cropped clear down to the sod—that's all I saw.

"Uhhh . . . Bob'll know we ain't rustlers cuz . . . there'd be nothing to steal on a grubby little spread like this?"

"My Lord," my brother groaned. "I knew you was blind, but I thought you could smell, at least."

I sucked in a long, deep snort—and was rewarded with singed nostrils and a soured stomach.

"Sweet Jesus, how'd I miss *that*?" I swept off my hat and waved it before my face. "What do you think ol' Bob raises down here? Polecats?"

"Something close to it. Don't you remember . . . well, hey there, little feller!"

Someone, it seemed, had gotten a whiff of *us*.

Standing on a shelf of exposed granite at the top of the bluff was a shaggy black and white dog. It returned Gustav's greeting with a single bark, then turned tail and darted over the hill.

At last I knew why Bob Harris wouldn't have to worry about rustlers, and why Suicide had said the spread had a "little herd," "of sorts." I knew, too, who my brother had been about to mention: Kaiser Wilhelm, the orneriest and by far smelliest of all the animals we'd looked after as boys back on the family farm.

When we crested the hill, we beheld a host of Wilhelms and Wilhelminas spread out in the valley before us—hundreds of grazing, bleating, *reeking* goats. There was a small farmhouse, too, and a barn and a stable and what looked like a half-built windmill water pump. The herd-dog was streaking toward the house yipping and yapping.

A dark silhouette appeared in the doorway.

As Old Red and I rode down into the dell and on into the barnyard, the shadowy figure took on a definite shape—and a lovely one, at that, for stepping outside came a beautiful young woman. Yes, her blond hair was frizzy and her gingham dress grimy and her face haggard, I saw upon coming closer. But all this was but a smudge on a fine piece of china. There was no missing the splendor of what lay beneath.

To say Gustav sat up and took notice would be an understatement. The second the woman moved into the light, he went bolt upright in his saddle, muttering something I couldn't make out.

"Hush, Gus," the woman snapped.

She was looking down as she said it, though, and I quickly realized it wasn't my brother she was talking to—it was the whimpering dog that was now dancing around her feet.

Old Red cleared his throat and tried again to speak. "Lottie. It's me."

"Gus! Hush!" the woman hollered at the dog. She hadn't heard Gustav at all.

A thickset man appeared behind her. He was half sodbuster (the half with tattered overalls and square-toed work shoes) and half cowpuncher (the half with the battered Stetson and the bowed legs). Surprisingly enough, he was *all* smiles, though I could tell from the quizzical wrinkling of his eyes he had no idea who we were.

"Help you, boys?" he said.

Gustav swept off his hat and forced his lips into a trembly little crescent, the best stab he could make at a smile.

"Hello, Bob. Hello, Lottie."

Man and woman alike looked like they'd just seen a ghost—and I'm not just succumbing to cliché there. The gal went pale and took a step back, bumping into the fellow standing stiffly behind her, his smile now an O of slack-jawed shock.

"Gus?" the woman said.

Suddenly she was running toward my brother.

He fairly threw himself from the saddle to meet her.

Then, there before my eyes, was a sight I hadn't seen in nearly ten years: my brother with his arms around a woman.

The last time, it had been our dear *Mutter* he'd been holding, her clinging tight as Gustav got set to go off in search of work as a drover. My mother had wept then, and this young Lottie, whoever she was, did the same now. It almost looked like Old Red himself was on the verge of tears, though I had to dismiss that as a mere mirage, the man being no more capable of crying than a stack of pancakes.

Yet why was he wiping a sleeve across his face as he and Lottie ended their embrace? Why did he suck in a snorking sniffle? Why did his eyes seem to glisten as he beamed (Gustav Amlingmeyer . . . *beaming*!) at the woman before him.

I looked over at the stocky goat rancher, Bob, certain that this was his wife Old Red had just wrapped himself around. There wasn't the slightest hint of resentment on his round face. Rather, his grin returned, bigger than ever, even as his wife took Gustav's hands in hers.

My brother tried for another smile. Again he couldn't quite pull it off, though he seemed to be getting better with practice.

"Oh, Gus," Lottie said. "Welcome back."

There was so much warmth and affection in her words—and my brother responded to them with such an air of tender contentment— she might as well have said "Welcome *home*."

13

A HOME ON THE RANGE

Or, Bob Talks Goats, and Gustav Gets Mine

Usually, it's my brother who hangs back, silent, when there's social-izing to be done, and I'm the one slapping every back. Out there on that goat ranch, it was just the opposite: Gustav was receiving such a warm welcome I almost expected his friends to break into "For He's a Jolly Good Fellow," while I might as well have been his pack mule for all the attention I was getting.

Just because I note it, though, don't think I was jealous. To the contrary, it warmed the cockles of my heart (whatever they are) to see Old Red greeted with such affection. More than once, Doc Watson described Sherlock Holmes as a friendless fellow who "loathed any form of society," and I'd always assumed such a brand belonged on my brother, too. There were folks he tolerated and a few he trusted, but I would've been hard-pressed to name more than two of whom he was genuinely fond.

After a round of merry my-Gods and look-at-yous, Bob and Lottie finally noticed the beefy, devilishly handsome cowpoke watching the reunion from atop his chestnut mare.

"Surely that couldn't be Otto," Bob chuckled. "You said he never stopped talkin', Gus."

"No, I said he never shut his mouth," Old Red said. "You can see he's been usin' it for plenty of eatin'. Why, if his head was half as full as he keeps his belly, he'd be the smartest man alive."

"Hey!" I started to protest.

"Oh, don't let this old grouch fool you," Lottie said, jerking a thumb at Gustav. "We could always tell he was proud of your book smarts."

"Oh, you could, could you?"

I looked at my brother.

"I never said any such thing," he grumbled.

"You didn't have to," Lottie said, and she and her husband snorted and shook their heads in a "Same old Gus!" sort of way.

Bob started toward me with arm outstretched. "I'm Bob Harris, by the way."

I slid from my saddle, and Bob gave me a handshake so firm you could use it as an anvil.

He nodded back at Lottie. "That's Mrs. Harris, case you couldn't guess."

"Can you believe it, Gus? He finally made an honest woman of me." Lottie threw me a grin and a wink. "And let me tell you—that took some doin'."

"Lottie was a friend of Adeline's," Old Red explained gingerly.

A *co-worker* of Adeline's—that's what he was really saying. Another of the Eagle's soiled doves.

"Ma'am," I said, tipping my hat and dipping my head, the same as I would upon meeting Mrs. Grover Cleveland or Mrs. J. P. Morgan or any Mrs. Hoity-Toity you could name.

"Sir," Lottie joshed me back with a little curtsy. She was still smiling, but there was the stilted strain of effort to it now—a stiffness that had set in with but one word.

Adeline.

It turned Bob to a waxwork, too, and we spent the next long, painful moment just standing around waiting for the black cloud to blow over.

Gus the goat dog broke the silence with a growl aimed my way, and Lottie bent down to ruffle his mottled chocolates-and-cream coat.

"Don't mind him. He's standoffish at first, but once you get to know him, he's just a big, fuzzy puppy." Her smile broadened, loosened, *lived* again. "Why, how else do you think he got his name?"

Everyone but the Guses got a laugh out of that. Yet there was something tolerant, even pleased about the way my brother rolled his eyes.

"Well, go on, go on," Lottie said, flapping her hands at us like she was chasing chickens out of the corn crib. "I may be an old harlot, but I know my duty. Bob, you show our guests around while I whip up something to eat."

"Oh, please, Lottie," Old Red said, "you don't have to—"

"Now, now, Brother—one mustn't be an ingrate. And anyway, I've got a reputation to live up to, thanks to you." I swept my hat off and held it over my heart in a gesture of beseeching solicitude. "I'm mighty partial to biscuits and gravy, ma'am."

"I aim to please," Lottie said, and she gave me another wink.

Yes, she was a friend of my brother's. Yes, I'd treat her like a lady. But at such a moment as that, it was hard not to look on her in light of her former profession—and think she'd probably been a "good earner" for Ragsdale and Bock.

Once our ponies were unsaddled and watered and turned loose in the corral, Bob took us on a walking tour of what he called the Lucky *Two* Ranch. It was a small operation—fifty acres and five times as many goats—but Bob took obvious pride in it. It's the rare cowhand who doesn't dream of running his own outfit one day, and Bob had pulled it off, in a modest sort of way.

"So," Gustav said as we took in the sight (and smell) of Bob's grazing herd. "Goats?"

Bob chortled and shrugged. "Why not? Actually, they're a better fit for the Hill Country than cattle, and you know the bottom ain't finished droppin' out of the beef market—not now that you can get your head everywhere but the moon by rail. You said it yourself all them years ago, Gus. The days of the big cattlemen are through. The ones that can't accept it, they're just clingin' to something dead and gone."

"That's easy to do," Old Red said dolefully. Then for once he seemed to recognize what a soggy-wet blanket he was, and he put a look on his face that aimed for chipper inquisitiveness . . . and only missed by half a mile. "So what breeds we lookin' at here? Angoras, mostly?"

"That's right," Bob said, and he launched into a lecture on the fascinating ancestry of the Mexican/American short-haired Angora goat.

My brother managed to work in questions here and there—about breeding and feeding and mohair and the like—but it was all I could do to keep my eyes open. Eventually, my stomach got to rumbling so loud Bob made a crack about a thunderstorm rolling in, and I made my escape with an excuse about hurrying up the grub.

Gus the mutt followed me back to the Harrises' little homestead, and as we reached the barnyard, he raced ahead into the house to announce my arrival. Lottie was telling him to shut up when I walked in.

"Sorry about all the barkin' and growlin'," she said to me. "He'll get used to you sooner or later."

"Oh, that's alright, ma'am. It's nothin' new to me."

Lottie smiled, the grin crinkling her skin with wrinkles even as it flushed up a youthful glow.

"I tell ya," she said, "I love Gloomy Gus to pieces, but it'd take a saint to put up with that man's cussedness night and day."

"Just call me St. Otto."

I walked over to the dining room table (the "dining room" being, well, the table) and started setting out the cutlery and plates stacked there.

After a final "Hush!" for Gus, Lottie got to stirring a musky-scented stew simmering atop the potbelly stove in the corner.

I didn't bother asking what kind of meat was in it.

"So how have things been for your brother, anyway?" Lottie asked.

Mangy Gus curled up by her feet, black eyes fixed on me.

"Oh, we've had our share of bad breaks the last five years, but we ain't licked yet. In fact, I would say things was finally lookin' up if only Gustav wasn't so down. No matter how things go for us, he's still a Gloomy Gus."

"I'm sorry it's not a cheerier picture than that." Lottie kept poking at the stew with her spoon, though surely it was stirred up plenty. "I've thought about Gus a lot since he left. I always hoped he'd find himself some kinda happiness somewhere."

"We're workin' on it."

I stepped back from the table to admire my handiwork.

Mangy Gus growled at me.

"Howzabout when he was with Adeline?" I said. "He seem happy then?"

"Happi*er*, I guess. The four of us had some laughs. But your brother was always the last to join in and the first to stop. I remember Adeline sayin', 'Gus, if I had a nickel for every time you smiled . . . I'd have fifteen cents.'"

I cut loose with a chuckle. That was the sort of thing I wish *I'd* said. "What was she like, anyway? I barely know a thing about her."

Lottie finally stopped stewing over her stew and looked up at me. "She was a scared farmgirl is what she was. Not the brightest you'd meet, but sweet as could be. She stayed sweet, too. Despite everything."

"And she loved my brother?"

Lottie gave the stew another useless stir. "I think Gus was the first kind man Adeline ever met. The first who didn't treat her like some sow in the pen. She'd have done anything for him. Would've made him a good little wife." Locks of long hair were falling over Lottie's face like a veil, and she pushed them back with an angry sweep of the hand. "God knows that girl didn't deserve what happened to her."

"Yeah . . . well . . . ," I said, all too aware I'd asked a yes-or-no question and heard neither back. "I reckon nobody deserves *that*."

Lottie's eyes flared up so fiery hot it hurt just to look at them, like staring into the sun.

"I know a few who do," she spat, "and if they were here right now, I'd do 'em myself."

I was still groping for an appropriate reply when Bob stomped in, wide-eyed and grinning.

"Guess what, Lottie? We've got us a new partner!"

He was in so jubilant a mood he didn't see—or let himself see—the scowl on his wife's face.

"What are you talkin' about?" Lottie asked.

"Gloomy Gus, of course!" Bob boomed, and right on cue my brother trudged in after him. "I asked if he'd come in with us on the ranch, and he said yes!"

"I did *not* say yes," Gustav said, speaking to me.

Bob made a beeline for a can of peaches on the table. "Maybe you didn't say yes, but you didn't say no, neither—and that's as good as a yes from you!"

Old Red kept his eyes on me. "All I said was it's a generous offer."

"*What* was a generous offer?" I asked.

"Well," my brother began.

"You've seen the place, Otto," Bob cut in. He somehow managed to pop half a peach in his mouth, chew, swallow, and lick his fingers even as he went on talking. "It's more than one man can manage. In fact, I was just about to hire up for the fall shearin'. If you two was to settle in, I wouldn't have to. I couldn't pay more than six bits a day to start, but if you stuck around through the end of the season? Why, you could come in halvsies with us on the whole spread!"

He glanced over at his wife, and she gave her blessing with a nod.

"Leave those peaches be, Bob" was all she said.

Me, I had a little more to say on the matter.

"Sweet Jesus, Brother . . . have you forgotten why we're here?"

"Of course I haven't!" Gustav barked back.

"Then tell 'em." I nodded first at Bob, then Lottie. "Tell 'em right now."

"Yes, Gus," Lottie said quietly. "I think you should."

Her husband swallowed hard and wiped a sleeve across his syrup-smeared chin.

"Lottie. Bob," Old Red said. "Why don't you have a seat?"

The three of them slowly settled in around the table, and though I hadn't been invited, I joined them. As we took our seats, Mangy Gus skulked off and curled up in a corner. He seemed to sense that something bad was approaching fast, and Lottie and Bob did, too. All of them slouched. All of them looked down.

I knew exactly what was coming, of course—the next *two* things, really. My brother would tell his friends why we were back in San Marcos . . . and just like that, they wouldn't be his friends anymore. Surely they harbored no love for Ragsdale and Bock, but that wouldn't matter. Out here all alone in the hills, they couldn't afford to piss off Ike Rucker or the cattlemen and cowboys thereabouts. Farmers and ranchers alike depend on the goodwill of their neighbors. Bob and Lottie wouldn't have a choice.

It would be a sad thing to see, all this cozy camaraderie brought to such a swift end. But I had my silver lining in sight: a future that was far, *far* removed from the smell of goats.

"Here's the thing," Gustav said. "I come back to find the man who killed Adeline. Find him and see justice done . . . if I can, and it looks like you're the last folks I can turn to for help."

Bob and Lottie looked at each other long and hard. It wasn't at all the sort of look I'd been expecting, though—one filled with fear and regret and self-recrimination.

No, it looked more like simple surprise, at first, and then maybe . . . relief?

Lottie reached out to take my brother's hands in hers. "You can count on us, Gus."

"That's right," Bob said, and he put a hand atop the others in the middle of the table. "There's nothing Lottie and me won't do to help you. *Nothing.*"

14

STONEWALL'S SECOND JOB

Or, Lottie Gives Us a Lot to Chew on, but It Doesn't Go Down Easy

Gustav thanked Bob and Lottie for their willingness to help.

I cursed them.

Silently, of course, and with feelings that went so far beyond mixed you could call them scrambled.

Did I want my brother to find Adeline's killer? Certainly, yes.

Did I want him settling down to *raise goats*? Dear Lord, no.

If this selfishness in any way betrayed itself upon my face, no one seemed to notice. Old Red and his friends just huddled in closer around the ranch house's rickety table while I rode out a churning in my gut that was only half due to hunger.

"Why come back now?" Bob asked. "After all these years?"

"I've picked up a trick or two lately," Gustav said. "Had a few experiences along the lawman line."

Usually here he'd evangelize a bit on behalf of his hero. Yet he made no mention of Mr. Holmes—and, what's more, he shot me a glare that warned against jumping in with any embellishments of my own.

"Before that," he went on, "it didn't even occur to me that I *could* do anything about Adeline. Now . . . well, I still don't know if I can, but at least I know how to try."

"You said we're the last people you can turn to for help," Lottie said. "Who else have you talked to?"

Old Red's eyes met mine again, though this time he wasn't gagging me but whipping the gag off.

"Brother," he said.

As is his way, he was leaving tale-telling to me. Though it made me feel like a phonograph machine for him to crank up and switch off as he pleased, I obliged.

It took me fifteen minutes to talk it all through: our first run-in with Ragsdale and Bock; Milford Bales's words of warning; the solitary nugget we were able to mine from Big Bess (that another chippie from the old days, Squirrel Tooth Annie, still worked at the Phoenix); the trap Stonewall and his bosses had sprung on us; the breakfast we'd (unintentionally) bought for Ike Rucker; Suicide's help getting us to the Lucky Two; and my brother's inexplicable interest in raising stock animals that smelled like outhouses with mange.

Actually, I kept that last item to myself, more or less, merely concluding with "And then we followed our noses here."

"It's too bad it was Big Bess you bumped into instead of Squirrel Tooth," Lottie said when I was through, her face puckering with disgust. "I could've told you that fat bitch was trouble."

Bob placed a hand on his wife's shoulder, a gesture that said either a comforting "There, there, dear" or a more reproachful "Your petticoats are showing."

"Well, you won't get another shot at Squirrel Tooth now, that's for sure," Bob said to Old Red. "You were lucky to get away from the Phoenix once. You set foot within a mile of that place again, Stonewall'll squash you flat."

Lottie reached up and patted her husband's fingers. She looked calm now, her expression smoothed like wrinkled bedsheets flattened by a gliding palm.

Bob took his hand away.

"So," Lottie said to Gustav, "what do we do?"

"Well, the first step's easy enough: You talk, I listen. Nobody's given me any straight answers yet about the night Adeline died. I need you to lay it all out for me. Every detail, best as you can remember."

Lottie nodded, then took in a couple deep breaths as if preparing for some great exertion. A load to lift, a row to hoe—or something long buried to dig up.

"It was a Tuesday night," she said. "Slow, like always. You and Bob wouldn't be back till Saturday with the rest of the Lucky Seven boys, so me and Adeline were bored outta our skulls. Then Gil Bock called Adeline over and sent her upstairs alone, and we all knew what that meant. She was gettin' dressed for a house call. Sure enough, when she came down again, she was all prettied up proper for a trip to the Star. She gave me a smile and a wave, and she and Stonewall headed out the door. That was the last time I—"

"Hold on," Old Red said. "Stonewall went with her?"

"Oh, yeah. He always came along when we got sent out. He was our 'escort.' Or guard, more like. Made sure no one gave us any trouble . . . and we didn't do any business on the sly." Lottie squirmed in her seat. "Adeline . . . she . . ."

"I know," my brother said brusquely. "Adeline never passed up a chance to turn an extra buck. It was the only way to build up her nest egg. She told me. It didn't bother me none."

A quaver in those last words gave the lie to them, but none of us was going to call Gustav on it. Lottie just tried to forge on. She didn't get far.

"Well, Stonewall did what he could to keep us gals from puttin' out on the side . . . unless it was . . ."

Lottie's mouth hung open for a moment, as if the words she was trying to say had stolen her breath away.

"Unless it was what?" Gustav prodded her.

"You gotta understand, Gus," Bob said gently. "We couldn't tell you before."

"Couldn't tell me *what*, dammit?"

"That Stonewall was doin' Adeline every chance he got!"

The words exploded out of Lottie with a force that hit my brother like a cannonball. He seemed to be thrown against the back of his chair, and as Lottie went on he slumped down limply, pale and silent.

"He made all of us give him freebies, but Adeline . . . he had a special hankerin' for her. He didn't like it when you started hangin' around, but there was nothing he could do about it. Ragsdale and Bock wouldn't have tolerated it. You were a steady-payin' customer, and that was that. Stonewall could take it out on Adeline, though. Scare her, play with her rough, anything he wanted so long as it didn't leave a mark. Bringin' pain to that girl got to be like a second job for him, and he worked it hard."

My brother's eyes had taken on the glazed, distant quality that so often comes over them when a thought grabs hold. But there was something different about it this time—a blankness, an emptiness. Wheels weren't turning behind those eyes. They were stuck on one awful thought, bogged down like a chuck wagon in mud.

"Why didn't you tell me? Why didn't *she* tell me?"

"Adeline was afraid for you, Gus—afraid of what Stonewall would do if you two tangled," Lottie said. "She made me swear not to say a word."

"But after she was dead—?"

"That would've been the worst time to tell you," Bob said. "You were drinkin', actin' crazy right up to the time you left San Marcos. No good would've come of it. Just bad."

"It makes it all so simple," Old Red said. "It was him. Stonewall. He wanted Adeline's money or he wanted *her* or both, and she said no. So he killed her."

Bob shook his head. "I don't think so, Gus. Lottie and me have talked this through again and again, and it just don't figure thataway. Stonewall wouldn't risk crossin' Ragsdale and Bock, for one thing. They're bread and butter to him. And if he'd known Adeline had a stash to steal, he could've got it without killin' her. Bullyin' women's what he does best."

"He never bragged on doin' it, neither," Lottie said. "And if he *had* done it, you can bet he wouldn't have been shy about it. The things he used to say to us . . ."

She wrapped her arms around herself as if to stifle a shiver.

"Well, Stonewall had to say *something* about how Adeline died," Gustav said. "That night, at least."

Lottie nodded. "Yeah. He did. Came back about an hour after he and Adeline left and went straight to Ragsdale and Bock. They did some whisperin' behind the bar, then Stonewall ran out again with Bock at his heels. They were back around dawn, and that's when they finally told us . . . after the last customer cleared out. Adeline was dead. She'd slipped around behind the Star, probably to do some off-the-books business, and someone knifed her."

"They said she was killed *outside* the hotel?" Old Red said. "Not inside? By some out-of-towner guest?"

"That's right."

My brother glanced my way.

"Funny Big Bess didn't remember that," I said.

"Yeah. Funny." Gustav turned back to Lottie. "Seems like they swept things up pretty fast after that. By the time I got to town, Adeline was already underground."

"For good reason," Lottie said, and her arms coiled even tighter around her sides, as if she was trying to keep something from busting out—a sob or a scream or her breakfast. "Adeline wasn't just knifed, Gus. She was cut all to pieces. 'Butchered like a hog,' that's how Stonewall put it. They had to clean it up fast, cuz when a person's done like that—even a whore—it sets folks to talkin'. So Ragsdale and Bock had her boxed up and buried the same day. No service, nothing."

Lottie's face hardened, her sadness baked away by a rage still blazing inside her after all these years.

"I saw the blood, though. The next time I had to pay a call at the Star. The stain around back . . . I don't know if they ever bothered scrubbin' it away. Ragsdale and Bock probably didn't want it gone. It'd make a good warning to the rest of us."

"My God," Old Red muttered.

He'd gone so slumpy it looked like he was melting.

"Butchered like a hog," he said, and he closed his eyes.

"So," I said softly, carrying on when it became plain my brother couldn't, "Ragsdale and Bock were able to keep the law out of it?"

Bob shook his head. "They didn't have to bother. Kaz Cerny, the old town marshal—the one before Milford Bales—he was worse than Ike Rucker. Practically lived at the Golden Eagle. And the county sheriff serves as county coroner, too. So there was an inquest, but Rucker was runnin' it and Cerny did most of the talkin'. Which wasn't much. The whole thing didn't last five minutes. 'Murdered by party unknown' and then *whack*—a bang of the gavel and it was off to the Eagle for an afternoon quickie."

"I had to do Rucker once after that," Lottie said. "Took all I had in me not to rip the bastard's balls off and stuff 'em down his throat."

Bob winced. I fidgeted and looked away. Old Red blinked and sat up straight again as if waking from a dream.

"How long were you at the Eagle after Adeline died?" he asked Lottie.

"A while."

"I got her outta there quick as I could," Bob threw in. "Never was as good at pinchin' pennies as you, but five or six months of scrimpin', and we was out here with our goats. We ain't laid eyes on Ragsdale or Bock or any of that ever since."

My brother nodded slowly. "For that I'm glad," he said. "So that's it, then? The whole of what y'all know about Adeline?"

"I wish it was more," Lottie said.

"Well, there might be other ways y'all can help." Gustav took a sudden interest in a knot in the tabletop, tracing over it with his forefinger a few times before speaking again. "Could you come up to town tomorrow night? Meet us at the springs around sundown, say?"

Bob turned to Lottie.

"We could maybe get Frank Kurtz to look after the place while—"

"Yes," Lottie said to Old Red.

"Good." My brother peered past her at the stove and did his feeble best to brighten. "Now what say we dig into that stew, huh? I'm hungry enough to eat a horse."

How about a goat? I almost asked. I managed to restrain myself.

As we ate, Bob lightened the mood with tales of Gustav's days on the Lucky Seven: his feuds with the foreman, his feats of derring-do (including saving Suicide when he was thrown from a saddled bull), how he came to be called "Gloomy Gus" (guess). There was no mention of San Marcos or the Star or Adeline, though. The very things Old Red was no doubt brooding on anyway.

By the time I was setting aside my spoon and patting my bulging belly (goats tasting a hell of a lot better than they smell), the light streaming in the windows had gone early-evening gray. It was time for us to go, Gustav announced. Despite Bob's insistence that we stay the night, he couldn't be swayed—our ponies were due back at the livery that night.

The real reason to go I could see in Old Red's eyes. The wheels were turning again. Spinning so fast, in fact, his pupils were practically spiraling like pinwheels.

He didn't say a word as we saddled our horses. Nor did Lottie, who'd come out to the corral with us. When at last we were mounted and ready to ride, she stepped up to Gustav and leaned against his leg, hands on his thigh.

"I'm glad you came back, Gus."

"I just hope you still feel that way when this is all over."

Lottie held my brother's gaze, her body so still it seemed to have roots right down into the ground. "I will."

Then she let go and stepped back.

Old Red tipped his hat to her, I did the same, and with a final "Good night!" we were off.

We had to move fast to make the most of what light we had left, which meant my brother was spared my many questions and protestations. (I mean, really . . . *goat ranching*?) When darkness finally fell and we did slow down, all our attention was on keeping to the trail that took us past the Lucky Seven and the other spreads south of town.

We'd been ambling along a good half hour in total silence when Gustav snapped up tall in his saddle, his gaze sweeping the pitch-black woodland to our right. I followed his line of sight and caught a dull gleam in the darkness.

Then the gleam moved, and there was much rustling of brush as something big came toward us out of the thicket.

Something*s*, actually: three mounted men riding abreast.

They were wearing gunnysack masks.

"Stop right there," one of them said, voice deep and rough, "or I'll blow you outta your damn saddles."

The gleam, I now saw, was moonlight reflecting off the twin barrels of his sawed-off shotgun.

15

THE END OF OUR ROPE

Or, We Are the Guests of Honor at a Necktie Party

The fellow with the scattergun did all the talking in his low, rough rumble.

"Gun belts. Off. Slow."

"Hands behind your backs."

"Over there."

His two compadres, meanwhile, threw our Colts in the brush and tied our hands together and led our horses beneath a big oak tree without so much as a jingle of spurs, let alone a word. So it was the froggy-talking man I tried reasoning with.

Alright. *Pleading* with.

"Just hold on, would ya? If you got a beef, lay it out plain. We can talk it through. Whadaya say, huh?"

I tried to meet the man's gaze, make contact with something behind his ghostly-gray mask, but I couldn't even see his eyes at all—just a pair of ragged holes as black as tar.

His body was mostly hidden, as well. All three men wore oversized slickers buttoned to the neck with the collars turned up. Which left nothing to judge them by other than general size. Yet though they differed slightly in build, none was excessively tall or short or broad or lean. They weren't excessively anything, really, except unfriendly. Unfriendly and quiet.

Froggy just sat in his saddle, shotgun in his left hand, reins in his right, ignoring my chatter. So I stopped wasting my breath on him. I had so little left to spare.

"I'm sure you're a decent feller," I said to the man holding our horses. "You don't wanna be party to nothing like this. It ain't right, and you know it. Why don't you say so to your friends?"

He chose not to. He chose, in fact, to go on saying nothing at all.

I can't say I was surprised. I didn't really entertain the delusion that I could talk my way out of what was coming. I was just angling for a stay of sentence. A minute's conversation might be enough.

I'd managed to keep my wrists a couple inches apart as they were cinched together, so there was a little play in the loops—literal wriggle room. And wriggling I was, too, groping for loose ends, hoping I could snake my hands free in time to . . . something.

The third masked man had moved off somewhere behind us, and I twisted in my saddle, thinking to aim some wheedling his way while keeping my fumbling fingers from his line of sight.

When I saw him again, he was back on horseback, riding up close—the better to toss knotted ropes over the branch above us.

"Oh, no you don't!" I cried out as the man whipped off my hat and slipped on the noose. "Don't you do it!"

"It's alright, Brother," Gustav said, his voice flat but steady. Tense but calm. Or maybe just resigned.

"These bastards are fixin' to hang us!"

Old Red lost his lid and gained a loop of rope as I just had.

"It's alright," he said.

I was in no frame of mind to debate his definition of "alright." I was clawing at the rope holding my hands now, not even worried that one of the masked men might notice. What would they do? Shoot me before they hung me?

"Ain't you got the balls for a fair fight?" I spat at the fellow holding our bridles. I was tempted to kick at his cloth-covered face but thought better of it lest he let loose and set us to swinging early.

I turned to face the shotgun man again, coarse hemp scraping at my Adam's apple. "Yellow son of a bitch! Why don't you take off that mask and face us like a man!"

The black holes of his hood stayed pointed at my brother. "You shouldn't have come back," he croaked.

My hands moved a little further apart. A loop was finally working loose. A few more seconds and—

The man who'd noosed us unholstered his six-gun.

The bridle man let go and scurried aside.

"No, goddamn y—!"

They didn't even let me finish.

The shotgun man gave a nod and his chum with the gun pulled the trigger and everything exploded.

I can't even recall hearing the shot at all. I remember only the jerk of sudden motion as my pony bolted and the grunt-shriek-squeal that popped up from my gut. After that, all was blackness.

For about three seconds.

Because I'd closed my eyes.

I opened them again when the up-down jostle of a galloping mount beneath my butt made it clear there was actually something still to see. This is what I quickly discovered: Either the Afterlife looks remarkably like the Texas Hill Country at night from atop a runaway horse, or I was still in the Duringlife . . . for the moment, at least.

A sudden tug on my neck nearly yanked me back out of the saddle. It didn't last, though, and I straightened up again, my throat burning. But I knew another such tug—perhaps a stronger, longer one—was sure to come along quick, for my noose was dragging along loose behind my spooked pony. All it had to do was tangle in the hooves or catch in some brush and my neck would be just as broke as if I'd dropped from the gallows.

"Whoa. Whoa! *Whoa*, dammit!" I roared, and I leaned back in the saddle as far as I dared.

A good cutting horse, accustomed to the feel of cowhands working rope up top, would've known just what do to, but a rented-out nag from some livery wouldn't have the saddle sense God gave a groundhog. Certainly mine, with her reins hanging loose and a gunshot still ringing in her ears, had no intention of slowing down, even if she was charging down a narrow trail in the dead of night.

My hands were flopping like fish now, struggling to work free of the rope around my wrists. The knot was more slack than ever, with maybe six inches of play between my hands. For all I knew, a pull the wrong way would just cinch it up tight again, yet I had no choice but to try.

Then the fingers of my left hand brushed over something stubby flapping loose, and after a few frenzied fumblings I managed to clamp onto it.

I'd found one of the loose ends of the rope. If I worked back, fingers crawling along the hemp like a spider, I could latch on to the knot itself. Assuming I recognized the hitch—and if there's one thing a cowboy knows, it's knots—I could untie it in no time.

Which was exactly what I had. My pony was skirting the tree line, and perhaps thirty feet ahead I spied a long, thick shape stretching out over the trail. If I didn't duck quick, I'd be brained on a branch as big as the one I'd almost been hung from.

I tilted forward and tucked myself down.

Then a strange thought occurred to me. I can only convey it to you now as "Awwwww, fudge *this*," though it wasn't words so much as a simple (and some might say simple-minded) impulse.

I straightened my back and pushed down on the stirrups, lifting myself as high out of the saddle as I could.

Now, I'm sure there are more painful ways to dismount a horse than a branch across the chest. Being shot from the saddle by a harpoon might sting a mite more. Maybe. Believe it or not, though, there are advantages to being chopped down by a tree.

For one thing, I was removed from my pony's back quickly and cleanly, without a broken neck or (should I have tried hurling myself from the saddle trussed as I was) crushed legs.

For another thing . . . well . . .

Anyway, it didn't kill me.

For the briefest of moments, I dangled limply over the branch like a damp sheet on the line. Slowly, I came sliding off, the rough bark scratching and gouging what of my chest it hadn't pulverized. Then I dropped to the rocky ground, landing on my tailbone.

I didn't even have the wind left in my lungs to yelp. I just sort of puddled there on the trail, collapsing in a panting heap as my horse's hoofbeats faded into the distance. It would've been a welcome luxury to pass out, and I think my brain was flirting with the notion when a single, searing thought burned through my pain and snapped my eyes open wide.

"Gustav!"

I squirmed and cursed until I was up on my knees, then whipped around to peer back at the big oak that was now a hundred feet behind me. I expected to see a slender figure swaying there, limp, broken, alone. A sob was already welling up in my chest when I spotted my brother.

The sob turned into a laugh that sliced through my bruised chest like a Bowie knife. Not that I minded.

Old Red was riding toward me—his hands, untied, on the reins. There was no rope around his neck.

When he was close enough, he slid from the saddle and stomped up, shaking his head. He squatted down to give me a fast, fuming once-over.

"Christ, Brother," he sighed once he was satisfied my head wasn't about to fall off. "I *told* you it was gonna be alright."

16

FALSE FRONTS AND BACK DOORS

Or, Old Red Yanks the Mask off One of Our Attackers

My throat was rubbed raw and my butt was bruised black. Yet when it comes to pains in the neck *or* ass, nothing can top my brother.

"You couldn't undo this yourself?" he griped as he freed my hands with one ungentle jerk of the rope.

I pulled the noose over my head and threw it into the bushes beside the trail.

"I was gettin' it loose. Another minute and—"

"Another minute? It was a granny knot, ya idjit! You were supposed to untie it in five *seconds*."

"What are you talkin' about?"

Old Red turned and headed for his horse.

"'The grand thing is to be able to reason backward,'" he said, quoting Guess Who for the first time in ages. "Thinkin' ass-backwards is more your line than reasonin' backward, but maybe that's close enough. See if you can work it out before I get back."

"Where the hell you goin'?"

"Great day in the morning," Gustav groaned as he hoisted himself up into the saddle. "You'd have thought the man had landed on his head."

He went galloping off into the darkness.

When he rode back a minute later, at least one of the puzzles he'd left me with solved itself: He was leading my runaway pony by the reins.

As for the the Mystery of the Sloppy-Ass Knots, it still had me mystified—though, in my defense, I'll say that the Mystery of Standing Up Without Fainting was still proving quite a challenge, too.

"So?" Gustav said, tossing me my reins.

I shrugged—and nearly passed out from the pain that went shooting down my backside.

It was going to be a long night.

"What does it tell you," Old Red said, "that our nooses weren't actually hitched to anything and our hands were tied with knots a five-year-old should've been able to untangle?"

"Can't you just tell me?"

Old Red spun his hands in the air instead, coaxing me to trot out a deduction.

"Alright," I sighed. "They never meant to kill us. It was just another warning."

Gustav nodded. "Yeah? And?"

"And . . . I feel extremely warned."

Old Red rolled his eyes. "Didn't you even ask yourself why they was wearin' masks?"

"I just assumed they *didn't want us to know who they were.*"

"And why should they care if we did?"

"Cuz otherwise we'd . . . oh. Right."

The answer had been staring me in the face. Literally.

My brother knew our "lynching" was phony from the get-go—because there's no need to hide your identity from a man you're about to kill.

"Brilliant deducifyin'," I said, putting on a look of misty-eyed admiration. "Why any man with a mind like yours would for a moment entertain the notion of herding goats is beyond—"

"Feh," Old Red spat, and he wheeled his mount and set off up the trail without another word. Assuming "feh" even counts as one in the first place.

He was headed north. Toward town.

Extremely warned or not, he wasn't turning back.

Nor was I—though I gave myself another moment to recover before forging on. The way my keister throbbed, stretching out on a featherbed would've been purest agony. A saddle might as well have been the rack. Still, I managed to get astraddle of it somehow.

When I caught up to Gustav, he was crawling around nose to the ground beneath the hanging tree. Our little Vigilance Committee was long gone.

"Too dark to read sign," Old Red said. "Found this, though."

He tossed me my Stetson. His was already back atop his head.

"Nice to have my hat back," I said, "but I'd rather it was my Colt."

"No such luck." Gustav stood and got atop his horse again. "They threw 'em so far into the brush we couldn't find 'em in broad daylight."

"Which means we gotta ride the rest of the way unheeled."

"Unless you tucked a couple spare six-guns in your socks."

I slumped in my saddle—then sat up ramrod straight as another bolt of pain raced along my tailbone.

"So," I grated out, "you got any notion who them fellers was?"

"Oh, I got more than a notion."

"You mean you know?"

"Well . . . 'know' is a mighty strong word."

Then, as he so often will, my brother ended the conversation by simply moving off with no apparent worry in the world about my following.

"You know," I called after him, " 'jackass' is a mighty strong word, too, but I ain't afraid to use it."

Old Red shushed me and kept going.

I shushed and followed.

Risky as it was leaving the trail at night, it would have been riskier sticking to it, given our popularity thereabouts. So before long, we were groping our way through the bramble, headed for the river. We had to lead our horses on foot, it was so dark, and that, combined with the water's serpentine slithering through the hills, added hours to our journey north. By the time we rode into town, branch-scraped and chigger-chewed, I was so achy-tired only the pain in my posterior kept me from nodding off on the hoof.

Before we could collapse into our saggy hotel bed, though, we had to return our rented mounts. It took some pounding on the stable doors, but eventually the liveryman opened up.

"Who the hell . . . ?" he muttered as he leaned out, lantern in hand. He was half-dressed and half-asleep, and his hair was standing up so straight it could have been a gray crown. When his droopy eyes found their focus, they widened in surprise. "Oh. You. You're late. That'll be extry."

Once the horses were in the livery and the "extry" in the man's pocket, I started shuffling off for the Star. Gustav lingered, though.

"Tell me," he said, "anybody come 'round askin' about us today? Wonderin' where we was goin'? When we might be back?"

The liveryman rubbed his stubble-covered chin and tried to look thoughtful—which was enough right there to slap the BS brand on whatever he was about to say.

"No, sir. Not that I recollect."

"Not that you recollect. Right," my brother said. "Would there be another livery in town these days?"

"Sure. Some Polack opened a place over on Fountain Street a couple years back."

"Good," Old Red said. "We'll be takin' all our business to him from now on . . . ya damned snake."

The liveryman looked like he was about to protest, then changed his mind and flashed us an evil, yellow-fanged grin. "Hey, it's no skin off my nose—I figured I'd never see you two again anyhow. I'm just glad I got my horses back!"

"Why, you nasty old backstabber—"

I took a step toward the man, right fist readied for a roundhouse, but he was already on the move, hopping backward and slamming the doors in my face. On the other side of the thick wood, I could hear him dropping the bar in place with a phlegmy cackle.

I battered the door with kicks and cusses, but my brother just turned and walked away.

"Where you goin'?" I said. "This SOB knows who jumped us. Shouldn't we get in there and beat it out of him?"

"I never knew a liveryman who didn't keep a hogleg handy," Gustav said without slowing down.

By the time he reached the first corner, I was at his side.

When we got to the Star, Old Red steered us to the alley that ran along and behind the hotel. At first, I assumed this was just more precautionary creeping, but the way my brother froze when we got around back reminded me where we were.

Here Gertrude "Adeline" Eichelberger had been butchered five years before.

There wasn't much to see there in the dark. An ash heap, a rotting mattress, a back door for deliveries (and sneaking in floozies). Directly behind the hotel was an empty lot overgrown with weeds, while the backs of other businesses stretched off to the north, east, and west in a T.

It was the Star's back wall Gustav stood and stared at. If there were still any stains there after all this time, I couldn't see them.

A beam of orange light cut through the alleyway into the little field behind us. Dawn was coming on. Old Red turned toward the light . . . then stopped again.

He was facing one of the other buildings now—its fresh-painted, neatly swept back landing was maybe fifty feet away. There were other, nearly identical posterns to either side of it, yet this one alone held my brother mesmerized.

"What are you lookin' at?" I asked.

"These days? I wouldn't know," my brother said, "but it used to be a barbershop."

It took a moment for that to sink in. When it did, though, it sank good and deep, and it hit bottom hard.

"Are you sayin'—?"

Gustav nodded. "That's what I'm sayin'."

"Well, my oh my."

Before Milford Bales became town marshal, he'd been a barber—and the back door of his old shop wasn't thirty steps from the very spot Adeline had died.

I'd just passed the night without a wink of sleep, yet for the first time in hours I felt truly awake.

"Did Bales know Adeline?" I asked.

"Not that I ever heard."

"He have any truck with crib gals?"

"If he did, he kept it quiet."

"Well, he'd have to, wouldn't he? Respectable feller like him. You don't get to be postmaster or town marshal without puttin' up a few false fronts."

"Or puttin' on a few masks," Gustav said, and he gave me what some writers like to call "a significant look." Which is to say he stared into my eyes long and hard, as if trying to push a thought into my head through sheer force of will.

Funny thing, too. It worked.

"Say," I said. "That feller with the shotgun and the deep voice . . ."

A word popped into my mouth I hadn't been expecting, and I paused a moment to sample the taste of it. It tasted real, true, right. So I started again.

"That feller with the shotgun and the *phony* voice. He held his reins here, didn't he?"

I held up my right hand.

"And his scattergun here."

I held up my left.

"He sure did," my brother said. "A southpaw, I'd bet."

I thought back on the hand I'd seen all atremble as it hovered next to a holster the day before.

A *left* hand.

"Them fellers found us by askin' someone in town," I said. "Which means it probably wasn't anyone off the Lucky Seven. They already knew we'd be passin' thataway."

"That's right—and didn't you hear? When the two of 'em was on foot gettin' the nooses on us?"

I tilted my head and closed my eyes, as if whatever sound my brother was speaking of might yet be echoing around for me to hear. After a few seconds, I gave up.

"I didn't hear nothing."

"Exactly," Gustav said. "*No spurs.* The rope was stiff, too. New bought. Never used. Them slickers didn't have a spot on 'em, neither."

I nodded. I hadn't seen it till just then, but there'd been clues scattered around like Hansel and Gretel's trail of bread crumbs, and they led to one and only one conclusion.

We'd been ambushed by townsmen. Not just that—one townsman in particular.

"Looks like your pal Bales went to an awful lotta trouble to put a scare in us tonight," I said. "Makes me wonder why he'd bother."

"Makes me wonder, too. A lot."

Old Red turned toward the Star again. The morning light had spread now, and with it more detail emerged from the shadows.

Warps in the wood. Chips in the paint. No old bloodstains yet, but maybe that was just a matter of time as the darkness lifted.

"Like I said a while back—'know' is a mighty big word to bandy about," Gustav said. "But 'think'? 'Suspect'?"

My brother gave one quick, firm nod, like a straw boss giving his approval to a new-built corral.

"Those'll do just fine."

17

CUFF

Or, We Dig for Dirt on Bales but Dredge Up an Old Devil Instead

Gustav's gotten pretty good at picking locks with a length of wire—the one and only of his tricks he'll credit to a magazine detective other than Mr. Holmes. (In this case, the rival being the American dick Nick Carter, whom my brother refers to only as "Blockhead Numero Uno.") After less than a minute of fiddling, Old Red had us through the Star's rear door, and we made our way to the second floor via a musty, unpapered back stairwell.

Once we were in our room, our duties on watch were sorted out quickly.

"Gimme two hours," Gustav said, and he collapsed onto the bed already snoring.

I tried to pass the time working on my new story for Mr. Smythe, but I didn't get far with it. Every six words or so, my pencil would slip from my weary fingers—and my thoughts slide into half-dreamed horrors.

A woman gutted-out hollow like a butchered hog.

Baby-faced Milford Bales bathed in blood.

My brother hanging from a tree, eyes abulge.

Me herding goats.

After falling asleep and jerking awake what seemed like a thousand times, I switched places with my brother and let the nightmares play out uninterrupted for the rest of the night.

I first stirred around noon facedown in a pillow. When I rolled over to breathe, my tailbone sent such a lightning bolt of pain racing through me, my hair should've stood on end, and I nearly passed out again before I was even fully awake.

"Still smarts, huh?" Old Red said.

"Brilliant . . . deduction," I gasped. "Sweet Jesus . . . I think I broke my butt."

"Better that than your neck."

I reached around and gently copped a feel of my right cheek. The slightest pressure was all it took to bring tears to my eyes.

"That's entirely open to debate," I said.

Once I'd managed to oh-so-gingerly drape my aching carcass in clean clothes, we limped off to the nearest gunsmith's shop. We needed new artillery, and the quicker we got it, the better.

For once, it wasn't a Peacemaker I picked out for myself. On the spur of the moment, I bought a short-barreled Webley—a "British Bulldog." Old Red glowered with obvious disgust as I slipped the gun into a new-bought shoulder holster that better suited the city duds I'd struggled into that morning.

"Man's gotta move with the times, Brother," I said.

Gustav gave me a "Feh" and put his own iron the only proper place for it, in his mind: in a gun belt, hanging at his hip.

"Mind if I ask you a question?" he said to the gunsmith.

"Cash-payin' customers can ask anything they want," the man said with a grin. "Cuz at least I know they won't be askin' for credit."

Old Red forced up a chuckle that sounded about as jolly as a cat ridding itself of a hairball.

"It's your town marshal I'm wonderin' about. Milford Bales. What do folks 'round here make of him?"

The gunsmith's grin wilted.

"Allow me to correct myself. Cash-payin' customers can ask me about anything . . . *except politics*."

"It ain't politics I'm interested in. It's Bales."

The man crossed his arms and shook his head. "Sorry, cowboy. Gunsmiths can't afford to choose sides."

"I ain't askin' you to . . . oh, forget it."

My brother spun on his heel and marched out the door.

After that, we headed to a cozy little café not far from the Star. There we got eggs, bacon, hot cakes, coffee—and much the same answer when Gustav asked about Milford Bales.

"Well, he's always been decent to *me*, that's all I know," said the (till then) friendly fellow who'd been serving us, and he streaked away like a squirrel with its tail on fire.

"Well, hell," Old Red grumbled. "Ain't there nobody in this town willin' to say boo about Milford Bales?"

"Oh, I'm sure there's somebody." I pointed a half-eaten strip of bacon at my brother's clothes. "They're just not gonna say it to a feller who looks like he oughta be bulldoggin' steers. Tell you what—let *me* handle this."

"And exactly how do you intend to handle it?"

I stuffed the rest of the bacon into my mouth. "Observe."

I scooted away from our table and approached a cigar-chomping gent dining by himself nearby.

"Pardon the interruption, sir." I pointed at the newspaper spread out before him—the *San Marcos Free Press*. "Would you happen to know where that's printed up?"

The stogie-sucker peeped up from the front page just long enough to confirm he wasn't hearing voices. "East on Fort, north on Cedar, right side of the street."

"Thank you."

The man grunted.

I could see why he was eating alone.

"Well, there you go," I said as I slid back into my seat. "Love Bales or hate him, the local newspaper's gotta have *something* to say."

My brother gave me an approving—and begrudging—nod. "It's gratifyin' to see you actually think every once in a while."

"It's gratifyin' to hear you actually say something nice every once in a while," I replied. "Too bad I'm still waitin'."

We found *Free Press* HQ sandwiched between a butcher shop and a Chinese laundry. The building was a small, creaky-floored, poorly lit affair chockablock with printing equipment, leaning towers of musty paper, and, buried here and there beneath the clutter, what I assumed were desks and chairs.

Three men were hard at work on the next edition: one stooped over a typesetter's table picking letters from long trays, another cranking sheets off a clattering printing press, and a third—the only one not apron-clad and ink-stained—pacing back and forth between the first two, periodically peering over their shoulders to point out their mistakes.

It wasn't hard to deduce who was in charge.

Despite the disorder all around him, the editor and/or publisher was an extraordinarily prim-looking gentleman himself. He wore a long frock coat, a double-breasted vest, and a red ascot wrapped around a starched collar so high it just about tickled his earlobes. His bearing was plenty starched, too: The man carried himself with a stiffness some would describe as "dignity" and others (mostly cowboys) as "having a corncob up your ass."

He didn't hear my first demure coughs over the racket of the printing press. So eventually Gustav lost his patience and barked out a booming hack of the sort you'd expect from a tubercular mule.

The gentleman turned to face us. "Yes?"

He was exceedingly fair, I now saw, with thinning blond-white hair and sallow skin and a mustache so light and overtrimmed it could have been a stray strand of silk stuck to his upper lip. His pale blue eyes flicked from me to (with a noticeable souring of expression) my brother.

"Good afternoon, sir!" I said. "My name is Otto Amlingmeyer, and this is my brother Gustav. We're colleagues of yours, of a sort, and we're hopin' we might impose on you for a wee bit of assistance."

"What sort of assistance?"

His accent was English.

His sneer was universal.

"Well, you see, sir . . ."

A grin came to my lips I couldn't keep down. Words were forming I'd waited a long, long time to speak, and my mouth just couldn't get them out without a smile.

"I'm a writer under contract to Smythe & Associates Publishing of New York City. At the moment, I'm workin' on a story about San Marcos. Naturally, I figured this'd be the place to turn for insights into your fine community, and I only need trouble you for a few minutes to chat. Who knows? You might even end up in the story yourself!"

The newspaperman pursed his lips so tight they went white.

It took me a moment to realize this was his rendering of a smile.

"Come with me."

He led us to his private office: a jumble-covered writing table jammed into a corner. The Englishman took the only seat, then held out his hand to offer us thigh-high piles of newspapers for our own (dis)comfort.

Once Old Red and I were roosting precariously upon our perches, our host introduced himself properly. He was Horace Cuff, editor and publisher of the *Free Press*. He'd come to San Marcos from Dallas by way of New York and, before that, London, where he'd newspapered in a variety of positions he outlined for us in droning, catatonia-inducing detail. Apparently Mr. Cuff didn't just think he should be in my story, he felt he ought to *be* my story.

Fortunately he ran out of biography before either Gustav or I could topple off our rubbish heap dead asleep, and I was able to slip in a question. I thought it best to ease around slow to the real matter at hand—Milford Bales—so I began by asking about San Marcos. Cuff's views were nothing new, though I must say the pomposity with which they were relayed was all his own.

San Marcos was "maturating," Cuff told us, moving from unruly youth into civilized adulthood. Soon the town would "wipe the last muck from its shoes" and claim its place as a proper little city.

"Sounds like you'll have paradise on earth once the cattlemen finally dry up and blow away," I said.

Like all humorless men, Cuff was armor-plated against sarcasm, and he answered with a fervor that made it plain he hadn't noticed mine.

"No, San Marcos will never be paradise. There's only one of those, and the larger a city grows, the further it seems to drift from it. In fact, all the great metropolises, I've found, are far closer to hell than heaven. It's something my friends here must guard against."

"Guard against how?" Old Red asked.

Cuff eyed him as if wondering whether his dignity could survive parlay with someone so far beneath it.

"By denying sin a toehold," he said. "Crime, degeneracy, moral decay . . . London and New York are awash in it all, and it saddened me to find Dallas no better. It's too late for them. Not so for San Marcos. Here, fortunately, it's wickedness on the decline, not virtue."

"Who's to thank for that?" I asked. "San Marcos cleanin' itself up, I mean? The town marshal?"

Cuff gave a reluctant nod. "To some degree, I suppose, but Brother Landrigan deserves most of the credit."

"Brother Landrigan?"

Cuff nodded again, eagerly this time, and a rush of color came to his pinched, pallid face.

"Yes. The man's a dynamo—a dynamo powered by the Holy Spirit! It's my great privilege to be a member of his flock."

I stole a rueful peep over at Gustav. He responded with a here-and-gone grimace.

If there's one thing we absolutely cannot abide, my brother and I, it's having our souls saved. The way Cuff was starting to talk, a sermon couldn't be far off.

"Brother Landrigan is a tireless crusader for decency," the Englishman enthused. And I mean really *enthused*—he didn't so much say the words as "Hallelujah!" them. "He's cleansing this town just as surely as he cleanses hearts of sin. Why, the marshal wouldn't even *be* marshal if Brother Landrigan hadn't backed him. It was Brother Landrigan who set the man's sights on a higher purpose in the first place. The same could be said of me. I was languishing in despair until I heard Brother Landrigan speak. That's why I took over the *Free Press*. He convinced me to come and serve His purpose here."

You could hear that capital *H* in "His" just from the way the word popped off Cuff's mouth. What wasn't so obvious was who he was referring to: Brother Landrigan or God. I almost got the feeling they were, to Cuff, one and the same.

"Does Brother Landrigan do any street preachin'?" my brother asked. "With a choir, maybe?"

"Indeed he does. You've seen him?"

"We have been so blessed, yes," I said.

We'd not only seen Brother Landrigan, we'd been damned to hell by him: He was the fire-and-brimstone-breathing sky pilot spreading the Bad News outside the saloon the day before.

Old Red and I traded sour looks again.

This time, Cuff noticed.

"So," he said, "you say you're a writer working on a magazine story." He turned to Gustav—and turned frosty cold while he was at it. "Why is it *you're* here?"

"Oh, my brother travels everywhere with me," I said. "You could call him my muse . . . but mostly he just totes the luggage."

I laughed at my own joke.

If I hadn't, no one would.

"Tell me again," Cuff said. "*What* sort of story have you come here to write?"

"Local history," I said. "Speakin' of which, would you mind if I was to do a little perusin' through your back numbers? To soak up more flavor of the place, you understand."

Cuff looked back and forth between me and my brother, weighing, I assumed, how much we'd worn out our welcome: just a tad around the edges or clear to tatters.

"You're sitting on 1892," he finally said. He nodded at the papers propping up Old Red, then pointed at more piles strewn about willy-nilly nearby. "1891, '90, '89, '88."

"Thank you, sir," I said. "I think we can manage from here. Wouldn't want to take up any more of your valuable time."

"How . . . considerate of you."

Cuff made "considerate" sound like something you wouldn't let a fellow call your mother.

"Interestin' bird, that one," Old Red whispered as the man went back to browbeating his staff.

"Yeah. Half peacock, half cuckoo," I said under my breath. "So where should we start—under your ass or mine?"

"Neither." Gustav reached out and patted the stack for 1888. "October third. That was the day after."

I didn't have to ask the day after what. I just got to work.

I found the October third edition quick enough. It was the *head-line* I was hunting that was nowhere in sight. I scanned the October fourth and fifth editions with the same result.

There was nothing, not a word, about the murder of Gertrude "Adeline" Eichelberger.

"Any chance you're misrememberin' the date?"

"No, there is *not* a chance," Old Red snapped. "They just didn't think it was news."

"Yeah, you're probably right. Still, long as we're here I may as well . . . ahhh."

At last, I'd found something about Adeline . . . or so I thought at first. I'd spotted a couple of the words I'd been looking for, but the date, the story, the *everything*—it was all wrong.

My "ahhh" became a "Huh?"

Gustav leaned so far off his stack it nearly toppled over.

"What is it?"

I gave the paper in my hand a shake.

"This here's the *Free Press* for October second. Morning edition. Folks woulda got it more than half a day before Adeline died. And lookee here . . ."

I pointed to the headlines. The words, of course, would mean nothing to my unlettered brother, but the placement of them would. They were on the front page, up top, big.

" 'Whitechapel Fiend Strikes Again!' " I read out. " 'More *Prostitutes Butchered.*' "

I glanced up at Old Red to make sure he'd caught the full weight of it.

Indeed he had—right in the gut. He opened his mouth as if to speak, but no sound came out.

I went on. " 'Authorities Helpless to Stop—' "

And here Gustav got his breath back enough to utter three words heavy with dread.

Even an illiterate cowhand who couldn't find all of England on a map—even *he* knew who the Terror of Whitechapel was.

"Jack the Ripper," my brother said.

18

THE SERMON, PART ONE

Or, Cuff Fills Us In on the Ripper—and Rips into Mr. Holmes

I read the article to my brother as Cuff and his minions went about their business not thirty feet away. My voice was as low as I could keep it and still be heard above the clanking and rattling of the printing press, and the hushed, whispery tones made it seem like I was unspooling a spook story over a cattle drive campfire.

A few days before, the article said, the Ripper had claimed two more victims, bringing his official tally to four. The women were again members of London's "unfortunate class," and had been, yet again, slashed to death while making their rounds. One had been horribly mutilated, as well. Just how horribly was left largely to the reader's imagination, though the word "eviscerated" popped up to offer a none-too-subtle hint.

Eventually the article trailed off into a long regurgitation of the case to date and various windy proclamations of resolve from Ripper-hunters both amateur and professional. I stopped about halfway through.

"Heck of a coincidence," I said.

Old Red shook his head. "I can't figure it for a coincidence at all."

"But how could it not be? It ain't like the Ripper squeezed in a trip to San Marcos between killings."

Gustav squinted and stroked his mustache as if mulling over that very idea. "Could be whoever killed Adeline wanted to make it look random-like. The work of a lunatic. To hide the real why of it. Or could be a *real* lunatic read that there story and got . . . you know . . ."

My brother spun his hands in the air listlessly, too lost in other thoughts to chase down the word he wanted.

"Inspired?" I suggested.

He nodded.

"Don't that seem a tad far-fetched?" I said. "Some asshole all the way out here in the West hears tell of a crazy Englishman and sets out to copy his every move?"

Old Red gave me a droopy-lidded glower. "What do you think *I* been doin' the past year?"

"Hmmm, yeah, well . . ." I cleared my throat and tried another tack. "All the same, we been drawin' a bead on Milford Bales, and he don't strike me as the madman type. A nasty SOB maybe—when you're around, anyway—but not a madman."

"He never seemed the lawman type neither, but look at him now. Besides, to get away with murder all these years, you'd have to be pretty good at buryin' things down deep."

"I suppose. Only bein' loony ain't some secret you can tuck out of sight, like rustlin' or diddlin' the neighbor's wife. Sooner or later, crazy's gonna show."

Gustav's eyes widened, a new thought hitting him hard. "What if it *did* show . . . five years ago? Only I was so drunk when it happened I didn't even remember come morning?"

"You mean the time you took a swing at Bales? You think he let something slip?"

"I don't know, dammit." Old Red looked away and pounded a fist on his thigh, his anger turned inward. "One less shot of rye, and maybe we wouldn't be here now. Maybe I would've known the truth five—"

The sound of approaching footsteps clamped his lips tight.

Horace Cuff loomed up behind us.

"Local history?" the Englishman sniffed, cocking a disapproving eyebrow at the article I'd been reading.

I shrugged and dredged up a chuckle. "Guess we let ourselves get distracted."

Cuff told us what he thought of such distractions (and the sort of person who's susceptible to them) with a wrinkle-nosed sneer.

"I wonder, Mr. Cuff," my brother said. "Was you still journalizin' in London when all that Ripper stuff was goin' on?"

Cuff's whole face wrinkled with revulsion now.

"Yes, and before you ask—because certain people always ask—*no*, I did not write about 'that Ripper stuff.' I refused. In fact, it's part of the reason I came to America. Fleet Street may have been eager to wallow in such salaciousness, but not I. I left for New York a few months after the Ripper appeared."

"A few *months*?" I said. "Why, that whole business would've been about through by then anyway, wouldn't it? As I recall, ol' Jack stopped of his own accord after the sixth killin'."

"The fifth," Cuff said. He gave his head a quick shake and straightened his already impressively stiff spine. "I've said all I intend to say on this subject."

"Oh, yeah. You made that right plain," Gustav said—and God bless the single-minded little so-and-so, he forged ahead anyway. "I'm curious, though. There was a feller in London at the time—the best crime-buster the world ever knew, to hear some tell it. Mr. Sherlock Holmes. How come he didn't catch the Ripper?"

"Because," Cuff said with a smugness so thick it practically oozed out of him like syrup, "he made no attempt to do so."

The Ripper was someone Cuff didn't care to talk about, but Mr.

Holmes? The way the man carried on now, we couldn't have shut him up had we tried.

"Oh, there were rumors of a confidential inquiry on his part, but even if true—and I imagine they weren't—it came to naught. No, it's more likely, I think, that the man simply couldn't pull himself from his needle without a fee to collect. Either that, or it was plain coward-ice. Imagine the blow to his standing—and his bank account—should he involve himself in so very public a mystery only to fail."

Cuff's gaze lifted away from Old Red and me, drifting off to something beyond us, distant. The Promised Land, maybe. He cer-tainly had the air of a prophet about him now . . . even if it is hard to picture Moses in an ascot.

"Sherlock Holmes," Cuff intoned, somber and slow, "was the em-bodiment of everything misguided about our modern age. Mind de-void of soul, so-called progress that masks moral rot, the hubris of science. He claimed to see things others couldn't, but the yawning emptiness within himself—the emptiness only God's grace can fill? That he was blind to. It came as no surprise to me when his foolish 'adventures' destroyed him. Logic is not wisdom, and a rational mind without a repenting heart is worse than worthless. Those are truths someone like Sherlock Holmes could only understand once he felt for himself the full agony of perdition's flames."

I waited for my brother to jump to his hero's defense. There'd been a time when he wouldn't even admit that Holmes was dead— sure, everyone else in the world thought he'd gone over a Swiss water-fall, but had anyone actually seen the body? So I couldn't believe Old Red would let some prig say Holmes was roasting over Beelzebub's own barbecue pit.

Yet he just stared off the same direction as Cuff, like he was trying to spy with his own eyes whatever vision it was that had transfixed the man so.

Myself, all I saw that way was a wall.

"Well." I slapped my hands on my knees and pushed myself to my feet. "I think we best be goin'."

"No . . . not yet," Gustav muttered, tearing his gaze away from Infinity. "We ain't done researchin'."

"I rather think you are," Cuff said. He'd returned to the Here and Now a lot quicker than my brother, and what he found awaiting him there—namely, *us*—was obviously not to his liking. "This is not a public reading room. It is a private place of business, and it's been disrupted enough by your presence. I would ask you to leave now."

"Look, mister . . . I don't mean to come off pushy," Old Red said, "but if we could just have ten more minutes to—"

Cuff turned toward the typesetter and printer still slaving away behind us. "Mr. Littlefield. Mr. Maleeny. Would you show our visitors to the door?"

The men glanced at each other, neither looking anxious to play bouncer. Nevertheless, when Cuff prodded them with a tart "If you please?" they reluctantly started toward us.

"Thank you ever so much, Mr. Cuff." I tugged my brother to his feet. "Your hospitality's something we won't soon forget."

Gustav said not a word as the newspapermen escorted us outside. He just stared ahead, blank-faced, looking like a man who's had the rug not only pulled out from under him but rolled up and dropped on his head. I fancied I knew just what was gnawing at his mind . . . and his confidence and even, I dare say, his soul.

He'd put his faith in something, and of late that faith had been foundering. Now we learn that Sherlock Holmes, the great sage of observation and logic, had failed when he'd been needed most? That either the Method had proved useless against the Ripper or the Great One had simply turned tail and run?

Well, if that was true—if lunacy could trump reason, and our killer was indeed a lunatic—then what chance did we have?

How can you deduce the hows and wherefores of what a madman might do . . . except perhaps go mad yourself?

19

THE KRIEGERS

Or, Old Red Admits He Doesn't Know Jack

Thanks largely to my busybody brother, I've been thrown out of more places than most folks ever get into. Only once, though, have I received an apology midboot.

"Sorry about this," whispered the typesetter—I'm not sure if it was Mr. Littlefield or Mr. Maleeny—as he helped escort us from the offices of the *San Marcos Free Press*. "Mr. Cuff's a bit . . . well . . ."

"Loco?" I suggested.

"Prickly," the printer corrected.

"Oh, I know the type."

I peered around him at my brother.

Gustav was squinting and blinking, momentarily blinded by the brightness of the sun outside. Yet there was something about him that seemed stunned, too—distant and oblivious.

"You should try the Kriegers. Fredericksburg and Comal," the typesetter said. Then he threw in another whispered "Sorry" before puffing himself up to bellow, "And stay out!"

The newspapermen marched back into the building and slammed the door.

Out on the sidewalk, a prim and proper couple stopped midstroll to stare at us.

"Good afternoon," I said, tipping my hat. "May I interest *you* in a set of genuine leather-bound encyclopedias?"

The gentleman and his lady made for the hills.

"So," I said to Old Red, "got any notion who Fred and Comal Krieger are or why we should 'try' 'em?"

"Fredericksburg and Comal ain't people. They're streets. Thisaway."

Gustav started up the sidewalk, moving fast.

I caught up and matched him stride for stride.

"So who would the Kriegers be, then?" I asked.

"I have no idea."

"Not that that's slowin' you down any."

"Feels better goin' fast," my brother said without looking over at me. "Almost like we're actually gettin' somewhere."

Before long, we were scuttling past snug houses with shrub-studded yards set off by picket fences as white and straight as sets of perfect gleaming teeth. One home, though—the one we found casting a shadow over the corner of Comal and Fredericksburg—was considerably grander than its cozy neighbors, with so much curlicued ornamentation upon its gables and veranda it made a gingerbread house look about as fancy as a sharecropper's privy. Posted in front was a large sign, which I dutifully read out for my brother.

SAN MARCOS'S BEST
(SAN MARCOS'S ONLY!)
PHOTOGRAPHY & CUSTOM FRAMING STUDIO
MORTIMER KRIEGER, PROPRIETOR
"EXCELSIOR!"

Gustav just grunted, then bounded up to the porch and knocked on the door.

"Got any idea what you're gonna say to this Krieger feller?" I asked as I came up the steps behind him.

"I ain't worried about that," Old Red said. "You're doin' the talkin'."

"Well, thanks for givin' me so much no—"

The door swung open.

The first part came easy. It's not hard to figure "Good afternoon, ma'am" is the best way to start when greeting a matronly middle-aged woman.

After that, I was winging it.

"Would Mr. Krieger be available?"

The woman was silent. Which isn't to say she didn't say anything. Her lips were moving, so I knew there were words floating around there somewhere. They just never made it so far as my ears.

"Pardon?"

The woman repeated herself . . . and I still couldn't make out a sound. Fortunately she stepped back and swept an arm out behind her, which was easy to interpret even without words.

"Thank you, ma'am."

Our hostess offered up a small smile as Gustav and I stepped past her. She was a well-proportioned if unremarkable specimen of perhaps forty-five years of age, with curly black-gray hair and delicate features that fairly screamed gentility (if "GENTILITY!" is something that can be screamed). Her rather shapeless black-and-brown tea gown so matched the murky interior of the house that the woman almost literally faded into the woodwork.

To be fair, though, she'd practically have to light herself on fire *not* to fade into the woodwork in such a place, so gloomy was it. Between the dark mahogany paneling and the walls papered in velvety red paisley, the house had all the warmth and cheer of your average bear cave. Further back, beyond the foyer, black banisters and crimson-carpeted steps curled up to a second floor so shadow-shrouded I wouldn't have been surprised to spy stalactites hanging from the ceiling.

The lady closed the door behind us and spoke/whispered again.

"You'll have to excuse me, ma'am," I said, tilting an ear her way. "I can't seem to catch anything more quiet than a thunderclap today."

Then at last I heard it—a tiny, distant voice, like one of Swift's Lilliputians talking from under a teacup.

"Are you here for a sitting?"

She swiveled as she spoke, hand held out to a closed door to her right—the studio, I was guessing.

"No, ma'am. We're here on other business."

She pivoted the other way, gesturing toward a door directly opposite the first.

"You'd like to join the subscription library?"

Bull's-eye.

"Yes, indeed, ma'am. We've heard ever so much about it . . . haven't we, Gustav?"

"Talk of the town," my brother muttered.

"Come with me," the woman said.

At least I assume that's what she said. I couldn't make it out. Anyhow, she opened the door and gestured for us to follow her through.

We did—and from drab darkness, we stepped into a miracle.

Everywhere I looked, floor to ceiling, were books books books—more than I'd ever seen altogether at once. Andrew Carnegie may be sprinkling the East with public libraries, but out here in the West they're still a rarity, as are bookstores any bigger than the back corner of a general store. Stumbling into such a treasure trove in someone's home was like opening a tin of stewed tomatoes and finding the crown jewels.

Old Red and I were stunned so silent it was actually possible to hear our hostess speak.

"Please, make yourselves comfortable. My husband will be with you shortly."

With that she went gliding out of the room.

"Quite the little firecracker, ain't she?" I walked to the nearest bookshelf, pulled down the first volume within easy reach, and found myself holding *The Works of Edgar Allan Poe*. "I didn't think I'd get a word in edgewise."

"The lady's got 'the grand gift of silence,' that's all," Old Red said, appropriating a compliment Holmes once paid Watson. "I just wish that gift wasn't so danged rare."

I slid Eddie Poe back in his slot.

"This better?" I said.

My brother either didn't hear me or (about a thousand times more likely) chose to ignore me.

I drifted over to a table covered with newspapers. "They got the *Free Press* for the last week or so. Could be they keep the old ones stashed away, too."

Gustav started flipping through a book big enough to crush a Chihuahua. Maybe he was looking for pictures.

"I ain't interested in that rag now," he said.

"Well, why the hell are we here, then?"

Fortunately I'd merely mumbled this to myself, for at that very moment the door opened and a nondescript man sidled into the room. And when I say "nondescript," I mean it—even such a word as "sidled" imparts too much character to him. He was an average-looking man of average height and average build, dressed with the tasteful blandness expected of your average middle-aged, middle-of-the-road Everyman.

We were face-to-face with mediocrity incarnate.

"Good afternoon, gentlemen. I'm Mortimer Krieger," he said, and you'll have to excuse the lack of adjectives describing his voice. To tell you the truth, I can't even remember what he sounded like. "I apologize for keeping you waiting. I was attending to a client in my studio. An engagement of the utmost delicacy." He leaned forward slightly, his voice dropping to a near-whisper. "A *memento mori*."

"Ahhhh," I said in a sympathetic, say-no-more kind of way.

My brother said more.

"A what now?"

I stifled a sigh.

"Keepsake commemoratin' a dearly departed," I explained.

"Oh." Old Red looked at Krieger. "You're talkin' about a death portrait."

The photographer nodded. "Just so."

Old Red scowled.

Our family never succumbed to the fad for death portraits, though our resistance might have been more a matter of circumstance than sensibility: We lacked the ready cash for photographs of any kind, and when one of us died it was rarely in a way that made for a pretty picture.

My brother jerked his chin at the door.

"The 'dearly departed' ain't over there in your studio, is he?"

"No," Krieger said, unruffled by my brother's bluntness. There are advantages to having no discernible personality. "A member of the family was simply making arrangements for me to visit the home before the wake."

"Ahhhh," I said in a neutral, no-accounting-for-taste kind of way. (Amazing how many meanings you can shoehorn into an "Ahhhh," isn't it?)

Gustav was still scowling.

"*De gustibus non est disputandum*," Krieger said to him with a smile I might have labeled "sly" had it come from someone I credited with a capacity for irony. "There's no accounting for taste . . . even in how we deal with death. *Now*"—Krieger's smile grew larger, yet at the same time emptier—"how may I help you?"

Leave it to my brother to wipe anyone's grin away quick.

"You got anything on Jack the Ripper?"

"E-excuse m-me?" Krieger stammered, hazel eyes (or were they blue?) abulge.

"Allow me to explain," I said, throwing Old Red a glare that thanked him for his customary subtlety. "You see, I'm a writer under contract to Smythe & Associates Publishing of New York City, and . . ."

I proceeded to explain that I was working on an article about Mr. Krieger's fair city, and as part of my portrayal of a leading citizen—Mr. Horace Cuff of the *San Marcos Free Press*—I was in need of information on the outrages that had driven him from the practice of his profession in his native land. So it wasn't the Ripper himself I was interested in so much as his depiction in the press. Having heard much local talk of Mr. Krieger's impressive private library, I'd come to him to appeal for aid.

Krieger's alarm quickly evaporated, and by the time I was through he was nodding knowingly—if also sorrowfully.

"We might have something of the sort you're looking for. There's a small stock of penny dreadfuls and detective magazines and other such low entertainments. However, you must understand—these things don't belong to *me*. They're the property of the subscription library, for members' use only."

Old Red waved a hand at the books all around us. "You sayin' all this ain't yours to do with as you please?"

Krieger shook his head. "It was once, but I couldn't keep it all to myself. I handed over the collection when we founded the subscription library. I'm merely a caretaker now."

"Well, we're just askin' for a peek at one or two books," I said. "Surely, as caretaker, it's within your power to—"

Krieger was shaking his head again. "I'm sorry, but no. I can't make exceptions. This isn't a public library. The books are for dues-paying members only. Although . . ." Krieger rubbed his nondescript chin, then brightened. "Yes, why not?"

"You have an idea?" I asked dutifully.

Krieger's face may have been flat and bland, but his business instincts, I now sensed, were plenty sharp.

"All you have to do is join the library and you can look at whatever you want!" he said.

"Now, why I didn't think of that?"

That was a rhetorical question, of course. I didn't think of it (or suggest it, anyway) because I knew it would cost us big. What I hadn't reckoned on was *how* big.

Two one-year memberships: forty dollars.

Two "reading room fees" (necessary, Krieger said, because we weren't San Marcos residents and therefore couldn't remove books from the premises): four dollars.

Two "one-time processing surcharges": one dollar.

The air we were breathing: free, believe it or not.

Grand total: forty-five bucks.

This was a sizable dent in the money we had left from the sales of my stories, and before forking it over, I peeked at Old Red for the go-ahead. He gave it to me with one jerky, sour-faced nod, and we were quickly forty-five dollars the poorer . . . without yet being any the wiser.

I filled out some forms with our names and local address and whatnot while Gustav pretended to skim a randomly chosen book. (I had to stifle a snort when I saw it was *Principles of Domestic Science: A Manual of Practical Housewifery*.) When I was done, our host offered me his hand.

"Welcome to the San Marcos Subscription Library," he said as we shook. "Now if you'll just wait here a moment, I'll have a look through our archives and see if I can accommodate you."

"He don't 'accommodate' us," Gustav said once we were alone again, "I want that money back."

"I already want that money back. In fact, I never wanted it gone. Forty-five bucks to look at some books? What do you think we're gonna find in 'em, anyway?"

"Pages." Old Red shrugged. "Words."

I didn't bother with a "hardy har har." My brother wasn't just making a bad joke. He was admitting what I already knew: There was every chance no book on earth could help us.

A moment later, Mr. Krieger returned.

"I'm sorry. This was all I could find."

He handed me a single, slender, well-worn book. I looked down and read out the title.

"*The Whitechapel Mystery: A Psychological Problem* by Dr. N. T. Oliver."

"Psycho logical?" my brother muttered skeptically. "What the heck does that mean?"

"Psychology is a new field of science," Krieger said. "The study of human behavior."

Gustav actually perked up upon hearing that. "So this Dr. Oliver's tryin' to figure the Ripper out scientific-like?"

"I assume so," Krieger said. "I haven't read it myself. Does it sound like the kind of thing you're looking for?"

"Not really," I said at the very moment Old Red was popping off with a "Yessir!"

"Well. I'll leave you to it."

Krieger backed out of the room and was gone.

"Alright—now we're gettin' somewhere," Old Red said.

"We are?"

"*We are*," Gustav said. "The killers and thieves Mr. Holmes rounded up always did things for a reason. If you could put your finger on their purpose, you could put the finger on them. But the Ripper, or anyone tryin' to act like him, ain't got no reason I can see other than . . . *fun*, I guess you'd call it. And that don't leave no trail to backtrack. There ain't no *why* to nothing."

I gave the book a little waggle. "You think we'll find a why in here?"

"We'd better."

Old Red stomped off and plopped into one of the room's over-stuffed armchairs.

I sighed and took a seat myself and commenced to reading.

It didn't take long to know that the why Gustav wanted so bad wasn't there.

The *who*, though—that seemed plain as day.

20

PSYCHOLOGICAL PROBLEMS

Or, Our First Stab at "Psychology" Just About Drives Us Nuts

It wouldn't be entirely accurate to say there was no why to be found in *The Whitechapel Mystery: A Psychological Problem*. True, I couldn't find the why we were looking for—the one that might explain a man turning mad dog—but there were plenty of others. They started cropping up from the first sentence, and all were aimed at the author, Dr. N. T. Oliver.

"Why can't you use words a fellow can understand?" came first. Followed by "Why don't you just say what you mean?" Then on to "Why would anyone read this tripe?"

After that it was all one big what: namely, "What the hell is this SOB talking about?"

"While alienists would attribute the horrific Whitechapel murders of recent months to the specific, exclusive 'psychoses' or 'mania' of a single dement," the book began (more or less), "psychology, as a natural science devoted to the phenomenological study of, as James put it, 'finite individual minds' (plural) must take a broader view, and the treatise which follows will, I hope, serve as contraindication to conclusions that discard empiricism in favor of quasi-metaphysical tenets that . . ."

Oh, I give up. Even faking this much required the borrowing of a thesaurus, and it *still* doesn't get across how deep the hogwash was we had to wade through.

I would provide some actual quotes from the book itself, but I have neither a copy at hand nor a mind equipped to memorize long stretches of what was, to me, not just Greek but Greek as babbled by Athens's resident village idiot. Certain phrases I have retained, though: "transcendental ego," "elementary units of consciousness," "deterministic assumptions," and, most puzzling of all, "the Spatial Quale."

To describe the book as highfalutin doesn't do it justice—the falutin was so high-flown it left earth altogether, outward bound for parts unknown. If Dr. Oliver in any way explained the "psychology" of the Whitechapel killer I can't even say, for I'm in need of a separate book entirely to explain the psychology of Dr. Oliver.

In fact, the only parts I could understand at all were the letters reproduced in the book—the ones written by Jack himself and sent to the police. That I had an easier time following the thoughts of a "Ripper" posting letters "from hell" than a (one assumes) qualified doctor/scientist is something I prefer not to dwell upon.

Gustav did his best to ride it all out with me, but his best didn't get him far. Four turgid, interminable pages into it and he was rolling his eyes and telling me to "skip to the parts in English."

Such parts I never found, aside from Saucy Jack's contributions.

"*That* they call scientific?" my brother finally spat. "It ain't nothin' but a buncha two-dollar words glued together with horseshit."

"You're bein' overcharitable. It's *all* horseshit. I mean, my God . . . I feel like I know less now than I did before we started."

This set me up for an easy jab of the "You can't take nothing from nothing" variety, but Old Red was too incensed to notice the opening.

"Psycho logical," he fumed. "Ain't nothing logical about it I can see. If that's the best science can do, I may as well try hoodoo."

"Now, now. Don't go speakin' blasphemy. Holmes's method's plenty scientific."

"Yeah," Gustav said bitterly, sinking deep into his plush seat, "and just look how far that's got us."

I had no ready reply. Griping about detectiving's always been *my* job.

While Old Red slumped there silently, I skipped to the index at the back of the book hoping to find entries for "Holmes, Sherlock" or "Prostitutes, Explanation for Murders of" or even "Sense, Common." There was nada on anything of use . . . while "the Spatial Quale" got its very own chapter.

I flipped to the front to see who'd put out such an unreadable brick of BS as this. I could only hope it wasn't Smythe & Associates Publishing of New York. My pride wouldn't survive the blow.

As I flicked past the first page, I noticed something I'd overlooked before: a little yellow sleeve glued to the paper. Sticking out of it was a small, stiff card.

"What's that?" Gustav asked.

"Index card." I slipped the paper from the sleeve. "I'm guessin' Krieger uses . . . whoa."

Old Red sat up straight.

"What?"

"Looks like these are for trackin' who's borrowed which books. Only this one's just been out to one member . . . and he's had it three different times."

I held up the card and pointed at the name printed neatly on line after line.

"Milford Bales . . . Milford Bales . . . Milford Bales."

Gustav snatched the card from my hand. Sure, he can't read a word, but he still likes to see things with his own eyes.

"Might just be another coincidence," I said, not even half believing it myself.

"Like Adeline dyin' forty feet from Bales's barbershop? Then Bales doin' us like he did last night?"

Gustav gazed hollow-eyed out one of the room's high-arched windows. Outside, the bright shine of the clear-skied afternoon was giving ground to twilight.

"Pile up enough coincidences," my brother said, "they make a fact."

"That don't sound like something Mr. Holmes would say."

I thought I heard a "fff"—the beginnings of an emphatic "Feh!"—but the door opened before Old Red could finish.

"Gentlemen," Mr. Krieger said. "How goes your research?"

"Can't say we think much of the book," Gustav said, "but *this* makes for mighty interestin' readin'."

He gave the index card a wave.

"Oh," Krieger groaned with a rueful shake of the head. "I really must change that system. Not everyone would want their reading habits to be public knowledge."

"Oh, I'm sure the marshal wouldn't mind," Old Red said. "Readin' up on murders and such would just be part of the job for him. Why, I bet he's in here all the time lookin' over all kinds of gruesome whatnot."

Krieger spread out his hands helplessly, lips pressed together in a prim pledge of silence.

"Protectin' folks' privacy, huh?" my brother said. "I understand. So let me ask you something you *can* talk about: When did Milford Bales become town marshal?"

"He was first elected in the fall of 1890, and he was reelected last year." Krieger turned to me. "I thought you said you were doing research related to Horace Cuff."

I shrugged. "We got sidetracked."

"Did you now? If I may ask, Mr. Amlingmeyer—what kind of

writing do you do again? These questions, your interest in Jack the Ripper . . . it doesn't seem to fit."

As will sometimes happen when I'm stuck for a fast answer, I reluctantly resorted to the truth. Of a sort.

"To be honest, sir, we haven't been entirely forthcomin' with you. It's not an article about the town or Mr. Cuff we're here for. I write what I guess you'd call 'low entertainments.' 'Detective yarns' others might call 'em. True-to-life stuff, such as Dr. John Watson has in *Harper's Weekly*. We're here in San Marcos to look into an old case."

Krieger didn't look pleased, but he didn't rush to show us the door, either.

"What kind of case?" he said.

"Murder, I'm afraid."

"A murder? In San Marcos?"

"It was five years ago," I said.

"You wouldn't have known her," Old Red added, voice flat. "Just a poor farmgirl. They didn't even write it up in the paper."

"I see," Krieger said, nodding gravely. "I must say . . . Kriegers have been in San Marcos from the very beginning. I suppose you could call us one of the town's first families. So you can imagine how displeased I'd be to see the community painted in an unflattering light."

I smiled reassuringly . . . which can be tricky to pull off when lying through one's teeth.

"You have nothing to worry about. I have been charmed—absolutely *charmed*, sir—by the beauty of San Marcos and the warmth of its people. In fact, I'm thinkin' of callin' this case 'Death Comes to Paradise.' "

"Where would this 'case' appear?"

"In a special issue of *Smythe's New Detective Library*. That's where all my other yarns have been published."

Or *will be published*, I should have said—but why muddy the waters with wearisome details?

Krieger closed his eyes, his already colorless, characterless face going slack. "Amlingmeyer . . . Amlingmeyer . . . ," he said slowly, chewing on each letter like he was trying to taste the sound of it.

His eyes popped open and met mine. " 'On the Wrong Track'?" he said.

I blinked at him, stunned. "Yessir. That's one of mine."

"We got in a copy on Wednesday," Krieger said. "It's already been checked out."

My fingers took to tingling, then my face, and a lightheadedness came over me it usually takes half a bottle to bring on. It was a good thing I was already sitting or my knees would've buckled.

At last, it was real. Something I'd written had been published—printed out in something other than my shoddy chickenscratch. If Gustav and I hadn't been making our way to Texas the past week, I might have had copies of my own already.

I looked over at my brother, an idiot grin glued to my face. Old Red scowled it right off.

Something was stuck in his craw. Something uncommonly bothersome even for a craw as sticky as his.

He jerked his head at the nearest window—and the graying sky beyond—then flicked the index card back to me and got to his feet.

It was time to meet up with Bob and Lottie.

"Well, thank you for your help, Mr. Krieger," I said. "We best be goin' now."

I walked *The Whitechapel Mystery* over to Krieger, and the two of us shook hands again.

Gustav was already halfway to the door.

"That's really all you need?" Krieger asked. He actually looked disappointed by our departure—a first for us in San Marcos. Whatever his misgivings, meeting a bona fide (dime) novelist seemed to have put them to rest. "There's nothing more I can do to be of service?"

Old Red paused in the doorway.

"Mr. Krieger, what we need now ain't in no book."

Then he looked at me again—looked at me hard, in a way that made a promise.

"*Any* book."

He was through with research and data and talking and thinking. Maybe even through with Mr. Holmes.

As of this moment, my brother was ready for *action* . . . and he was going to see that we got it.

21

THE PLAN

Or, Old Red Hatches a Plot to Net a Soiled Dove

I t would take ten minutes of fast walking to get to the meeting spot: the San Marcos Springs, headwaters of the San Marcos River. I proposed to pass the time discussing my brother's plan of action—his response being, "There ain't no plan yet . . . but there will be if you shut up and let me think." After that, we made the trip in silence, aside from some huffing and puffing on my part.

By the time we got out to our rendezvous, it was dusky-dark. I was a little disappointed to have lost the light, for I'd pictured the springs as bubbling, roiling, geysery things, clear-pure and alive.

As it turned out, I wasn't missing much, sightseeing-wise. The springs were hidden beneath a swampy, brackish lagoon, and if not for the name of the place—Spring Lake—you'd have had no idea it was anything other than an overgrown pond. Down at the bottom, seething-hot streams gurgled up through invisible cracks in the earth, but the surface was as smooth as black glass.

Bob and Lottie were waiting for us in a beat-up buckboard at the southern end of the lake, near where the river snakes off into the hills. I waved and smiled, but my heart didn't know whether to soar or sink.

We had allies at last. Faithful friends.

Faithful, generous *goat-ranching* friends in the market for a partner.

"Really, now. A cowboy travelin' on foot?" Bob chided my brother as we came up close. "What would the boys in the bunkhouse say?"

"They'd say we were smart not to waste money on rented mounts when we ain't left town all day," I said.

Bob gave my suit and lace-up shoes a scornful squint. "Oh, I ain't listenin' to you. You look like a damned banker today. What's the matter with you, Gus—lettin' your brother strut about in public kitted out like that? It's positively shameful."

Gustav let all this hot air blow right by. "Thanks for comin'." He turned to Lottie. "I'm gonna need both of you before the night's through."

"Good. I didn't come all this way just to keep Bob company," Lottie said. "What are you thinkin'?"

"Well, I got some notions as to who it is we're huntin' for, but I ain't ready to take that head-on just yet."

My brother's gaze flicked my way, and I nodded my agreement . . . not that Old Red would need it to do as he saw fit. Still, it was a relief to know he wasn't simply taking us gunning for Milford Bales. Go after a town marshal, you'd best have more backing you up than a couple former cowboys and a reformed harlot. You'd better have you some *proof.*

"So we're gonna go about it roundabout," Gustav went on. "Like this."

It wasn't a bad plan, really. In fact, the only part I objected to was Step One: Old Red and I were to sneak back into town unseen—by lying in the back of Bob and Lottie's wagon under a tarp fished from the jockey box.

If you don't understand what I disliked about this, I can only assume you've never stretched out in the bed of a buckboard under canvas that's normally used to cover loads of fresh-shorn goat wool.

Needless to say, by the time we pulled around behind the Star, my suit stank of Angora so bad I could have taken shears to it and sold it as fleece. I would've changed into something less goaty the second we got to our room, only Gustav and I sneaked up the back stairs with company—Lottie was sticking with us while Bob got Step Two rolling solo.

We let our guest have the room's one chair, and she perched upon it stiffly, face grim. When her gaze fell upon our unmade bed, she looked like she wanted to spit on it. It took me a moment to realize why, oaf that I am.

This room was nothing new to Lottie. For all I knew, she'd spent time in that very bed, staring up at the cracked ceiling, praying for escape that came only after her best friend was hacked to death not fifty paces away.

Old Red, of course, couldn't be counted on to lighten a mood—if anything, he dependably darkened them, and this night was no different. He just hovered by the window, staring down into the black alley below, looking sour and saying nothing.

We'd been waiting maybe half an hour when the knock finally came: four light raps on the door, just as we'd agreed out by the springs. Bob was back.

"It's all set," he whispered when I opened the door a crack. "Come on."

We followed him down the hall into another room—the one he'd just rented posing as a rancher in town on business. A *lonely* rancher.

"Didn't take much wink-winkin' to get the clerk to talk turkey," Bob told us. "I laid out what I wanted, slipped him a couple greenbacks, and he said he'd 'ring for room service.' It shouldn't be long now."

"You sure he didn't suspect nothing?" Gustav asked.

"Hey, who spreads bullshit better than your ol' pal Bob?"

My brother looked at me.

"Let's just hope it didn't get spread too thick," I said.

After that, we were on to Step Three: waiting again. Old Red resumed his watch by a window, and it wasn't twenty minutes before he spotted someone moving around down in the alley. It was time to see if his plan was going to pay off.

Just in case it didn't, Gustav and I drew our guns.

Soon we heard footsteps out in the hall. They sounded slow, hesitant—not like the brisk, businesslike gait of a good-time gal anxious to get another unpleasant job over and done with.

The steps came closer, drew even with the door, stopped.

Then . . . nothing. No steps, no knock, no "Anyone home?" Just silence.

Someone was out there, though. Doing what we were.

Standing.

Listening.

Perhaps, as in my case, sweating. A lot.

At last, there was a knock.

Bob looked over at my brother. Gustav and I were side by side, pressed against the wall so as to be out of sight when the door swung open. Lottie was in the far corner, well out of the way should Ragsdale and Bock have sent us Stonewall in lieu of the strumpet we wanted.

Bob had asked for a skinny gal, preferably a blonde. Like a chippie he used to do at the Golden Eagle years before. That one, she was an animal—in all the right ways, ho ho. Squirrel Tooth Annie, they called her.

Old Red gave Bob a nod.

Bob put on a smile and stepped over to the door.

I kept my eyes on that grin of his. It was my canary in the coal mine. It died, I knew there was trouble.

Bob opened the door.

"Well well," he said, smile holding steady. "Come on in."

He stepped back, and a tall woman moved past him into the room. She had her back to me as Bob closed the door, but it was plain she was a bony-thin thing—sure as heck not Stonewall in a dress and shawl.

I lowered my Bulldog and let out a sigh of relief . . . which was what spun the woman around and set her to screaming.

"No!" she shrieked when she saw me and Gustav. "Stonewall! *Stonewall!*"

Bob got an arm around her as she dashed for the door, but she opened wide and sank big buck teeth into his wrist. He let go with a howl.

I tried next, jumping over to block the door, and took a kick to the giblets for my trouble. I spent the next few seconds so blinded with pain I was only barely aware that the screeching nutcracker who'd sent me to my knees was now clawing at my brother's eyes.

As Old Red hopped back out of scratching range, another shape swooped into the fray, wrapping itself around our wildcat from behind, pressing close to one ear.

"Annie, stop. Annie, it's alright. Annie, it's *me.*"

The woman twisted to look over her shoulder. Then the whole of her was spinning around, pressing into Lottie, sobbing.

I started to get to my feet, then thought better of it on the advice of my stomach, which was threatening to evict my last meal if I didn't hold still a little longer. Next to me, Gustav was tenderly testing the red-raw flesh of his face, apparently worried there wasn't enough left on the bone to hold his eyeballs in place.

"Good God," Bob croaked as he plopped himself onto a chair and checked his wrist for blood. Somehow, Squirrel Tooth Annie's bite hadn't broken the skin. "If Custer'd had her at the Little Big Horn, it's Crazy Horse would've got scalped."

"It ain't her I'm worried about now," my brother said. He'd holstered his Colt for the fracas, but now he drew it again and leaned in close to the door.

The three of us listened for a moment, but there was nothing to hear beyond Squirrel Tooth Annie's weeping and Lottie's quiet words of comfort.

"Neighbors ain't complainin'," I said.

Bob grunted out a gruff chuckle.

"That's the Star for you. A ruckus like that'd be a soothin' lullaby compared to some things you might hear." Bob's blubbery face reddened, and he glanced over at my brother. "No disrespect intended."

"Don't bother apologizin'. It's true." Old Red turned to the women. "Ain't Stonewall supposed to hang around in case there's trouble?"

"He doesn't wait in the hall," Lottie said. "Even for this place, that'd be too obvious."

"Especially these days," Squirrel Tooth Annie added, her voice breathy and tremulous.

"Whadaya mean?" Gustav asked her.

She wiped a sleeve over her thin, sniffling nose. There was nothing even vaguely squirrelish about her until she talked: Her two front teeth were huge. One was slightly crooked. Both were gray. Taken together, they looked like a couple gravestones side by side in the boneyard.

"Things ain't been the same since Milford Bales became marshal," she said. Her voice gained strength—or perhaps just hardened—with each word. "Used to be the law didn't give a shit what we did, but Bales . . . can you believe he actually arrested me once? For 'soliciting,' he said."

"Arrested you?" My brother's eyes narrowed. "What'd he do?"

Squirrel Tooth put her hands on her hips, shooting for spunky-sassy even with puffy red eyes and tear tracks on her gaunt cheeks.

"What do you think he did? The son of a bitch put me in jail! Ragsdale and Bock had to send Stonewall over with fifty bucks bail to get me out. They said it was more than my scrawny old ass was worth, but I worked it off quick." The woman cocked her head to one side. "You're Gloomy Gus, ain't you?"

"Yup."

She looked over at Bob.

"And Bob Harris. I'd just about forgot what you two looked like."

"Well, now you got something to remember me by," Bob said. "I'll be the feller with the tooth marks in his arm."

"Who'd you think we were, anyway?" Old Red asked.

Squirrel Tooth let her fists drop from her hips, her arms going slack. "I thought it was my time to go. Like Adeline."

My brother was nodding along, understanding, unsurprised—until Squirrel Tooth went on, adding three words that changed everything.

"And the others."

Gustav froze so solid it was actually Lottie who got in the obvious question first.

"There've been other murders?"

"I don't know about *murders*," Squirrel Tooth said. "Gals just . . . go. Disappear. And I've been thinkin' for a long, long time that . . . that *I* was gonna be next."

She started to sway as she spoke, knees going wobbly.

Lottie swooped to her side again.

"For Christ's sake, Bob," she hissed.

"Oh. Sorry."

Bob hopped off his seat like a frog from a frying pan, and Lottie settled Squirrel Tooth in his place.

"Lay it all out for me, Annie." Old Red pushed past Bob and knelt down before Squirrel Tooth. "Please. I need to know *everything*."

Squirrel Tooth looked at Lottie.

Lottie nodded.

Squirrel Tooth talked.

"It happens in October . . . always October. Stonewall takes one of the gals out on a job, and she doesn't come back. 'She run off with a drummer,' he'll say. Or 'She run off with a cowboy.' Or just 'She run off.' You know how it is"—she looked up at Lottie and flashed a quick, quivery smile—"some of us really do get out clean. Others die of this or that. But there's always fresh stock comin' in to replace the ones that go. So by the time Stonewall's sayin' it again—'She run off'—it's mostly new gals he's sayin' it to. Kids, practically, and they ain't got no idea. Me and Big Bess, though, we've been around since it all began, so we know the truth of it: October's when they thin the herd."

"Who'd they do it to, Annie?" Lottie asked. "Who 'run off'?"

"The first was Belle, almost a year to the day after Adeline died. Then a year later it was Billie Jo, and Sunshine after that. Then last year, it was a gal you never knew—Sissy, her name was."

"Sunshine?" Lottie whispered. "Even little Sunshine?"

Squirrel Tooth reached up and took Lottie's hands in hers.

"So the last one was October of '92," Gustav cut in, flinty and cold. "Ain't nobody disappeared this year?"

Squirrel Tooth shook her head. "Not yet—but we're just barely into October, and I figure it's gonna be me or Big Bess this time. We're old and poxy and worthless, us two. It won't be long 'fore Ragsdale and Bock rid themselves of us one way or another."

"Why don't you just get out?" I asked. "Run off for real?"

Squirrel Tooth scowled at me as if she wanted to sink in those big chompers and crack my thick skull like a walnut.

"Run off to where? No man wants me, and I don't want no man." She turned away, talking to Lottie now. "Besides, you know I've got the kinda habits you can't feed out on some dirt farm. I tried savin' up money, like Adeline done, but it's no use. It all goes up my arm."

Squirrel Tooth leaned into her old friend, fresh tears welling in her eyes.

"Oh, sweetie," she moaned, "it's a wonder I'm still alive at all."

Lottie kissed the top of her head, looking like she was on the verge of sobbing herself. Then she looked over at my brother, and it wasn't tears in her eyes but rage.

The two of them held the gaze a moment, Lottie fire, Gustav ice. Some understanding passed wordlessly between them, and my brother turned and marched stiffly toward the door.

"Wait here," he said to no one in particular. "This won't take a minute."

He left, closing the door firmly behind him.

"Where's he goin'?" Bob asked me.

"You're askin' the wrong person."

We both turned to Lottie.

She just smiled—but, oh, *what* a smile—malicious and bitter and gleeful and wild.

It was a wolf grin. The kind with blood on the fangs.

Seeing it, I knew where Gustav had gone . . . and what he was about to do.

I tore out of the room and raced to the back stairwell and fairly threw myself down the steps. And before I was even halfway down, I heard it.

Muffled curses, scuffling feet, something heavy hitting the ground. Then thrashing. Then gurgling.

When I got outside, I found Stonewall hunched over Old Red, his big paws wrapped around my brother's neck.

22

BUMP BUMP

Or, We Put an Old Enemy's Feet to the Fire

It was too dark to make out more than thrashing shapes back there behind the hotel. Yet that's all I needed to see.

The silhouette the size and shape of a grizzly had to be Stonewall. The slip of a shadow on the ground beneath him had to be Gustav.

And the moist, burbling sounds that little shadow was making? That had to be choking, though it was getting awfully close to a death rattle, too.

I whipped out my new Bulldog and stepped toward Stonewall's broad, stooped back. My finger twitched on the trigger.

That's all it did, though—twitch. It didn't tighten.

I flipped the gun around and brought the butt down on the back of Stonewall's head.

Bob came charging out the Star's back door just as Stonewall went crashing to the ground . . . or almost to the ground, seeing as he had my brother to land on.

"Holy shit!" Bob gasped. "Is Gus alright?"

"I don't know! If he ain't been choked to death, he mighta just been crushed!"

After some frantic heave-hoing, we managed to roll Stonewall over on his back.

Old Red sat up, gulped in a lungful of air, and showed us he was alright by immediately starting carping.

"Jesus," he wheezed, "couldn't you have pushed the big bastard off me *before* you brained him?"

I scooped up Gustav's Peacemaker, which was lying on the ground just outside the stairwell.

"You're welcome." I stomped over and offered my brother the gun. "What the hell were you tryin' to do back here, anyway?"

Old Red snatched the Colt from my hand. "Talk."

"Talk, huh?" I nodded at his iron. "With that?"

Gustav pushed himself to his feet and delivered a none-too-gentle nudge to Stonewall's side.

The man-mountain's blubber jiggled for a moment, but beyond that Stonewall didn't move.

"I wanted to talk so's he'd hear me," Old Red said.

"Well, I guess he had a thing or two to say to you, too, didn't he?"

My brother gave Stonewall another toe-prod. This time, the big man moaned.

"The conversation ain't over." Gustav turned to Bob. "You'd best go fetch the wagon. We're leavin'. All of us."

"You mean"—Bob looked down at Stonewall—"*all* of us?"

"What do you think 'all' means?" Old Red snapped.

Bob put his hands up in surrender. "Alright, alright. I didn't know Stonewall counted as an 'us,' that's all. Won't take ten minutes to collect the wagon from the livery."

He stepped into the alley running along the Star and was promptly swallowed in darkness.

"Why don't you go up and tell Lottie and Squirrel Tooth what's goin' on?" I said to Gustav. "I'll keep an eye on Stonewall."

"Feh. He ain't in no condition to cause trouble now. You run on upstairs. I'll wait here."

"It ain't the trouble *he'll* cause I'm worried about," I said, and I crossed my arms and planted my feet.

Old Red stared my way a moment, silent. There wasn't enough light to see more than the general shape of him, an outline that was only slightly lighter than the blackness all around. His face was a smudge, a gray blur revealing nothing.

"Get Stonewall out of sight soon as Bob's back," he finally said. He turned and headed for the stairwell. "I don't want any fuss when I bring the women down."

As my brother's clomping footfalls faded away up the stairs, Stonewall groaned and started to stir.

"You are one lucky SOB, you know that?" I said to him. "It'd be poetic justice, you dyin' on the very spot Adeline got done in."

Stonewall struggled to his hands and knees, then looked up and told me I'd committed an unmentionable sin with an immediate relation and should now repeat the act solo. (His phrasing was a tad more concise than that.)

I laughed. "There you go—that's the spirit! Pull yourself together. Get your strength back." I walked around behind him, put a foot to his massive, meaty cheeks, and shove-kicked him to the ground again. "Cuz I reckon justice ain't done with you tonight. Now stay down, or I'll finish hammerin' out what little brains you got. I've already had two goes at it since I come to town, and I'm thinkin' the third time'll be the charm."

Stonewall repeated his earlier suggestion.

He stayed down, though.

When Bob pulled around in the buckboard a few minutes later, he threw down some rope from the jockey box, and I tied Stonewall's hands together. After a little lively debate as to my brother's exact meaning—get Stonewall out of sight *how?*—we loaded our prisoner in the wagon bed with the tarpaulin pulled up over him. To keep him out of mischief, I slithered in beside him and pressed my Bulldog into his side.

"You're makin' a big mistake, asshole," Stonewall growled, his onions-and-beer breath actually worse than the tarp's stifling goat-stink. "Anything happens to me, you're gonna have a lot of people gunnin' for you."

"Well, then"—I pressed my iron deeper into his soft flesh—"I sure hope we don't hit no potholes."

What followed was one of the most excruciatingly uncomfortable experiences of my life to date, and bear in mind I'm a fellow who used to spend twenty hours out of a day sitting in a saddle. There I was, lying under stinking canvas trying to hold a gun on a *reeking* man, and as if that weren't bad enough, Gustav and Squirrel Tooth eventually wriggled in behind me.

"Oh, you gotta be kiddin'," I groaned.

"Ain't got no choice—can't none of us be seen leavin' town together," my brother said. "Get us rollin', Bob!"

I heard the snap of reins, and the wagon jerked forward.

"You're gonna regret this!" Stonewall hollered. "You're all gonna—!"

I gave him another gouge with my gun.

"Bump *bump*," I said.

Stonewall shut up.

After that, no one spoke for a good quarter hour—at least not loud enough to be heard over the rumbling roar of the wagon wheels. I would say I now knew how a sardine in a can feels, only you'd have to be a sardine packed in goat piss during an earthquake to come even close to what I was going through.

And I was expecting it to go on all night, for it would take hours to get the wagon back to Bob and Lottie's spread. So I was mightily surprised when the wagon lurched to a halt and Lottie called out, "You can come out now. We're here."

I threw off the canvas cover and sat up.

"Here" appeared to be nowhere. Bob and Lottie had lit up a lantern, but its light didn't stretch far, and all I could see was the dim outlines of looming trees.

Then a sound reached my ears through the chirpings of a million crickets: the low gurgle of slow-moving water.

Memory sketched in the landscape around us.

We were back at the springs.

"Someone oughta keep watch a ways down the road," my brother said, sliding out of the wagon bed. "In case anybody else comes out from town."

He turned toward me.

"Bob volunteers," I said.

Bob hopped down from the driver's seat.

"If you insist," he said, and he scurried off into the moonlit gloom of the trail.

I'd volunteered the right person. Bob wasn't just willing to take watch. He was anxious for it—grateful to escape whatever was coming next.

Beside me, Stonewall was trying to struggle up into a sit despite his bound wrists. I didn't stop him—though I certainly didn't offer any help, either. When he finally got himself upright, I saw the first real fright on his face.

It was seeing Lottie that put it there—her, and the way she was staring at *him*.

"What you lookin' at, bitch?" he snarled through an unconvincing sneer.

Lottie didn't flinch.

"A dead man," she said.

Then she moved off into the trees, taking the lantern with her.

My brother pulled out his Peacemaker and waved it toward the lake.

"Alright . . . over there."

"And if I won't go?"

Gustav straightened his arm, bringing his .45 in line with Stonewall's mouth.

"Then it'll be all the easier to cart your lousy carcass down to Bob and Lottie's and let the wolves have at it."

"Alright, alright." Stonewall started scooching out of the wagon bed.

Squirrel Tooth was the last to get out of the buckboard. I helped her down—something a child could've done, she was so light. The poor woman wasn't just skin and bone. She felt more like skin and toothpicks.

I worried at first she wouldn't hold up under Stonewall's hateful glare—she wasn't half the woman Lottie was, literally or otherwise. But she didn't seem to notice Stonewall at all, so glassy-glazed were her eyes. Something in her had shook loose, come unanchored. When Old Red and I started marching Stonewall out toward the water, she didn't so much accompany us as float along behind like a leaf caught in the breeze of our passing.

Gustav had us stop sixty feet or so from the wagon, close enough to the spring pool to skip stones off its black waters. A dead tree was stretched out in the brush nearby, and my brother ordered Stonewall to sit up against the splintered stump and stretch out his legs. It took a little more persuading of the Colt-waving variety, but Stonewall finally plopped his bulk against the rotting wood.

"Untie his hands," Old Red said to me.

"About damn time," Stonewall grumbled.

"Then hitch him to that," my brother went on.

He nodded at the tree stump.

I can't say who looked unhappier about that, Stonewall or me. Neither one of us liked the way this was shaping up. Stonewall, of course, had no choice in the matter. Me, I didn't have any such excuse, but I went along with it anyway.

Just as I got Stonewall's hands tied behind him, his arms wrapped back around the stump, a light came flickering through the thicket.

Lottie was returning with the lantern—as well as a small stack of wood that she dumped on the ground not far from Stonewall's out-stretched legs.

She'd been out gathering kindling.

"What's that for?" I asked. "We didn't come out here for a barbe-cue."

"Don't be so sure," Old Red said.

Lottie looked over at my brother and grinned. It was a grin I was learning to worry about.

"Take off his boots," my brother said to me.

"Excuse me?"

"You heard me."

I started to reply that I had indeed—it was *understanding* him I couldn't manage. I held my tongue, though.

Gustav and Lottie had cooked up some kind of contrivance while upstairs at the Star. A trick to scare Stonewall into talking. That's what I had to figure.

That's what I had to *hope*.

I crouched down next to Stonewall.

"Socks, too," Old Red said.

As I wrestled with our prisoner's prodigious (and prodigiously odiferous) feet, Lottie put down the lantern and headed back toward the wagon. Squirrel Tooth, meanwhile, began fashioning the fire-wood into a little wooden teepee atop a bed of twigs. Contrivance or not, the women knew their parts.

Once I had Stonewall unshod, I turned to find Squirrel Tooth us-ing the lantern flame to light up a handful of dried-out leaves. When they were smoking and crackling, she put them under the kindling, and within seconds the whole heap was ablaze.

"Alright, Stonewall," my brother said, "now we're gonna have us a talk."

"No, asshole . . . now *you're* gonna listen," Stonewall rumbled back. "You've screwed yourselves but good. All of you. Let me go, clear outta the county, and maybe you'll live, but so much as lay a hand on me and . . ."

Stonewall's lips kept moving for a moment, though he no longer had the breath in him for words. He was staring at something off to my left, and when I followed his wide-eyed gaze I saw Lottie stepping into the circle of yellow-gold firelight. In her hands was what looked like a couple daggers joined together with a bent branding iron.

She was holding a pair of sheep shears—or goat shears, more like. Huge, razor-sharp scissors for cutting through thick wool.

Lottie crouched down and slid the blades into the fire.

"I say again: We're gonna have us a talk, Stonewall," Old Red said, "and you'd best pray God I believe what you tell me."

23

BURNING QUESTIONS

Or, My Brother Tries to Tear Stonewall Down Any Way He Can

I don't know if Stonewall took Gustav's advice about saying his prayers. Somehow, he didn't strike me as a praying man.

I'm not usually one myself. Yet I had a favor to ask of the Almighty, and I sent it silently heavenward.

Please, Lord . . . let this be a bluff.

Lottie was fiddling with the shears, searching for just the right angle to leave them in the fire so the flames would lick at the blades but leave the handles untouched. When she got them just so, she looked pleased, like a lady admiring her fine china spread out for the Christmas feast.

"Alright, you know what I wanna hear," Old Red said to Stonewall. "Who killed Adeline?"

"If I knew that, you can bet the SOB would've been dead a long time ago," Stonewall said with grim conviction. Once he'd swallowed his panic at the sight of those shears, he'd become quite earnest indeed. "Nobody slices up one of our gals and gets away with it."

Lottie scoffed.

"It wouldn't set a good example," Stonewall went on, eyes locked on my brother. "Customers think they can get away with hurtin' whores, it'll start costin' you quick."

"You lyin' sack of shit," Lottie hissed, looming up over him. "What about all the hurtin' *you* done?"

"Lottie," Old Red said, and that was all it took to pull her back, if not calm her.

"Lyin' sack of shit," she muttered.

My brother turned to Stonewall again. "But someone *is* hurtin' your chippies. More than hurtin' 'em. You're losin' one a year, come October, and you're either doin' the hurtin' yourself or givin' 'em over to him who does."

Stonewall glowered at Squirrel Tooth. She'd backed away from the rest of us, retreating out toward the shadows, face blank. The sparkle of reflected firelight in her eyes was the only life left in her to see.

"You're gonna believe that dried-up old hophead?" Stonewall said to my brother.

"You bet we are," Lottie snapped.

Stonewall nodded Lottie's way while still holding Gustav's gaze. "And that one there? Take it from me, Gus—you can't trust half the things that come outta her mouth. Why, your Adeline wasn't cold in the ground before she bolted outta the Eagle, and she's spent the last five years sloppin' goats. So if she's told you she knows what goes on at the Phoenix, well, you can bet the tricky bitch is just tryin' to—"

Lottie lunged toward him again. "Liar!"

"*Lottie*," my brother said, her name coming out hard and cold this time.

It was too late. Her leg was already swinging up.

Stonewall was almost able to jerk his head aside in time. Almost.

Lottie's kick caught him across the nose.

There was a sickening splintering sound, and Stonewall sagged, moaning. Only the tree stump behind his back kept him from falling over entirely.

Lottie reared for another kick, but Old Red grabbed hold and pulled her away. She screamed and flailed as she was dragged back, her screechings only slowly finding shape in words.

"Make him answer! Make him answer! Make him answer for what he done!"

Gustav shoved her at Squirrel Tooth, who wrapped her friend in her spindly-thin arms.

"He's just gonna keep lyin', Gus," Lottie sobbed. She looked down into the fire, face aglisten with tears. "You're gonna have to do it. It's the only way."

My brother followed her gaze.

The shears were red hot.

Old Red pulled out a handkerchief, draped it over the handles, and pulled the blades from the fire.

Stonewall looked up. Blood from his crooked, gashed nose flowed down over his mouth, drenching his thick black beard.

When he saw the shears in my brother's hands, he folded up his legs, sweeping his naked feet away from the hot iron. He may have even whimpered, I'm not sure.

"I swear I don't know nothin'," he said, words slurred, teeth mottled red. "I swear it!"

I didn't believe him for a second.

"Brother . . . don't," I said anyway.

Old Red was still crouched by the fire, the glow from the flames gleaming orange-red across his face.

"I'm gonna give you a place to start, Stonewall . . . and where it goes from there is up to you," he said. "What happened that night?"

Stonewall spit out his answer so fast he was spitting foamy blood, too.

"I took Adeline over to the Star for some drummer. A salesman just passin' through. I was supposed to wait around back for her, but . . . and I can see how you might hold this against me, Gus, and I'm truly sorry . . . but I used to slip away to attend to my own business long as I was out from under Mr. Ragsdale and Mr. Bock, and that's what I did that night."

"What sorta business?"

"You know what line I'm in. A feller owes money and he hasn't been payin', he gets a reminder. That kinda thing."

"I don't wanna hear about this or that 'kinda thing,' " Gustav said. "I wanna hear what you did that night. *Exactly.*"

The shear-blades were already cooling in the night air, going from red to amber to near black. They were still hot enough to brand a man, though—to make skin sizzle and cook—and Stonewall knew it.

"I swear to God, Gus, I don't remember! I beat the shit out of some dumb son of a bitch, but you can't expect me to remember who after all these years. All I know is, I came around back of the Star wonderin' if Adeline was even gonna be there . . . she used to slip off on her own business, too, you know. And I found her there by the stairs, sliced up something awful. Dead. I went straight to the Golden Eagle and told Mr. Ragsdale and Mr. Bock what had happened, and that was that."

"And that was that?" Old Red spat. "You go moseyin' off when you're supposed to be lookin' after a 'good earner' and she gets killed and Ragsdale and Bock don't skin you alive? Bullshit! Your bosses weren't mad at you cuz you brought 'em something they could profit from. You didn't just find Adeline dead. You caught her killer in the act, didn't you? Then you and them leeches you work for—you cut some kinda sick deal with him!"

Stonewall pushed back into the dead wood behind him. "That's crazy, Gus. You're just makin' that up."

"Am I?" My brother looked down at the shear-blades—pondered on them, it seemed like—before speaking again. "Tell me about Milford Bales."

"The marshal? What's to tell? Ragsdale and Bock hate his guts, and he hates theirs. Him and that loudmouth preacher Landrigan are the biggest enemies they've got around here. Surely you don't think . . . that milksop . . . a killer?" Stonewall made the sound of a laugh, though a laugh it was not. "Jesus. You *are* crazy."

Gustav slumped, his head hanging, and I thought maybe it was over. He'd got all he could from Stonewall, and now it was time to figure out our next move.

But my brother already knew it.

He slid the shears back into the fire.

"Someone's gonna have to hold him down," he said.

Lottie didn't pause a second. As soon as Old Red spoke, she was starting toward Stonewall.

Squirrel Tooth just sort of swayed in place like one of the trees rustling in the soft night breeze.

"Brother," I said. "Look at me."

Old Red kept watching the shears, waiting for them to fire up red again.

"Look at me, dammit!"

There was a twinkle I needed to see in him. The little sly spark that would tell me this was all sham. A ruse.

As Gustav picked up the shears again and turned back toward Stonewall, he finally did look my way—with eyes that were dull and flat, hardened with resolve. It lasted all of a second, that look, but that was all it took.

I stepped toward him and made a grab for the shears. "You ain't doin' this."

I got hold of the handles, but Gustav's grip didn't loosen no matter how hard I tugged. It was like the metal was a part of him now.

That metal was hot, too. Even with a hankie wrapped around the handles, they were getting hard to hold, and I could feel the heat off the blades spread across my belly.

"He knows who done it," Old Red said. "I'm sure of it. All we gotta do is get him to say the name."

"So find a way. *Another* way. Do it like Holmes would. Use your brain."

Gustav tried to spin away with the shears, but I managed to hold him in place.

"It's Holmes brought us here!" he roared. "The Method ain't workin'!"

"It's what we got!"

"It ain't enough!"

Old Red wrenched the shears to the left now, then the right, then the left again, and I felt a searing pain slice across my stomach. I cried out and pressed my hands to my belly, and my brother was so stunned he let loose of the shears, too.

They spun to the ground a few feet away.

I looked down, peeling my hands apart slowly, afraid they might be the only thing keeping my insides inside. Through my shredded shirt I could see blood and—fortunately—two long, ugly scratches.

I was just cut, not gutted.

"Jesus, Otto . . . ," Gustav said.

A bulky shape went crashing into the underbrush nearby.

While we'd been scuffling, Stonewall had pushed himself to his feet, got his bound hands up over the stump. He was making a run for it.

He didn't get far. Lottie was on him fast, and it was only after the first shrill scream—*Stonewall's* scream—that I knew she'd picked up the shears.

"Bastard! Bastard! Bastard!" she shrieked.

Her right arm swung, swung, swung, and kept swinging even as Stonewall slowed, then went to his knees, then toppled with a splash into the headwaters of the San Marcos River.

When Old Red and I came stumbling up to the water's edge, Lottie was still there, hacking at the shredded flesh that had bathed her in blood.

24

ACTUAL ANSWERS
Or, We Get Set to Bury a Body and Find a Skeleton in the Closet Instead

The body was half in, half out of the water, and the moon and stars mirrored on the smooth black surface took on a pinkish tint as blood billowed out into the lake and drifted southward into the San Marcos.

Lottie was kneeling in the mud, face in her hands, Squirrel Tooth Annie by her side. It had been Squirrel Tooth who'd stopped all the frantic stabbing, wrapping her arms around Lottie and squeezing tight. Now, though, Squirrel Tooth just hung around her friend's shoulders as limp and lifeless as a ratty old shawl.

The shears lay in the shallows, streaked with dark stains even fresh spring water couldn't wash away.

"It wasn't supposed to turn out like this," my brother muttered.

"Well, how the hell *did* you see it turnin' out?"

Gustav gave me a droopy-shouldered shrug. "Different . . . better . . ."

There was a rustling in the brush behind us, and Bob stepped out of the shadows.

"Did I hear—?"

He stopped, going stiff at the sight of Stonewall facedown in Spring Lake.

"Shit," he said, the word coming out in a long, slow, descending sigh. He looked over at his wife but made no move to join Squirrel Tooth at her side. "What happened?"

"Don't look to me to talk for you this time," I said to my brother. "This mess ain't mine to explain."

Old Red nodded. "Stonewall made a run for it," he said to Bob, "and Lottie . . . stopped him."

"Why didn't one of—?"

Bob finally seemed to notice the position of my hands: pressed to my stomach over blood-speckled rips in my shirt.

"You alright?"

I brought up my hands and checked the palms. They were striped red up the middle but were mostly dry—the bleeding wasn't any more than a trickle.

"No, I ain't alright," I said, "but I ain't dyin', either."

"Stonewall had a blade hid on him?"

I jerked my head at Gustav. "You're supposed to be askin' him the questions, remember?"

"Come on," my brother said, sloshing into the water beside Stonewall. "It's gonna take every one of us to get this back in the wagon."

That much he was right about. Never has the term "dead weight" been more literal. Even drained of half his blood, Stonewall seemed to weigh a ton.

Old Red led the way, his hands under Stonewall's shoulders. The women grabbed hold by the wrists, Bob and I the ankles. Yet every few steps, someone would lose their grip, an arm or leg would go flopping loose, and the whole bloody thing would hit the ground. Eventually, Bob asked why we didn't take the hint and just plant Stonewall where he'd plopped.

"Think, Bob," my brother growled. "People come out here for picnics, for chrissakes. Sooner or later, he'd be found, and that we can't have—not if we like our necks unstretched. Just buryin' him ain't good enough. We gotta vanish him."

After that, no one lost their hold, and we finally made it all the way out to the road.

"I know this won't sit well with you," Gustav said once we'd hoisted the corpse into the buckboard, "but Lottie, Annie—I think you two oughta ride under the tarp with Stonewall."

Lottie hadn't said a word the last few minutes, simply doing what was asked of her in a hollow-eyed daze. My brother's words roused her as hard and fast as a slap.

"Are you serious? All the way back to the ranch"—she waved a crimson-smeared hand at Stonewall's mangled remains—"lyin' next to *that*?"

"I can't," Squirrel Tooth mumbled. "I won't."

"You got to," Old Red snapped. "Anyone lookin' for Stonewall's gonna be lookin' for you, too, and you know you ain't got the nerve to lie us outta this. And would you just look at yourself? You, too, Lottie."

The women glanced down at their muck- and blood-covered dresses.

"It's gonna take a miracle to get that wagon down to the Lucky Two before dawn," Gustav said. "You wanna pass someone on the road lookin' like you just stepped out of a slaughterhouse?"

"No. You can't make me," Squirrel Tooth said, shaking her head. "I won't do it."

"*Annie.*"

Lottie spoke the name sharply, like she was talking to a dog lifting its leg inside the house.

"Gus is right," she said. "We don't have any choice."

"No . . . I'll just go back to the Phoenix and . . . I can say someone jumped us and . . . and I got away, but Stonewall—"

Lottie clapped her hands on Squirrel Tooth's bony shoulders and shoved her against the back of the wagon.

"Get up there, you dumb hoppie! Climb up or I'll throw you up!"

Bob took a hesitant half step toward his wife. "Ease up, Lottie."

"Ease up, hell!" she screeched. "I ain't gonna hang for that bastard! He ain't worth it!"

"You shouldn't have killed him, then," Old Red said.

Lottie spun on my brother with her hands up, the fingers curled like claws poised to swipe for his throat. Her beauty was a thing that seemed to come and go, and there was absolutely no trace of it now: She was all wide eyes and teeth and wild hair and blood.

"What was I supposed to do? Just let him get away cuz you were squabblin' with your idiot brother? Anyway, it's not like what you were gonna do to him was any better!"

"That was to get him to talk," Gustav shot back, "and he sure ain't talkin' now, is he?"

"How 'bout before things got outta hand?" Bob asked. "Did we get anything out of him at all?"

He was obviously trying to get us on a different track, avoid a head-on collision. He didn't put himself between his wife and his friend, though. He hung back a few paces. Out of range.

"No," Lottie snarled. "We didn't learn a damn thing."

"Oh, I ain't so sure about that," Old Red said, and he whirled on Bob so fast the man actually took a step back. "When did you and Lottie move out to the Lucky Two?"

Lottie's eyes flashed with anger—or a signal.

Bob saw it but couldn't make sense of it.

"About four and a half years ago," he said helplessly, gaze swinging back and forth between Lottie and Gustav. "Why?"

"Look, Gus—" Lottie began.

"Is that your recollection?" my brother asked Squirrel Tooth. "Lottie left the Eagle six months after Adeline died?"

The gaunt, ghostly woman peeped sheepishly at Lottie, then shrank back against the buckboard.

"I don't remember. I guess I'm just an addled old hophead, like everyone keeps sayin'."

"What's this all about, Brother?" I asked.

"Money." Old Red turned to Bob again. "Stonewall said Lottie left the Eagle five years ago. Right after Adeline died and I left town. So I gotta wonder . . . if that's true, how'd you come up with the cash for the Lucky Two so fast? When we was workin' the Seven together, you never had the coin in your pocket to put up a jingle. Then all of a sudden you got enough to buy your own spread?"

"I was savin', too," Lottie said. "Just like Adeline."

Gustav kept looking at Bob. "Funny you never mentioned it before."

"You can't go by Stonewall's say-so anyway," Lottie went on. "Us gals was just cattle to him. He wouldn't remember our comings and goings any more than you'd remember some heifer."

My brother was still staring at Bob, gaze pinning the man in place like a butterfly in a glass case.

"But y'all said Adeline *was* special to Stonewall, in some sick way. Her bein' murdered? The first of five? I think he'd remember that well enough."

"What the hell are you sayin', Gus?" Lottie snapped. "Are you suggestin' we'd—?"

"Stop it, Lottie," Bob said, voice calm and even. Resigned. "He knows."

I knew by then, too, though my brother had to lead me there on a leash.

The money Adeline had been socking away so she and Gustav could run off together—it had done just what it had been saved for. Only for somebody else.

Even the name of the goat ranch made sense to me now. It wasn't just a goof on the Lucky Seven. The Lucky Two—that was Bob and Lottie.

The unlucky ones were Adeline and my brother.

"I should've seen it right off," Old Red said, finally looking at Lottie again. "Who'd be most likely to know where Adeline kept her kitty hidden? Who could get at it easiest without anyone bein' the wiser? Adeline's best friend at the Eagle, that's who."

"Alright . . . what if it's true?" Lottie said. "I *was* Adeline's best friend. Don't you think she'd want that money to help me? For all we know, it saved my life."

A few feet away, her husband was wilting, practically melting with humiliation. Lottie was doing just the opposite: straightening her back, stiffening her neck, making herself into something stiff and unyielding and impervious to shame.

"I don't know what Adeline would've wanted," my brother said to her. "I just know you never asked *me* about it."

"We almost told you, Gus. Right before you left San Marcos," Bob said. "Except you were still so crazy with grief, we didn't know what you'd do. You might've blown it all on liquor or paid some gunny to go after Ragsdale and Bock or who knows what, and do you think any of *that* would've made Adeline happy?"

"How much was it?" I asked. "Adeline's stash?"

Lottie gaped at me angrily, as if one of the horses hitched to the wagon had just butted into the conversation. She obviously couldn't see what business it was of mine.

My brother knew, though.

"Tell him," he said.

"She'd saved three hundred and nine dollars and some odd cents," Bob told me. "In a cigar box under the floorboards."

I sighed.

That nest egg was a good three hundred bucks more than Gustav and I had when we'd hit the trail together five years before. How many indignities, how much pain would that money have spared us?

"Believe me—it's torn us up all these years," Bob said to Old Red. "We were truly happy you came back. We finally had a chance to make it up to you."

"Oh, I get it now," I said. "That's why you were so eager for us to come in with you as partners. You were gonna give us a slice of what you stole."

"Well, now," Bob mumbled, "I wouldn't say—"

He stopped himself.

I wouldn't say "stole," he'd been about to say—but what else would you call it?

"Goin' halvsies on the Lucky Two—that was Bob's notion of makin' amends," Lottie said. "Showin' up today. Helpin' you find Adeline's killer. That was mine."

Old Red jabbed a finger at Stonewall's naked feet poking out from under the tarpaulin.

"This is help?" he scoffed. "There we are, finally closin' in on some actual answers, and Stonewall ends up dead? It makes me wonder if helpin' is what you really had in mind."

"Well, I'm sorry," Lottie spat, about as sorrowful as a hissing cat, "but like I said already, what was I supposed to . . . hold on."

She tilted her head to one side, taking in my brother from a new angle, looking for something she couldn't quite see before.

She saw it, too—and she sure as hell didn't like it.

"Why, you ungrateful little shit—"

"For all I know, my gratitude's exactly what you was countin' on," Old Red said.

"What are you two talkin' about?" Bob asked.

"Don't you see?" Lottie said. "He's sayin' I killed Stonewall cuz we had something to hide."

"Well, did you?" my brother asked her.

"Oh, come on now," Bob said. "We already come clean about the money."

"You thick-witted *moron!*" Lottie raged. "He ain't talkin' about the money no more!"

Her meaning dawned on Bob so slowly I could actually see the precise moment the man's heart broke in two.

There were his thick brows beetled in confused concentration. There they were lifting higher as the truth took form in his mind's eye. Then there they were sagging again, along with the rest of his face, as he saw it all.

"Oh, Gus," he moaned. "How could you think such a thing of us?"

Old Red shrugged. "Lottie did a pretty good job on Stonewall with them shears, and y'all sure stabbed *me* in the back. Why not Adeline, too?"

Lottie stepped toward my brother, her right hand whipping up high. It was plain what was coming, but Gustav didn't jump back or turn aside or make a grab for the woman's wrist. He just stood there, expressionless, and took the blow like there was no avoiding it—a slap from the Hand of Fate itself.

And what a slap it was. It rang out through the still night air as sharp as a gunshot, and the rest of us flinched even if Old Red didn't.

"How dare you?" Lottie brought up her hand again. *"How dare you!"*

The second smack never came. Lottie turned aside and pitched forward into Bob's arms, sobbing hysterically.

Bob steered his wife around to the front of the wagon, glancing back over his shoulder just once to shake his head at Gustav. He looked like an old dog that's just been kicked for reasons it can't understand.

"You know, I was at the Eagle the night Adeline was killed," Squirrel Tooth said, "and Lottie was busy workin' the whole time Adeline was gone with Stonewall—that I remember plain as day. There ain't no way she could've snuck out and done what you're hintin' at. I'd have told you that, too . . . if you'd bothered to ask."

She climbed up into the wagon bed then, disappearing under the tarp. The thought of crawling under there with Stonewall had her in hysterics just a few minutes before, but now, it seemed, she preferred a dead man's company to ours.

In case there was any question, her head popped out a moment later, and she added a final afterthought for my brother's benefit.

"Asshole."

She ducked back under the canvas.

"I suppose you agree with her," Old Red said to me.

I shrugged. "I *was* taught never to contradict a lady."

"Yeah, well . . . I reckon I wouldn't give her any arguments either," Gustav mumbled.

A moment later, Bob came shambling around to join us again, alone this time.

"Alright, boys," he said, "you can leave the rest of the tidyin' to me."

"You'll put out the fire?" Old Red asked.

"Yup."

"And gather up Stonewall's shoes and socks?"

"Of course."

"And the shears?"

Bob's lips curled down at the corners, but he didn't have the strength left to even hold onto a scowl. He shook his head, face going slack.

"Dammit, Gus . . . I'm really *not* a moron," he said. "I'll gather up everything and get it down to my spread and bury it—and Stonewall— out where even the goats never go. No one'll catch sight of the women on the way, either, don't you worry about that. It's all gonna be taken care of."

He drew in a deep, *deep* breath that swelled his big balloon-round gut and practically lifted him up off his feet.

"Then that's it. We're done. I'm truly sorry . . . about everything . . . but you're on your own now."

"Well, what the hell else is new?" Gustav said, and he turned and marched off down the trail toward town.

Bob and I stood there together, watching him disappear into the gloom, waiting to see if he'd turn back to say more.

He didn't. He let his walking do the talking, the steady, fading trudge of footsteps in the dark the only indication that my brother was still there at all.

25

ROOM FOR WORSE

Or, I Awake from One Nightmare into Another

Well . . . good-bye," I said to Bob before dashing off into the darkness after Gustav. I didn't have time for more. Or the words for it.

We'd practically accused him and his wife of murder, they'd both admitted to theft, and now the man had to drive all night by lantern light with a bloody body and a hophead chippie hidden in the back of his buckboard. "No hard feelings" just didn't seem to cover it.

After a quick sprint—and several toe-stubs on rocks and gnarled roots along the trail—I was shoulder to shoulder with my brother.

"Thanks for waitin' for me," I panted.

Of course, Old Red hadn't slowed in the slightest, nor did he bother looking at me now. He just kept charging ahead at a quick-time march just shy of a gallop.

"Ease up before you walk smack into the side of a tree," I said.

My brother ignored me.

"I said slow down."

I was ignored again.

"You're pushin' too hard, Brother. Every which way."

This time, Gustav *sped up.*

I reached out and took hold of his left arm.

He jerked free and kept going.

"Slow down? Ease up? Feh!" he spat. "Don't you remember what Squirrel Tooth said? Beginning of October, every year, some gal goes missin'." He finally looked at me, his gaze holding mine so long I started worrying we were *both* going to walk into a tree. "He's due, Otto. Any day now, he's gonna do it again."

"And breakin' your leg out here is gonna stop him how?"

My brother looked over his shoulder, and I glanced back, too.

Bob and Lottie's lantern was just a smudgy circle of light now. The wagon—and the people around it—we couldn't see at all.

"That's what you get for diggin' your spurs in so deep," I said. "We've lost the only friends we had around here."

"Good," Old Red said, and he slowed down at last.

"Good? How do you figure that? And don't tell me it's cuz *they* might've killed Adeline. You said yourself someone's been doin' away with a gal a year, and Bob and Lottie wouldn't have no reason to—"

"I know that, dammit! Lottie was at the Eagle the night Adeline died, and Bob was out at the Lucky Seven with me. Neither one could've done it."

"Then why in God's name would you accuse them of it?"

"Because we killed a man tonight. And not just any man—Ragsdale and Bock's straw boss. They'll know who's to blame, too. One way or another, they're gonna come gunnin' for us, and they ain't gonna care who gets caught in the crossfire."

Gustav glanced back again, but there was nothing behind us to see anymore.

We'd rounded a bend in the road. The lantern light was lost to us.

"It'd be best," Old Red said, "if Bob and Lottie steered clear of us."

"Spittin' in their eye was the only way you could get that to happen?"

"It worked, didn't it? They'll be safe down on their ranch. Squirrel

Tooth, too." My brother narrowed his eyes, scowling into the darkness ahead as if he could see through it to something even darker—something infinitely *black*—waiting on down the road. "Things around town are about to get pretty bad."

I gave my blood-crusted shirt a little flap. "And so far it's been a barn dance?"

Gustav shrugged and favored me with a sentiment that sums up much of his outlook on life: "There's always room for worse."

After a brisk trot of maybe ten minutes, we hit the northeastern outskirts of San Marcos. From there, we slowed to a slink. It was a little unnerving sneaking around back of the hotel again—if anyone was out hunting for Stonewall and Squirrel Tooth, this was the place to start. But we made it inside without being spotted . . . or spotting anyone spotting us, anyway.

"There other hotels in this town?" I asked as we slipped up the back stairwell.

"Sure. A couple."

"Well, don't you think it's time we moved over to one or the other? Seems to me we're pushin' our luck stayin' here."

"Yeah . . . you're right," Old Red said, sounding vaguely surprised. "We'll clear out tomorrow."

You might think I'd find it gratifying, my brother listening to my advice, for once. It actually unsettled me, though.

If *I* was the only one thinking straight enough to keep us out of danger, we really were in trouble.

"You take the bed first," Gustav said after we crept into our room with guns drawn, half-expecting an ambush that didn't come.

"You sure?"

"Go on. Clean yourself up and get some rest. I ain't gonna be fallin' asleep anytime soon."

When I returned from the WC, Old Red braced the door with our chair, turned the gas lamp down to a soft amber glow, and seated himself on the floor nearby.

Looking at him there, propped up stiff and still, back against the wall, eyes gazing at nothing yet seeing far too much, I knew he was right. For him, there'd be no sleep—no rest—for quite a spell.

"I am sorry, you know," he said as I stretched myself out on the bed. "About you gettin' hurt . . . and the rest of it."

I ran my fingers lightly over my stomach. The wounds had cleaned up quick and easy—they weren't much worse than cat scratches, really.

All the same, absolution was something I wasn't ready to offer.

"I know," I said, and my eyelids slammed shut.

If Old Red said anything more after that, I didn't hear it. Sleep came to me fast. As did the nightmares.

Vivid as my dreams must have been, given all the tossing and turning and pillow punching I did that night, all I can recall of them is this: Gustav taking shears to a young sheep, only the wool he's shaving off turns into clothing, and the sheep becomes a man, and then it's not a shirt being cut away but skin tearing off in long, bloody strips, and the bleatings turn to screams, and a hand grabs my shoulder and shakes hard.

The hand was real.

"Otto," Old Red said. "Otto, wake up."

I jerked my face out of the covers smothering me and found myself sideways on the bed, my feet hanging out over the side.

"Thanks for wakin' me," I groaned. "I was dreamin' I woke up with a big ol' soup-strainer mustache and my new suit had turned into ratty puncher duds and I was a scrawny little thing with no more meat on him than a chewed-over chicken bone and I had a horrible temper and no sense of humor. It was terrifyin'."

I rolled over to look at my brother . . . and had to wonder if I was really awake at all.

For one thing, sunlight was streaming in through the window. It was morning. Gustav had let me sleep all night.

Yet even more miraculous was his appearance. His clothing was unstained and unwrinkled. His boots were freshly shined. His hair was combed, his face shaved, his mustache neatly trimmed.

He almost looked . . . well, he'd never pull off handsome with his high forehead and, shall we say, generously proportioned nose and ears. But presentable—that he could manage. Just about.

"Sweet Jesus." I rubbed my eyes and blinked at my brother like he was a mirage. "You goin' to Sunday school or something?"

"Yes."

My hands fell to my sides. My jaw just about fell to the floor.

"Is that a yes to the Sunday school or a yes to the something?"

"The Sunday school. Or Sunday service, more like. I did me a lot of thinkin' last night, and . . . well . . . I think I'd like to hear what Brother Landrigan has to say this morning."

I gave my left thigh a vicious, twisting pinch. It hurt.

"No . . . definitely not still dreamin'," I said. "You ain't really gettin' religion on me, are you?"

Old Red growled at me—and I mean a real, rabid mongrel "grrrrrr"—and stomped toward the door.

"Service starts in twenty minutes. Meet me on Fort Street in ten, if you wanna come along."

He was gone before I could tell him to wait. Which was alright, actually.

I didn't know if I wanted him to.

26

THE ASSEMBLY
Or, We Return to the Fold—and Find a Wolf There Ahead of Us

My dear old Mutter was a good Lutheran woman, and she did her best to put the love of God in all us young Amlingmeyers. Unfortunately her "best" meant hours in a wagon every Sunday, heading into town rain or shine (or snow or gloom) to hear doddering, drooling old Reverend Kracht drone out homilies so bone-dry they'd have made hard tack seem like cherry pie. The reverend was ever exhorting us, in his plodding way, to think of eternity and the afterlife, and in a fashion he succeeded: I often wondered who would die first, him of a coronary or me of boredom. As it turned out, he won that race, and in the pulpit, to boot.

Our uncle Franz was a lot livelier on the subject of salvation, but sadly this was because he thought Jesus lived in a hollowed-out oak behind our outhouse, and nearly every day he spent an hour or two back there praying and singing hymns underneath the tree . . . right up to the day he hung himself from it.

After all this, frankly (and hopefully no offense), churches and God-talk gave me the heebie-jeebies, and I think it was the same for Old Red. Once we were out on the trail just the two of us, we never darkened the door of a house of worship, nor had we spent more than five minutes in the last five years discussing the mysteries of the spirit. God may be everywhere and in everything, but we'd done a pretty good job of avoiding Him so far.

All good things must come to an end, though. I was going to church.

I found Gustav waiting a little ways off from the Star, a greasy-bottomed paper bag in his hands. Our faith in the Almighty may have been in question, but of my brother's faith in *me* I saw proof positive: He'd been so sure I'd show up, he'd bought me doughnuts.

I wished my faith in him could be as firm.

"Thanks," I said, and half a cruller disappeared into my mouth.

"Can't have your stomach growlin' all through the sermon. Uhhh . . . speakin' of which . . ."

Old Red glanced down at my belly, looking sheepish.

I gave my breadbasket a gentle pat.

"Oh, don't worry about that," I said, doing my best not to spray Gustav's (for once) tidy clothes with crumbs. "I'm healin' up fine. Just itches today, that's all."

"Alright, then."

My brother nodded brusquely and hustled off up the sidewalk.

"So," I said, striding after him, "why in God's name do we care what Brother Landrigan's got to say in God's name?"

Old Red chewed on that while I chewed on my cruller, and a dozen paces were behind us before he answered.

"It occurred to me that Stonewall might've been tellin' the truth."

"About what?" I was about to ask.

Gustav cut me off before I could get out the first word. "Now hurry up and eat. We'll be there in a minute."

In other words, shut up.

I obliged. The questions could wait. My empty stomach couldn't.

While out hunting up doughnuts, Old Red had apparently scouted out the way to Brother Landrigan's church, too, for he walked with the quick, straight step of a man who knows where he's going. He zipped first around the town square and then down one of the side streets shooting off it like the spoke of a wagon wheel. Then he turned again, and my own zip faltered.

We were about to pass Ragsdale and Bock's wallpaper store.

I slapped the sugar from my fingers and slipped a hand under my jacket. My brother might have given me guff about buying a shoulder holster the day before, but it sure was handy having a rig for my iron I could actually wear to church. Unless he had a .45 stashed under his hat, Gustav wasn't packing at all.

"Don't worry—Ragsdale and Bock ain't around," Old Red said as we hustled by the store. It was dark inside, and a sign in the window said CLOSED. "They got other things on their minds today than sellin' wallpaper."

"Oh, sure. It's the Sabbath. I bet they're slippin' on their choir robes even as we speak."

I knew exactly what my brother meant, though. It had to be very, very clear by now that Stonewall and Squirrel Tooth weren't coming back to the Phoenix. Which made it equally clear to me that their bosses would soon be coming after *us*.

I had to figure we were safe for the next couple hours, though. Even lowlifes as bold as Ragsdale and Bock wouldn't gun us down on the steps of the town's most popular church.

Brother Landrigan, it turned out, presided over the towering white tabernacle I'd noticed our first day in San Marcos. Dozens of parishioners were making their way inside with the slow, stately steps so many folks seem to deem appropriate for entering or leaving the house of the Lord (and which I always suspected had less to do with reverence than with the ladies' rib-crushing corsets).

As we reached the edge of the herd, I came to a stop, putting an arm out to force my brother to rein up, too.

"Something just occurred to me," I said. "Everyone's been tellin' us Milford Bales and Brother Landrigan are thick as thieves. So don't you think Bales'll be here this morning?"

Old Red nodded slowly. "Yup."

He took a big step into the oozing-slow molasses flow of the crowd. I sighed and joined him.

As we shuffled toward the doors, we were greeted with friendly grins and nods from some of our fellow churchgoers. They uniformly wore the upright, straitlaced look of any prosperous Protestants come Sunday morning, and it occurred to me that among them would be the selfsame folks who'd scowled at my brother's drover duds Thursday, Friday, and Saturday.

I suppose your "Sunday best" doesn't always refer to just your clothes.

Were these people Baptists? I wondered. Methodists? Presbyterians? Landrigan sure hadn't sounded like Reverend Kracht when we'd heard him ranting outside a saloon a few days before, so Lutheran seemed a stretch. And given the man's emphasis on hellfire and being saved by "the blood of the Lamb," it was a safe bet he wasn't Mohammedan, Hindu, or Hebrew, either. Or Unitarian, for that matter.

I craned my neck and went to tippy-toe in search of a sign or cornerstone that would tell me the name of the church. We were almost inside by then, though, and there was nothing in sight.

"Looking for someone, Mr. Amlingmeyer?"

Old Red and I turned to find Mortimer Krieger, the photographer/amateur librarian, behind us with his wife on his arm. We offered the couple our good mornings, which they returned with prim little smiles.

At least, I *assume* Mrs. Krieger wished us good morning. Her lips moved, but I couldn't hear her voice, and for all I knew she was whispering, "Oh, God . . . these dumb-asses again."

"To be honest with you, sir," I said to her husband, "I was tryin' to figure out what this church is called. My brother and I were just out for a morning stroll when we saw the line here and, being devout Christian men, decided to sample the services. Certainly the size of the crowd and the beauty of the church speak well of the congregation, but other than that this has been a real leap of faith, so to speak."

Mr. Krieger chuckled.

Mrs. Krieger just kept smiling in a way that looked more waxy and masklike with each passing moment.

"In that case, Mr. Amlingmeyer," Mr. Krieger said, "it's my honor to welcome you to the Shepherd of the Hills Assembly of the Living God."

"Ahhh," I said, nodding as if this actually meant something to me. Which it did not.

"What denomination is that?" Old Red asked bluntly.

"Its own. Our minister, Brother Landrigan, built all this himself," Mr. Krieger said, and he held up his hands and gazed past me and my brother.

We were just reaching the bottleneck that had been slowing the throng so—the doors into the sanctuary—and I turned and looked ahead again.

Stretching out before me I could now see a long, red-carpeted aisle. At its end was a blocky altar set between a white pulpit and a lectern upon which rested an open Bible only slightly smaller than a steamboat. Hovering just beyond and above all this was an enormous pair of stained-glass feet, though I couldn't yet see who they belonged to. As they were clad in sandals, I could only assume it was Jesus and not Brother Landrigan himself.

All in all, the place made Reverend Kracht's drafty, rough-hewn church seem about as awe-inspiring as a trapper's lean-to. To add to the impressive (and, for me, oppressive) atmosphere of unearthly grandeur, an unseen pipe organ was filling the air with the low, spectral tones of "Though Your Sins Be as Scarlet."

I can easily imagine how the place would give the faithful goose bumps. Me it gave the creeps.

"Five years ago, all this was just an empty lot on one of the town's most notorious blocks," Mr. Krieger said. "Now *that's* progress, right, dear?"

He patted his wife's hand.

"Yes," she said.

As we passed through the doors two by two, I noticed something large and dark looming over us, and I looked up to see the low-hanging bottom of a balcony jutting about a quarter-way into the sanctuary. The organ, I could now tell, was up there, a little closer to heaven so as to better rouse the Lord should He (like me) be tempted to sleep in come Sunday morning.

"Your Brother Landrigan," Old Red said to the Kriegers. "Where'd he come from?"

"I believe he had a small congregation up in Dallas originally," Mr. Krieger said, "but it was here his message really took root. Martha and I decided to give him a try when we noticed the pews of the Presbyterian church were half empty . . . and growing emptier every week."

Mr. Krieger's soft, bland, eminently forgettable face momentarily took on some character—in the form of a smirk. "A smart business-man always follows the flock."

"Sure," I said. "More sheep to fleece."

Mr. Krieger's smile froze. "Yes . . . well . . ." Something off to our left caught his eye, and, looking grateful for the distraction, he brought up a hand and waved. "You might have an admirer here today, Mr. Amlingmeyer. It's Mr. Coggins there who checked your book out from our library."

"Mr. *Coggins*?"

The name rang a bell, though faintly—the chime of it was nothing but a muffled echo until I turned to see who Krieger was waving at.

Sitting in one of the rows nearby was the mousy little clerk from Ragsdale and Bock's wallpaper store. He was staring at my brother and me so wide-eyed I almost expected him to duck under his pew.

I waved at him, too.

He hurriedly hid himself in a hymnal.

"You know Mr. Coggins?" Mr. Krieger asked as we continued up the aisle.

"We've met," I said. "In the course of our inquiry."

Mr. Krieger nodded sagely and shot me a conspiratorial wink. "Of course," he said, voice going as whisper-quiet as his wife's. "His employers. Don't think that hasn't been a topic of gossip around here."

"How do *you* feel about a member of the congregation workin' for men like that?" Gustav asked.

"Well . . ." Mr. Krieger shrugged. "There's nothing in the Bible against selling wallpaper."

Most of the pews we'd been passing were full up, but now we came to one that was half empty, and Mr. Krieger stopped and motioned for his wife to scoot in and have a seat.

"Would you care to join us?" he said, still keeping his voice low. "I know it's hardly a topic worthy of church, but I'd be most curious to hear how your investigation's proceeding."

"Maybe later, Mr. Krieger," Old Red said, his eyes locking on something up ahead, on the other side of the aisle. "Right now I see someone else we should say hello to."

I followed his gaze and spied Horace Cuff sitting alone in the very first pew before the pulpit. The newspaperman's face was pointed straight ahead, away from us, but I recognized his slender build and his fair, wispy hair, and, most of all, his bearing. Even sitting, the man looked stiff and steely, all straight lines and right angles like the big-city "skyscrapers" he no doubt loathed. He was passing the time before the service by reading from the Bible, holding the book up directly before his eyes so as to spare himself the indignity of tilting his head.

Gustav and I headed up the aisle toward him, and the closer we got to the front of the sanctuary, the less crowded grew the pews.

Whatever sort of "Assembly" this turned out to be, its members had this much in common with Lutherans and schoolchildren: Nobody likes to sit in the front row. Except for Cuff.

As we drew up behind the man, a sudden, thunderous blast brought the congregation to its feet—and almost had me taking *to* mine. As in bolting through the nearest exit. Or, failing that, stained-glass window.

It was music, though you'd have been excused for mistaking it for artillery fire. The organist was pounding at the keys with such gusto it's a wonder flakes of chipped ivory weren't drifting down on us like snow, and a moment later a chorus of booming voices started bellowing out "Come, Christians, Join to Sing."

Old Red and I turned to gawp at the source of the din: a choir up in the balcony, beside the organ.

When Brother Landrigan had called down damnation on us a few days before, he'd had perhaps twenty followers with him. The chorus now was at least twice as large. The members, men and women alike, were garbed in golden robes, and each clutched a big black songbook. All stood with mouths open wide and eyes pointed down at their hymnals.

All but one, that is.

It took me a moment to notice him, what with his badge and holster traded in for a flowing gold frock, but the spite on his round baby face—that remained the same.

Milford Bales was glaring down at us, mouth so scowl-twisted he couldn't even sing.

Seeing him there glowering amidst the choir was like gazing up at a cloud and spotting an angel giving you the finger.

Or maybe a demon.

27

THE SERMON, PART TWO

Or, Brother Landrigan Fires Up His Followers, and Gustav Sees the Light

I felt so exposed and vulnerable there under Marshal Bales's hateful stare I might have ducked for cover behind the altar if Gustav hadn't hopped into the nearest pew and pulled me with him. We got out of the way just in time, too, for a dark-clad figure was barreling up behind us with all the unstoppable force of a locomotive at full boil. If we hadn't cleared the aisle, I think he would've rolled right over us.

Nothing was going to keep Brother Landrigan from the pulpit.

He took the steps up to the altar with big, bounding strides, then whirled around with a spin that set the long folds of his black robes to flapping like bat wings. It'd been too dark to gauge his looks when we'd run across him on the street Thursday, but now I could see how comely the man truly was. Not that he was handsome, exactly. He had one of those blocky heads that looks like it belongs on a totem pole, the features strong and deep and sharp-edged. It was the kind of face that fills men with admiration and women with fluttery awe.

"My friends," Landrigan intoned, holding both hands up high, "be seated."

We all did as we were told, including Old Red. I turned around first, though, looking up into the choir loft to make sure a certain baritone wasn't hurrying toward the stairs—and us.

Bales and I locked eyes, but he made no move to leave his pew. When he sat, I sat.

With that, the service commenced.

It followed a general form I remembered well—talk, stand, sing, sit, repeat. But I felt none of the old tedium that had made Reverend Kracht's services such a trial. Brother Landrigan infused his every action with a thespian's flair for drama. When he was singing, he looked joyful. When he was listening, he looked thoughtful. When he was speaking, his face seemed to find a new expression—a new *emotion*—for each and every word.

I kept dreading the look his face would take on once he spotted me and Gustav. Yet when his eyes did at last pass over us, all he did was smile. If he remembered us from our brief meeting three days before, he didn't seem to hold our lack of reverence against us.

Horace Cuff, on the other hand, wasn't so forgiving.

The Englishman didn't notice us for the first hour or so of the service—nor would he have noticed the Battle of Gettysburg in the row behind him, so mesmerized was he by Brother Landrigan. Eventually, though, Cuff was called up to do a reading himself, and when he laid eyes on us, his narrow face pinched with such disgust you'd have thought someone had set a couple dung-smeared pigs loose in the pews. He managed to wipe away his revulsion as he stepped to the lectern, and by the time he was orating from Second Corinthians, he looked so solemn and sanctimonious he could've stepped right down from the stained-glass mural filling the wall behind him.

"Would to God ye could bear with me a little in my folly and indeed bear with me," he began in a voice that trilled and warbled with exaggerated quavers. "For I am jealous over you with godly jealousy: for I have espoused you to one husband, that I may present you as a chaste virgin to Christ. But I fear, lest by any means, as the serpent beguiled Eve through his subtlety, so your minds should be corrupted from the simplicity that is in Christ. For if he that cometh preacheth another Jesus, whom we have not preached, or if ye receive another spirit, which ye have not received, or another gospel, which ye have not accepted, ye might well bear with him."

Cuff peered down at the page, pausing a moment as (I learned with later research) he skipped over a long passage delving into the particulars of some obscure pissing match betwixt the ancient church elders.

"For such are false apostles, deceitful workers, transforming themselves into the apostles of Christ," he went on. "And no marvel; for Satan himself is transformed into an angel of light. Therefore it is no great thing if his ministers also be transformed as the ministers of righteousness; whose end shall be according to their works."

It seemed a strange choice for a reading, given that Brother Landrigan—a maverick preacher without affiliation with a big denomination—might have struck some folks as a "false apostle" himself. It made sense, though, when Cuff retook his seat (after another long glower at us) and Landrigan finally launched into his sermon.

I can't remember all of it word for word. There were a *lot* of words to remember—great torrents gushing out as Landrigan shook his fists and banged on the pulpit and threw his arms up to heaven. I've seen plenty a street-corner sky pilot preach up a storm, but this was a regular typhoon, a hurricane fit to rival the deluge Noah rode out.

The theme was indeed false prophets, but not the ones you might expect: the pope or Joseph Smith or the other usual targets when preachers start throwing around the word "heresy." No, the blasphemy Brother Landrigan railed against wasn't religious at all.

"My friends, what cursed mankind?" he asked at one point, brow furrowed. "What unleashed evil upon the world? What did the serpent offer Eve?"

He paused, scanning the congregation, pretending to search for an answer he already had tucked away like the proverbial card up the sleeve.

"Knowledge!" he bellowed. " 'For God doth know that in the day ye eat of the fruit of the tree in the midst of the garden, then your eyes shall be opened, and ye shall be as gods!' And who is telling us this now? Where do we hear this sweet solicitation, this seduction, this flattering, *foul* lie?"

Brother Landrigan was obviously a big believer in rhetorical questions. I could see why, too.

One row up from us, Cuff was nodding rapturously, knowing the answer but content—thrilled, in fact—to let the man in the pulpit toss it down to him. Out of the corner of my eye, I could see a woman across the aisle from us nodding, too, and from somewhere just beyond her I heard a man hiss out a half-whispered "Yes!"

I didn't have to turn and stare. I could *feel* the frenzy building up in that church. It was like being on the trail with a herd right before a stampede or squall. There's a million tiny pinpricks all over your skin, as if your whole body's fallen asleep. Except it's the opposite—your body's so awake it hurts, because it senses something's coming your mind hasn't grasped yet.

Then it came, there in the Shepherd of the Hills Assembly of the Living God. Brother Landrigan leaned forward, seeming to loom so far out into the pews I was almost afraid he'd fall on us, and he brought the storm.

"I'll tell you who's lying to us, my friends! The serpent Thomas Edison! The serpent Nikola Tesla! The serpents George Westinghouse and Alexander Graham Bell and Charles Darwin! All the serpents who tell us that with logic and science we can see all! *Know* all! These are the angels of a false light . . . the light of electricity and wire and 'progress.' Well, I say unto them: Take heed, serpent! Take heed, liar! Your end shall be according to your works! *You will get exactly what you deserve!*"

"Take heed," Cuff blurted out. He'd finally unlocked his stiff body, and it was rocking slightly, the wood of the pew creaking beneath him. "Take heed!"

Somewhere behind me, a man called out, "Amen!"

"Hallelujah!" a woman threw in. Then a man, too. Then another woman.

I'd never experienced anything like it. The services of my youth were so sedate they'd have made your average quilting bee look like a night at the Phoenix. The most spontaneous thing that ever happened was an occasional snore or the eruption of an insufficiently clinched fart, and the majority of both came from Reverend Kracht himself. Just singing with too much enthusiasm was enough to get you stares.

Here, though, the whole point was enthusiasm, passion, sensation. I heard feet thumping the floor, spontaneous praisings to the Lord, wails, cries, snippets of song. Walking in, the congregation had looked as straitlaced as any other, but those laces weren't just loosening up now. They were being ripped clean away, and something bound up tight inside—something *wild*—was breathing free.

Brother Landrigan knew just when to slip the leash back on, though.

"The truth is," he said, suddenly calm and dryly amused, "no man, no matter how clever, could ever hold a candle to God. Or even a lightbulb."

A ripple of chuckles spread through the sanctuary, followed by sighs and the sound of a hundred numb fannies shifting on hard wooden benches. The sermon's climax was past now, and Brother Landrigan's deep voice turned tender—yet with an undercurrent of soft, almost sad menace.

"Any light but the Lord's is puny and impure. At its heart will be a shadow, a darkness only He can penetrate. That darkness is Eve's curse—the stain of sin upon us all—and there's only one way to wash it clean."

Landrigan stepped from the pulpit and walked to the altar, then turned to face his parishioners again. Behind him, stained glass stretched all the way to the ceiling, a thousand jagged shards of color arrayed to display Jesus on a grassy hillside, a crock in one hand, a lamb cradled in the other.

The preacher stretched out his arms.

"The blood of the Lamb," he said.

A cannon blast of a chord exploded out into the sanctuary, and everyone leapt to their feet for the song some of the choir had treated me and Gustav to a few days before.

> *There is a fountain filled with blood*
> *Drawn from Emmanuel's veins.*
> *And sinners plunged beneath that flood*
> *Lose all their guilty stains.*
> *Lose all their guilty stains.*
> *Lose all their guilty stains.*

After but one verse, though, the music came to a stop.

"Friends," Brother Landrigan boomed out even as "guilty stains" reverberated in the rafters, and he looked straight at me and Gustav. It wasn't some passing glance this time. It was a gaze, one he held and held and kept holding so long it made my eyeballs itch.

"If there be any among us today called by the Holy Spirit to renounce sin and accept the salvation of Jesus Christ our Lord, let them come forward now!"

I peeked over at my brother, thinking I'd flash him a jesting "Shall-we?" waggle of the eyebrows. He hadn't acknowledged my presence in any way throughout the service, being too busy eyeing Cuff, pretending to sing (him being unable to actually read from the hymnal, of course), and watching Landrigan with a fascination that bordered on fixation.

And he kept right on ignoring me—even as he pushed past me out of our pew.

"What the hell are you doin'?" I whispered.

Gustav didn't answer. He just headed up the aisle, climbed the steps to Brother Landrigan, then fell to his knees and wept.

28

DIRTY LITTLE SECRETS

Or, Old Red Is "Saved" in More Ways Than One

Let us pause here for a brief moment of sacrilege.

God, to me, is like Sherlock Holmes. I've read about Him. I've heard a lot of talk about Him. But I've never seen Him myself, and His existence I have to take on faith based on published reports. In *Harper's Weekly*, say. Or the book of Genesis.

At least with Holmes, I've met folks who knew the man personally. Jehovah, on the other hand . . . Well, while I'd never be so bold as to say the Man Upstairs isn't home, I've also never known him to answer when any of my friends or family came around looking for help.

I've always assumed Gustav shared my uncertainty on matters ecclesiastic. My brother neither hosannaed in the highest nor looked askance at those who do, and his problems he always chose to meet head-on without any bowing on bended knee.

So you can imagine my dismay seeing him down on both knees before an altar, nodding tearfully as a preacher asked him if he repudiated Satan and accepted Jesus Christ as his lord and savior.

"Hallelujah!" a man proclaimed.

"Praise Jesus!" a woman called out.

"Holy shit," I whispered.

Brother Landrigan helped my brother to his feet, and the two exchanged a few quiet words as the choir launched back into "There Is a Fountain Filled with Blood."

> *Dear dying Lamb, Thy precious blood*
> *Shall never lose its power*
> *Till all the ransomed church of God*
> *Be saved to sin no more.*
> *Be saved to sin no more.*
> *Be saved to sin no more.*
> *Till all the ransomed church of God*
> *Be saved to sin no more.*
>
> *E'er since, by faith, I saw the stream*
> *Thy flowing wounds supply,*
> *Redeeming love has been my theme,*
> *And shall be till I die.*
> *And shall be till I die.*
> *And shall be till I die.*

As these cheerful sentiments shook the walls, Old Red wobbled weak-kneed back to our pew and stepped in next to me, eyes downcast. I had a lot to say to him, though you could boil it all down to a simple "*Huh?*" Now obviously wasn't the time even for that, though, and I just passed him a handkerchief so he could wipe the tear tracks from his face.

He dabbed at his cheeks, blew his nose, and handed the hanky back to me, all without meeting my gaze.

"This is a joyful day for you," Horace Cuff said, turning around to offer Gustav a bony hand. "Congratulations, brother."

It chilled me in a way I can't quite explain, hearing someone else—someone like Cuff—call Gustav "brother."

Old Red just nodded and shook the man's hand, attempting a smile that never got past a quiver of the lips.

Then, once again, the hymn came to a sudden halt, and Brother Landrigan took a step out toward the pews and raised his arms, the palms turned downward. He bowed his head as a signal for the rest of us to assume an attitude of prayer, and the congregation—and my brother—did as directed. I kept my eyes on Landrigan. With his long black robes dangling from his outstretched arms, he looked like a big buzzard alighting on a fresh carcass.

"Dear Lord," he said, "we humbly beseech thee to watch over your disciples as the shepherd keeps watch on his flock. Strike down the wolf, drive away the wicked, and always, in everything, guide us toward righteousness. In Jesus' name we pray. Amen."

Landrigan dropped his arms and went swooping up the aisle to the strains of "The Son of God Goes Forth to War." Once he'd left the sanctuary, the music stopped, and there was a moment of complete and utter silence. Then the organist eased into a quiet, slow-tempoed tune I didn't recognize, and gradually, as if blinking their way out of a deep sleep, the congregation started to murmur and stir.

"Alright, Brother," I whispered as the pews behind us began to empty, "would you mind tellin' me what you're—?"

"Were you raised Christian?" Cuff asked, turning to face Gustav again.

"Yessir," Old Red said. "Lutheran. It didn't really stick, though. Howzabout yourself, if I may ask?"

"I'll share my dirty little secret with you." Cuff leaned toward my brother and lowered his voice. "I was raised Catholic."

He said "Catholic" the way some folks might say "cannibal."

He straightened up again, smirking. "I suppose I could say the same you do of Lutheranism: It 'didn't stick.' I wandered godless through this dark world for many a year before Brother Landrigan brought me to the light."

"Yes, Brother Landrigan's quite . . ."

My brother rubbed his chin, hunting for the right word and finding nothing in his sights.

"Overwrought?" I suggested.

"Rousing," Gustav growled before turning back to Cuff. "Was that a typical sermon for him?"

"Oh, yes! That's what's made Brother Landrigan such a powerful tool for the Lord."

I was about to agree that the preacher did indeed seem to be quite the tool, but Old Red jumped in first.

"Well, he sure got to me. I'm just grateful y'all are so openhearted here. For a saddle bum like myself to wander in and find himself welcome . . ."

Cuff smiled smugly. "We are all God's children."

"You're right, sir. You're right. That's how Jesus Himself went about it, ain't it? He didn't look down on the lepers, the tax collectors." My brother shrugged casually, carelessly, but his eyes were sharp as razors. "The whores. He didn't judge, did He?"

"Oh, Jesus judged," Cuff said. " 'If thy hand offend thee, cut it off. If thy foot offend thee, cut it off. If thy eye offend thee, pluck it out.' That was Jesus, too."

"You done any pluckin' yourself lately?" I asked.

Before Cuff could give me more answer than a scowl, someone came up the aisle behind us. I glanced back and caught a glimpse of bright robes and a dark glower.

It was Milford Bales—and he wasn't alone. Behind him was another member of the choir, a somber-looking fellow so young and gawky I pegged him for a soprano.

I half-expected the marshal and his pal to grab me and Gustav by the collar and hustle us out to the gutter where we belonged. Instead, Bales just swung around next to Cuff and pointed a frown at us. His youthful, golden-robed compadre stopped in the aisle alongside our pew.

"Mr. Bales," Cuff said by way of greeting. "Tommy."

The lawman and Tommy—whoever the hell he was—ignored him.

"Was that some kind of playacting up there, or were you serious?" Bales asked my brother.

"You know me to do much playactin'?" Old Red replied.

Bales narrowed his eyes. "So you're truly repentant? You're here to sincerely seek forgiveness?"

"I'm here to set things square."

I didn't think it possible, but Bales narrowed his eyes even further. They were now no more than little folds of fat I could hardly believe the man could see through.

"That's a tall order," Bales said. "You've got a lot to make amends for."

My brother squinted back at him. "Don't we all."

"Some more than others, Amlingmeyer."

"You got that right, *Marshal*."

By this time, Tommy and Cuff and I were doing some squinting of our own, though none of us was shooting for steely-eyed intimidation. We were just plain confused. Bales and my brother were doing so much talking in between the lines there didn't seem to be anything *on* the lines but gibberish.

"Well, what have we here?" a jovial voice boomed, and we all turned to find Brother Landrigan striding up to join us. "I don't recall scheduling a prayer meeting after the service today." He clapped a hand on Tommy's back and beamed a blinding smile at Bales. "Or are you two recruiting for the choir?"

"Milford was just welcomin' me into the fold," Old Red said.

"Good, good."

Landrigan nodded, still smiling, but up close I could see he wasn't as accomplished an actor as I'd at first thought. An undercurrent of anxiety swirled just beneath his cheer. His rictus grin twitched, his eyes darted.

"I've got some welcoming to do myself," he said, turning to Old Red. "Would you care to join me in the parsonage for a chat, Mr. Amlingmeyer? We've got a lot to talk about. A lot to *pray* about."

"I don't think that's such a good idea," I was about to say.

Bales piped up first . . . to say the exact same thing.

Landrigan eyed Gustav warily, like a cowboy taking in a snuffy bronc he's been tasked with breaking.

"Oh, we'll be alright."

He stretched out one arm, inviting my brother to slide out into the aisle and walk away with him.

Old Red did indeed move toward him—but only to look down at the clunky black shoes poking from under the man's robes. Then he swiveled around to eyeball young Tommy's feet, too. Cuff and Bales he didn't bother with.

"Did you know drovers pride themselves on havin' small feet? Means they don't walk where they're goin'. They ride." Gustav looked back up at Landrigan. "You and Tommy here—you got yourselves some big ol' walkin' feet. Especially you, Reverend. Stick them things into stirrups, and they'd dangle there like a couple loaves of bread balanced atop a fence rail. I know that for a fact . . . because I've seen the like before."

"Uhhh," Landrigan said.

" 'Course, a lot of fellers have big feet," Old Red went on. "What's more tellin' is that you ain't asked the marshal *why* you shouldn't be alone with me."

"Oh . . . hmmm . . ."

"I assume it has something to do with you callin' me 'Mr. Amlingmeyer' a moment ago. Cuz I didn't tell you my name when I was up there with you durin' the service."

"I . . . ummm . . . perhaps . . ."

My brother waved a limp hand at Landrigan, signaling him to stop. "Yeah, yeah," he sighed, "I figured as much."

A look of grim chagrin spread over Landrigan's face—then spread to Bales's and Tommy's.

He knows, they were plainly thinking. Which told me all *I* needed to know.

The fellow with the rope and the one who'd held the bridles. The men who'd helped Bales lynch us.

Tommy and Brother Landrigan.

A curse slipped from my lips so foul I was lucky the chapel's stained-glass Jesus didn't step down to slap me.

"Well," Landrigan said, and even in so small a word as that I could hear the change coming over him—his voice deepening, his tone toughening, his whole being smoldering with a rekindled flame. "It appears the marshal was right about you two all along. You need to go. Now."

"Oh, they're leaving, alright," Bales said. "Leaving *town*. There's gonna be a train at the station in two hours"—he wrapped his chubby fingers around Gustav's forearm—"and you're—"

My brother tore his arm away.

"Get your damn hands offa me!"

There was a sudden flurry of motion. Cuff hopping back agasp, Bales making another grab at Old Red, Tommy scooting along the pew behind us to get at my brother's other arm.

I cleared my throat and slipped a hand under my jacket.

"Y'all ever hear of a shoulder holster?" I said.

Everyone froze.

I smiled.

"Thought so." I nodded first at Bales's choir robe, then Tommy's. "And it sure don't look like you ladies are packin' under your evenin' gowns. So I'd suggest y'all back off so's I don't have to profane the house of the Lord by whippin' out my hardware."

Tommy looked to Bales.

Bales didn't move.

"You think I might be bluffin'?" I said to him. "Well, good for you. You might look like a two-year-old with a tin star pinned to his bib most of the time, but I reckon there's more to you than meets the eye. Only the thing is—"

There was a sharp *click-clack* as I thumbed back the hammer on my Webley.

"I *ain't* bluffin'."

Bales stepped away from Old Red, and his young friend did likewise, but Brother Landrigan stood his ground, eyes alight with righteous indignation.

"Go! Leave this place and never return!"

"That's the general idea." I put a hand on Gustav's shoulder and gave him a gentle push. "Let's get gone, Brother."

We moved out into the aisle and started backing away.

"The next time I lay eyes on you, you're going to jail," Bales spat at us.

"I can only hope so," Old Red shot back. "Only you might be surprised who ends up on which side of the bars."

Bales, Landrigan, Tommy, Cuff—they all stared at him like he was a madman. I guess they were giving me the same look, for who'd follow a madman but another?

My brother spun on his heel and broke into a scurry. I uncocked my Bulldog (few things ruin your day faster than shooting yourself in the armpit), and hurried after him. The church had already cleared out but for a few pop-eyed stragglers, so it was an easy dash down the aisle and through the doors.

Once we were outside, our scurry became a full-on foot-pounding, arm-swinging sprint.

The time hadn't just come to check out of the Star. We needed to grab our things and look for a hole to hide in. Preferably a deep, dark one.

Where we'd find such a hideaway was just one of a dozen questions I was longing to throw at my brother, but we were far too busy tearing up and down the sidewalks to pause for any talk beyond the occasional "Gangway!" and "Comin' through!" We didn't even slow down for our usual creeping and gun-drawing before barging into our hotel room and grabbing for our carpetbags.

Which explains why it took us so long to notice the bulky shape under the blankets on the bed—and even longer to notice all the blood.

29

OBVIOUS (AND NOT SO OBVIOUS) FACTS

Or, I Lose My Stomach for Detecting, and an Acquaintance Spills Her Guts

There was a body under the bedsheets. A big one. That much was clear. What wasn't so clear was what to do about it.

The first two steps came easy enough: (1) jump three feet in the air shrieking "Shit!" and (2) shut the damn door. After that, though, I was stumped.

As was, it seemed, my brother. The two of us just stood there staring at the bloody heap on our bed.

"I can't believe it," I said. "I know we parted on bad terms and all, but to go and do this . . ."

A different (though very familiar) kind of incredulity—the "Are you crazy or just plain stupid?" kind—shoved the shock off Gustav's face.

"What are you talkin' about?"

"Bob and Lottie dumpin' Stonewall on us 'stead of buryin' him," I said.

"You think Bob 'n' Lottie drove around back of the Star in broad daylight, dragged Stonewall up here with only Squirrel Tooth to help 'em, picked the lock on the door, and plopped the body here in our room? All just to spite us?"

"Well . . . I suppose it don't sound so likely when you put it like that, but I don't know of any other dead bodies floatin' around town just now."

"That's the problem, ain't it?" Old Red said, and he turned again toward the round-bellied mound under the sheets. "Someone can always go and make more."

He took in a deep breath, steeling himself, and started toward the bed. He moved slowly, and not just because he wasn't anxious to get where he was going—he was trying to keep his boots out of all the blood smearing the floorboards.

It wasn't easy.

When he was close enough, he pinched one corner of the bedsheet and gently lifted it up.

"Awww, hell," he sighed, peering down at a face I couldn't yet see.

"Awww, hell *what*?"

With a quick flick of the wrist, Gustav threw off the rest of the bedding.

"Uh!" he huffed out, sounding like he'd just taken a punch to the stomach, and even he—rawhide-tough witness to so much death he could just about compete with the Grim Reaper himself—was forced to look away.

Me, I didn't just look away. I *stumbled* away, barely making it to a chair before my legs buckled.

It had been Big Bess, the gargantuan good-time gal from the Phoenix, under the sheets—and much of what belonged under her *skin* wasn't any longer.

I couldn't (and wouldn't if I could) tell you exactly which pieces of her had been pulled out and strewn about. Suffice it to say she'd been gutted, and Big Bess was a woman with a lot of guts.

"Sweet Jesus," I gasped. "He's been here. The killer. Not only did we not stop him, he butchered a gal right in our own room."

Gustav was hunched over, hands on his knees, face still turned away from the bed.

"Maybe," he said.

"Good Lord, what else could it be? Big Bess dropped by to apologize and accidentally gored herself on the doorknob? No, *he* was here, Brother"—I pointed uselessly at the thing neither of us could yet bear to look at again—"and he left us *that*."

"Maybe," Old Red said again, and his next words he spat out like a curse. " 'There is nothing more deceptive than an obvious fact.' "

It was a Holmes quote, of course, and I might have been glad to hear it—comforted that my brother had a grip on the Method even now—but for two things.

First off, it was my least favorite of Holmes's little truisms. A false-ism, it seemed to me. A bullshit-ism, even.

Then there was what Gustav said next.

"And the only 'obvious fact' here is *we* killed Big Bess."

"Now, don't be like that. You don't have to feel guilty cuz some crazy bastard went and—"

"I ain't talkin' about what I *feel*, ya idjit!" my brother thundered. "I'm talkin' about what this is supposed to look like!"

His meaning sank in quick—and just as quick, I hopped to my feet.

I'd been in such shock I actually forgot to panic. But that was over now.

"We gotta go," I said. "We gotta *run*, and I ain't just talkin' about out of the Star."

Old Red shook his head. "No."

"Listen to me, Brother. You're right about Bess there. Someone's stickin' our heads in the noose again, and there's only one way to get 'em out. We can't get rid of that body, and sure as hell no one's gonna believe we didn't kill her. So we ain't got no choice. We gotta put San Marcos a long, long way behind us."

"No!" Gustav snapped up straight, his expression a muddle of revulsion and rage and regret that came close to agony. "If we run now, this follows us forever. We won't have just come here and failed. We'll be wanted for murder, and everything I hoped for and you hoped for . . . it'll all be impossible. Our lives'll be over whether we're caught or not."

He paused to suck in a deep breath. When he went on, he was calmer—though not anywhere near calm.

"It ain't just about avengin' Adeline anymore. It's the only way to save *us*."

I knew he was right . . . dammit. Turn tail, and we were ruined. Yet a part of me—like nine-tenths of me—wanted to light out of there and never look back.

Only there'd be looking back. Back over our shoulders. Back at our mistakes. Back at how close we'd come to being something other than drifters.

Besides, that other one-tenth that wanted to stick with my brother, no matter what? It always won out anyway.

I slipped off the chair and crouched down by our carpetbags.

"I'll get us packed while you do what detectin' you can. But don't dilly-dally, you understand?"

"I never dilly-dally," Old Red grumbled, and he finally turned himself toward the bed again.

How exactly he went about inspecting Big Bess's mangled remains I couldn't say, for I made certain I couldn't *see*, keeping my back to him as much as was possible. I *heard* plenty, though—a moist, sticky sound, like someone peeling a half-chewed licorice whip off a strip of soggy flypaper.

"Throat's cut," Gustav said. "It's a clean cut, too. Not hacked or gashed."

There were more soft, squishy sounds that made me thankful I had nothing but nice, bland doughnuts in my stomach—and even those I was having a hard time keeping down now.

"Same with her stomach. Straight lines. And her hands are covered with blood."

"What were you expectin'? Cookie crumbs?"

Old Red grunted sourly, and I heard footsteps and the creaking of floorboards.

I risked a quick glance back.

My brother was backing away from the bed, eyeballing the blood on the floor, tracking the splatter and flow of it around his half of the room.

I got back to stuffing my carpetbag full of clothes. When it was filled, I snatched up my brother's and kept at it till it was full, too.

"Done," I said, hopping to my feet, both bags in hand.

Gustav was kneeling, still staring at the floor, and he pushed himself up with obvious reluctance.

"Alright . . . I reckon that'll have to do."

He turned and took in Big Bess one last time, holding his gaze steady on the mess that had been made of her. He was fixing the sight in his mind, like a photographer hovering over his camera while the light burns into the plate.

"Let's get the hell outta here," he said.

I didn't ask where the hell we'd be getting *to*. First things first. We had to get clear of the Star.

My brother moved to the door and cracked it open. After a quick peep around, he hurried out, waving for me to follow.

The hallway was empty.

We locked the door behind us before making for the stairs. It felt more than a little futile, doing that, for surely what was in that room we couldn't lock away forever.

But a day? Maybe two? That at least we could hope for. It might even be enough.

We slipped into the back stairwell we'd come to know so well and started spiraling down fast.

"Smart thing would be sneakin' outta town and comin' back after nightfall," Old Red said. "We wouldn't last long 'round here while there's light."

He was right about that, too—more right than he knew.

All of two steps into the sunshine behind the hotel, and a gun butt came crashing down atop my brother's head. Before he even hit the ground, the business end came swinging around to practically poke me in the nose.

"Marshal!" Bales's friend Tommy called out. The gawky young man had traded his choir robes for street clothes—and a deputy's six-pointed star. "Marshal, come quick! I got 'em!"

30

TEXAS JACK

Or, The Killer Still Doesn't Have a Face, but He Finally Gets a Name

My brother wasn't knocked out. He just wished he was.

"Damn," he moaned. "Give a man a chance to surrender, why don't you?"

He was on his knees behind the Star, a steadying hand on the ground the only thing keeping him from flopping face-first into the dirt.

His other hand was pressed to the top of his head. Or the top of his hat, more like. The blow from the deputy's gun butt had come down on Gustav's white Stetson, smashing the crown into a dimple like a hammer hitting a mound of mashed potatoes.

"Marshal!" Tommy hollered again, a note of growing panic in his reedy voice. I couldn't help but notice that his gun hand was shaking—this being a point of general interest to me, as said hand was pointing a Colt at my picture-perfect features, and stray bullets are hell on a fellow's profile.

I dropped the carpetbags I'd been toting and put up my hands.

"Steady there, Tommy . . ."

I was still inside the stairwell, and if I'd whirled around and bounded up the steps, I'd have had a good chance of getting away. Yet the thought that I could make a break for it didn't occur to me till this very moment. At the time, it just seemed to me if Gustav was caught, I was, too.

"We won't be no trouble," I said. "No need to be nervous."

Tommy *meant* to wave the gun at me now, though he'd gone so slick with sweat I was almost more scared he'd throw the thing at me than shoot me with it.

"Who's nervous? You're the one who oughta be nervous!"

"Oh, I am, Tommy. I promise you. I am."

"Stop calling me Tommy!" the deputy squeaked.

His boss might have seemed about as rough and tough as cotton candy, but compared to young Tommy, Milford Bales was Wyatt Earp.

"Look . . . uhhh . . . *friend*," I began.

The sound of approaching footsteps silenced me.

Bales rounded the corner from the alley. He was still in a black suit of the sort you might wear to church, but now there was a badge pinned to his sack coat and a holster around his well-padded waist.

"What happened?" he asked Tommy.

"They came sneaking out the back here not a minute after you left. I apprehended them."

"Oh, is that what you did?" I said. "Gosh, I don't think I've ever been 'apprehended' before."

"Shut up," Bales snapped.

"Not just yet, thank you. I'd like to point out that none of this strong-arm stuff is necessary." I stuck out my right foot and gave one of our carpetbags a nudge. "See that? We was leavin' town, just like you told us to. You wanna escort us over to the train station, fine, but there ain't no need for gunplay."

"We'll see about that."

Bales bent down and pulled Old Red's Peacemaker from its holster, then stepped up close and groped under my coat to relieve me of my Bulldog.

"Think you can hold 'em here another couple minutes, Deputy?" he said once he had us unheeled.

Tommy straightened up to his full height and nodded firmly. I almost expected him to salute.

"Of course, Marshal."

"Alright. I'll be back."

Bales marched back into the alley. If he was headed to the hotel's front desk to get a passkey, it was all over.

Or maybe, I realized with a queasy churn in my gut, it was all over already—because Bales had done in Big Bess, and we were caught in a web he'd woven for us himself.

I nodded down at my brother.

"Mind if I help him up?"

I could practically hear the gears turning in Tommy's head as he thought it through. *What would a* real *lawman do?*

"You got the gun," I reminded him.

"Okay. But no tricks."

I got my brother to his feet. He was wobbly but surprisingly steady for a fellow who's just had his hat nailed to his head.

I wondered if he was steady enough to run.

"Say," I said to Tommy, "how long you been a deputy, Deputy?"

"Shut up," he barked. Or yipped, more like. He wasn't so much a rottweiler as a shivery little Chihuahua.

"Fine. You don't gotta tell me. I thought you seemed a tad green, is all. Like you could use a few pointers. I've done some detective work, you know, so I could tell you a thing or two."

Tommy tried to shoot me a steely glare, but it merely made him look cross-eyed. "What are you talking about?"

"How you got the drop on us, for one thing. That wasn't too bad, the way you had yourself hid outta sight back here . . . except you almost undid it all comin' at my brother like that. Believe me—I've had some experience thumpin' fellers with gun butts." I shook my head and tut-tutted. "And boppin' a man over the brainpan when he's wearin' a big ol' Boss of the Plains? Please. He may as well have had a pillow strapped to his head."

"So what would you do? Tap him on the shoulder and ask him to take off his hat?"

I had to smile. The kid had some spunk after all. More importantly, he was starting to listen to me.

"Actually, if you're quick about it, you *can* take a man's hat off before you hit him," I said. "Just grab the brim and flip. Or if that don't suit you, don't hit the man at all. Most of the time, just tellin' a feller you got a gun on him is enough. Though you'd wanna fix your stance first."

"My stance?"

"Yes, your stance! The way you're holdin' your body—chest square to us, elbow bent, gun out. You fire a .45 like that, the kick'll pop it right outta your hand. I mean, just look at how you got your feet set."

God bless the lad, he looked.

I clenched my fist and started forward.

A hand shot out and clutched at me, bunching up my shirtfront and holding me tight.

It was my brother.

He looked into my eyes and shook his head.

Not yet.

By the time Tommy looked up again, it was all over.

"What's wrong with my feet?"

"On second thought," I sighed, "your way's as good as any."

The clatter of quick footfalls echoed down the stairs behind me, and a moment later the marshal came charging from the stairwell. We were about to find out if he'd gotten into our room.

"You sick son of a bitch!" he spat, and he sent Old Red back to the ground with a roundhouse to the jaw.

I took that as a yes.

I balled up a fist again and started for Bales.

"Don't," Tommy said, his Colt level with my head, and even with the shrill screech to his tinny voice, that was warning enough.

"Why would you do it?" Bales roared at my brother. "Why? *Why?*"

Gustav was sprawled out in the dirt, and when he rolled over and looked up, there was blood and grime on his face—and a crooked, sneering smile.

"Feh. And you accuse *me* of playactin'."

Bales looked like he wanted to squash my brother like a scurrying bug.

"Get these animals in a cell," he said, and he whirled around and stalked back toward the stairs again.

"What did you find up there?" Tommy asked him.

Bales paused half in, half out of the darkened stairwell, rubbing the bruised knuckles of his left hand.

"Another one. Just like before."

Then he stepped into the shadows and was gone.

"Alright, you two—move," Tommy snapped. I must admit, he almost sounded like a real lawman, for once. Which is to say, he sounded like he couldn't stand the sight of us.

"You alright?" I asked Old Red as I hauled him to his feet yet again.

My brother put a hand to his chin and gave it a waggle. When he was sure his jawbone wouldn't pop out, he shrugged.

"Don't hurt any worse than the top of my head."

"Well, that's a relief. Who wants to get hung with a busted jaw?"

"*Go.*" Tommy waved his gun at the alley. "That way."

We picked up our carpetbags and started off.

"What'd the marshal mean when he said 'just like before'?" Gustav asked. "Which 'other one' was he talkin' about?"

"Just shut up and walk," Tommy said. "No distractions."

I looked back and gave him an approving nod.

"Now you're gettin' the hang of it!"

"The next one of you that talks," the deputy said, "I'm shooting."

I kept my compliments to myself after that.

Old Red and I spent the next few minutes on parade through the streets of San Marcos. No one could have known what we were accused of yet, but that didn't matter. Marching at gunpoint was enough, and we passed under one cold, scornful stare after another.

Once we'd withstood the disdain of what seemed like every upright citizen in the county, it was almost a relief to finally tromp into the marshal's tidy little office . . . until we saw who was waiting for us inside.

Leaning back in a swivel chair, his long legs propped up on what had to be Bales's own desk (none other being in sight), was Pete Ragsdale. Like always, Gil Bock was beside him, as unshakable as a pudgy shadow. Both were dressed with their usual overformal flair—top hats, frock coats, ties, checked trousers—with a little something extra to show they were in a festive mood: Each wore a big yellow daisy in his lapel.

"Well well well," Ragsdale drawled through his perpetual lip-curled sneer. "Would ya look what the fudgin' pussy dragged in."

Gustav started toward him fast, flying by me before I could get a hand on him.

"You bastards—"

"Hold it right there!" Tommy hollered, and I was relieved to learn my protégé could muster the menace to get my brother to stop. Packing a stingy gun's an old mack tradition, and I was certain Ragsdale wouldn't pass up a chance to claim self-defense.

"I didn't think even you had the gall for this," Old Red snarled at him.

Ragsdale threw up his hands and beetled his brow, putting on a show of mystified perplexity. "The gall for fudgin' what? We're just here to talk to the fudgin' marshal. Three of our fudgin' employees have gone missin' in the past twelve fudgin' hours." He swept his feet off the desktop and sat up straight. "Hey . . . *you* wouldn't know anything about that, would you, Gus?"

"Exactly which employees are you talkin' about, Mr. Ragsdale?" I piped up. "From what we've heard, you two have been losin' 'em pretty regular-like goin' on five years now."

Ragsdale's smirk puckered and petrified, while Bock's dead eyes finally came to life, widening ever so slightly as they darted toward his partner.

We were closer to the truth than they'd thought—and they didn't like it.

Ragsdale recovered first, leaning back and throwing his heels up on Bales's desk again.

"So, Deputy," he said, "whadaya got these two fudgewits in for, anyway?"

"You can ask Marshal Bales about that," Tommy said. "And you can get your ass out of his chair, too."

Ragsdale chuckled and raised his hands in mock surrender, as if he'd just been told "Stick 'em up!" by a four-year-old waving a pinewood gun. He did as Tommy told him, though, pushing himself to his feet and stepping away from the desk.

I resisted the urge to give Tommy a round of applause.

"Alright, let's go." The deputy jerked his head at a narrow staircase in a back corner of the room. "Up there."

Gustav and I dutifully trudged off toward the steps, passing so close to Ragsdale and Bock we were practically treading on their toes—and for a second there I was tempted to try it.

"Don't worry, Gus," Bock said with his usual deadpan flatness. "You won't be here long."

Ragsdale burst out laughing, though I had no idea what the joke was. I got the feeling I wouldn't find it funny even if I did.

A minute later, Tommy was locking us in upstairs. It was a small jail, with just two cells, each barely bigger than a horse stall. The one Old Red and I ended up sharing had but one bunk and one iron-barred window. I felt like a turkey crammed into a birdcage with a canary.

After heading back downstairs with our bags, Tommy exchanged a few more words with Ragsdale and Bock, though all Gustav and I could make out were muffled *mph-mph*s. A door opened, there was another couple minutes of *mph-mph*ing, and the door slammed shut.

Then Milford Bales came upstairs alone.

"Well, there you are, at last," he said, glaring at my brother through the bars. "Where you belong."

"Don't bother," Gustav jeered back. He'd appropriated the bunk for himself, sitting atop it with his legs stretched out and his arms folded. "There ain't nobody but us around to hear."

Bales shook his head sadly. The rage that had overtaken him back at the Star was gone. Now he just looked drained and disgusted.

"I'm still willing to make this as easy on you as I can, Gus. For old times' sake. Just come clean. Admit what you did. Then we can get this over with."

"Oh, come on, Milford," Old Red said. "You got us where you want us, so you may as well cut the crap."

Bales blinked at my brother a moment. If he knew which crap to cut, he sure wasn't letting on.

"So you're not going to own up to anything? Even now?"

"Tell you what," Gustav said. "You want me to start ownin' up to stuff? Fine . . . only you go first."

The marshal gaped at him again. "You are one crazy SOB, you know that? Well, I guess it doesn't matter if you can admit it or not." Bales pulled a slip of folded paper from his coat pocket and gave it a little wave. "This is as good as a confession."

"Oh? And what is that supposed to be?"

Despite Old Red's sneering tone, he let himself be lured off the bunk. I joined him as he stepped up to the bars.

Bales unfolded the paper. It was covered with scratchy-scrawled writing.

"I guess you thought you'd be out of town by the time Horace Cuff found this slipped under his door at the newspaper," the marshal said, "but then, you don't know Horace very well, do you? If he's not at church, he's at his office. He went straight there after the service this morning. Then he came straight to me with this."

"Are you gonna tell us what the damn thing says or not?" Old Red growled.

Bales shook his head and sighed. "Gus . . . this is getting ridiculous."

"I couldn't agree with you more, Marshal," I said. "Tell you what, though—just for a minute, why don't you pretend we *don't* know what that is and read it out for us, hmmm?"

Bales looked back and forth between me and my brother as if trying to decide which of us was the bigger loon. Eventually he cleared his throat and brought the note up to eye level.

" 'From Hell (a.k.a. San Marcos),' " he read. " 'A woman's work is never done, and neither is mine—except what I work on is women, ha ha. It's been five years since I plied my trade here, and in that time I've picked up a trick or two. For proof, you can look to my lucky Star. Don't bother looking for *me*, though. By the time you see this, I'll be gone again. But fear not—or fear do, if you be a whore. As long as there are soiled doves to pluck, Texas Jack will be on the job. Send word to the barber: I'll be back one day for another trim, snip snip.' "

Bales refolded the letter and stuffed it back in his pocket.

"It's signed 'T. J.,' " he said.

While the lawman had been reading, my brother had sagged more and more against the bars, until now he gripped them with both hands as if they were the only things keeping him upright.

"My God . . . it's so obvious I didn't even see it," he said. "It looks like *I* killed Adeline."

"Looks like?" Bales scoffed.

"That note don't prove nothin'," I shot back at him. "You know yourself Gustav can't write a word."

"But *you* can," the marshal said. "I talked to Mortimer Krieger this morning, too. He told me you and your brother dropped by yesterday. Came in with some wild story about being writers or sleuths or something, investigating a murder . . . wanting to see anything he had on the Whitechapel killer. You even joined the library so you could take a look at his Ripper book. And the membership form you filled out—for yourself, Otto?"

Bales patted another of his pockets, signaling that the form was right there, safe and snug.

"The handwriting matches the note."

There was a long pause while my brain worked through these words, rejected the only possible interpretation, tried again, came to the same conclusion, then finally ground to a smoking, spark-spewing halt.

"That's impossible," I managed to mutter.

Bales barked out a mirthless, incredulous laugh, like I'd just told him the same bad joke twice.

"Oh, it's possible, alright. So possible it's true."

"You really believe that, don't you?" Old Red said, eyes unfocused, voice hoarse. "You haven't been tryin' to run us off cuz you're the killer or you're coverin' for him or any of that. You been doin' it cuz you think *I'm* a killer."

"You actually seem surprised," Bales said, looking something close to astonished himself. "But . . . don't you remember?"

"Remember what?"

"Five years ago. The last time I saw you before you left San Marcos. You came into my barbershop drunk, raving, practically foaming at the mouth."

Old Red's knuckles whitened, tightening around the gray iron bars. He wasn't just readying himself for his knees to give out any-more. It was more like the whole world was falling away beneath his feet.

"That's when you admitted it to me, Gus," Bales said. "You told me *you* killed Adeline."

31

CONFESSIONS

Or, We Learn Why Bales Is So Bitter, and It Sours Me on Him Even More

Gustav staggered back from the bars and plopped down onto the little cell's lone bunk.

"You really don't remember, do you?" Bales said to him.

"Of course he don't," I said. "Cuz it didn't hap—"

"Otto," Old Red cut in, and when I looked at him he held up a hand and shook his head. "Tell me what *you* remember, Milford."

Bales scowled at him, nose crinkled as if at the smell of bullshit. A heap of it. Yet something drew the lawman on.

"I was sweeping up in the shop one night, maybe four or five days after Adeline died. And I heard noise in the alley out back, off towards the Star. It sounded like shouting and sobbing. Some kind of argument. I tried to ignore it, at first. I didn't want to go out there. Not after what I'd seen . . ."

A fire lit up in the marshal's eyes.

I'd hoped it was the benefit of the doubt that had kept him talking, but it was looking more like a reckoning now. Bales wanted to rub my brother's nose in his own dirt.

"Oh, yeah—I saw the body," he said. "When I came in to open

the shop the next morning, it was still back there in the alley, waiting for the undertaker. Old Marshal Cerny had a deputy there, and the son of a bitch was letting kids take a peep for a nickel apiece. I went to chase 'em off, and that's when I saw . . ."

His eyes went glassy, losing focus. Or focusing elsewhere, more like. On a picture seared into his mind.

"Anyway," he said, and suddenly he was back with us, staring hard at Old Red. "A few nights later, I hear that commotion back there, and I start thinking, 'What if the killer's come back? What if another girl's getting murdered, and I'm just standing around with a broom in my hand?' So I took a look. And it was you, Gus. Alone. Behind the Star."

"What was I doin'?" Gustav asked. He truly had no idea.

"Blubbering, ranting . . . though I couldn't understand a word. You were so soaked, the whole alley reeked of rye. So I got you to come into the barbershop, thinking we could talk things through. Friend to friend."

Bales's thick lips puckered like he'd just bitten into a rotten lemon.

"I didn't really know you at all, did I? You never even told me about you and Adeline until that night. You were pacing around, bawling, and that's when it came out."

The marshal clasped his hands together, face contorted in anguish like a bad actor in an amateur melodrama. He wasn't just going to tell us what Gustav had said all those years ago. He was going to show us.

" 'If I loved her, Milford, why'd I do her like that?' " He aimed a beseeching gaze heavenward. " 'I'm sorry, hon! I am so, *so* sorry!' "

Bales locked eyes on Old Red again, and his tone went icy cold.

"I asked what you were sorry about, and that's when you said it. 'She's dead because of me, Milford. I killed her.' Just like that, plain as can be, you admitted you murdered Gertie."

My brother had been listening with an air of weary forbearance—

Job taking another whipping from Jehovah because, one way or another, he figures he must deserve it.

One word snapped him out of it.

"I murdered *who*?"

Bales looked both flustered and defiant. He knew he'd made a mistake—but part of him *wanted* to make it.

"Adeline," he said.

Gustav shook his head. "No. You said Gertie. That's what her family called her. That's what I called her."

Bales couldn't hold it back another second. The truth he'd wanted to spit in Old Red's face ever since he first saw us—he finally let it fly.

"And it's what *I* called her!" he roared. "You think you loved her? You don't know what love is, you sick bastard! *I* loved that girl! Me! And you're finally gonna pay for what you did to her!"

My brother didn't just slump back into the bunk. He collapsed into it. Even old Job didn't have to take a blow this low.

"Oh, Gertie," Gustav moaned.

"So that night . . . when she was in the alley behind the Star"—I turned to Bales—"she was comin' to the barbershop. To see *you*."

"Oh, didn't he tell you that part?" Bales sneered, jerking his thumb at my brother. "She'd been meeting me over there for months, whenever she could slip away. Only that night, I wasn't there . . . and Gus was. Gertie always swore she hadn't told a soul about us, but I guess he found out somehow—and he tore that poor, sweet girl apart!"

"Bull—!"

"*Otto*," Old Red said, cutting me off yet again.

After that, though, he seemed to have a hard time getting out more words. Not that there weren't any to say. It was more like there were too many, and he had to pan through them to find the right ones to start with.

"The night. . . ."

It came out a croak, and Gustav cleared his throat and tried again.

"The night you and I talked in the barbershop. After you heard me say . . . whatever I said. What happened then?"

Bales shrugged.

"I took a swing at you, you took a swing at me, we struggled."

He spoke carelessly, as bored with his own words as Old Red had been mindful. He'd said what he'd been itching to say for so long. Now that he'd scratched the itch, he was losing interest.

"Eventually, you got your hands on a pair of scissors, and I thought it was all over. You were going to slice me up, too. But I guess killing a man in a fair fight just isn't your way. You dropped the scissors and stumbled out."

"Yeah . . . yeah," Gustav said slowly, perhaps catching glimpses of memories long lost in an alcohol fog. "Then after that . . . what? You went to Marshal Cerny?"

"Of course. He thanked me, too—and then didn't do a thing about it. You left town a few days later, and that was that, far as he was concerned."

"But not for you."

"No. I couldn't stop thinking about it. That I could know a man, think of him as a friend, and he could do *that*. I even tried reading up on it. To try and understand you. But nothing I ever saw made a lick of sense."

My brother nodded limply.

"*The Whitechapel Mystery: A Pscyho Logical Problem*," he said.

The marshal looked startled, as if Gustav had just told him his mother's maiden name or that he had a mole on his unmentionables— something he couldn't possibly know. Then he must have recalled that we'd done some snooping around the Kriegers' library, and he relaxed and rolled his eyes.

"Yeah. That thing. I may as well have been reading Mother Goose, for all I got out of it. No, the only grip I could get on you, Gus, didn't come out of any book. It came from Brother Landrigan. He led me to repentance and salvation and acceptance . . . of a sort. There's no understanding evil, look at it all you want. It just is, no rhyme nor reason. If any good was going to come of what happened to Gertie, I'd have to make it myself." Bales tapped the badge pinned to his coat. "And the first step was making sure Kaz Cerny wasn't wearing this if another lunatic like you showed up."

"But *I* showed up again, Milford," Gustav said. "How come you didn't arrest me the second you saw me?"

Bales waved the thought away—though a trifle too quick, it seemed to me.

"I had no proof."

"You're the town marshal. Your word alone might've been enough to . . ."

Old Red let his words trail off, and he gave Bales a sidelong, sizing-up sort of look. Then he shook his head.

"You didn't *wanna* testify, did you?" he said. "You steered clear of the Eagle all them years ago, did your dirty business in your barbershop, for chrissakes. And even now that you've repented and been saved, hallelujah, you're still tryin' to protect your precious reputation. Cuz love Gertie or not, you don't want folks knowin' you was ever mixed up with a low-down whore. So you got your pals to help run me and my brother out of town when you thought—truly believed—I was a mad-dog killer. What the hell kinda lawman does that?"

The marshal's face went so red-hot I half expected him to blow up like an overstoked boiler.

"Face it, Milford—you ain't changed," my brother pressed on. "You think that badge made you something new, washed you clean? Well, it didn't. You're still just a haircutter pushin' a broom."

"Are you through?" Bales growled.

"Yeah," I threw in. "Are you through?"

"For the moment," Gustav said.

Bales opened his mouth.

I opened mine faster.

"Well, it's about time. Because I have been waitin' and waitin' and waitin' for you to swing back around to *the point*. And since you never did, I guess it's up to me."

"And the point is?" Bales asked.

"That my brother is not a murderer," I told him, "and that you, marshal, are a goddamn moron!"

"E-excuse me?" Bales spluttered, so surprised he wasn't even angry yet.

"No, I don't believe I will. Not while I'm in a jail cell because of your stupidity."

"Otto," Gustav said once again, but it came out more of a groan this time. He knew there was no stopping me until I'd worked off my head of steam.

"You're so twisted up with grief you got your head worked up your ass," I raged at Bales. "I mean, please! That 'confession' Gustav made?" I popped my eyes and clapped my hands to my face, mock-shocked. "Goodness me! Do you mean to say he allowed himself to become *visibly agitated* merely because the gal he loved had just been *murdered*? Well, no wonder you pegged him for the culprit. Cuz, of course, only a cold-blooded killer would get shit-faced and start actin' nuts if his fiancée—yes, I said *fiancée*, Marshal—was *hacked into mincemeat*!"

"Listen, Amlingmeyer," Bales began.

"And that badge of yours?" I sped on. "The one you wanted in case another lunatic came thisaway? Well, you been wearin' it while some madman killed four chippies right under your nose—and that ain't even includin' Adeline and Big Bess!"

"I don't know what you're babbling about."

"Well, you wouldn't, would you? You big—!"

I felt a hand on my shoulder.

Gustav had sprung up from the bunk.

"Otto here might not be puttin' it the way I'd have liked"—my brother's grip on my shoulder tightened to a painful pinch, then let loose—"but it's true you misunderstood me, Milford. Gertie's blood *is* on my hands, but not cuz I killed her with 'em. I thought we needed more money 'fore we married, so I let her keep on . . . you know. And it got her killed. I'm sure that's what I was tryin' to say that night—I should've got her away from Ragsdale and Bock first chance I got. And you know what? If you truly cared for her, like you say? You should have, too."

The angry flush on Bales's face had faded to pink. He wasn't boiling anymore, but he was still asimmer.

"So you're trying to take it back," he said.

"I can't take back a confession I never made!" Old Red snapped, exasperated at last. "And if you'd bothered checkin', you'd know I not only didn't kill Gertie, I *couldn't* have. The night she died, I was asleep in a bunkhouse ten miles outside town. You can ask Suicide Cheney or Joe Koska down on the Lucky Seven. You can go out and ask"—there was a pause so brief I'm sure only I noticed it—"Bob Harris. They'll all tell you the same thing. I didn't even know Gertie was dead for days."

"I always knew your pals would cover for you," Bales said, shaking his head. "It doesn't prove a thing."

"Milford, I don't have no pals around here anymore."

"Look, Marshal," I said, "have you even asked yourself why we're here? If Gustav really killed Adeline . . . Gertie . . . *her* . . . if he'd done it, why on earth would he come back to San Marcos?"

"Because he thought he got away with it."

I barely reined in a "Sweet Jesus!"

"He came back," I said slowly, with as much patience as I could muster, "because he aimed to do what he couldn't five years ago. We're here to find the killer."

"Well, if that's true," Bales replied, mimicking my overdeliberate, explaining-math-to-a-halfwit cadence, "then why is there another dead prostitute in your hotel room?"

"Someone put her there," I said, my words coming out now like molasses in January. "You think we're so stupid we'd leave a body in our room while we went to church?"

"It's . . . not . . . that . . . you're . . . stupid," Bales said. "It's . . . that . . . you're . . . *crazy*." He turned his glare on Gustav. "And now you're done."

He turned and stomped toward the stairs. "You're crazy . . . you're done"—that said it all, as far as he was concerned.

"What we told Krieger about bein' sleuths?" I called after him. "That's true! We've been railroad dicks and we've caught killers and I know it doesn't look like it but we're actually good at this stuff! Believe it or not, you need our help!"

Bales reached the top of the steps.

I turned to Old Red. "You gotta show him I ain't lyin'."

Bales stopped on the first step down.

Old Red said nothing aloud, but his eyes were talking plenty.

I can't, they told me.

"Go on, Brother," I said. "You can do it. I know you can."

Even if you don't.

Bales muttered something and started down the stairs again.

"You don't wanna believe me about Gertie, fine," Gustav called after him. "I can understand. Big Bess, though—at least hear me through on that."

Bales tromped out of sight.

"Dammit, Milford!" Old Red grabbed the bars of the cell door and gave them a rattling shake. "I know who killed her! And if you give me just two more minutes, I can prove it, too!"

Bales's footsteps faded.

Then stopped.

Then grew louder again.

Bales reappeared at the top of the stairs.

"Two minutes," he said, pulling a watch from his waistcoat pocket. "Starting *now*."

32

TWO MINUTES (PLUS)

Or, We Try to Fill Bales In While the Town Gets Set to Rub Us Out

You know, I threw two minutes out kinda off the top of my head,"
Gustav said. "It might take more time to talk through than
that."

Ten seconds into my brother's bluff—if it was a bluff—and already he seemed to be losing his nerve.

Bales looked up from his watch and scowled at him.

"How about *five* minutes?" I suggested.

Now he scowled at *me*.

"Four?" I tried. "Three and a half?"

The lawman tucked his watch away.

"Just talk," he said to Old Red.

"Right."

My brother took in a deep breath and shot me a look that said,
Remember, now—if this doesn't work, it was your *dumb idea*.

"One of the reasons it's been so hard to get a handle on who killed
Gertie," he said to the marshal, "is there don't seem to be no why to it,
beyond sheer bloody-mindedness. But with Big Bess, the why's plain
as day. You're lookin' at it right now."

He spread out his arms and swiveled first this way, then that.

Us in a cell.

"We been sniffin' around, and someone wanted us to stop . . . wanted it bad enough to kill a woman just to get at us. And when you ponder on the *how* of Big Bess's death, that tells you who it was."

"It does?"

"Yup," Gustav said. "Just take her innards, for instance."

Bales suddenly looked like he really, *really* regretted putting away his watch.

"Her . . . innards?"

Old Red nodded. "You saw Big Bess on that bed. Her guts 'n' such was spread out careful-like, orderly—and the slices up her belly was clean, not jagged. If there'd been any struggle, she'd have been hacked up every which way, and her bowels would've been spilled all over. So it wasn't the guttin' that killed her. It was that slit throat. She was awake when it happened, too—she wasn't rapped over the head or nothin' first."

"How could you know that?" Bales asked.

Unless you were there when it happened, he didn't bother adding.

"Didn't you notice?" my brother said, and I caught just a hint of the old curt cockiness that used to come over him when he'd get to stringing out deductions. "Her hands was covered in blood. After she was cut, she pressed 'em up over her throat. Only that didn't do no good, of course. That was a deep slice. Clean, too. From here to here"—Gustav put a finger to the left side of his neck, then pulled it across to the right in one smooth motion—"straight as a razor."

"That means something?"

"Well, of course, it does! Bess didn't see it comin'. The feller who done her in—he was standin' behind her. And if you think on that, you'll see it weighs against me or Otto bein' the killer."

Bales furrowed his brow and cocked his head . . . then grunted and shrugged. "Alright, I've thought on it, and I don't see how it means a thing."

Old Red grabbed hold of the bars again, hard, as if he wished they were the marshal's shoulders—so he could give the man a good shake.

He was getting riled up. Which was good news, I had to think. Like water to a fish or dirt to a worm, irritation is my brother's natural element. Better to have him vexed than dispirited.

"I'll just have to keep thinkin' for the both of us, then," he said. "Cuz here's what ain't occurred to you: Big Bess *let* someone stand behind her long enough to draw a blade and cut her throat. So she either trusted the man or had to act like she did, and she sure as hell had no reason to let her guard down around me and my brother. Surely even you've heard about the flap at the Phoenix Thursday night—and how we were to blame for it. Would she come to our hotel room, alone, after that? *Could* she, without her bosses knowin' of it? No, sir. She was just payin' a call on a customer, far as she knew. And that tells us who killed her."

"It does?" Bales said. Or maybe "It does." It was hard to tell if the question mark was there or not.

"Word is Stonewall's gone missin'," Gustav said with an offhanded dryness I had to admire. "So who'd be escortin' Big Bess to the Star? Who's got an arrangement with the hotel for comin' and goin' on the sly—and probably borrowin' passkeys whenever they need? Who'd love to see me and Otto strung up like piñatas on account of all the snoopin' we been doin'?"

"Ragsdale and Bock," I said. Not that we weren't all thinking it already, but *somebody* had to come out and say it.

Old Red nodded. "It was Ragsdale slit her throat."

"Why Ragsdale?" Bales asked. I liked the way he asked it, too. For the first time, it sounded as if he actually thought my brother might have a decent answer.

Too bad the answer he got was "Bess's butt."

Bales frowned, his eyes going into a twitchy squint, and Gustav pressed ahead fast before he could turn on his heel and leave.

"That caboose of hers had considerable size to it, you know. So much so that a feller like Gil Bock—a squat SOB with stubby arms and a tub gut—he couldn't even *reach* Bess's neck from behind, let alone cut it as clean and even as it was. Nah. It'd have to be a taller man with long arms. Bock was there, I'm sure of that. No one could hoist Bess's body onto the bed without help, and him and his partner ain't never any further apart than a pair of prairie oysters in the same sack. But it was Ragsdale did the killin'."

Bales snorted and shook his head in amazement. "For someone who never used to talk, you can pull some pretty good flimflam out of your ass. But you're forgetting one thing."

"If it's that 'Texas Jack' poppycock you're talkin' about, I ain't forgettin' it," my brother shot back. "I just ain't got to it yet, so thanks for bringin' it up. Now, here's the way you oughta look at it . . ."

He launched into a lecture just like his old deducifying self.

That old self being a smug little know-it-all, but I was pleased to see him nonetheless.

"Ragsdale and Bock wanted Bess's body found in our room—and soon, too, before we could cause 'em more trouble. So they whipped up that note knowin' Horace Cuff would bring it straight to you. As for the handwritin' matchin' my brother's, that don't mean diddly. You know Ragsdale and Bock got their grubby fingers in all kinds of nasty business around this town, and you can bet that includes forgery."

Bales shook his head again—though this time he looked less amazed than disappointed. "That's a mighty big stretch, Gus."

"Well, let me shorten it up for you, Milford." Gustav waggled a pointed finger at the staircase. "Our carpetbags are just down them steps, and in one or the other you'll find a new detectivin' tale my brother's been workin' on. He's got him a contract with Smythe & Associates Publishing, Limited, of New York City, you know."

As he spoke these last words, Old Red puffed himself up with a pride he's usually loath to admit merely for *my* benefit. He even got the full company name right.

On a better day, I would have smiled.

"So that story of his was just sittin' there in our room," he said, "waitin' for whoever might make use of it."

"As a sample of your brother's handwriting?"

"Yup."

"Which Ragsdale and Bock took the time to study and copy . . . after disemboweling Big Bess on your bed?"

Gustav blinked. "Something like that," he said with as much conviction as he could muster—which wasn't much.

Bales didn't seem much convinced, either. "Tell me again why Ragsdale and Bock would go to all this trouble on your account?"

"Tell him," Old Red said, and as always he turned to me when there was yarning to be done. "About the *real* Texas Jack."

I sketched it out quick as I could—and as vague, too, when it came to how we'd learned certain things. Bad enough that we had Big Bess hanging over us. We didn't need Stonewall up there as well. One of the two alone was enough to crush us.

To his credit, Bales went a bit green as I told him of the chippies who'd been disappearing, one a year around the anniversary of Adeline's death—and Jack the Ripper's spree in London. Some part of him seemed to accept that it couldn't all be lies.

"How'd you dig this up?" he asked when I was through.

I shrugged. "We tried."

Bales looked stung. "If something like that was really going on at the Phoenix, wouldn't Ike Rucker have noticed?"

"Feh," Old Red spat. "You know the man. Would he *want* to notice?"

Bales dropped his gaze, staring down at the floorboards so long he almost seemed to have fallen asleep standing up.

The man was thinking. At last.

When he looked at us again, his eyes were neither friendly nor hostile. Anguished uncertainty, that's what I saw there.

He was sitting on a fence—a wrought-iron one, hard and sharp and impossible to stay perched on long.

"You know all this sounds insane, don't you?" he said.

"Any more insane than a madman comin' back for a holiday in the very town he first killed in . . . with his kid brother along for the ride?" I replied. "Then leavin' bodies lyin' around even though the local law's been givin' 'em the evil eye?"

"Now *that* sounds crazy," Gustav threw in. "It only makes sense if we came back to find the real killer."

Bales combed chubby fingers through his close-cropped hair.

"I don't know what makes sense anymore . . ."

A door creaked open down on the first floor, and the muffled buzz of low-talking chatter drifted up the stairs.

"Marshal," Tommy called out, and after a few clomping steps his head poked up in the stairwell. "He's ready for you."

"I'll be down directly. I'm almost done here."

"Yessir."

Bales turned back to us as Tommy stomped away. "The coroner's downstairs. I've got to go."

"You'll think on what we told you?" Gustav said. "About what's been goin' on around here?"

"I don't know, Gus. I gave you a lot more than two minutes, and even after all that . . . everything you said . . . you couldn't *prove* anything."

"Oh. Noticed that, did you?"

Old Red sighed and slumped up against the bars. He'd been given one last chance to Holmes us out of our pickle—and he'd failed.

"You know, Milford," he said, "you might make a decent lawman yet."

Bales turned and headed down the stairs without another word.

As he went, Gustav trudged over to the cell's small, barred window and stared down at the street below. I joined him.

Together, we watched Bales walk out with the county coroner.

Who was the county sheriff, too, remember.

Ike Rucker.

They were walking west down Fort Street the last we saw of them. Headed for the Star.

The marshal's office was a narrow little affair across the street from the gold-domed county courthouse, and while we were watching Bales and Rucker stroll off together, I noticed a small crowd gathering on the courthouse lawn. It was mostly men milling about, maybe two dozen, but there were a few women, too, and a couple kids playing tag. It was hard to tell from a distance, but it looked like a strange mix of folks, a real gumbo. I could make out bowlers and bonnets and straw hats next to Stetsons and flat caps and even a lone sombrero.

One of the ladies spread out a blanket on the grass, and a dapper gent in tweed stretched out on it with a bottle of soda pop in his hand.

"Bit late in the day for a church picnic, ain't it?" I said.

"They ain't out for a picnic. They come for the *show*."

"The show? What sh—?"

That's when I noticed where those folks had chosen to gather: around the biggest tree in sight.

They were claiming front-row seats.

Sooner rather than later, they figured, there was going to be a hanging.

33

THE SHOW

Or, Darkness Falls, and the Odds We'll Live Out the Night Do Likewise

By the end of the afternoon, there were so many people clogging the streets around the courthouse you'd have thought the circus was coming to town. Indeed, the vendors who work the crowds at a parade weren't ones to miss this opportunity, and the vigilantes-in-waiting feasted on peanuts and popcorn and Dr Pepper while waiting to see justice done.

And the pushcart men weren't the only ones hawking their wares. Even from a distance, it was easy to pick out a Bible-brandishing Brother Landrigan gliding through the throng, eyes blazing like hellfire. I spied Horace Cuff, too, the lanky Englishman marching behind Landrigan so stiff-spined he could've been a soldier on review—a platoon of one. He eventually peeled himself from Landrigan's coattails, though, pausing to pull out a notebook and interview local notables on hand for the evening's entertainment.

Mortimer Krieger was there to record the proceedings for posterity as well, setting up a tripod-mounted camera atop the boxy, hard-topped wagon he'd arrived in. The camera, I couldn't help but notice, was trained on the towering oak that seemed to be the maypole around which this grim fandango was being danced.

The men calling the tune were there for a time, too. Pete Ragsdale and Gil Bock spent nearly an hour strutting around the town square, mostly mingling with the cowhands who'd started drifting in as (I assumed) word spread to the surrounding ranches. I could see Ragsdale slapping backs, passing out flasks, waving a pointed finger at the very jailhouse window at which I stood. Bock just drifted along beside him, utterly impassive but for one fleeting moment—he must've spotted me watching, for he raised a hand and flipped me a pudgy little bird.

The cowboys, meanwhile, threw looks our way that went from dirty to filthy to (the more they partook from Ragsdale's flasks) unprintable. They'd degraded Big Bess in a thousand ways, these dirty-faced boys, yet now they fancied themselves her champions—and avengers. What Bales and his buddies had been playacting at a couple nights before, these yahoos would gladly do for real.

I spotted Freckles the Kid, the itchy-fingered little so-and-so from the Lucky Seven, among them. My brother's old pal Suicide Cheney, too. If Suicide was inclined to talk sense to anybody, it didn't show, for he kept throwing back his head with flask in hand like the other punchers. I couldn't really blame the man. Try to defend us once the rush came, and he'd just live up to his name.

All these observations I made alone, for not two minutes after Marshal Bales left the jail, Old Red was asleep on the bunk. It didn't surprise me, exactly—he was going on thirty-six hours without a wink. Yet I found the timing difficult to fathom.

Sleeping through a lynching would be hard enough. But your own . . . ?

As the light of day faded, the crowd's restlessness grew. The gestures got bigger, the milling more frenzied, the noise louder. Whether they knew it outright or not—could admit it if it was put to them—the people gathered outside were waiting for the dark.

It was almost upon us.

Gustav stirred at last.

"I wouldn't think an up-and-comin' young city like San Marcos would tolerate lynchings on the courthouse lawn," I said as he joined me at the window. "Ain't good for their image."

"Neither are mutilated whores," Old Red pointed out. "Kill one in a back alley, whoop-di-do. Do God-only-knows with four others, that's fine, too, long as you do it quiet. But all that?" He nodded down at the roiling chaos below. "That's what you get when you're gaudy about it."

"What they got in mind ain't exactly subtle."

Gustav gave a grunt of agreement.

"So," he said, "what'd I miss?"

I filled him in as the sky outside went from amber-orange to ashy gray to black. Before I was done, Ragsdale and Bock swaggered from the square, satisfied, I suppose, that the seeds they'd planted would soon bear fruit. And Mr. Krieger, having lost the light, was packing up his camera gear. He could always come back in the morning . . . provided no one had cut us down yet.

Yet despite these departures, the swarm kept swelling. People were arriving on horseback, in surreys and wagons, on foot—every which way but hot-air balloon. It was like the proverbial moths to the flame only backward, the irresistible enticement now being the anonymity of encroaching darkness.

"Y'know, we oughta be proud," I told my brother. "Something finally brought the town folk and the county folk together . . . and it's us!"

Old Red "Feh"ed me.

"They ain't as far apart as they like to think," he said. "Overalls or frock coats, it don't matter. Hell, loincloths or crowns. Underneath the wrappin', people are all the same."

"Oh? I can name one feller who ain't—and I betcha he's down there this very moment."

"The killer, you mean?" Gustav shook his head. "He ain't so different. Everybody likes 'em a little blood. Him just a bit more than's polite."

"My word," I marveled. "That is without a doubt the sourest thing I ever heard you say, and you've said some doozies."

Old Red jerked his chin at the crowd below. "If that's the way we're gonna go, don't you think I'm entitled?"

"Well, I can see how gettin' lynched might bring out the cynic in a man," I conceded, "but I've always believed it biases the judgment to theorize before you have all the facts."

Gustav gave me that special glower he reserves for the rare occasions on which I quote Holmes back to him.

I smiled. "We ain't hung yet."

Not that I really gave us a snowflake's chance in hell, let alone a whole snowball's. But my brother was such a black cloud I couldn't help but play the little ray of sunshine.

Then, with the suddenness of lightning or the flare of a photographer's flash powder, the whole town square lit up. And stayed lit.

The streetlamps had all been switched on at once.

The swiftness of it left the crowd speechless, stunned, and looking down from above I saw a sea of open mouths and blinking eyes— hundreds of people rudely shaken awake from the same dream.

For a second, stretching out interminably into two, I allowed myself the hope that the mob-spell had been broken. In the stark white glare of the lamps, I thought, the men and women below might look upon each other, see themselves, and feel shame.

Sometimes you're a little ray of sunshine.

Sometimes you're just a fool.

I found out which I was pretty quick.

A chorus of voices rose up out of the silence, and though the words themselves I couldn't pick out, the tune I recognized. It was the hymn "Lead, Kindly Light," and I knew who was doing the crooning before I even spotted them.

Brother Landrigan and his choir had laid claim to the courthouse steps.

They soon had competition for the crowd's attention, though. The cowboys congregating along the northern edge of the lawn—the side closest to the jail—responded with a sort of hymn of their own: the trail version of "Buffalo Gals." And by "trail version," I mean the one with lyrics that'd make a sailor swoon. Suffice it to say, the young ladies being serenaded ("San Marcos gals," that night) weren't being asked to *dance* by the light of the moon.

As the church choir and the ranch hands battled for the mob's ear—and soul, Brother Landrigan would no doubt say—cackling laughter burst out here and there around the square, followed by a murmur of voices that quickly built back up to a roar. Soon enough, the carnival mood had returned full force, and all was as it had been before. The streetlamps had changed nothing, except to corral the darkness in spastic shadows that were all the blacker and sharper-edged for the harshness of the unnatural light that made them.

"God damn it," Old Red muttered, and when I followed his gaze I noticed two familiar figures lurking at the eastern edge of the bedlam.

Lottie and Bob were back in town.

"At least they had the good sense to leave Squirrel Tooth at home," I said.

"I *hope* that's where she is. I wish that's where they were, too."

Gustav cursed again.

Hoping and wishing never had done much good, in his experience.

The cowboys' serenade had long since disintegrated into guffaws, huzzahs, and wild, unintelligible howls, and now the choir's "Lead, Kindly Light" faded away, too. Brother Landrigan stayed where he was atop the steps, though, launching into pop-eyed writhing that could mean only one thing: He'd converted the courthouse facade into a pulpit.

Again and again, he pointed a wagging finger toward the north. At us.

"What do you think he's callin' us?" I asked my brother. "'Snakes' or 'serpents'?"

Old Red didn't answer.

"'Snakes' would get more of a rise out of folks. They got them things all over down here. 'Serpents,' though . . . it sounds more biblical-like, wouldn't you say?"

Gustav did not say. Anything. He just stared down at the preacher as if hypnotized.

"Brother," I said, and the somber tone of my voice was enough to break the spell, pull Old Red's eyes away from Landrigan. "When you went up to the front of the church this morning. Repented, saved your soul, whatever you wanna call it. Was that a bluff or not?"

Gustav pondered on that a moment, then shrugged. "Can it be both?"

Before I could reply—with a firm "No"—three loud raps sounded out downstairs.

Someone was knocking on the marshal's front door.

My brother and I froze, listening intently to muffled voices, the creaking of hinges, a sudden burst of sound as the din from outside came crashing into the office. Then the door slammed shut, and there was quiet again . . . for all of three seconds.

"Hey, give that back!" we heard Tommy shout.

"Butt out, kid," someone snarled—a someone who was stomping up the stairs to the cells. "It's time the grown-ups took over here."

Ike Rucker appeared at the top of the steps. His right hand was clutching a large metal ring with two keys on it.

"Alright, boys," he said. "You're comin' with me."

Tommy came slinking up the stairs behind him.

"I can't let you do that, Sheriff. Marshal Bales told me not to—"

"Shut up, kid," Rucker said, and he walked over to our cell and tried one of the keys on the lock.

It worked.

"Let's go." Rucker swung the door open, then took two steps back and drew his .45. "Move."

Gustav didn't move. I didn't move.

Tommy just watched from the top of the stairs.

"Go where?" I asked.

"To the county lockup," Rucker said. "You'll be safer there."

"You dirty son of a bitch," Old Red snarled.

"What's the matter?" I asked him.

My brother didn't take his eyes off Rucker.

"Where do you think the county lockup *is*, Otto?"

"I don't know. I suppose it must be . . . awww, hell no."

"Hell yes," Gustav said.

Rucker's jail was in the county courthouse.

Old Red had summed it up beautifully, so I borrowed his words.

"You dirty son of a bitch."

"You can't take them out there," Tommy said, still not getting it. "That crowd'll string 'em up for sure."

"You just let me worry about that," Rucker replied, and he flashed me and Gustav a toothy grin.

He wasn't worried about any lynching.

He was counting on one.

34

LAW AND DISORDER

Or, Tommy Uses His Noodle, and Our Troubles with Rucker Come to a Head

Staring down the barrel of a six-gun is no fun, I assure you. On the other hand, letting Rucker walk us out of that jail? That would have been sticking our heads in a cannon . . . with a lit fuse.

So it wasn't as hard as you might think to just stand there when the sheriff snapped out another "Move!"

"Why would we set foot outta this cage knowin' what's gonna happen to us out there?" I asked.

"Because you *don't* know what's gonna happen out there. Whereas this is a dead certainty."

For what felt like the thousandth time that week, a Colt was pointed at my forehead. I was beginning to think I had a bull's-eye pinned up there.

"If you don't do as I say," Rucker growled, "I'm gonna paint the wall behind you with your brains."

Yet still Gustav and I didn't move—except, in my brother's case, to shake his head in disgusted wonderment.

"Here you are cleanin' up after your pals Ragsdale and Bock, but do you even know what they've been up to? The things they've done?"

"Look," Rucker said, "if you think I ain't got the eggs to pull this trigger, just take a peek at that crowd outside. No one around here's gonna complain if I put lead through both your heads."

"Milford Bales might," Old Red said.

Rucker chuckled. "I ain't scared of no barbers. And guess what—Bales ain't around anyway, is he? He don't even know what's happenin' here. Instead of bein' on hand for the damned *riot*, he had to go off 'investigatin'.'"

The sheriff snorted to show what he thought of lawmen who'd waste their time on such useless pursuits.

"I'm here," Tommy said.

Rucker didn't even bother looking back at him.

"And a very nice doormat you make, too," he said.

"But the marshal told me—"

"And now the *sheriff* is telling you something else. So do yourself a favor and run home to mama."

"But—"

"This conversation is done, you understand?" Rucker thumbed back the hammer on his .45 just in case anyone didn't. "You two. Out. Now."

Gustav and I looked at each other.

Would Rucker really gun us down in cold blood?

Dear Lord, yes.

We put our hands up and started for the stairs, Old Red in the lead.

"So," I said to Rucker as he swiveled to keep his sights squarely on my skull, "you already tell the boys out front we're comin', or is this gonna be more of a surprise party?"

"Shut up," Rucker said.

Tommy scuttled out of the way as we neared the top of the staircase, and Old Red slowed to look him in the eye.

"You let him do this, Tommy, our blood's gonna be on *your* hands, too."

"He'll learn to live with it," Rucker said. "Anyway, he's got his own blood to worry about. You get me, kid?"

He most certainly did. In more ways than one.

"What the hell?" I heard Rucker snarl just as I started down the stairs.

I whirled around to find Tommy snatching off the man's hat.

"Are you cra—?"

The sheriff got no further before the butt of Tommy's gun came down atop his head. He dropped his Colt (which, by a happy miracle, did not go off), stumbled forward a half step, and toppled to the floor.

"I'm sorry I'm sorry I'm sorry!" Tommy jabbered as the sheriff fell. "You didn't give me any choice!"

Rucker was in no condition to accept apologies. He just lay there facedown on the floorboards.

"Nicely done, Deputy! See how much difference that hat trick makes?" I said. "Only now you mighta hit him *too* hard." I crouched next to Rucker and wrapped a hand around his wrist. "Yup. No pulse."

"What?" Tommy bawled.

"I think you killed him."

"Oh, God!"

Tommy knelt down to check for himself.

"I sure am sorry," I said, "but you gotta be extry careful with the ol' gun butt to the noodle."

"Hey," Tommy said, finally noticing that Rucker wasn't behaving much like a corpse, what with him breathing and having a heartbeat and all.

That's when my brother—who'd slipped behind the deputy and picked up Rucker's Colt—whipped off Tommy's hat and very carefully but very firmly gave him the ol' gun butt to the noodle.

Tommy pitched forward, crossing Rucker like a *t*.

I checked to make sure *he* was breathing, then gave the young man a pat on the back. "Like I said, Tommy . . . I sure am sorry."

Gustav rubbed the back of his head. "I ain't."

Within a minute, we had the lawmen locked up in our old cell. (We gave Tommy the bunk, of course. Rucker got the floor. Still face-down, too.) Then we hurried downstairs, retrieved our holsters and carpetbags from atop the marshal's desk, made sure the front door was locked, and headed past the staircase praying there was another way out.

There was: a back door at the far end of a dusty storeroom. We hurried toward it—then froze side by side as I reached out for the knob.

"So . . . ," I said.

Gustav nodded slowly. "Yeah. So . . ."

So where the hell were we going?

So what the hell could we do?

So, in a nutshell . . . *what the hell?*

I looked at my brother.

He looked at me.

I said nothing.

He said nothing.

It was like we were in a staring contest, only the object wasn't forcing the other fellow to blink. It was forcing him to make a decision.

Which had never been necessary before. Gustav led, I followed, that had always been the way of things.

It would be now, too, I decided . . . whether my brother would lead or not.

What would Old Red Amlingmeyer do? I asked myself. Not the Old Red before me—the one so unsure of himself he'd look to *me* for guidance.

No, it was the other one I was thinking of. The old Old Red. The one I'd been writing about. The stubborn, ornery, single-minded, Sherlock Holmes–worshipping *hero.*

Then I knew. I knew, and I hated it—but the old Old Red always got his way.

"Alright, fine—if you insist," I said. "We pay a call on Ragsdale and Bock."

"It's the only way," Gustav said so firm and clear you'd never have known he hadn't insisted at all. Why, he almost sounded like Old Red Amlingmeyer. "They're up to their eyeballs in this thing, that we know. So if we only get one more shot, it oughta be at them." He threw his carpetbag aside. "May as well leave these here. We're gonna have to do us some serious skulkin', and they'd just draw attention."

"Makes sense." I tossed my own bag next to his. "You ready?"

"Are you kiddin'?"

"Yeah. Me, neither."

I opened the door. Just a crack at first, so as to peek out at the alleyway behind the marshal's office. My brother pushed in beside me to take a look, too.

It was dark back there but not pitch black, and after a moment we were satisfied no one was outside to ambush us. So out we slinked, and from there we skulked.

For all of twenty feet. We were slipping between two of the buildings across the alley, making for a quiet cross-street to the north, when a shape appeared up ahead. And when I say "a shape," I don't mean a triangle or an octagon. This was the shape of a man—and another such shape quickly loomed up behind it.

Gustav and I pressed ourselves into the shadows, backs literally to the wall.

The shapes started toward us, one large, one small. They seemed to be slightly crouched, and what little light there was, they avoided.

They were skulking, too.

"You sure the jail'sh thish way?" the big one "whispered" not half as quiet as he seemed to think.

"Sure I'm sure," his runty buddy replied. "If there'sh a back way in, we'll fetch along the resht of the boysh."

"And the rope," the big one giggled, and he tripped over his own feet and stumbled into his pal's back.

"Jeshush, Kettle-Belly! You can't shneak no better than a three-legged elephant."

Kettle-Belly laughed.

They were soused, that much was plain, and they hadn't spotted us, though that wouldn't last long. Even with the two of them seeing double. They were so close now, in fact, we couldn't even turn tail without revealing ourselves.

We could either fight—and give ourselves away to god only knew who else—or we could . . . something else.

"Hey," Kettle-Belly said, peering down the alley toward us. "Who'sh that?"

Something else finally came to mind.

"It'sh no good, fellersh," I said, lurching out of the darkness. "If you're aimin' to go in the back way, you can forget it. I jusht tried myshelf, and that weashel Balesh hash a deputy on the back door with a damned shotgun."

"Really?" the little fellow asked.

As I drew closer, the shapes took on some definition, and I saw just what I'd expected—two men wearing cowboy-style denims and boots and Stetsons.

And gun belts, of course.

"Really," I told them.

"Awww, heck," Kettle-Belly groaned, and he stood up straight—or as straight as he could in his state—and started staggering back up the alley.

His friend reluctantly turned to go with him, then stopped and looked back at me.

"*Really?*"

I threw him a big, swaying, sham-drunk shrug. "Why would I lie?"

The cowboy grunted and set off after his compadre.

"Drunk *and* stupid," I said as my brother stepped from the shadows. "Our luck's finally turnin' around."

Gustav scooted past me, moving quick toward the end of the alley.

"We're gonna need more than dumb luck to do what we gotta tonight."

Before setting off after him, I patted myself on the back. Who else was going to do it?

Over the next few minutes, we cashed in a heap more of our dumb luck. There was a steady trickle of riders and wagons and folks on foot headed for the town square, but time and time again we managed to find cover before anyone spotted us.

Finally, after ducking into what seemed like every doorway and alley San Marcos had to offer, we reached Ragsdale and Bock's wallpaper shop. A light glowed in one of the windows on the second floor. The rest of the store was dark.

The front door was unlocked, and Gustav and I slipped inside. The only illumination to navigate by was a dull gray glow through the front windows and a little yellow line of light up high in the back. Between them was a long stretch of nothing we had to shuffle through blind.

While my brother moved so silently I could only take it on faith he was still there at all, I walked into a display case, knocked over what I assume was a sample book, and set the floorboards to squeaking like an old rocking chair rolling over a mouse. If there'd been a bucket of marbles and a bass drum on the premises, I surely would've upended the former over the latter one way or another.

After every stumble and bump, I'd stop and listen for noises from upstairs—voices, footfalls, the cocking of guns, the sharpening of knives, the bubbling of boiling oil—but I heard not a thing . . . until *I* got started moving again.

After what seemed like a journey on par with Lewis and Clark's, I made it upstairs to that bar of light, and I could make out the dim outline of Gustav's boot toes beside it.

It was the glow of lamplight under a door.

We were just outside Ragsdale and Bock's office.

"Shall we?" my brother whispered.

"Let's."

My Bulldog was already in my right hand. My left groped down and found the doorknob.

I flung the door open, and Old Red and I charged through.

"Make a move and you're dead!" I hollered.

I needn't have bothered. Ragsdale and Bock were there, alright, but they weren't going to be doing any moving. Not till someone came to haul them off, anyway.

They were both dead already.

35

THE THING

Or, Gustav Tries One Last Deduction, and It's Full of Holes

A wispy-thin haze of smoke floated over the room. Through it, I saw what could have been the office of your average small-town attorney or registrar of deeds.

Filing cabinets and gas lamps along the walls. Pictures and calendars nailed up willy-nilly. A worn-out rug on the floor. A couple desks. A few chairs.

Two cadavers.

Pete Ragsdale's lanky body was hunched over one of the desks, facedown in a pool of blood. Gil Bock lay on the floor nearby, both his broad belly and his wide-open eyes pointed at the door I'd just come busting through. He had three gunshot wounds I could see— one to the right shoulder, one that clipped off most of his left ear, and another that put a hole the size of a dime just above his right eye.

"I'll be damned," my brother muttered.

Me, I didn't know whether to curse or applaud. I'd weep no tears for Ragsdale and Bock, that was for sure. Though it was them we'd been counting on to clear us . . . somehow. Now we just had two more murders to swing for.

"I'll be damned," Old Red said again.

He started toward the bodies slowly, almost reverently, like a pilgrim approaching some holy shrine. As he moved, he tilted back his head and sucked in a long, deep sniff.

I took a smell myself, catching both the acrid scorch of burnt gunpowder and the earthier odors that linger when the soul departs and the bowels unclench.

When Gustav reached Ragsdale, he sent a lone finger gliding through the red ooze atop the man's desk. He stared down at the stain on his fingertip a moment, then smeared it with his thumb.

"You know, I was beginnin' to think I'd dreamed the son of a bitch up. That it was just Ragsdale and Bock all along. But this was *him*. We smoked him out of his hole after all."

"Just in time, too. You been sayin' from the beginning we ain't got no new trail to follow. No fresh data. But now?" I jerked my chin at the bodies. "That's pretty damn fresh."

Old Red nodded. "We didn't miss him by half an hour."

"Well, this is it, then. It's just me and you and a roomful of clues. If the Method's ever gonna clear this mess up, now's the time."

"Yeah," Gustav said. *"If . . ."*

And he just stood there not moving, not acting. Afraid to try. There'd be no excuses now. Either he and Mr. Holmes could do it or they couldn't.

Gentle coaxing, words of wisdom—it all eluded me just then. A kick in the ass, though? That'd be easy.

So I gave him one. Literally.

Not hard, mind you. Just the side of an ankle to the back of the pants. Enough to spin my brother around eyes aflame.

"What the hell you waitin' for?" I said. "Deducify!"

Old Red glared at me like he was thinking of adding another carcass to the pile.

"Feh!" he spat.

Then he turned away and got to work.

He started with Ragsdale. The man was slumped forward but still seated, one arm stretched out over the desk, the other tight to his side. He hadn't been wearing his lid, for once—his top hat, like his partner's, had been placed just-so on the desktop.

Gustav got a fistful of straw yellow hair and lifted up the head.

Even painted red with blood, the expression on Ragsdale's face was unmistakable. He'd died as he had lived: sneering. I almost expected him to tell me to go fudge myself.

There was a hole in his forehead dead center, directly above his long nose. Around the wound was a circle of flaky black.

"Muzzle was close," Old Red mumbled. "Little gun, though, or the back of his head woulda been blowed out. A .22, I'd . . . hel-lo."

Something on Ragsdale's right cheek sparkled dully in the gaslight. Gustav bent in close, then pinched the little whatever-it-was and pulled.

It wasn't just on Ragsdale's face. It was *in* it. Embedded. Once my brother slid it out, he held it up to the light.

It was a sliver of glass, dagger-ended like an icicle, about two inches long.

Old Red and I both looked down at the desktop.

"Where'd that thing come from?" I said. "Ain't nothin' glass on the desk there."

"Not now, there ain't." Gustav deposited the little shard in a shirt pocket, then lowered Ragsdale's face with a gentleness the SOB never earned in life. "Whatever it was, the killer took it."

He moved over to Bock's body and knelt down beside it. He didn't stay there long, though.

"Yeah, it's like I figured. Three shots, no powder burn." He stood up. "Bock died second."

There were chairs in front of the desks, and my brother walked over to the one facing Ragsdale and plopped himself down on it.

"I figure it like this," he said. "The killer was sittin' here, talking to Ragsdale and Bock. About us, most likely. Congratulatin' themselves on gettin' us out of the way so smooth. Then the feller seated here, he hands something to Ragsdale. Something made of glass."

Old Red acted the moment out, leaning forward and stretching his left arm toward Ragsdale's body.

"Ragsdale takes it in hand, the two men are face-to-face, close, and . . ."

Gustav whipped up his right hand, the forefinger and thumb jutting out to form a gun in the manner familiar to little boys everywhere.

"*Blam*. One shot, and Ragsdale's dead. But Bock, he's harder. The man's on the go, runnin' for the door or reachin' for a gun of his own. So it takes two shots to put him on the floor, and a third to the head to finish him. Then it's time to tidy up."

My brother stood and stepped up beside the desk again.

"He lifts Ragsdale, and he takes the . . ." Old Red shrugged. "Thing. Only Ragsdale, he'd pitched forward onto it, broke part off, and the killer don't notice. He's in a hurry, and the *thing* is probably drippin' with blood. A little sliver'd be easy to overlook. So off he runs, and twenty-some minutes later, in *we* come. Then . . ."

He spread out his hands and shrugged.

Then . . . here we are. Making guesses.

I held out a hand. "Lemme see that sliver."

Gustav pulled it from his pocket and dropped it into my palm.

The glass was flat and smooth and thin. Most of it was stained red with blood, but the wider end—the part that hadn't been buried in Ragsdale's flesh—was clear as air.

I pictured everything it could have come from. Spectacles, a drinking glass, a whiskey bottle, a hand mirror, even a magnifying lens of the sort Mr. Holmes used to favor. None fit. The glass was too even, too transparent, not warped or tinted in any way.

I handed it back to my brother.

"Yup," I said. "That's glass, alright."

I do what I can in the deducifying department. Which isn't much.

Gustav sighed and held the little shard up again, squinting at it with one eye. Then his other eye popped open, and suddenly he wasn't looking *at* the glass. He was looking *through* it.

He lowered the sliver and walked to the wall. There were pictures all around—Andrew Jackson and Grover Cleveland and Custer's Last Stand and a sultan's harem of lovelies blessed with ample flesh and decidedly unample attire to cover it.

Yet one section of the wall was even more bare than those painted ladies. It jutted up into the clutter maybe eighteen inches across and three feet high. No battle scenes, no presidents, no pulchritude. Just gaudy red paisley wallpaper.

Old Red stopped before the blank spot and ran a hand down the wall.

"Hole . . . hole . . . hole . . . hole," he said.

I squinted at the wallpaper.

"Bullet holes?"

"Nope. Nails." Gustav waved me over and pointed to a photograph hanging nearby. "What's that say on there?"

It was a group portrait of a dozen grinning men in baseball uniforms—and two very familiar gents in top hats and overcoats.

"Looks like Ragsdale and Bock sponsored a local team. 'San Marcos Gamecocks,' it says on their jerseys."

There was a date on the photograph, too, written in by the photographer: April 1892.

Old Red pointed at another framed photo hanging nearby. "How about that?"

Again, it was a group picture, except now the men (much the same bunch as before, I noted) were toting tubas and trombones and such instead of gloves and bats. They all wore frilly, military-style uniforms except for the bandleaders, who were attired—as always—in long frock coats and black top hats.

This time, the handwritten date along the bottom read "July 4, 1893," and the name of the outfit was printed in fat letters on the side of a bass drum. I had to angle my head to the side to read it, as the glow from the nearest gaslight was throwing a glare across the photograph.

"'The Marching Beavers,'" I said. "Them two sure did rub the townsfolks' faces in . . . what is it?"

My brother had stepped up so close to the photo he nearly stubbed his toes against the wall.

"Hel-lo," he whispered.

He tapped a fingernail against the smooth glass covering the picture.

"It was one of the Marchin' Beavers?" I said, craning my neck to see who he was pointing at.

Gustav shook his head slowly, his expression going slack, distracted, like he was doing sums in his head.

"It ain't the Marchin' Beavers that are important," he said. "It's the photo."

"Well, the photo's *of* the Marchin' Beavers, ain't it?"

"I said forget the damn Beavers! I'm talkin' about the photo!" My brother pointed at the blank spot before us, giving each little hole in the wall its own jab. "And that one, and that one, and that one, and that one. One-two-three-*four*. The one that was on the desk, too—the *thing*. But most of all, I'm talkin' about the man who took 'em."

"You mean the man who *took 'em*?" I pantomimed pressing a camera button with my thumb. "Or the man who *took 'em*?" I swiped an imaginary picture off the wall and tucked it under my jacket.

"Good God, Otto—don't you see how it all fits together?" Gustav said. "They're the same man."

36

MY CONSTITUTIONAL

Or, A Quiet Evening Stroll Turns into a (Search) Party

We ain't got no choice," Gustav said.

"I know."

"Killin' Ragsdale and Bock, collectin' them pictures—he's tyin' up loose ends."

"I know."

"Whatever evidence there is to find, it's gonna be gone forever lickity-split."

"I know."

"If one or the other of us don't get over there quick—"

"Oh, my God! I know I know I know! You can shut up about it now!"

My brother pressed his lips together tight.

For a few seconds.

Then—

"We ain't got no choice."

I sighed.

"I know."

It wasn't me he was trying to convince. It was himself. And who could blame him, really? It's not easy for a sane man to talk himself into suicide.

"So?" I said, turning this way and that. I was wearing Bock's shirt, tie, vest, frock coat, and top hat. His pants I couldn't work with: They barely reached past my knees, and Ragsdale's were too tight around the waist. So I was stuck with my own, though they didn't match the rest of the suit. My hair and eyebrows were slick with thick-slathered black shoe polish retrieved from a drawer in Bock's desk.

Old Red gave me a look that drained the few drops of confidence I had in me.

"Well," he said, "don't stand under any streetlamps."

"I wasn't plannin' on it."

I started toward the office door.

"You remember how to get there?" Gustav asked.

"More or less. Don't worry—I won't stop anyone to ask for directions."

"Alright, then. See ya there."

I paused in the doorway and looked back at my brother. This might be the last time I'd lay eyes on him, and I meant to leave with a few well-chosen words of parting.

They didn't come. Seeing Ragsdale and Bock stretched out in their soiled underthings sucked the sentiment right out of me.

Old Red was pulling on Ragsdale's coat, and it fit him like a glove . . . a huge, baggy, shapeless one draped over a midget's pinky.

"Don't stand under any streetlamps," I said.

"Ha," my brother grunted.

I left.

A moment later, I was back on the streets of San Marcos. They were deserted but for the occasional stragglers late for the lynching on the courthouse lawn. I passed them with head high and gait steady. No skulking for me, an upright citizen taking his evening constitutional.

Gustav and I had to get halfway across town. Skulking would get us killed, we figured. Better to be individuals with nothing to hide than a pair creeping around like rats in the shadows. Maybe.

When I hit Austin Street, I figured I was home free. It was the last major avenue leading down to the courthouse, and once I was across I'd have but a quarter mile of narrower, darker, tree-lined lanes between me and my destination.

I moseyed out into the street whistling "Ta-ra-ra Boom-de-ay."

I didn't even make it to the first "boom."

A howl went up to the south like the roar of some monstrous beast, and when I turned that way I saw a crowd surging up the thoroughfare. As it approached, little rivulets of grim-faced men spilled off down side streets. Spreading out for a search.

The lynch mob had discovered it had no one to lynch . . . and there I was frozen in the street before it. Under a streetlamp, no less.

Run, and I'd be a coon with a hundred hounds on its tail. So I stood my ground and prayed anyone in the crowd I actually knew was off searching to the south, east, or west.

A trickle of sweat and shoe polish ran down the back of my neck.

"What's going on?" I called out when the throng was within hailing range.

"Jailbreak!" a burly merchant type barked back. He was carrying a cheap revolver of the sort one orders from Montgomery Ward, and this, in his mind at least, made him the leader. "Have you seen two men come this way? Little fellow and a big one? Red hair?"

I considered—for all of one second—pointing north up Austin and trying a "They went that way." Best not to call attention to myself, though, even for a moment.

"Haven't seen a soul," I said.

The merchant scowled—and immediately took to eyeballing the dark doorways and alleys further up the street.

The first wave of vigilantes swept past me.

A group broke off and headed east, the way I needed to go. So I mingled in and joined the search for myself.

As I marched alongside my new comrades, I noticed one—a wobbly-woozy man in a white seersucker suit—squinting at my clothes. I could only assume something about my duds struck him as familiar. It'd be just my luck to end up next to Ragsdale's dentist or Bock's cousin Buck.

A distraction was in order.

"What'd these desperadoes we're after do, anyway?" I said.

The man blinked, dragged his droopy-lidded gaze from my suit to my face, blinked again, then gave me a lopsided smile. "Damned if I know, but when we find 'em—whoooooooeeeee!"

"They murdered a whore," someone said. "Cut her up something awful, I heard."

I half-turned my head and caught sight of Mr. B, the barkeeper Old Red and I traded gossip with our first day in town, tramping along behind me.

See what I mean about my luck?

"That's terrible," I muttered.

I pointed my eyes straight ahead and did my best to keep them there.

"Hey," the seersucker man said. "Hey, let me ask you something."

I slipped my right hand under my coat. The fingertips brushed against the hard leather of my shoulder holster.

"Yeah?"

The man waved a floppy hand at the voluminous waistcoat covering my not-quite-so-voluminous waist. "Is that houndstooth?"

"Uhhh . . . yeah."

The man nodded and grinned again. "Nice," he said. "Who's your tailor?"

When I told him it was no one local, I'd bought the suit in Chicago, he looked genuinely disappointed. I couldn't have been more relieved.

Over the next few minutes, our party shrank considerably, splintering further at every intersection, and I managed to separate myself from Mr. B. Yet the fellow I *really* wanted to see again had yet to appear.

Just as I reached Comal and Fredericksburg streets, a man stepped up beside me and matched his pace to mine. "Maybe we oughta go door to door," he said. "Warn folks there's killers on the loose."

"Good idea," I said, and I had to fight back a smile as I said it.

The voice I recognized. The face I almost didn't.

When I looked over at my brother, I saw that his mustache was gone.

I tapped a finger against my upper lip.

"Wallpaper scissors and soap," Old Red whispered.

"Ouch."

"You ain't kiddin'." Then, louder, "Why don't you and me start over there?"

We veered away from the last six or seven searchers, headed toward the home of Mr. Mortimer Krieger.

Mr. Mortimer Krieger, who was the only professional photographer and framer in San Marcos.

Mr. Mortimer Krieger, who had a sample of my handwriting thanks to the membership forms I'd filled out for his library.

Mr. Mortimer Krieger, who knew our address in town thanks to those same forms.

Mr. Mortimer Krieger, who could copy Jack the Ripper's writing style because he had a book full of Saucy Jack's letters.

Mr. Mortimer Krieger, who'd kept an eye on us in church while Ragsdale and Bock did their dirty work at the Star.

Mr. Mortimer Krieger, who'd done away with Ragsdale and Bock to keep his secret safe.

Mr. Mortimer Krieger, who was a homicidal maniac.

Or so my brother had deduced, all from a blank space on the wall and a sliver of glass. Proving any of it would be something else entirely. Which was why we'd risked everything to get to Krieger's mansion.

It was our last hope—and our last stand, too.

37

A DOZEN LUCIFERS

Or, Old Red Sheds New Light on Things, and I Make an Explosive Discovery

This much my brother and I knew: Knocking on the door hat in hand would *not* be the best way into the Krieger household.

"Fancy place like this," Gustav murmured as we passed through the gate into the yard, "maybe there's a coal chute."

"I'm too big."

We peeked back to make sure none of our fellow posse members were looking our way, then darted around the side of the house.

"Storm cellar?" my brother said.

"I don't see one."

We passed a coal chute half-hidden between two rose bushes.

"*I'm too big*," I said before Old Red could point it out.

"Servants' entrance, then."

We circled around toward the back door—and nearly ran smack into Mortimer Krieger carrying a crate out to his photography wagon.

As we hopped back the way we'd just come, a dozen reinforcements from the courthouse crowd turned onto the block.

"*Coal chute.*"

"I'm too big," I said, "but what the hell."

We did a hunchbacked waddle-scoot to a small wooden flap low to the ground along the side of the house. We both stripped off our bulky overclothes as we went: This was going to be a tight squeeze.

After a little fiddling, Gustav got the flap open, and we peered in at . . . nothing. It was so dark inside, we couldn't even see the chute itself. I had to stretch my hand into the void and feel the ramp just to reassure myself it was even there.

"You first," I whispered.

My brother didn't argue. We could hear more voices from the street now, and one of them was saying, "I'll go tell Krieger."

Old Red shoved his legs down the chute, wriggled for a moment, then slid into oblivion. I didn't wait for any signal to follow. I just stuffed our coats and hats in after him, then dove in headfirst.

There was only one problem.

I was too big.

Head, shoulders, and chest passed through just fine, but my midsection—alright, my *gut*—got jammed, leaving my legs jutting out betwixt the bushes.

I writhed. I squirmed. I struggled. Yet there I stayed, stuck half in, half out of the house like the cork in a whiskey bottle.

I heard a rusty creak behind me, then footsteps. Someone had come through the gate and was approaching the front porch.

Hands clamped onto me tight.

By the wrists, fortunately, rather than the ankles. My brother had climbed back up the chute and was trying to yank me down.

"For chrissakes," he hissed, "suck in your blubber."

I sucked, Gustav tugged, and a second later we were both sliding down into the coal bin.

Or at least I assumed it was the coal bin. I still couldn't see a thing, and it sure wasn't lumps of coal I'd landed on. It was my brother.

"Get offa me," he whispered hoarsely.

"Hold on."

We lay still, listening for the inevitable "They're over here!" and "Anyone know how to tie a noose?"

Instead we heard muffled knocking, footsteps on the floorboards, the low burble of distant talk.

"I'm turnin' to jelly down here," Gustav groaned.

"Hush."

The conversation faded away fast. Then the door closed and more footsteps click-clattered overhead. They were measured steps—unhurried, unpanicked.

"I think we're alright," I said.

"Speak for yourself," my brother wheezed.

I rolled off him onto what felt like a dirt floor.

"You got any lucifers?"

Old Red drew in a deep breath before answering.

"I did. I just hope they ain't squashed to a pulp like most of *me*."

A moment later, a match flared to life.

The bin we'd landed in, I now saw, was empty but for our borrowed coats and squashed-flat top hats. Nearby, a furnace gleamed dully in the dim light. Gustav knelt down beside it and tried to open the little door on the side, but it was rusted shut.

"Hel-lo," my brother said. Not like he was surprised, though. He was greeting something he knew already, something he'd expected to see.

"Hel-lo what?"

"Only rich folks would bother with one of those things this far south. Takes a lotta money to put one in, and they ain't cheap to run, neither. But this one ain't even been used in years."

"Yeah? And?"

"Just notin' some data."

Old Red put out his match with a sudden snap of the wrist. For a moment, the world around us vanished. Then another tiny flame flared up, and my brother moved off, holding up his match like a wee tiny torch.

We were in a low-ceilinged cellar, the far end swallowed in darkness somewhere beyond our sight.

"We could cover a lot more ground if you'd share some of them lucifers with me," I pointed out.

"Maybe—but I ain't got more'n a dozen of the things left, and I sure ain't gonna waste any lettin' you burn the place down."

I cursed myself for never taking up smoking.

For the next minute or so, we shambled along the wall, passing hazy shapes and shadows that flickered and rippled in what little light we had.

Cobwebs. Dust-smothered trunks. Sheet-draped furniture. A stand-up mirror, the glass cracked. A stuffed alligator, three feet long, spilling cotton from its broken tail. Shelves lined with Mason jars filled with . . . what?

I stopped, staring at the pulpy purple-red clumps floating in amber fluid.

"Tell me that ain't what I think it is."

Gustav brought another new-lit match in close.

"It ain't what you think it is," he said. "Unless you thought it was jarred tomatoes."

"Oh."

I felt both relieved and disappointed. It would've been nice had those jars been pickling indisputable proof—even if it had made me puke.

We turned to move on, then froze as footsteps clacked across the floorboards and came to a stop not a foot above our heads.

We'd been talking low all this time, moving careful and quiet, but maybe not quiet enough.

My brother and I stood there stiffly, both of us uselessly looking up.

"Shit," Old Red hissed with a start.

He jerked his hand down, and the light snuffed out.

The match had burned down to his fingertips.

We spent the next few seconds in utter darkness, the silence so complete I could hear my heart beat. Actually, I'm surprised everyone in the house couldn't hear it, it got to thumping so. Fortunately, whoever it was above us clomped off before it could hammer its way clean out of my chest.

Another lucifer flashed to life, and Gustav started toward a cluttery pile of canisters and boxes and bottles a few feet away. As we drew closer, I could see they were clustered around a half-opened door.

There was another room off the basement.

The largest of the cans was on its side, the lid off, and a grayish powder spilled out onto the dirt floor.

Old Red crouched down and brought his match in close.

"What's this say?" he asked, pointing at the big, blocky black lettering wrapped around the canister.

I had to step around him and straddle the can to get a good look at the label.

"DANGER," I read out. "MAGNESIUM. HIGHLY—"

That's as far as I got.

The next word was EXPLOSIVE.

38

THE DARK ROOM

Or, We Finally Get a Glimpse of the Big Picture

I lunged out and smothered my brother's match in my palm.

I did my best to smother my resulting yelp, too.

"FLAMMABLE?" Gustav guessed in the dark.

"Even better," I whimpered. "EXPLOSIVE."

Old Red was quiet for a moment.

"You know," he finally said, "one of these days I really do need to learn myself how to read."

"If you could just pick up the word 'danger,' it sure would help."

I moved slowly away from the canister, trying to shake the pain out of my hand.

"You know much about magnesium?" my brother asked.

"I know it explodes."

Gustav grunted out a "hmm."

"Hold on a tick," I said. "Come to think of it, I do know something about it. Photographers use it for flash powder. That'd explain why Krieger's got so much lyin' around."

"Yeah . . . but not why it's lyin' in a heap on the floor."

A spark burned a hole in the darkness, and I saw Old Red squat down distressingly close to the ground—and the magnesium—with a fresh-struck match.

"Hel-lo," he said.

The silver-gray magnesium powder wasn't just spilling from its can. It ran off in a sprinkly trail along the floor.

"Well, would you look at that?"

Gustav pointed at the checked trousers he'd borrowed off Ragsdale. The rolled-up cuffs were covered with fine gray powder.

I glanced down and saw my own shoes and pant legs were dusted up just the same.

"The stuff must be spread out all over down here," I said, "and you been tossin' around spent matches like you was Johnny Appleseed plantin' trees. We're lucky we ain't been barbecued half a dozen times over."

"Yup. Looks like Krieger's got the place rigged to blow."

My brother turned to the pile of cans, bottles, and boxes nearby. Some were labeled MAGNESIUM, others ETHER, still others a seemingly benign PAPER. All of it, I had no doubt, would burn but good.

"Sweet Jesus," I said. "There's gotta be an easier way to get rid of evidence."

Old Red shrugged. "Depends on the evidence."

He started toward the door just beyond the clutter.

As he stepped up close, something glistened, oily and metallic, at eye level—an open padlock hanging from a latch. Gustav lit a fresh match (after carefully snuffing the old one and depositing it in a pocket) and pushed the door all the way open.

A swirl of bitter-pungent vapors assaulted my nostrils. It was a harsh, chemical smell, a perfume of vinegar and kerosene with a subtle splash of decay.

Something else swirled out with it. Not so much an odor as a feeling, that queasy unease that wells up from some deep part of the soul that knows no words—the animal part that can sniff out menace before you even lay eyes on it. Dread, I guess you'd call it.

Old Red walked through the door.

I didn't follow my brother so much as the light.

The room beyond was long and narrow, the far end draped in impenetrable darkness. For all I knew, there was *no* end, and the room simply stretched on forever, a black tunnel to nowhere.

Just beyond the door was a table covered with beakers and tongs and shallow tubs. Exactly the sort of thing you'd expect to see in the "dark room" of a professional photographer. A few feet away, against the opposite wall, was something equally innocent: shelves lined with books.

Gustav and I moved closer, and I began reciting the titles. They started out innocuous enough—*Justine, Juliette, Fanny Hill*—but turned more lurid the further we went.

"*The Romance of Lust. Memoirs of a Coxcomb. The Lustful Turk. My Secret Life.*"

Old Red waved a hand at the rest of the books. "So they're all of a kind here?"

"Sure. I don't see no Bibles or cookbooks or . . . wait."

A section of slender, tattered, obviously well-read volumes caught my eye.

"*'Leather Apron,' or, The Horrors of Whitechapel,*" I read out. "*The History of the Whitechapel Murders. The Whitechapel Atrocities. The Whitechapel Terror. Jack the Ripper; or, The Whitechapel Fiend.*"

There were four or five more, all of them variations on the same words.

Whitechapel. Jack. Ripper.

"That cinches it," Gustav said grimly.

"Not in a court-of-law way, it don't. We still ain't got proof positive."

"Feh," my brother said. Then he said, "You're right."

The already low light of his match flickered and dimmed, and he put it out altogether with a quick shake.

"How many of them things you got left, anyway?" I asked.

Old Red's face appeared in a fluttery yellow glow. "After this one? Three."

"*Three*? Shit."

If we didn't find what we were looking for in the next couple minutes, we'd end up feeling around for it in the dark.

A hatbox was on the shelf, acting as a bookend, and I quickly slid it out and tossed off the cover. Inside was an assortment of "postcards" of the kind you'd never mail to your Aunt Polly. Yet they weren't anything I hadn't seen before, thanks to bunkhouse pals who collected such "Parisian novelties."

Gustav snatched the hatbox from my hands. "Alright, alright—that ain't nothing." He shoved the box back on the shelf. "Dammit, there's gotta be some real evidence down here somewhere."

He whirled around and took a few fast steps that almost put out his match. The crackle of breaking glass stopped him in his tracks.

"Christ almighty . . ."

When the light flared up stronger again, I saw what my brother was looking at.

There was a blank space beyond the worktable and shelves, all of ten feet where there was nothing but dirt floor and magnesium powder—and, strewn about willy-nilly as if tossed carelessly through the door, five photographs, the frames shattered. Just past the scattered pictures, at the edge of the light, a single wooden post jutted down into the middle of the room.

It was a beam, one of the big oaken shafts that made up the skeleton of the house. Attached to it were what, at first, looked like rusty-brown tin cups hanging from an iron loop about five feet off the ground. The wood beneath the ring, I noticed, was splotched with dark stains.

It took me a moment to realize I was looking at manacles. And dried blood.

And, at last, *proof.*

Old Red knelt down and picked up the nearest of the photos. It was a group portrait, like the pictures of the San Marcos Gamecocks and the Marching Beavers. Only this one showed a gaggle of young women lounging around a bed, all of them clad in white chemises or knickerbockers. They looked weary and worn, but most managed to work up a sleepy smile.

Squirrel Tooth Annie was among them, as was Big Bess. I recognized the bed, too. It was the big four-poster in the "Bridal Suite" at the Phoenix.

Written across the bottom of the picture were the words "A happy staff! September 1892."

We sorted through the other photographs, finding them much the same. Tired women gathered around a big bed. Squirrel Tooth and Big Bess were in them all. The other gals came and went.

As for the inscriptions on the photos, only one thing about them ever changed. It was always "A happy staff!" Always September. The years, though, went from 1889 to 1893—that last with a smear of blood on the fracture-webbed glass.

"That's how he picked 'em. The gals he wanted for *that*." Gustav jerked his head at the post and manacles. "They'd round up the chippies for him to choose from like heifers at auction. We must've come to town right before this year's cull: He'd taken the new picture but hadn't got around to the choosin' yet. That's what he was pretendin' to do when he plugged Ragsdale, I'd wager. He was sayin', 'That one there. She'll do.'"

"But there ain't no picture for '88, when Adeline died," I pointed out.

Old Red nodded slowly. "She was different. The first. Practice. Krieger set out to be Jack the Ripper, only it didn't go so smooth for him as for Jack. Stonewall either saw him at it or caught him red-handed. And it wouldn't be Ragsdale and Bock's way to take it to the law, nor to pass up a buck, neither. So they started in with blackmail, and from there it turned into more of . . . a business arrangement."

"One girl a year," I said. "Must've cost Krieger plenty."

"No coal for the furnace, lettin' folks buy into his private library, turnin' part of his fine old house into a photography studio." My brother nodded again. "Yup. He was bein' bled dry."

"Well, I guess he finally stopped the bleedin'—only now his 'fine old house' is about to go up in flames, and if it does, we won't have squat to prove any of this."

"Yup."

My brother put out his match and didn't hurry to light another. We'd run through two just looking over the pictures.

There was only one left.

I've never experienced such a total darkness as at that moment. It was the kind of black that makes you forget what light is. It wasn't just complete. It seemed infinite.

"Ain't no way around it," Gustav said. "We've gotta—"

There was a shrieking-loud squeak somewhere above and behind us—the squealing of rusty hinges—and light spilled down into the cellar.

Old Red hurried to the dark-room door and pushed it closed as far as it would go. Then he crouched down beside the keg of magnesium in the doorway just as we heard the first step on the stairs. I crept up behind him.

We watched as light spread across the basement, listened as the footfalls on the creaking stair-slats grew louder. Then at last we saw Krieger.

Mrs. Krieger, gliding through the cellar with an oil lamp in her hand. I'd been so preoccupied with her husband, I'd forgotten the lady entirely.

She was wearing a black cape over a dark blue walking dress, and her graying hair was pinned up in a mound so big it was less "bun" than "loaf." The lamplight shining up from beneath accentuated the long, straight lines of the high collar squeezing her neck, making her head look like a hot-air balloon straining to escape her body.

Her expression was placid, blank even, free of fear or suspicion. She hadn't heard us.

Indeed, she moved with her usual ghostly grace, quiet and calm, the only sound a soft shushing from her skirts as she knelt before the biggest of the basement's steamer trunks. After setting the lamp down atop another locker nearby, she unclamped the trunk's locks, lifted the lid, and reached inside.

A moment later, when Mrs. Krieger closed the steamer and stood to go, I caught a glimpse of something pure white and pillowish tucked under one arm. She took a single step toward the stairs, then seemed to change her mind, turning and moving deeper into the cellar instead.

She didn't go far—just a few feet—and she stopped and shook out the white material she'd been toting. It was long and billowy, and she pressed it close against her body.

Her back was to us, yet I finally got a good look at what she'd come down to fetch, for Mrs. Krieger was staring into the cracked glass of the big mirror propped up not far from the coal chute. The flowing white fabric looked like a shroud at first, but the more I stared the more I could make out sheer lace and the sheen of satin.

It was a wedding gown. Seeing herself with it—recalling herself *in* it—put a wistful smile on Mrs. Krieger's chalky face. Then the smile was gone, and I noticed something else in the mirror.

Two sets of eyes glistening in the gloom, reflecting the glow of the lantern. Two ghoulish faces striped by the light cutting through an open door.

Our eyes. Our faces.

She could see us.

"Oh," Mrs. Krieger said.

Her wedding dress dropped to the floor.

I stood and stepped around Gustav into the full light, talking fast in hopes of heading off a scream.

"You have nothing to fear from us, ma'am, I assure you. But my brother and I do have reason to believe you're in great danger. If you'll just hear me out, I can explain why."

She turned to face me, and I was heartened by how serene she still seemed, how poised.

I might actually pull this off, I thought.

Then Mrs. Krieger drew something from a pocket concealed beneath her cape, and once she had it out in the open—and pointed at my chest—I knew why she could stay so cool.

She was the one holding a gun.

"Uhhhh, Mrs. Krieger," I said, unsure what words might follow, except perhaps "please don't."

"MORTIMER!" the lady boomed. **"THEY'RE HERE!"**

39

ONE IN A MILLION

Or, I Try to Open Mrs. Krieger's Eyes, but It's Me Who's Blind to the Obvious

Ma'am, you gotta listen to me," I said. "If you'd just step into this dark room here and take a look at—"

"Oh, I never go in there."

Mrs. Krieger actually smiled shyly, apologetically, a proper hostess sorry to be interrupting a guest. Even one she was pointing a shooting iron at.

It was a dinky little thing—a short-barreled .22 with no trigger guard. Useless at a distance, but deadly up close. And Mrs. Krieger was close enough.

"Now . . . your guns," she said. "Would you put them on the floor, please?"

I pulled my Bulldog from its shoulder holster, bent down, and gently settled it on the ground.

"Do you have any idea what your husband's done? What he is?"

"Guns, please!" Mrs. Krieger chirped, swiveling her iron to the left, toward my brother.

I glanced back at him as I straightened up. He was still on the other side of the doorway, where the lantern light couldn't fully reach him. His arms—and his holster—remained draped in blackness, but it was plain to see he wasn't giving up his Colt.

"**MORTIMER!**" Mrs. Krieger bellowed.

There was no response—no distant "*Coming*," no scurrying footsteps on the floor above. Wherever Mr. Krieger was, whatever he was doing, he seemed to be out of earshot.

Mrs. Krieger brought her left hand up to brace her grip on her gun.

"I really must insist," she said to Old Red. "I may be a lady, but I'm not afraid to use this."

"So we've seen." My brother unbuckled his holster and let it drop to the floor. "I gotta say, though—that didn't look like nothing no lady would do."

Mrs. Krieger relaxed, going back to a one-handed hold on her gun. "Even a lady is expected to protect her husband," she said.

Which was when the truth finally chiseled its way through my granite skull.

Ragsdale's and Bock's hats on their desks: removed for a lady.

The little pocket gun that had killed them: a lady's weapon.

The lady in question: standing right before me.

"Ragsdale and Bock . . . that was *you*?"

"Mortimer's arrangement with the gentlemen had grown rather strained," Mrs. Krieger explained pleasantly, as if making small talk while waiting for the crumpets to come off the stove. "So he thought it best if *I* ended the alliance. It being, as your brother said, not something one would expect of a lady."

"Protectin' your husband's one thing"—Gustav nodded back at the darkness behind him—"but do you know what's gone on down here? *In your home?*"

"I don't need to and I don't care to," Mrs. Krieger said. "All men have a darkness inside them. For the sake of civility, they keep it out of sight. But in private . . . from time to time . . . well . . ." The corners of her mouth turned down in a dainty grimace. "It's distasteful, but

it's a wife's duty to tolerate such things. Better that my husband in-
dulge himself safely here at home than out on the streets. That's a les-
son we learned five years ago."

Old Red's eyes went wide—and my own just about popped from
my skull.

" '*We* learned?' " I said.

"How long have you known what your Mortimer really is?" Gustav
asked.

The lady favored us with another prim smile. "That's between me
and my husband." The smile faded.

"MOOOORRRRRRR-TI-MEEEEERRRRRRRRR!"

Again, there was no response from upstairs.

"Oh, for heaven's sake," Mrs. Krieger fumed. "What am I to
do?"

At last I understood the poor woman's dilemma.

She was such a dutiful wife, she didn't want to kill us without
hubby's permission.

"Martha? What are you shouting ab- . . . oh."

Hubby was at the top of the stairs.

My brother glared at him with a murderous, barely reined-in rage.
He would've shown his fangs, if he'd had any.

For his part, Mr. Krieger merely seemed embarrassed.

"Goodness me," he said as he came down into the basement. His
doughy-bland features were pinched, his body stiff. He didn't look
like a madman so much as an overfed Shriner fighting to hold back a
belch at a buffet lunch. "This *is* awkward."

"Oh, we do so hate to be an imposition," I said. "Perhaps we'd
best be on our way."

Mr. Krieger waggled a thumb at the top of the stairs. "They'd love
that out there, believe me. Half the town's looking for you, and the
prevailing attitude seems to be 'shoot on sight.' No, I think you'd be
better off staying here with us."

He moved out to the middle of the cellar as he spoke, stopping next to the lantern-topped trunk. My Bulldog was lying in the silvery dust nearby, and he picked it up and pointed it at me.

"Just look at you, Martha," he said, beaming at the missus. "Now you've captured a pair of escaped prisoners. You're becoming a regular Annie Oakley!"

"Oh, Mortimer," Mrs. Krieger said, and it wasn't just her voice that got smaller. The whole of her seemed to shrink, not cringing but somehow contracting. Suddenly, the woman looked like a child trying to hold up a cannon.

"The best little wife a man could have," Mr. Krieger said.

It was hard to tell by lantern light, but I think the lady blushed.

It was sweet . . . like a mouthful of treacle. Somehow, I managed not to throw up.

Mr. Krieger's dewy-eyed adoration turned into a smirk.

"Too bad about your mustache," he said to my brother. "The black hair suits you, though."

"Just ask your damn questions," Gustav growled back.

"Questions?" Mr. Krieger put on a look of mock-puzzlement. "What makes you think I've got questions?"

"You ain't shot us yet," Old Red said. "You're gettin' set to skedaddle, start over again somewheres else. So you wanna know—you *gotta* know—how we figured out what a mean-crazy piece of shit you really are. Cuz you can't leave that trail for anyone else to follow."

Mr. Krieger nodded genially. "Yes, that's it exactly. Do tell."

"Why should we?" I asked.

"Well, there's always *this*."

Mr. Krieger gave my gun a lazy little joggle.

"So?" I said. "You're gonna kill us anyhow."

"I don't see why we should," Mr. Krieger said with a shrug. "After all, we don't really have to, do we? The mob outside might very well do it for us. And even if they don't, no one's going to believe what two notorious killers have to say. So come now. Please. If you take a chance on us, we'll take a chance on you."

I threw Gustav a look of the "How dumb does he think we are?" variety.

He ignored it.

"Alright," he said to Mr. Krieger. "You got a question, I got a question. What say we trade answers?"

"Done—but I'll claim the home field advantage, if you don't mind. And the I-could-still-kill-you advantage. My question comes first. What led you to me?"

"Tell him, Otto."

Right up to the end, Old Red was still delegating tale-telling to his flannelmouthed brother. Only this time there wasn't any tale to tell, it seemed to me.

"Well, we went by Ragsdale and Bock's office and saw the bodies, and there was some pictures missin' from the wall, and . . . uhhh . . ." I threw up my hands helplessly. "The sign out front says you're the only photographer in town."

Both Mr. and Mrs. Krieger kept staring at me expectantly long after I'd stopped speaking.

"That's it?" Mr. Krieger finally asked.

"There was a mite more folderol to it," I told him, "but yeah. Boil it down, and that was it."

Mr. Krieger shook his head in befuddled dismay. "What are the odds? After so much, to lose everything because of something so . . . *capricious.*"

"If random-like's what you mean, that's just how it works some-times, I'm learnin'," Gustav said, "and that plays into my question for you. My brother and me, we've pinned down most of the who and how of all this now, but the thing I still can't figure, the one thing I wanna hear you account for, Krieger, is—"

"Oh, my. Is that really the time?" Mr. Krieger cut in, glancing down at an imaginary pocket watch in his palm. "I'm afraid we'll have to finish this conversation later." He snapped the "watch" closed. "*Much* later."

Usually there was so little character to the man's face you could forget what he looked like between blinks. The truly strange thing about it now was that it didn't change. I'd like to write that the beast within him showed itself at last—that the man's eyes glowed with a feral hunger, that he cackled like a coyote, that he was slavering with bloodlust—but it wouldn't be true.

Mr. Krieger just kept smiling insipidly as he told us we were going to die.

"I suppose 'capricious' can cut two ways. Now, out of the blue, we have two sets of bones for the cinders. It'll be even more convincing that way, don't you think, Martha? Bales and everyone else—they'll assume these desperate fugitives did us in and made off with our wagon."

"There!" I said to Mrs. Krieger. "Don't you see what kinda man he really is? What kinda *monster*? There's no lie he won't tell, nothing he won't do, if it suits him. How long do you think it's gonna be before he turns on *you*?"

The lady was behind and to the right of Mr. Krieger, her wedding gown crumpled at her side. All she had to do was shift her hand six inches, and her .22 would be pointing at her husband's heart instead of mine.

Instead she just tittered girlishly.

"Don't be silly. I'm his wife."

"One in a million, isn't she?" Mr. Krieger said fondly. "Alright. It's time we were going. All of us."

He brought up his gun and took aim.

For whatever reason, he decided to shoot me first.

40

THE FIERY PIT

Or, Our Last Chance for Salvation Goes Up in Smoke

I got set to dodge knowing it would do me no good. To my left were trunks and chairs and other assorted bric-a-brac. To my right was the pile of magnesium canisters and ether bottles and other assorted explodables. And the Kriegers were no more than twenty feet off anyhow.

Left or right, forward or back, I was dead.

There was a rustle of movement behind me, a scratchy scraping sound followed by a soft *shhhhhhh*.

"I got one more thing to say, Krieger, and you'd damn well better listen."

Gustav held up his last match. Lit.

"Pull that trigger, and we *all* die."

As one, Mr. and Mrs. Krieger dropped hollow-eyed gazes to the ground—and the magnesium powder they'd apparently forgotten all about. It was everywhere. On every*one*.

Old Red moved slowly out of the dark room and started sidling toward the stairs. "Come on, Brother. We're leavin'."

"Good idea. I think we done wore out our wel—"

The tiny flame of Gustav's lucifer fluttered and dimmed as I stepped up close.

I'd stirred up enough breeze to just about put it out.

Old Red and I froze for a moment, and the fire grew brighter . . . while moving to within an inch of my brother's fingers.

We had to move fast. Only we had to move slow.

"Just get to the stairs," Gustav whispered to me. "Then we got a chance."

We edged away from the Kriegers side by side, fearfully watching them fearfully watching us. They still had their guns up, ready to shoot, but so long as we had that powder beneath us, they didn't dare.

Just as we reached the first step, my brother let out a growl—a long, raspy *grrrrrrrr*.

The flame had reached his fingertips. He was burning.

"Get ready to run," he grated out through gritted teeth.

"Too late," Mr. Krieger sang, grinning again. "You're snuffed."

The match had gone out.

"Go!" Old Red barked, flicking the still-smoking matchstick at the dark room.

It arced harmlessly into the gloom and disappeared.

We were all of three steps up the stairs when Mr. Krieger pulled the trigger. The Bulldog's kick was more than he was ready for, though, and the shot went wild, thumping into the ceiling nowhere near us.

The real surprise—for all of us but Gustav—was the flash of flame around Mr. Krieger's hand, and the scream that followed.

When Mrs. Krieger first got the drop on us, I'd put the gun on the ground. Into the magnesium. Now the sparks from the shot had turned the whole thing, for just an instant, into a brilliant little sun that lit up the cellar with harsh white light.

I stopped, staggered by the sight of it, and my brother shoved me toward the top of the stairs.

"Go go *go*!"

I stumbled upward, yet I couldn't help looking back.

Mr. Krieger fell to his knees, howling in pain, and the Bulldog dropped from his hand—along with his blackened, sizzling fingers. The gun metal was white hot and still sparking when it hit the dirt.

"Mortimer?" Mrs. Krieger said.

Then there was another flash of light, one that raced like a bolt of lightning along the floor. It started with the gun, then ran through Mr. Krieger to Mrs. Krieger and on.

Mrs. Krieger's wedding dress went up in flame like a pile of old newspapers.

Mr. and Mrs. Krieger did, too.

As they shrieked and thrashed, the flare continued around the room, leaving smoke and flames wherever it went. Sheets and furniture caught fire. The stuffed alligator was a ball of flame in an instant. The mirror all but exploded, spewing a million tinkling shards every which way. Then the magnesium flash was mere feet from the cans and jars piled up by the dark-room door, and I finally tore my gaze away and focused all my attention on the task at hand: getting the hell out of there.

Yet when the burst of light came, I saw it still, though I was at the top of the stairs with my back to the basement. The world around me bleached solid white, and then the heat came in a great gust that lifted me off my feet, hurling me forward and pelting me with chips of wood and dirt and hissing, sputtering chunks of I know not what (and I dare not guess). Finally, as I tumbled and screamed, the sound came, not so much as a boom as an angry roar—the kind you might imagine Satan himself making as he was cast into the pit. It was the last thing I knew for a time, for somewhere between flying through the air and slamming to a stop, I blacked out.

I awoke to ungodly heat and the smell of smoke. Someone had hold of my shoulders and was shaking me hard.

"Otto . . . Otto, you gotta get up," I heard my brother say— barely. It felt like a bale of cotton had been stuffed in my ears. "You gotta get us outta here!"

For a moment, I wondered how I could have my eyes closed yet see nothing but white. Then I realized my eyes *weren't* closed—and ever so slowly the brightness faded, and I could see.

I was stretched out on my back, Old Red kneeling over me. There was something peculiar about the way his own wide-open eyes seemed to peer past me, staring at some point to the side of my right ear.

"Gustav . . . ?"

"Oh, thank God!" My brother's grip on my shoulders tightened. "I can't see a damn thing, Otto! The blast blinded me, and this whole place is goin' up in flames!"

"Holy shi—"

"We ain't got time to moan about it! We gotta go!"

"Right."

I sat up—and nearly flopped straight back to the floor again. My head was spinning like a top.

"Help me up."

Together, we got me to my feet.

What I saw cleared my head fast.

We were in the hallway toward the back of the house, outside the kitchen. There'd be no escaping through the servants' entrance, though. The blaze in the basement was so intense it had shot straight up through the floorboards. The kitchen was a wall of flame.

I had no choice but to take us out the other way, through the foyer—or what I assumed was the foyer, since all I could see thataway were dim swirls of smoke in the darkness.

"Come on."

I pulled Old Red into the gloom and ashes, and for all intents and purposes, we were *both* blind. Within seconds, we were coughing so bad we could barely stay upright, too, yet I kept limping forward, tugging my brother along beside me.

I thought I was running us toward the front door, but it was solid wall we hit. We bounced back with stunned grunts, and I lost my grip on Gustav. I was able to grab him again quick, though, and I held tight with one hand while groping along the wall with the other.

My fingers found a doorknob, and I twisted and pushed.

We weren't out yet, though. By the time my eyes teared away the soot and adjusted to the light—to the fact that there *was* light again, though not much—we were in the middle of the Kriegers' library. The fire wasn't as far along there, but it was coming on fast: The floor itself was smoking, almost too hot to walk on.

"Don't move!" I hollered at my brother.

"I'm blind, not deaf!" he shouted back.

I let him go.

There was a reading chair nearby, and I hefted it up and wobbled toward one of the library's oversized windows. My first toss came in low, hitting mostly wood and plaster, only a couple chair legs busting through the glass. On my second try, the chair went sailing out onto the lawn.

I turned back to collect Old Red. All around him were pockets of fire, spots where the blaze below had eaten up through the floorboards. Any minute—maybe any *second*—the flames were going to reach the lowest row of books, and the whole room would go up like the tip of a match.

I ran over to my brother and started dragging him back toward the window. After a few steps, though, the heat under my feet flared up into agony, and there was a little flash of light from below.

My shoes and pant legs were sparking and charring. Gustav's, too. The magnesium dust we'd picked up downstairs was getting set to ignite.

I stopped and bent over, about to swat at the smoldering sparkles. But Old Red knew what was happening just from the pain and the crackle of cooking leather.

"Don't touch it! You get that crap on your hands, it'll burn clear to the bone! Just *move*!"

Move I did—right into the cloud of stifling smoke that had popped up between us and the window. There was no time to beat around blind looking for the windowsill. I just charged into the black eddies and jumped where I thought I should jump, towing Gustav along with me.

Something clipped me on the shoulder, whipped me around, and I lost my hold on my brother. I spun as I fell, crashing down onto something hard and soft at the same time.

There was no time to see what it was. I was outside, but I hadn't escaped the flames. I'd brought them with me.

My shoes were on fire.

I screeched and kicked, pure panicked animal.

"Otto! Otto!" Gustav was yelling somewhere close by, and simply hearing his voice reminded me I had a brain. I could do more than just react. I could feel the fear, the pain, and still *think*.

I thrashed out of my vest and wrapped it around my feet, and after some wriggling and tugging I managed to pull off my shoes and toss them away.

My feet hurt like hell, but at least they weren't frying any longer.

"Otto?" Gustav said.

He was on his knees on the other side of the chair I'd come crashing down on a moment before. His gaze was pointed over my head.

He was still blind.

"I'm here . . . I'm alright," I said, and I wormed over to him and touched his hand. "Come on. We'd better get back a ways before the whole house falls on us."

I pulled myself through the grass, Old Red crawling along beside me, following by sound. When we were far enough off, I turned and looked back at the Kriegers'.

The home's fancy facade was all aflame now, every eave and gable and turret burning, consumed by the inferno raging up from below. The heat of the fire had created a powerful updraft, and cinder-edged pages from burning books sailed off into the sky, some of them flying so high they looked like the very stars the smoke had curtained from view.

It was an awe-inspiring and awful sight. Beautiful, dreadful. But I didn't get much time to soak it in.

There were shouting voices and hurried footfalls out on the street. They grew louder fast.

"We just lost every scrap of proof we had, you know," I said.

"Oh, it probably don't matter," Gustav sighed. "I don't guess they're in the mood to listen anyway."

His face was as blackened as a minstrel's, his clothes askew, his sightless eyes watering. Yet a strange calm had come over him, a serene passivity. It was as if he was trying to fix his features in that expression of dignified repose that makes folks at a wake look down and say, "It's like he's just sleeping."

"Over there! It's them!" someone shouted, and then they were on us—black silhouettes that swarmed into the yard and tore us apart.

"Now, let's not be hasty, fellers" was all I got out before I was treated to my first kick. More followed. Lots more, from lots of different feet.

"What did you do? What did you *do*?" a voice kept asking, but the stomps and punches never stopped long enough for me to answer. I was hauled up, hands grabbing my shirt, my pants, my hair, yanking me this way and that so I could be spat upon and called "Killer!"

It was no use trying to run or fight back. I'd lost track of my brother, and everyone pushing in around me was just another part of the same big bloodthirsty thing—a wolf with a hundred heads. It wasn't going to stop snarling and snapping its jaws until Gustav and I were dead.

Then there was a swirl in the crowd, a chaos within the chaos.

"Stop it!" a woman shouted. "Let 'em go!"

"Yeah!" a man joined in. "They're innocent, dammit!"

Lottie and Bob came shoving through the throng.

The men who had hold of me didn't let go, though. They just swiped and kicked at Bob and Lottie, too.

"Get outta here, you crazy old whore!" one of them was dumb enough to say.

Lottie went at him with both claws.

It was two against an army—and then *three* against an army as Old Red's friend Suicide Cheney fought his way to Bob and Lottie's side, fists flying.

Then *four* as Brother Landrigan came wading in bellowing, "Stop this insanity!"

That brought *five* and *six* and *seven* and more as Landrigan's followers crowded in after him, trying to build a wall of bodies between us and the mob.

One by one, the men clutching onto me were peeled off and pushed away. The last one refused to stop getting his licks in, though, flailing at me as he raved and spewed spittle.

". . . meddlin' sons of bitches gonna beat out your brains stupid bastard . . ."

It was Sheriff Ike Rucker himself, and I can't tell you how much it saddens me to say I lacked the strength for a single swing at him. Not that it was needed.

A hand grabbed Rucker, jerked him around, then clenched into a fist that slammed into the man's mouth, sending blood and teeth flying.

As Rucker sank out of sight, I found Milford Bales standing before me.

"Order!" he bellowed, spinning away to face the roiling crowd. He drew his Colt and fired it once into the air. "Order! There will be order!"

He was still standing that way—gun up, shouting for order, the Kriegers' house a giant wick of flame behind him—when I felt my knees start to buckle.

Well, why not? I thought. *I've earned myself a good faint.*

So I had one.

41

THE BREAKS

Or, We Finally Get Some Good News, but Old Red Remains in the Dark

I awoke from my swoon stretched out on a jail-cell bunk. You might think finding myself in the clink would be a mite discouraging, but that wasn't the case at all. In fact, I took it as a sign that our luck was finally turning around.

Lucky Break #1: I was alive.

And, oh, *how* alive! Alive with stinging eyes, aching lungs, throbbing bumps and burns, and a splitting headache.

I summed it all up thusly: "Ooooooooooooooh."

"You awake, Brother?" I heard someone say.

Lucky Break #2: Gustav was alive.

"Yeah, I'm awake," I croaked. "Kinda wish parts of me weren't, though. How long was I out, anyway?"

"Long enough so you missed the sawbones they brought in to look us both over. He was a little concerned, you bein' out cold for such a spell, but I told him not to worry—you was just goldbrickin'."

"Gee, thanks. I'd hate for anyone to waste their time frettin' on my account."

I struggled up to a sit and saw Old Red in the little jail's only other cell, a few feet away. He looked like I felt—bruised, bloodied, and charbroiled—but what hit at my heart the hardest was the way he had his head cocked to one side, eyes pointed down.

He hadn't been looking at me. He'd just been listening.

*Un*lucky Break #1: My brother still couldn't see.

"What'd the doctor say about you?" I asked.

"Oh, I'm alright . . . though my eyes are still boogered up. Reet-inal trah-ma, I think the doc called it. On account of that magnesium goin' off. He thought it should pass by and by."

I didn't like the way Gustav stressed the "should" there. All too often, such shoulds never turned into dids.

"I was there when them magnesium kegs went off," I said. "How come you got it so much worse than me?"

Old Red shrugged. "I looked back."

Footsteps started clomping on the staircase nearby, and a moment later Lucky Break #3 appeared—Marshal Milford Bales.

He looked tired and rumpled, yet sounder than I'd ever seen him, somehow. Not stronger, exactly. Steadier.

He turned to me first. "Thought I heard your voice. How you feeling?"

"Like a million dollars . . . that's been run through a thresher and set on fire."

Bales smiled. "You're young. You'll heal."

He looked over at Gustav then, and his smile faded. My brother's just six years older than me, yet to see the haggard, empty-eyed little fellow slumped there staring down at nothing, you'd be excused for thinking that gap was measured in decades.

Yeah, I was young. I'd heal—but what about Old Red?

"You tell him?" Bales asked him.

Gustav shook his head. "Ain't had the chance."

"Alright. I'll do the honors." Bales turned my way again. "I'm holding you and Gus on suspicion of murder. Don't worry, though. I know you aren't killers."

"You do?"

"I do."

And Bales proceeded to unspool a whole roll of Lucky Breaks.

"Krieger had his wagon in back of the house when the fire started. The horse spooked and bolted, but it didn't get far, so I got a look at what Krieger was packing up. He was getting set to leave town, alright, and he was taking some . . . keepsakes, I guess you'd call 'em."

"What kinda keepsakes?"

"He was a photographer, Otto," Old Red said. "Think about it."

I did . . . and wished I hadn't pretty quick.

"Four different women," Bales said. "I sent Tommy out to the Phoenix with some of the more presentable pictures." He turned toward my brother again. "He just got back, Gus, and it just was like you said: They were all Phoenix girls who went missing over the last four years, always in October."

Old Red nodded glumly. "You know, I been thinkin'. Soon as you can, you oughta dig around where Krieger's dark room was. He wouldn't have bothered haulin' the bodies far."

"I was just waiting for the cinders to stop smoking," Bales said. "I've got more to tell you, too. I found something this morning in Pete Ragsdale's desk."

He reached into one of his coat pockets and produced two folded pieces of paper. He handed them through the bars to me.

I smoothed them out, gave a whistle, then let my brother in on the news.

"It's the membership form I filled out for you when we joined the library. That 'Texas Jack' letter, too—written out in someone else's handwritin'."

"Krieger's," Gustav said.

Bales nodded. "That's a safe bet—and easy enough to prove."

I handed the papers back to the marshal. "I wonder why Ragsdale and Bock didn't set a match to these the second they were done with 'em."

"They probably told Krieger they did," my brother said. "Only it wouldn't be like them to give up a hold on nobody. Who knows when a little extry dirt might come in handy?" He kicked at a nonexistent cat. "We should've found them things ourselves."

"Well, as I recall, you were a little rushed for time," Bales pointed out dryly. "It's better I found them, anyway. Makes for stronger testimony coming from me, don't you think?"

"Nice work, Marshal," I said. "You're turnin' out to be quite the lawman, after all."

I hadn't meant to hide any barb in it, but Bales winced all the same.

"Better late than never, huh?"

"Oh, I didn't mean—"

"It's alright, Otto. I can admit I've been a fool. After that talk we had here last night, I did some digging. It didn't take me long to realize I'd been on the wrong track about you two." The marshal shook his head and chuckled. "No pun intended."

"None detected," I said.

"I went to Mr. Coggins, the clerk at the wallpaper store," Bales explained. "I wanted to find out what he'd overheard when you two were in there having it out with Ragsdale and Bock the other day. He told me Gus was asking a lot of questions about Gertie's murder—which certainly didn't jibe with Gus being the murderer himself. What's more, Mr. Coggins had a dime novel he'd checked out of Krieger's library. He didn't start reading it until yesterday afternoon, but he recognized the heroes' names straight off."

"Why, of course." I beamed like a daddy gazing for the first time on his newborn son. "Big Red and Old Red Amlingmeyer in 'On the Wrong Track.'"

"That's right," Bales said. "Once I took a look at your story, I knew all your talk about being detectives was actually true."

"Yeah, well . . . don't believe everything you read," my brother grumbled.

"So," I said, "now all that's cleared up, I assume you'll be lettin' us outta here right soon."

Bales shook his head. "Not exactly. There's going to be an inquest—several, in fact—and you remember who the county coroner is."

"Oh. Shit."

Ike Rucker.

"I wouldn't worry about Rucker too much," Bales said. "Horace Cuff's preparing quite the story for the *Free Press*. He can't tie Rucker directly to any of the deaths, but the sheriff was close enough to Rags-dale and Bock to get some of the blood on his boots. If he knows what's good for him—and he usually does—he'll want all this to die down fast. In the meantime, I'm going to keep you two here until you're cleared. For your own protection."

I looked around at my cell—all thirty square feet of it—and tried to calculate how quick I'd lose my mind cooped up there. The answer being "It's half gone already."

"What if we don't wanna be protected?"

"Well, then there's the little matter of assaulting a peace officer, not to mention unlawful flight," Bales said. "Tommy's been very un-derstanding about the whole thing, but I don't know. Hit a man over the head, and sometimes he can't think straight for a while. He might wake up tomorrow and decide to press charges after all. Which would force me to reconsider my position on your escape—"

"Say, Marshal." I stretched out on my bunk, doing my best to look comfy-cozy and content. "Could you loan me some paper and a pen-cil? Long as we're makin' camp here, I may as well get me some work done."

Bales grinned and started off, then stopped halfway to the stairs. "A couple things still bother me, though." Slowly, reluctantly, he turned around. "Ragsdale and Bock's man Stonewall and a prosti-tute called Squirrel Tooth Annie—they've gone missing, too. Went to the Star Saturday night and haven't been seen since. You know anything about it?"

I wanted to steal a peep at my brother, try to read the look on his face, but that might have been what Bales was looking for—his way to read *me*.

"Nothin' more than what you just said," I replied, holding the marshal's gaze. "You got any theories?"

Bales peered over at Old Red, then back at me, not just looking at us but *into* us. Gauging who we were, how we were connected. Who owed what to whom.

"No," he said. "Nothing to speak of."

He turned again to leave.

"You said a couple things was botherin' you," Gustav said. "What's the other?"

Bales stopped without looking back. Even without having his face to judge by, I knew what he was thinking of.

Gertie. Adeline. The woman they'd both loved, and who may have loved both of them.

Or one of them.

Or neither.

"Forget it," Bales said, and he headed down the stairs.

Gustav just sat hunched on his bunk, staring at nothing. He stayed that way for a long, long time.

Forget it?

Never.

42

MEMENTO MORI

Or, Old Red Tries to Untangle Himself from the Last Loose End

Here's a little pearl of wisdom you can tuck away for a rainy day: If you ever get a hankering to write a novel of your own, you'd do well to get yourself thrown in the pokey. And not for some trivial, one-night-in-the-hoosegow kind of thing like public intoxication, either. Be ambitious. Get hauled in for murder. Because I've discovered there's no better place to get some good writing done than in jail.

My brother and I spent five days behind bars, and during that time I composed more than half of this book. Old Red, on the other hand, didn't do much of anything, beyond listen to the occasional Holmes story and sleep and brood. There's not much you can do when you're locked up and blind.

The doctor—a young fellow fresh from some eastern university—came by to check on Gustav often, but it was obviously out of his hands. My brother would see again soon . . . or he wouldn't.

We had other callers, too. Horace Cuff dropped in to interview us for the *Free Press*, though I didn't get the feeling he liked us any better now that we were, even by the reckoning of his own newspaper, heroes. Brother Landrigan came by as well, mostly to talk God to

298

Gustav. My brother's spiritual awakening in church (if that's what it had been—I still wasn't sure) represented unfinished business, as far as Landrigan was concerned, and he was there to close the deal.

Normally, I would've guyed the man a bit, sanctimony bringing out my sacrilegious side, but I gave him no guff. He and his flock had helped save our skins when the lynch mob got us, and Cuff told me what Landrigan had been preaching on the courthouse steps that night: the book of John, chapter 8, verse 7.

Let him who is without sin cast the first stone.

So I was actually respectful, for once. Not that it mattered. Brother Landrigan never got much more than grunts and nods out of Brother Gustav. Before long, the preacher stopped coming altogether.

Old Red perked up more for Bob and Lottie's visits, and all the bad blood from that dark night out at the springs seemed to be forgotten. They'd stay for hours sitting on chairs Tommy toted up, all of us (even Gustav) swapping stories and (all *but* Gustav) laughing. Bob even brought up his old offer again, with an approving nod from Lottie. Squirrel Tooth Annie would be staying on at the Lucky Two for a spell (this said in a whisper), but what they really needed was hardworking men. Partners.

Half the ranch was ours, should we want it.

"I don't know," my brother said. "Let's see how these peepers of mine heal up, huh?"

He dodged all other attempts to talk it through. The future was something he wasn't ready to face. It was the past he was still pondering.

"Say, Lottie," he said one day. "Adeline ever mention her and Milford Bales . . . you know? Doin' business?"

Lottie looked like she was going to bust out laughing. "Bales? With one of the girls? Never. I didn't even know he had balls at all till I saw him slug Rucker the other night. Why? Did Ragsdale or Bock tell you that?"

"Oh, we heard something of the kind somewhere or other," Old

Red muttered, and he quickly changed the subject to the myriad miseries of jailhouse food.

We only had one other visitor of note during those days. Sure, a few gawkers and curiosity seekers came by—townsfolk with nothing better to do than angle for a good gape like we were sideshow pinheads—but Bales only let one up to see us.

It was Mr. Coggins, the mousy little wallpaper salesman. He was clutching something in his hands: a thick magazine he held up for me to see.

Across the cover, in blocky black letters, were the words *Smythe's New Detective Library*. Underneath that, smaller but by no means small, was the title of that issue's main story hovering above a black-and-white drawing: two men in a furious fight atop a locomotive as it plunged over a mountainside.

" 'On the Wrong Track' by Otto Amlingmeyer," I read out for my brother's benefit.

I mashed my face against the bars, squinting at the illustration.

Yup—that was a mustache, alright.

"Oh, wouldn't you know it."

"What?" Old Red asked.

"They put you on the cover instead of me."

"So this is all *true*?" Coggins marveled.

"And I've got the scars to prove it," I told him. "Only I think they're all buried under new scars."

Coggins stepped up to my cell and passed the magazine through to me. It was lighter than I'd expected, and rougher, too.

Coggins pulled out a fountain pen. "Would you mind signing it?"

"My friend, nothing on this earth would give me greater pleasure."

Gustav mumbled something under his breath, but I paid him no mind. This was a moment of pure triumph, and no naysaying or needling would be allowed.

I John Hancocked the cover with big, swirling loops. "Here you go, sir."

I passed the pen back to Coggins. But when it came time to hand over the magazine, I hesitated.

It was a dream made manifest I was holding. The word made flesh—or cheap paper, at least.

Would it, I had to wonder, ever feel this real again? Or was this my one little brush with fame and fortune, and after that . . . goats?

Coggins cleared his throat, and I reluctantly slid the magazine back through the bars. Once he had it in hand, he turned toward Old Red—then quickly changed his mind.

He'd read my story, so he knew. Even before he'd been blinded, my brother was not an autograph-signing kind of fellow.

"Thank you." Coggins started backing toward the stairway. "I truly appreciate your—"

"Mr. Coggins, I gotta ask," I said. "Would you mind leavin' that magazine? Just for a day or so? I've never actually seen anything of mine in print, and I'd dearly love to—"

Coggins kept going.

"Oh, I'm sorry," he said, "but this might be valuable now."

And he hustled off down the stairs.

The inquests started the next morning. Rucker tried to herd them along quick, as Bales had predicted, but it still took days. There had to be hearings for Mr. Krieger, Mrs. Krieger, Big Bess, Ragsdale, Bock, and every one of the four skeletons they did indeed find once they dug under the rubble of the Kriegers' home. Nine deaths to make findings on, in all.

In the end, the pointing fingers just went in a circle—victims-killers-victims-killers—and nobody wanted to widen the loop beyond that. Circles are closed in on themselves, tidy, and San Marcos needed to see itself as a tidy town.

So at last, Old Red and I got the okay to hobble on our way. Just where we'd hobble *to* remained a thorny thicket, though, and it was decided—by Lottie, and nobody felt up to opposing her—that we would complete our recuperations as guests of the Lucky Two.

Milford Bales himself helped my brother into the back of Bob and Lottie's (freshly whitewashed) wagon.

"Thanks for all you did, Gus," he said, "and . . . I'm sorry for what *I* did."

Gustav turned his face toward Bales, though he'd gotten in the habit of keeping his eyes closed at all times.

"You already made your apologies good enough, Milford. And then some."

"Anyway," I threw in as I climbed up next to my brother, "what's a lynchin' or two between friends?"

Bales grimaced. "Is there anything you won't crack a joke about, Otto?"

I thought for a moment.

"Nope."

Bales smiled and shook his head. "If Rucker gives you any trouble," he said as he closed the gate on the bed, "just let me know."

There was no tremble in his voice, no strain, no extra effort at all. The words came to him naturally, easily.

He still dressed like a banker but for his brass star. Yet somehow he looked like a lawman now.

"Good luck," he said.

"Yeah," Gustav replied. Just that and no more: "Yeah."

We didn't head straight south to the ranch after that. We went north first, just a mile or so, to a little cemetery on a hill overlooking town.

We could have had quite the day visiting up there. Our old friends Big Bess and Pete Ragsdale and Gil Bock were all fresh-planted thereabouts, as were the four girls dug up from the Kriegers' cellar.

The Kriegers themselves were elsewhere—as in nowhere and everywhere. They'd been completely consumed in the fire, and now every time the wind kicked up, ashes from their house—and from *them*—went swirling through the streets. Mortimer and Martha Krieger would have no gravestones, no monuments. They were just dust to be swept off porches and wiped from windowsills and breathed in and sneezed out and forgotten.

But it wasn't any of these recent, not-so-dearly departed we'd come to call on, anyway. The grave we were looking for was five years old.

Bob and Lottie hung back by the graveyard's black iron gates, giving Gustav as much privacy as could be had. Which wasn't much. He had to trudge out to the plot with a hand on my shoulder, giving directions even with eyes squeezed tight.

"It's over in the southwest corner. On the other side of a toothache tree. You see it?"

"I see the tree."

Old Red's grip tightened, his fingers digging in so hard it hurt.

"Should be a row of markers just beyond. Ain't they there?"

"I don't . . . hold on."

I spied a line of small, brown humps barely visible through thick grass.

"Yeah. I see 'em."

That the undergrowth had sprouted so tall proved fortuitous, actually, for the flimsy wooden grave markers I found in the grass were decayed and faded. If they'd been out in the open entirely, nothing would've remained but rotting stumps.

The third one I uncovered had just two things written on it: ADE-LINE and 1888.

Old Red shuffled forward, arms out before him.

"Help me," he said.

I guided him down to his knees by the marker, and he groped around till he had his hands on it. He seemed shocked by the feel of it, at first—that this crumbling, pathetic little thing was all he could touch of the woman he'd known.

He bent forward, face pointed down at the ground. I thought maybe he was going to cry, but he just stayed like that a moment, and his eyes remained closed, and no tears came.

"We only figured out the half of it, you know," he said. "We got the who but never the why."

"You said yourself over and over, Brother: There wasn't any why. Not with a feller like Krieger."

"I don't mean why he did it. I mean why *her*?"

I shrugged. A useless gesture, of course, considering my brother couldn't even see it, but it felt like it had to be done. It was the truest answer I knew.

"Wrong place, wrong time," I said. "That's as close to a why as we'll ever get."

"Feh," Old Red said listlessly. He didn't even have the heart left for spite.

I groped around for a silver lining.

"Hey, at least Mr. Holmes came through for us. You can't deny the Method worked in the end."

"Did it?" Gustav said. "Seems to me it was luck as much as anything. If we hadn't stirred up all kinds of shit, we never would've had no clues at all."

"So? Maybe it wasn't all magnifyin' glasses and deducifyin', but it worked. Who knows? Could be we're comin' up with a method of our own."

Old Red grunted. "Stir shit up. That's quite a method."

"We do seem to have a talent for it."

My brother said nothing for a while. Did nothing, too. He just stayed crouched beside the grave, head bowed.

"You wanna be alone?" I asked him after a minute or so.

"No. I'm ready to go. Ain't nothing here but a piece of old wood."

He steadied himself against the marker as he stood, and for a moment I feared it would snap in half.

"I'm sure she loved you, Gustav," I said.

I don't know where it came from. I certainly hadn't thought it through beforehand. If I had, I wouldn't have said it.

"How would you know?" "Shut the hell up!" Yet another "Feh."

That's what I expected in reply. Instead, "It don't matter now" is what my brother said to me. "That's all done."

He turned his back to the grave, then just stood there. Yet as I stepped up beside him, I saw he wasn't waiting for me to guide him away to the wagon again. He was gazing off at the horizon.

He'd opened his eyes.

It was midmorning still, and the sun was shining warm and bright to the east—the way Old Red was facing.

"Clear day today? No clouds?"

"That's right," I said. "Can you see the light?"

"I . . . I don't know. I can't tell if I see it or just *feel* it."

He stretched out a hand and found my shoulder, and from the trembling of his lips I could tell he was trying to smile.

"Don't you worry, though, Brother," he said, eyes still open wide. "I ain't never gonna give up lookin' for it."

Acknowledgments

The author wishes to thank:

Jim Thompson and Bernard Herrmann—for inspiration.

Crafty Keith Kahla, editor and Texan—for pointing the way.

Elyse Cheney, agent and New Yorker—for cracking the whip.

Andy Martin, Hector DeJean, Kathleen Conn, and everyone else at Minotaur Books—for keeping this crazy cattle drive moving.

Big Red's Posse (you know who you are)—for giving me a reason to saddle up.

Sandra E. Cortez and the San Marcos Public Library—for helping me get my facts straight and forgiving me (I hope) when I chose to bend the truth.

India Cooper—for the sharpest eyes this side of Old Red himself.

Sophie Littlefield, Steven Sidor, and Ben Sevier—for timely words of wisdom and encouragement.

Everyone I'm forgetting to thank—for not hitting me the next time I see you.

Mark and Alyssa Nickell—for sweet relief.

Kate and Mojo and Mar—for the whole schmear.